PENGUIN BOOKS

SHORES OF DARKNESS

After working on local newspapers in Devon and the East End of London, Diana Norman became, at twenty years of age, the youngest reporter on what used to be Fleet Street. She married the film critic Barry Norman, and they have settled in Hertfordshire with their two daughters. Her first book of fiction, *Fitzempress's Law*, was chosen by Frank Delaney of BBC Radio 4's *Bookshelf* as the best example of a historical novel of its year. She is now a freelance journalist, as well as a writer of biographies and historical novels. Her novel *The Vizard Mask* is also published by Penguin.

Shores of Darkness

Diana Norman

PENGUIN BOOKS

PENGUIN BOOKS

Published by the Penguin Group
Penguin Books Ltd, 27 Wrights Lane, London W8 5TZ, England
Penguin Books USA Inc., 375 Hudson Street, New York, New York 10014, USA
Penguin Books Australia Ltd, Ringwood, Victoria, Australia
Penguin Books Canada Ltd, 10 Alcorn Avenue, Toronto, Ontario, Canada M4V 3B2
Penguin Books (NZ) Ltd, 182–190 Wairau Road, Auckland 10, New Zealand

Penguin Books Ltd, Registered Offices: Harmondsworth, Middlesex, England

First published by Michael Joseph 1996
Published in Penguin Books 1997
1 3 5 7 9 10 8 6 4 2

Printed in England by Clays Ltd, St Ives plc

To Harry Clifford

PROLOGUE

İF I BELIEVED in such things, I'd think that the spirit of my murdered aunt, Effie Sly, has begun to haunt me.

It was a strange business.

Today is the fourteenth of July, in the year of our Lord 1716. Ten years ago exactly, on 14 July 1706, Aunt Effie was strangled by 'person or persons unknown'. Except that I do know.

And this very afternoon, when we were at dinner in my hall, the sun darkened all at once. As we scurried for candles the oak that's stood beyond the lawn these three hundred years split in smoking halves. In the same instant, thunder rattled the pewter on the dresser and I swear I heard a voice call, 'Revenge.'

I could have said, 'Go back where you came from, Aunt Effie. For eight bloody years I chased your killer across seas and continents and near lost my own life doing it. You were avenged right enough, though maybe not as you'd wish. If that don't please you, I'm sorry. I'll do no more.'

But I hope I'm a rational man and don't spend time talking to demons. Instead, I sent John to the stables to help Bates soothe the horses while I went upstairs to see if the thunder had upset my daughter or my wife, who was in labour with our next child.

Jubah answered my knock, barring the door with her big black arms and telling me to 'get'.

'How's she faring?' I asked.

'Cussing. Where she learn to cuss so strong?'

'Give her my love.'

'She had it nine month since,' Jubah said, 'that why she cussing now. You get.'

I went down to go on with dinner. The storm was passing and thin daylight was beginning to brighten the coats of arms

1

in the little stained-glass panes round the mullions, throwing their reflections on to the floor in flimsy colours.

The heraldy is not mine, of course, but the De Marchmonts', one of those strong-in-the-arm, weak-in-the-head families that died out fighting for the wrong kings. This is royalist Devonshire and my neighbours, all High Tories, would leave me in no doubt the De Marchmonts spin in their tombs to see a low-born, jumped-up Puritan in possession of their house. But by the time I bought the place it had deteriorated into little more than a barn. The leaves of the great front door had broken away from their upper hinges and hens pecked at weeds growing between the flags. The farmer who owned it used the kitchen for a cow byre.

I restored the linen-fold panelling and the newel post of the staircase and the lovely plasterwork of the ceilings and leaded the cracks in the coat-of-arms panes so that they shouldn't be dishonoured – I have a weakness for those who fight lost causes, even if they are not mine.

Actually, I think the De Marchmonts rest easy at what I have done for their home; the hall especially has regained the dignity due to its fine, long, low proportions which I have left uncluttered apart from a chest, a refectory table with tapestried chairs and a settle, all of them oak, all dating from the time of England's first James and all going for a song now that fashion in furniture has changed to spindly elegance. Very pretty, of course, but I like a chair of substance under my arse.

Usually, I say, the hall keeps its ancient calm, but today, with the storm, a restlessness had entered it. The fire in the huge grate which I'd lit to warm our guest, always a cold mortal, was not drawing well and sent out puffs of smoke. Leaves skittered about that had blown through the windows before we could shut them.

I experienced an odd repulsion. Again I remembered the date and what happened exactly ten years ago. Aunt Effie. It's a name to cuddle into, to pat on its white-capped head, totally unsuitable to the woman I addressed by it – a malignant female who brought misery to so many of us and her own death on herself.

2

Whether it was Aunt Effie's ghastly presence or the sudden violence of the storm, I could see as I paused on the stairs that my two fellow diners had been affected by dissatisfaction. My young ward, James, slumped in his chair, unusually sullen, while our guest, Daniel Defoe, crumbled his bread and in his high, nervous voice lamented the lack of duty in the younger generation.

His complaint was not against James, who is generally an obedient boy, but his own eldest son with whom he has recently quarrelled over a matter of money.

'How goes it upstairs?' he asked me.

'No arrival yet,' I told him and poured him wine. As ever, he was dressed like a Christmas beef and cut a garish figure against the sombre oak of the panelling in his emerald green coat with its gilt buttons and tarnished cuff lace. His long wig's out of date and could do with a clean. He's been ill, he says, and needs a breath of our good, Devonshire air. He seems spry enough to me, apart from the hunted look that's usual with him.

I suspect he's come to lie low for a bit, escaping a creditor, or a libel action, or another of the troubles he's always tumbling into. I never knew a man who can write better theories on how the world should tick, nor one who spends more time tangled up in its machinery.

'I'd like more wine,' said James, surprising me by his demand since so far he has accorded with my views on continence. He's about ten years old now, maybe eleven. Since coming to us he's sprouted tall and is mature for his age. A handsome lad, dark-haired, fair-skinned, with a good blue eye; affectionate, perhaps too passionate, but with a saving interest in science and the natural laws.

I gave him another half-glass, not wanting to shame him by a refusal in front of Defoe, and suggested we drink to the safe delivery of mother and baby.

We raised our glasses. 'And for your peace of mind, may the child be an affectionate girl, not an ungrateful son,' said Defoe, returning to his theme of fatherhood and its sorrows.

The fire blew out more smoke, leaves chased back and forth

in discontent. As if spurred by the suddenly malicious air of the room, James asked: 'Since we talk of fathers, Guardian, who was mine?'

I stared back at him. For two years I've dreaded him asking, but I hadn't an answer ready. I've rehearsed fairytales and then dismissed them. Lies are unworthy of him, yet he deserves better than the truth. I cannot tell a boy so young he was conceived only for revenge.

He scowled at me, trembling, then turned to our guest. 'My guardian does not satisfy. Perhaps *you* can tell me who my father is, Mr Defoe. Or was.'

I watched Daniel prick up. He loves a drama. Being so old a friend, he knows some of our story. Not all, thank God.

'What have you heard, my lord?'

'They say I'm the Pretender's by-blow,' James told him, 'the Papist's bastard. Hobbledehoys shout it after me in the lanes. Greville Narracott twitted me that I was not invited to Court. He says his father says it's because the King fears I will become the centre of another rebellion.'

'When was this?' I asked.

'Yesterday, after service. Greville said I didn't petition for the King's health. But I was a-sneezing during the prayer.'

'I'll have words with Squire Narracott,' I said.

James sent his trencher spinning. 'Why not me? Why not words with *me*?'

'I have to consider.'

He stood up and threw his wine on the floor. 'You always consider. I demand you tell me the truth, I command it. I outrank you. You're only a commoner. I have estates . . .' His anger was bolting off with him and he couldn't rein it in, which was scaring him the more.

'This ain't one of them,' I said, 'Get to your room.'

'I –'

'Your room.'

As the lad ran out, the wind in the chimney moaned as if in triumph. After a while Daniel said, 'I was there, you remember. In the palace antechamber while Queen Anne lay dying.'

'I remember.'

'Granting the letters patent of his peerage was virtually her last mortal act.'

'Yes.'

'It was bound to lead to this interpretation. A mysterious, unknown boy of mysterious, unknown background raised all at once to an earldom? What else but that she was ennobling a bastard son of her brother's as compensation because she could not hand on the throne to that same brother? It was already being whispered then.'

'I know.'

'He has the Stuart chin. And eyes.'

'I know.'

'And Squire Narracott is right. King George is suspicious of the boy, more than ever since the Scottish rising last year. It was a nearer thing than people think. Without Argyll's prompt action we might even now have a James III on the throne.'

That I didn't know. Like everybody, I'd accepted the official version; shiftless Jacobites routed by model Hanoverian troops. But I could trust Daniel on this. His agency still has spies in Scotland.

'So if the boy *is* James Stuart's bastard,' Daniel went on, becoming desperate, 'he constitutes a threat. Monmouth was a bastard son too, and everybody remembers *his* rebellion.'

'Didn't you take part in it?'

He shuddered. 'A youthful indiscretion. I extricated myself when I saw which way the wind was blowing.'

A great one for watching the wind, our Daniel. I nodded. 'I'm bringing the lad up a loyal subject of King George.'

'And there's another mystery,' pleaded Daniel. 'For Queen Anne to name you his guardian . . .'

'Once a common dragoon sergeant and at that time her gardener. I know. It must have seemed odd.'

'Odd?' shrieked Daniel, 'Is that all you'll say? It seemed odd?'

Poor old Daniel. Information is his food and drink. But he won't get any from me. It's not that he was once a professional spy, it's because he's a scribbler. As well tell the town crier. He could no more help putting our story in print than a charger can resist battle trumpets.

I changed the subject and went into a dissertation on the drilling of crops that had him almost weeping with frustration.

He made one last feint. 'Tell me this at least, Sir Martin. Does the mystery of the boy have anything to do with that other business? You know, our search for . . .' he lowered his voice '. . . Anne Bonny?'

I shook my head. 'That came to nothing. I told you. Anne Bonny didn't exist.' I went to the stand by the front door and picked out a riding whip, 'Now excuse me. I mustn't keep the boy waiting.'

He sighed and nodded. 'Justice is best when summary,' he said, 'Not harsh, but firm. Even an earl must learn respect for his elders.'

I thanked him for his advice and went upstairs. Jubah stopped me in the corridor, so worried it frightened me: 'Does it go badly?'

'No, no. That babby still kicking his way out and his mother still cussing.' She crushed her apron in her hands. 'You won't whup the boy too hard, Sir Martin? He don't mean no disrespect. He only worried this child be a son and you love it more than him. Thrash him light now.'

'Jubah, I'm trusting you with my wife. You trust me with the boy.'

James was sitting on his bed. He'd been crying.

'You were rude, James. And you were rude in front of a guest.'

He nodded, miserably. His eyes on the riding whip, he said, 'I deserve that you should beat me, don't I?'

Like I say, too passionate. 'I don't intend to beat you. I propose we go for a ride while we discuss matters. Wash your face, fetch a hat and crop and meet me at the gates.'

Barty Bates saddled up Armchair for me and Picardy for James. He complained, like he always does: 'Sergeant, it don't do my bloody reputation no good you riding out in public on a bloody cart-puller like this four-legged fortune. They may have dumplings for brains round here but they know horseflesh when they see it.'

'We ain't charging the Frogs in Flanders, you grumbling bugger,' I told him, 'We're going alderman pace. Peaceful. Now get me up. And don't call me Sergeant.'

Barty was in my troop at Ramillies. When I found him again he was begging on the streets, as too many old soldiers have to. Like me he's a Londoner and as out of place among the bumpkinarchy as I am; though, unlike me, he cares what the yokels think of our stable, James's being the only hunter in it. My gallops are over; I've only one good leg nowadays and a swinger that's getting worse.

Waiting for James at the gates, I looked back at the house. It is still so enchanted a place for me that I'm afraid it will disappear one day. Decrepit as it had become when I first saw it, its bones were beautiful and it sat as comfortably in the combe as a fine old lady in her rocking chair. Mostly the estate's pasture but there's some forty acres down near the Dart suitable for drilling.

It was going cheap and I used my inheritance from Aunt Effie to buy it. This may account for her haunting. She always set her mind against other people's happiness, did Aunt Effie, especially if it was her money they were happy on. 'You've done your damage this day, Effie Sly, if that's what you wanted,' I said, 'Now leave me alone to pick up the pieces.'

I didn't want to be away long because of the baby. We rode towards Spitchwick and we rode in silence. I had a lot to consider. At the old pack bridge, James helped me dismount and we sat with our legs dangling to watch the shadow of the fish holding against the rush of water on the pebbles below. The storm had washed everything fresh and the scent of bracken was strong up here on the moorland.

I said, 'You ever embarrass me and a guest again, James, I'll knock you down.'

'I'm sorry, Guardian,' he said.

'I know you are. And, rudeness excepted, you were right; a man should know his parentage. What I'm going to do, James, is this: I'm going to write your history down, all of it I know.

7

And how I discovered it – that's important. And when I've written it I'm going to seal it in that little brass-bound box in my library and take it to Lawyer Pardoe in Exeter and tell him to give it to you on your twenty-first birthday.'

'But that's ten years off!'

'Haven't been neglecting your mathematics, then.'

To hell, I thought. Here I sit, delivering like Solomon, but I'm not *sure*. Even twenty-one is too young for that much hurt. To know you were conceived only to be an instrument of revenge, not just now but for the generations to come? That's hard.

He tossed a stone into the river. He was upset but keeping his temper. 'Why do I have to wait so long?'

'Because I hope by then you'll know your own worth. Not your estates' or your titles' or your birth's, yours as a man. A man's true measure is who loves him and why. To quote our mutual friend Defoe: "Titles are shadows, crowns are empty things."'

He finished the quotation, ' "The good of subjects is the cause of kings."'

I patted his knee. 'The same applies to earls. You're a fine boy in your own right, James, and you're going to be a fine man. Who fathered you makes no difference to that.'

He considered for a while. 'I don't have to be the cause of a rebellion if I don't want, do I?'

They hanged and quartered the Jacobite leaders last January and the account of their executions lost nothing in the telling. It must have been weighing on him.

I said, 'No question of it, that much I *can* tell you. Squire Narracott is a . . . I'll have words with Squire Narracott.' I'll make that bow-gutted, ale-swilling, piss-brained yokel wish he'd been born in another county; the reason we settled so far from London was to keep away from rumour-mongering clumps like him.

'Greville says the Narracotts can trace their ancestry back to the Saxon kings,' James said.

'Who were conquered by the Normans,' I said. 'So much for heredity. Proves my point.'

He laughed and seemed satisfied. He's a good lad. He chattered all the way home. I thought, Why give him pain? Why not manufacture a happy history for him? No, he's entitled to the truth.

As we rode through the gates, Jubah leaned out of the solar shouting. 'She a girl and she fat. Mother and babby doing fine.'

In my relief I noticed James's. Jubah was right; he'd been afraid a son would replace him in our affection. On our way upstairs to the solar he said, 'I wish I was your son.'

At least there was one truth I could tell him: 'We couldn't love you more if you were.'

Now here I sit, a new ledger before me, quills sharpened, inkpot open, candle placed. It's so quiet I can hear the beams creak as they dry out. Pastor Thomas has been and gone. The sheets are washed, afterbirth burned. Daniel Defoe has toasted the baby in so many drams he's had to be helped upstairs, while the lady herself is tucked up in bed with her mother and sister. The house smells of dill, which Jubah says hastens nursing women's milk. If Aunt Effie's ghost was here, it's gone again, content with the harm it's caused.

Reading over what I've put down already by way of practice, I see that Reverend Morton would have beaten me for not including some improving and uplifting moral. He ran a good school, did Reverend Morton, the Dissenters' Academy, and it was Daniel Defoe who persuaded Father to send me to it. He was educated there himself and, being our neighbour those days in Smithfield, he knew I'd profit from being taught not only grammar, but science.

I profited more from science than grammar, so the good Reverend's moralizing will find no place in my tale. What I will do, though, is distance myself from the events I put down and from the people who lived and died in forming James's history. I shall try to recreate what went on in their minds; Daniel Defoe has told me often enough what was going through his, the Highlander's was transparent – and I always knew what the Bratchet was thinking.

Then again, I have the Madwoman's diary, that terrible docu-ment which came into my hands on the same day I became

9

James's guardian, the day Queen Anne died. When necessary, I can interpose the Sir Martin Millet who sits at this desk now to explain the age of Queen Anne and its affairs; by the time James reads this it will be history to him, and, having been deliberately sheltered from fashionable society, he is mercifully ignorant of politics and life's other sewers.

He will learn that power makes great men careless of other men's lives, that they will commit any crime to hold on to it – and call that crime 'patriotism'. He'll learn the suffering that was inflicted on me, and even more on others, because of a single action that was taken to preserve a particular party in power. Most of all, he will learn the appalling price of sugar that is paid, not in money, but in flesh – and why I will never allow so much as a spoonful of it in my house.

But I'm unsure where to begin. With the Stuarts? No. I agree with Daniel who calls them 'an unchancy crew'. Of the fifteen Stuart sovereigns who ruled first Scotland and then all Britain, six died violent deaths. James II, Queen Anne's father, inherited all their obstinacy without any of their intelligence and England did well to rid herself of him in the Glorious Revolution of 1688. The Pretender, his son in exile, takes after him. He would be on the throne by now if he'd agreed to forswear the Roman Catholic religion and become a Protestant.

Not the Stuarts, then; Queen Anne was the best of them and she's dead these two years. No, we'll start the tale with Aunt Effie's murder, which is how I entered it. It may give her spirit some satisfaction to know that her death was one in a line which included princes'. Aunt Effie died because Queen Anne, despite seventeen pregnancies, had no child that survived beyond the age of eleven.

In any case, it's fitting to start there because women are the beginning and end of the story and, whatever else this manuscript does, it will profit James to know the importance of the other sex. Because he's had Jubah at his beck and call all his life, he's inclined to take women for granted, whereas I, deprived of my mother early, have a regard for them which makes me an oddity in a society that believes they were put on this earth only to provide various forms of gratification for the male.

10

Squire Narracott, for instance, who has his eye on my land, has already suggested we arrange a marriage between our two-year-old daughter and his fifteen-year-old son. I told him my wife would insist that the girl choose for herself when she's of age. He went off thinking me not only effeminate but dangerous.

Queens, sluts, good women, bad women, white women, black women, vengeful women, kind women, adventurous and brave women, they dominate this history.

Yet the one question James didn't think to ask was, 'Who is my mother?'

CHAPTER ONE

THE KILLING of Effie Sly, lodging-house keeper, took place on the night of 14 July 1706, in the fourth year of Queen Anne's reign.

Her murderer had come for the small brass-bound box in Effie's bedroom, but Effie was not one to give up possessions easily. She was a stout woman and she put up a fight; also, the fatness of her neck made it difficult to throttle. Even so, her assailant was taller, with hands that could wield a cutlass like a butterknife, and Effie's forty-eight years of gin drinking were against her.

The struggle knocked over the brass-topped table that Effie had acquired off an East Indiaman in lieu of payment, tipped her Dutch chamber-pot and spilled its contents, extinguishing the candle which had already fallen and was setting fire to the floorboards. Finally, Effie herself toppled and her killer's fingers squeezed the last of life out of her.

Dust and quiet settled back on the room. It might seem impossible that nobody had heard the struggle or the altercation that preceded it, but the house was deserted until Effie's lodgers should return from the various hostelries they patronized. In any case, this was Puddle Court just off the docks – in every sense one of the lowest parts of London. It was accustomed to the sounds of violence and its inhabitants found it wiser not to investigate them.

The only person to see the murderer leave the house was Effie's maid, returning from the shop down the alley with a jug of best cock-my-cap for her mistress, accompanied by Effie's dog. And the murderer saw her. The killing hands put down the box they carried, the eyes under the low hat-brim stared into those of the maid whose life at that moment was as good as ended – and doubtless would have been if, in that same moment, three roisterers hadn't emerged from the brothel next door to Effie's house.

The murderer picked up the box and ran off, to be followed by the maid, calling, in turn followed by the dog, wagging its tail, and the roisterers, staggering, but none caught up with the fleeing figure. As the coroner said at the inquest, it must have been a local man to know the alleys so well.

I know now that my aunt, Effie Sly, was among other things a government informer. There are hundreds, perhaps thousands, of such people: caretakers, letter-writers, footmen and maids, liverymen, lawyers, all of them men and women who are privy to the secrets and comings-and-goings of others. The London underworld, which has its own *lingua franca*, has a strange name for such informers. They are called Dark Lanterns. They are the natural descendants of the system set up by Elizabeth Tudor's spymaster which had its filaments all over the country so that a conspiracy against the Queen in, say, Warwickshire would send a tremor along the web and alert the great spider Lord Walsingham in its centre that there was a traitor to be racked.

In my day, the reign of Queen Anne, the spider who sat in the centre of this web was Secretary of State Robert Harley, the most devious of Her Majesty's ministers. It was inevitable, therefore, that a report of Effie's death should end up on his desk where, for a while, it was lost in the jumble of papers.

He didn't read it until three weeks after the murder, when, by coincidence, a Scotsman had come down from the Highlands to question a man in a pillory on what turned out to be a related subject . . .

If, James, you're ever faced with the alternative of imprisonment or a day in the pillory, choose imprisonment. For one thing, the pillory can wreck your back. Constables responsible for erecting the post, with its yoke for arms and head, in which the offender stands from dawn to dusk, take care that its height puts maximum strain on the spine.

The pillory can kill you. However worthy the cause or crime which puts you in it, you're victim to the universal law which demands that a crowd, presented with a coconut, has to shy something at it. Manure, rotten eggs or last week's cabbage, aren't so bad; it's the stones that do the damage. Dead kittens are harmless, but live dogs used as missiles hang on by their teeth and can claw your eye out.

In that sense, the man in the pillory on Cornhill just outside the Royal Exchange was lucky; for most of the day it had been raining God's own version of cats and dogs, soaking, warm, summer rain and only a few passers-by had felt impelled to keep their throwing-hand in. However, the lamentations and prayers emitted by the bent, rain-soaked figure indicated he was suffering to the depths of the pillory's intended purpose – degradation. Here was a man who had once walked the colonnades of the Royal Exchange where his fellow-merchants gathered under the columned portico, staring at him. No more would he share with them the right to vote or sit on a jury. No chance now to be Lord Mayor. He was branded an offender unworthy of trust or respect, sharing the punishment of homosexuals, perjurers, keepers of dishonest scales and anyone else the establishment wanted to humiliate.

The pillory's most dreaded time was approaching – the moment when schools disgorge their pupils. Moreover an obstinate raindrop was clinging to the end of his nose, tickling it into spasm, and in trying to shake it off – his fingers couldn't reach – he'd lodged a splinter in his neck from the rough oak collar around it. Into his misery came the voice of the Scotsman. 'Is it Master Foe of Freeman's Yard I have the pleasure of addressing?'

With his head at its present angle the pilloried man could make out a pair of large feet wearing pumps, calves encased in clocked hose, and bony, bare knees below tartan of which the predominant colour was red. Without these pointers, he could still have guessed at the nationality of the enquirer, as much from the voice's lilt as from the comments of the by-standers, who, used as they were to the cosmopolitan mix of merchants going in and out of the Royal Exchange, found the sight of Highlanders' filibegs irresistibly worthy of such shouts as, 'What's under the kilt, Kitty?'

Even in the profundity of his shame, the pilloried man's

15

interest was aroused. As we know, curiosity was, and still is, his weakness. He twisted his neck to peer through plastering hair into a pair of astonishingly blue eyes. 'De,' he said.

'Master Duh?'

'*De* Foe,' said the man in the pillory with emphasis, 'The name's Defoe.'

The Highlander took the right hand poking through the pillory's yoke and shook it heartily, causing Defoe's body on the other side to tilt eastwards. 'I've been fain to meet ye,' he said. 'I've enquired of every watch in the City to find a man who has the greatest knowledge of it. I'm told ye have grand acquaintance of its every stank and cobble and I'd employ ye in a search for a lassie that was here a whiles back.'

They were attracted to the pillory, Defoe thought. Sometimes they came to preach, or tell you their life's story, or mutter incantations. This one was a giant who wore a tattered thrum bonnet cocked over orange hair. The part of the plaid that went over his shoulder was neatly darned here and there but fastened with a jewelled dagger. Defoe said, 'I'm otherwise engaged, sir.' It didn't do to offend them when they were this size.

'I can see that ye are,' said the Highlander, 'but it'll no take much of your time to answer one or two questions. If ye can locate the lass, guidsir, I'm prepared to pay your caution money and free ye.'

Mad but splendid. 'My dear sir.'

The Highlander winked and gave his sporran a self-satisfied tap. 'There's thirty pound in English siller here awaiting the right answer.'

Defoe's head drooped again. 'Multiply that sum by ten, my good sir, and we'd be compacted,' he said.

'Three *hundred*? I've no that much. Losh, man, how'd ye come to such a pickle?'

Three hundred pounds would only liberate Defoe from his immediate debts; it would take five times that amount to satisfy all his creditors.

'Well, but a bawbee's better than a brackle as my dear mother used to say,' the Scotsman went on, 'Advise me and ye'll have thirty pound in siller and my gratitude. Anne was the lassie's name. She shipped into London from foreign parts mebbe four, five year ago, then vanished. Will ye enquire for her?'

A girl called Anne who'd disappeared years before in a city of nearly a million souls. Defoe humoured the idiot: 'Did she have another name?'

'Bard was the family, yet she'll mebbe have travelled under the name of Bonny. She'd have set out from Bohemia but my chieftain surmises she'd have taken ship in Hamburg.'

Until a few minutes before, Defoe had considered his position incapable of further humiliation; now he heard sniggering coming from the portico of the Royal Exchange behind him. To be in this condition and bantered by a bedlamite, a *tartaned* bedlamite, was Pelion piled on Ossa. 'Please go away.'

A hand the size of a spade clasped his left hand, causing him to tilt westwards. 'Master Foe,' the giant said, sternly, 'I'm ettling to be home, away from the clishmaclavers of this city life that suits me but ill. Yet my chieftain bids me find the lassie and find her I will. So far I've discovered nobody as will admit to knowing her. Now I need your aid, since ye're the man as knows the dark of this place and has agents everywhere, they tell me. I'll not leave till I get it. Do I have it?'

Anything, *anything*. 'Yes.'

'Ye'll make enquiries?'

'Yes.' Defoe felt a displacement of air and winced as the Highlander clapped him on the back, dislodging the rainwater that had settled in the open collar of his shirt so that it ran down his spine.

'Grand, grand. I'm to be found at the Fountain tavern in Cheapside. I'll await your findings. As quick as you please. I have to tell ye this is a confidential matter. We must be discreet, my guidsir. Good fortune to ye.'

There was another assault on Defoe's stiff shoulders and the pumps moved out of his sight. 'What's your name?' he shouted.

The answer came singing through the wet air. 'Ask for Livingstone of Kilsyth. Good day to ye, Master Foe.'

'De,' shouted Daniel Defoe. 'The name's *De*foe.'

Struggling to right his trunk against the wood of the pedestal, he craned his poor neck to watch the giant swing away, his figure startlingly outlined against the dignified, Portland stone frontages of Cornhill. The red tartan, rose-coloured jacket and orange hair looked as discreet as a fairground. *Did I dream the man?* No, more likely the man had dreamed him. There had been no questions as to why he, Defoe, occupied a pillory. He might as well have been a staging post at which the Highlander changed horses on an urgent journey. Only the young and the aristocracy possessed such absent-minded ruthlessness and Defoe was now prepared to swear that, for all the worn habit, the giant incorporated both of those enviable conditions. There had been a confidence in the 'Livingstone of Kilsyth' that spoke of castles perched on barbaric crags, tenantry, and a thousand years of breeding.

Well, he could save his breath to cool his porridge, or whatever it was Highlanders ate when they were home. Defoe could have told him that the pillory was only the first stage of his sentence. The rest was likely to extend in Newgate prison for life.

Defoe groaned as he stared downwards into the puddle at the pillory's foot which still shivered from the Highlander's step, distorting the reflection of the suffering face above it.

'Clishmaclavers,' muttered Defoe, 'Livingstone of Kilsyth.' Bard and Bonny and Bohemia. Like a tired dolphin he chased the alliteration through the sea of his mind and couldn't catch it. Something swam there, though.

The wench was dead, of course. But that was in another country, and besides, the wench is dead. Or worse. When they disappeared in this city they never resurfaced. If the Highlander but knew it, he wouldn't want her to. Then his own shame flooded away others'. Samson among Philistines, he allowed his head to hang so that he was blind to everything, unaware of handbells announcing the end of the school day until the shriek of joyful treble voices rang round his ears and the first mud pie splattered on his hair.

But that night when the bailiffs came to release him they were, to his amazement, polite. To his further astonishment, they escorted him, not back to his cell at Newgate, but to the royal palace of Kensington where a most important man awaited him.

'... And so, Master Foe, Her Gracious Majesty may, at my urging, be pleased to set aside your sentence and even pay sufficient of your debts to gain your release.'

Robert Harley's voice was one of those kept deliberately soft so that to hear what he was saying you virtually had to cease breathing. Defoe stopped panting and brought his bemused gaze away from the ceiling with its cupolas down to the ormolu writing table and the gentleman in mouse-coloured velvet who sat behind it. Everything in the room, the gentleman, his desk, the white panelling, the huge blue and white Chinese vases that stood in its niches, bespoke taste, riches, cleanliness. Only Defoe was foul. 'I beg your pardon, my lord?'

The small voice repeated what it had said and still didn't permeate Defoe's understanding. This neat, secret man was at the heart of the government which had brought him to trial; to appreciate that it might now be winding him up from the bottom of the well into which it had plunged him took adjustment.

He was distracted by the mud still dripping down his face from his hair, more especially by the state of his breeches. He had begged the bailiff to be allowed to clean himself and been refused. Through the windows open on to a terrace came the scent of roses and lavender refreshed by the rain, emphasizing his embarrassment at his own stink but ... *He means me to be shamed.* Defoe's wits were coming back. 'Do you say Her Majesty will forgive me, my lord?' Pounding hope in his brain forced him to hold his breath again to hear the reply.

'It was a foolish essay, Master Foe.'

It was a splendid essay, thought Defoe, a fine Whig attack on High Church Tories ...

Perhaps, James, at this juncture I'd better explain the difference between Whig and Tory as it was then. By the time you read this, their politics may have altered. They're already beginning to.

Even now, the division's clear-cut in country areas like ours. Squire Narracott is a typical High Tory, as his father was, as his son will be, a landowner, an unquestioning and regular attender of the established Church of England, fiercely patriotic, loyal to the Crown; generally a pain in the backside. It worried the Narracotts when James II was ousted, but they didn't oppose the Glorious Revolution because James was a Roman Catholic and was showing his intention of bringing up his baby son, now the Pretender, in the same faith. The Narracotts and their ilk can't abide popery; their memory's still haunted by Bloody Mary, two centuries back, who demonstrated the Christianity of the Catholic religion by burning Protestants alive.

In James's place they reluctantly accepted William of Orange's right to the throne as coming through his wife, Mary, James's elder daughter. On his death they were happier to welcome Queen Anne, James's second daughter, because she ruled alone and was at least in direct succession.

What made Narracotts and other Tories unhappy during Anne's reign was the war with France. They knew that the papist French king, Louis XIV, had to be stopped from annexing all Europe, they even cheered the victories of Anne's great general the Duke of Marlborough and our Protestant allies against the French tide when it threatened Flanders.

But as the war dragged on, the taxes they had to pay for it became heavier – and if there is one thing a Tory hates more than papism, it's taxation.

Whigs now. As I write, the only Whigs you've met are artisans. Save-the-Lord Cribbens, the weaver, is a Whig, so is Will Nutley, so is Margaret Bates, the laundress – descendants of those who opposed Charles I's 'divine right of kings' in the Civil War, believing that it's due even to the poor to choose their own form of government.

You've never seen them or their families at service in the parish church because they aren't Anglicans like you and Squire Narracott, but have gone back to what they believe is the 'pure' church as it was established by the simple followers of Christ in his lifetime. Puritanism has developed many branches, Baptists, Quakers, Presbyterians and other sects which refuse to conform to the state religion. They are the non-conformists and the extreme among them are as big a pain in the arse as the Narracotts and their ilk.

The High Tories call them Dissenters and hate them as much as popery and taxes.

But there was, and is, another variety of Whig you haven't met yet. At bottom, they hold similar beliefs to their poorer brethren in the country towns and villages, but these are mostly rich merchants and bankers, not landholders in the sense that Tories are, though they have their acres and build fine houses on them. They are men who congregate in what, in my day, was Jonathon's Coffee Shop and is now the Stock Exchange.

On the whole they supported the war and the Duke of Marlborough, a Whig himself, on the reasonable assumption that the total defeat of France would enable them to trade in markets that until then had been French.

Society, which was mainly Tory during Anne's reign, punished non-conformism by forbidding from public office any who did not take Church of England communion. But these Whig Dissenters were powerful men with a large representation in the House of Commons and they wanted office.

To Tory fury, they crawled through a neat little loophole in the law by occasional attendance at the established Anglican churches where, presumably with fingers crossed, they took the sacrament before returning to their chapels and tabernacles.

Today we're becoming used to one-party rule. But under Queen Anne there were both Tories and Whigs in the government because she insisted on choosing her ministers from the best men of both parties. A great one for tolerance, Anne, bless her. She herself was a devout member of the Church of England but her husband, Prince George of Denmark, who she made Lord High Admiral of England, was a Lutheran and worshipped in his own private chapel, only attending Anglican communion once a year.

Of course, James, this is a simplification; nothing in life is as clear-cut at that. But generally, it's safe to say, the Whigs of those days felt in constant danger of losing their freedom if High Tories gained control of Parliament.

And that thoroughgoing Puritan Whig, our friend Daniel Defoe, couldn't resist entering the fray. We know his forte is writing but he regarded himself then – I think he still does – as a merchant adventurer who used his talent with the pen only in good causes or, in his bankruptcies, to pay his bills. In this case he had published a pamphlet satirically attacking the High Tories by aping the violence of the language they poured out against non-conformists. He called it 'The Shortest Way with Dissenters', suggesting all non-conformers be hanged.

He'd been too clever – he often is. As he said to me later: 'The buggers took it seriously.' He was applauded by the High Tories and abused by fellow Dissenters. It wasn't until Secretary of State Nottingham, a fanatical Anglican, realized he and others like him were being parodied that a warrant was taken out for Daniel's arrest and he landed in the pillory. With this result . . .

A truly splendid essay, Defoe thought defiantly in that beautiful room in Kensington Palace. But he also thought of his family and his future and what this man who faced him, this most powerful of men, could do to them.

'It *was* foolish, my lord.' Doglike, he fixed his eyes on the bland face before him. It was rumoured this great man, too, was a Dissenter. A Tory, but a Dissenter. Formerly the Speaker of the House of Commons, now the coming man in Her Majesty's government. Could he . . . ? Would he . . . ?

'Like the Queen, I believe in moderation in all things.' Harley's words stole on to the air and with them came the whiff of fine port. Defoe noticed a half-empty decanter on a nearby table. Not moderate in quite everything, then. But it was a lovely word 'moderation', resonant with forgiveness, and allowing imprisoned men to go home to their families. 'Are you a moderate man, Master Foe?'

He was, he was. He could be moderate until their eyes watered. 'I *am*, my lord.'

Harley nodded. 'With an aptitude for words, it seems. Should you employ them in the cause of moderation, perhaps there could be some mutual benefit in our cooperation from time to time.'

Eh? Did the Tories think that he, a Puritan Whig, was a hired pen to write what they wanted him to write? A Defoe had his pride. 'I am always at your disposal, my lord, but I am first and foremost a merchant. If it's mutual benefit you suggest, may I expound on a project sure to quadruple investment – a waterproof overcoat invented by a friend of mine, a marvellous protection against –'

'You are a bankrupt, Master Foe.' The terrible phrase tiptoed across the desk and crawled over his flesh. 'How then can you be a merchant? But if you do not wish to cooperate . . .' Harley's white hand reached for the little bell on his desk.

Newgate. Defoe fell to his knees. 'Don't send me back, my lord. I'll serve, I'll serve. In any capacity. Only deliver me from my dungeon and my life is yours to make return as no man ever made. I have seven children, my lord. I shall dedicate my life to you. My lord, my lord.' He was crying at the horror of a return to Newgate, but also out of terror of a future to which he had just sold his soul.

Impassively, the Queen's minister watched him until his sobs subsided. 'Very well. I shall recommend Her Majesty to mercy. I think I can promise that your sentence will be set aside. You are free. You can make your own way home? Then au revoir, Master Foe.'

Defoe crawled under the desk and kissed the buckle of his deliverer's right shoe. He had a sense of displacement as he did it, the Puritan Whiggish gentleman he had once been standing aside in amazement at this other, broken self. He crawled back, got up and wiped his eyes. 'Yet tell me what you want me to *do*, my lord.' Even this moment of his deliverance had the uncontrol of the nightmare he'd been in these past weeks and he was a man who liked things specified.

Robert Harley didn't. 'These matters have a way of becoming apparent. Good night.' He watched the scarecrow bow its way backwards to the door and only when it turned to go through the door did he call it back. 'I believe you were approached by a Scotsman this afternoon, Master Foe.'

Defoe turned round, eager to share the joke. 'A madman, my lord. And careless. He'd lost a woman and wished me to find her. "Lost indeed," I told him . . .'

23

'Livingstone of Kilsyth is a Jacobite, Master Foe, a relative by marriage of Claverhouse, the rebel against our late king. We have been watching him. It is strange he should come to you for assistance.'

Defoe clung hard to the door handle. 'I never saw him before, my lord. I swear it. I had no notion. What could I do but hear the man, pinioned as I was?' Dear God. All he needed was to be suspected of sympathizing with the Pretender across the Channel. He heard himself jabber his loyalty to Queen Anne, the Protestant faith, all of it true, knowing he was protesting too much. 'I rode with the late, good King William to oust James, my lord, as did you. My devotion to the Protestant cause is on record.'

'Strange, though, that Kilsyth came to you. Why you?'

'I don't *know*.' He tried to calm down. 'I have a reputation, my lord, for a better knowledge of London than most. I believe I was recommended to him. As a merchant, I've had to do with low as well as high. And due to unfortunate circumstances I was forced into unwilling acquaintanceship with rogues . . .'

'That would be during your other incarceration in Newgate, would it, Master Foe?' came the soft voice. 'Your previous bankruptcy in 1696?'

Defoe gaped. Did this man know *everything*? 'Believe me, lord,' he begged, 'I know nothing of this Scotsman nor his strumpet, this Bonny or Bard or whatever she called herself.'

Harley's hand reached for the decanter and stroked it before pouring himself a dark, rich glass of its contents. 'But perhaps we *should* know more of this Jacobite of yours, Master Foe.'

'Not mine, my lord, I . . .'

'Perhaps we should find this woman for him and discover what it is he wants of her.'

Defoe watched the glass lifted and sipped from. 'Small chance of it, my lord. We don't know . . .'

'We know that five years ago she arrived in the City, calling herself Bonny. We know that she lodged for a while in Puddle Court before she vanished.' Harley sipped his port and the smell of its ancient fruit reached the nostrils of the man who

24

had neither eaten nor drunk for twenty-four hours. Defoe gulped, even as he registered the fact that Harley knew the woman's past address. The Scotsman didn't.

Over the rim of the winking crystal, Harley added, 'The woman who kept that lodging house was murdered three weeks ago.'

Mystery. Tired as he was, afraid and confused as he was, the old excitement tingled through Defoe. Some men dug up relics of the past, others explored foreign lands; for him the great adventure was to discover what lay hidden in the jungle of his fellow-creatures. 'You believe there to be a connection between the two events?'

'That is for you, Master Foe. Search the house if you wish.'

'De,' said Defoe, abstractedly, '*De*foe. Puddle Court, eh? I suppose I could. Yes, as soon as I can, I shall . . .'

'Tomorrow, Master Foe.'

Defoe looked up. 'My lord, I must see to my business. I owe you my life but I have other debts, some £1,542. 13*s*. 4*d*. If I don't settle I shall be re-arrested. I have a wife and seven children, my lord, whose education calls on me to furnish their heads, if not their purses.' He looked hopefully towards his new employer in a try for wages.

'Tomorrow, Master Foe. With discretion, if you please.'

The interview was like being lost in fog. At this rate the sale of his soul wasn't fetching much. He'd be back hiding in the cupboard listening to the bailiffs' tread on the stairs and the familiar 'Is your husband at home, Mistress Foe?'

Yet still he tingled with the desire to know why two such disparate men as a patched young Highlander and a senior minister of England had a mutual interest in a missing girl. 'She is of importance, then, Mistress Bonny Bard?'

Harley's expression didn't alter. 'We look forward to hearing your discoveries tomorrow, Master Foe.'

After a long march through great corridors a footman showed him out by a back porch into the care of a porter who took him to a lodge and gates that bore the insignia of William and Mary. Defoe's sense of direction, like all his senses, was wobbling. 'Which way to London?'

The porter pointed eastward along the dark village street beyond the gates. 'Along to the Gore and follow your nose.'

'But, but . . .' He would have to pass through notorious Knightsbridge. At night. 'What if there are footpads?'

The porter looked him up and down. 'Ask 'em if they can spare a couple of coppers.'

Limping home, Defoe tried to place the character of the man to whom he was now in thrall, and failed. Impossible even to pinpoint his age, other than putting it between thirty and fifty. Harley was one of those who'd always looked middle-aged, always would; the fixity of his pleasant expression preserved the face from wrinkles. It evaded Defoe's mind's eye as the personality behind it evaded his understanding. A secret, devious man with a reputation for cleverness that had taken him from a country member of parliament to one of the highest posts in Queen Anne's cabinet where he was known to have made the middle ground of politics his own. But whether he had taken it through conviction or because it gave him a basis of power that nobody else occupied was impossible to guess.

My master now. Defoe knew he had no alternative. He was forty-six, too old to recover from this bankruptcy as he had before. *I could have been Lord Mayor.* Now he wasn't even worth the attention of footpads.

He'd loved being a merchant, not just for the opportunity to make great wealth – though that too – but for the romance of it, to be able to say he'd ventured such and such ship abroad, to sit in his counting house in touch with all nations.

'A true bred merchant,' he used to tell his apprentices, 'is a universal scholar. He understands languages without books and geography without maps.'

Now there were no apprentices and no ships. He'd taken too many risks, become too excited at this project and that. Credit, his life-blood, had been stopped. His counting house had been shut up as if he were dead, which is what he might as well be. Here lies Daniel Defoe, mortally stabbed by his creditors.

Newgate. Criminals and whores went into that fever-ridden rat-hole for a set term of imprisonment, but a debtor went in until his creditors could be paid – which they couldn't or the poor debtor would have done so – and died. Sooner, rather than later.

Suddenly Defoe doubled up and retched until he had to sit down on a milestone near the turnpike to get over the nausea at the nearness of his escape from that awful death. It was late and there was no one around to see him. The sky had cleared and warm moonlight shone through the branches of a chestnut tree above him where a nightingale trilled its arpeggios. Rain had heightened the smells of the cow-patted, hay-ricked, honey-suckled countryside around him. Gratitude came over him for the man who had preserved him to sniff these free and lovely scents on this July night. *I'll serve and I'll serve.*

Robert Harley had hired himself a hack.

Sighing, Defoe got up, favouring his back. He wiped his hand across his mouth and down the seat of his disgusting breeches, which were further wetted by the milestone. They reminded him there was still a fortune to be made if he could only invest in Sutton's waterproof overcoat. And the words Bard, Bonny and Bohemia continued to play peep-bo at the edge of his memory. He pursued them all the way home.

By the next morning, Defoe had retrieved his confidence with a good night's sleep, as well as his sage-green velvet coat and Isabella satin waistcoat from under the floorboards where Mrs Defoe kept them away from the bailiffs' eye. Bathed, break-fasted and bewigged he stepped out of the attic in Clare Market in which the family was riding out its present difficulty, to set off eastwards towards Puddle Court.

His emergence was less glorious than his appearance – he stepped out through a back window on to next door's roof and from there, via other roofs, to an alley – but once on the ground he shook his frilled cuffs over his beringed hands, settled the curls of his wig and the sword at his hip and strode off, whistling.

After all, though one professional door had closed, another had opened. Writing, which had been his hobby, could yet be his lifeline with Harley's backing. *God who gave me brains will surely give me bread*. A fine summer's morning and a mystery to solve.

His route was deliberately erratic, to avoid creditors' eyes and pursuing bailiffs. He paused before shop windows that reflected the view behind him in each pane. At Booksellers' Row he resisted the siren call of the volumed stalls and made a fast crossing of the Strand to disappear under the clothes lines that stretched across Strand Lane, past the quill merchant's and the fish sauce shop into George Yard, where a quick dash took him through the front entrance of Charles the pipemaker's and out of the back.

He resurfaced in the City, if resurface is the word for the walk through that portion of it bordering the river. Dark passages and courtyards shut out sunlight, tunnels only occasionally evincing glimpses of a sky criss-crossed with spars and the cordage of ships. He had to skip to avoid water sloshing from fish tanks carried on the heads of scaly, besmocked porters who swore at him for getting in their way. Even he was lost in this maze but he knew whom and how to ask his way and at last came upon Puddle Court.

For the past ten minutes his hand had rested on the hilt of his sword and now he shifted it to make sure it would come easily out of the scabbard; the gentry of this area rose late, conducting most of their business in the dark, but it was well to be prepared.

The court had taken its name from Mr Puddle's famous dock, to which it had once been contiguous, but, after the Great Fire of 1666 had consumed it and two-thirds of the City of London, it had been rebuilt further back by a speculator who'd renamed it Grantley Court in the hope of raising its tone and its rents. He'd managed to put up one stone house before losing his money, after which less high-minded builders had taken over with wattle and river-mud and the court's former inhabitants scuttled back to it, resuming their rat-like existence under its old name.

Broken drainpipes directed last night's rain on to sunken, weedy cobbles, wetting forty years of debris. Defoe stood in the archway entrance, staring at the court's only elegant house which faced him at the other end. A leaning sign outside it read, 'Lodgings'.

He nodded. A girl fresh from abroad, perhaps at night, tired from her voyage, might well have wandered from the quayside and mistaken this house for a safe haven in which to find a bed. Whitened steps led up to a pillared door with a brass knocker. Long, curtained windows looked loftily across the ramshackle court below them as if trying to ignore it. The house exuded respectability.

Probably a brothel. Respectability and Puddle Court were incompatible. Defoe crossed the court, avoiding the two dogs, one living, one dead, that bared their teeth at him. As he approached the lodging house, the bulky figure of a beadle emerged from a doorway next to it. 'Stand back there. No entry. Agin the law.'

'Good morning, Bully,' said Defoe.

The beadle shaded his eyes against the morning sun. 'It's Master Foe, as I live and. Thought you was in Newgate.'

'*De*foe,' said Defoe, 'Her Majesty recognized her mistake. I'm on her business, Bully. What do you do here?'

The beadle pointed a stout arm at the lodging house, releasing a smell of old sweat and fresh ale. ' "Murder by person or persons unknown," ' he said, 'such was the verdick of the inkwitch. I'm stopping the willain coming back.'

'He's hardly likely to, is he?'

'Shows what a good job I'm doing,' said Bully. His hand groped the inner recesses of the doorway and came out holding a battered tin tankard.

'Thirsty work, is it?' asked Defoe with irony.

Bully drank, nodding. A woman with straggling hair and wearing a wrapper too small across the chest appeared behind him. 'More ale, Mr Bully?' The rarity with which residents of Puddle Court were on good terms with the law produced a tendency to fawn on it when they were. She spotted Defoe. 'If it ain't Dan'l Foe done up like a maypole. Thought you was in Newgate. How's your dad, Dan'l? Still in the candle trade?'

'Ain't talking to you, is he, Dan'l?' said the beadle. His face went blank as Cockneys' do when they were amused. 'Not

29

since that project of yourn to light London with whale oil. Would've put him out of business.'

Defoe gave up and relapsed into the *langue de guerre*. He jerked his head at the lodging house. 'Who got done, Bully? And who done it?'

'Madam as kept the place. Effie Sly.' The beadle wiped his mouth and leaned forward confidentially. 'Throttled. Mo'ucks, Floss reckons. Eh, Floss?'

Floss nodded. 'Mo'ucks.'

'Mohocks?' Defoe was incredulous. The aristocratic young ruffians terrorizing London at the moment, taking their cue and head feathers from a group of Mohawk Red Indians who'd been brought from the New World for display in the capital, were known to slit noses, rape girls and roll old women in barrels, but throttling wasn't their style. Moreover, they tended to restrict their atrocities to the better parts of town. 'Mohocks in Puddle Court?'

'What's wrong with Puddle Court?' demanded Floss, 'Ain't it good enough for 'em?'

'I'd back it against Mohocks,' Defoe assured her. 'Did you see 'em?'

Floss reluctantly admitted she hadn't. 'But some gentlemen friends did as was visiting us at the time.' She inclined her head towards Effie Sly's house. 'An' so did the slut next door.'

Bully held to the Mohock theory. 'They never took her chink, Dan'l. Proves it.' A local murderer wouldn't have left Effie's cash behind.

'What did they take then?'

'Papers. She had papers in a box and they was took.' Floss's face expressed admiration. 'Effie could read and write, Effie could.'

It was then, James, that I, Martin Millet, entered Puddle Court and this history. Only arrived back from Flanders the previous night, I hadn't been in England twelve hours before people were telling me of my aunt's murder. Waiting for me was a letter from Effie's lawyers.

If she keeps on haunting me for it, I can't say I loved Aunt Effie; as far as I know she inspired affection in very few. My father, her brother, forbade me to see her on pain of yet another whipping and wanted to bring her to trial for 'bawdiness, cheating and the monstrous impiety of consorting with Satan'. But Effie seemed to have friends in high places; the charges came to nothing.

I was prepared to look kindly on anybody my father hated – anyway, what boy wouldn't be intrigued by a relative consorting with Satan? And because they flouted my father, Effie encouraged my visits with sweetmeats or the occasional farthing which, to me, was riches.

Unusual in Puddle Court, she dressed cleanly and kept her grey hair washed and tightly curled; her bodices were so stiffly boned that, in advancing on you, she gave the impression of contained weight on the move, like a walking tree. Though her daily drink was a jug of gin, I didn't see her the worse for it. I don't think, either, I ever saw a smile or a frown crease her wide, flat face; its immobility was another thing which set her apart from other Puddle Courters, who raged or laughed immoderately – though never at Effie Sly; there was something in her blue and shallow eyes that sobered people into respect.

But she could be angry; I once heard hissing coming from one of the lodgers' rooms and Effie, on emerging from it, looked at me expressionlessly and said, 'He wouldn't pay.' Behind her a man cowered with his arm over his eyes as if to keep off demons.

Who the lodgers were I never knew. Mostly men, sometimes women, often of a class not to be expected in Puddle Court. They didn't stay long. While I doubt whether Effie's past qualified her for membership of the Puritan sisterhood – Mr Sly had been the last of several husbands, none of whom survived – hers wasn't a bawdy house, like Father believed; instead, I realize now, it was a staging post for those who wanted to leave the country quickly without benefit of passport. She knew most of the Thames's more dubious shipping masters; they were often with her in her front room holding muttered conversations while money changed hands. The lodgers certainly paid high for her travel arrangements on their behalf – if they didn't, Effie betrayed them to the authorities like the Dark Lantern she was.

31

For a small boy whose father believed that any ornamentation on dress or furniture was Satan's keyhole, Effie's house
was an eldorado of curios and knick-knacks, nearly all foreign,
some repellent. A stuffed snakeskin coiled along her man-
telshelf between soapstone idols with overmany arms, and
weird candles that, when lit, made your head float.

There was a long, thin painting on silk which depicted
eastern men and women doing the sort of things to each other
that my father would have killed me for knowing about. Em-
balmed in a bottle of green fluid was an embryo that Effie said
was a monkey's but looked like a human baby.

Altogether it was a house I wouldn't have liked to spend the
night in, and never did, but by day Effie allowed me to roam it
– as long as I never entered her bedroom. I did once, from
curiosity, but Effie found me there. I can't remember what she
said, or if she said anything, but her eyes haunted my dreams
for a week, as did the glimpse of a hanging over her bed on
which the Lord's Prayer was written backwards. I thought I'd
be damned just for seeing it.

I know now that my soul was no more imperilled in Effie's
house than it was in my father's loveless one. In any case, once
I began attending the Dissenters' Academy, I grew away from
both and found more pleasure in Nature's laws than I ever did
in God's or the Devil's.

The last time I saw Aunt Effie was after I joined the Dragoons, when I went to say goodbye before I embarked for Flanders. There was a different maid in attendance on her; there
was always a different maid there – she didn't keep her staff
long, didn't Effie.

This one seemed even smaller, younger, dirtier and more
browbeaten than the others; she followed me outside when I
left, plucking at my coat. 'Don't want to stay here,' she whispered, 'Give us work, master. Take us away.'

I pitied the poor child but I had worries of my own; I was
trying to find my mother before I embarked. Besides, I couldn't
afford a camp follower. I patted her grubby head, gave her
sixpence and left – and shall be sorry for it to the end of my
days.

Now I was back again, not best pleased. I'd seen some sinks in Europe while I was away but Puddle Court outstank them all. I'd wanted to unsaddle my past, all of it, and here it was summoning me back. Somebody'd murdered Aunt Effie and got away with it.

Bully stepped in front of me as I approached Effie's steps. 'Stand back there. No entry. Agin the law.'

'Cut off, Bully,' I said, 'She was my bloody aunt.'

Floss gave a light scream and flung herself at me: 'Mart, my hero, my little cunnyborough. It's years.'

'I am pleased to see you, Martin,' said a voice I recognized from the depths of Floss's bosom. Daniel Defoe. He and his family had been our neighbours during my childhood in Smith-field. I was pleased to see him, too, despite the fact that we'd parted on bad terms. He hadn't wanted me to volunteer. As a true Whig he approved of the war against France – in his opinion England had to defend the Protestant faith, not to men-tion trade – but for me to join it, he said, was a waste of a natural, talented engineer better employed in a diving bell project that Daniel was trying to initiate: 'Think of the sunken Spanish treasure ships still waiting to be raised,' he'd said. I was angry and young so I told him to stuff his sunken treasure, and marched off to follow Marlborough's drum.

'Are you well, Martin?' he asked anxiously now, 'You're limp-ing.' I could see he thought I'd aged badly. He hadn't.

'Middling, Mr Foe, thank you.'

'Accept my condolences for the death of your poor aunt.'

I shrugged. 'Haven't seen her in years. Seems like she left me all her worldly goods. I got a paper here from a lawyer.'

'All her goods, eh?' Beadle Bully, acting on the local wisdom that he who benefited from murder ipso facto done the murder-ing, became official, 'Then I must ask you, Martin Millet, where was you on the night of 14 July?'

Floss turned on him. 'You beef-witted bluebottle. Our Mart's been fighting the Froggies with Marlborough.'

'What's he doin' here then?'

'He's a fucking hero anyways.' Floss grabbed me again. 'Gave them fucking French what for, din't you, chucky?'

'Point is, did he give his aunt what for on the night in question? Come on, Marty lad. You count for your movements.'

'Movements?' I said, 'Bully, my only movements've been hobbling home from Flanders with a game leg. I got home in the early hours. Ask the Dutch packet's skipper. She's still docked in the Pool.'

'I will,' said Bully stolidly. 'Gawd help us, what's that?'

We all turned to where he was staring and I saw the Scotsman for the first time. He stood in the entrance to the court like a kilted maypole, then strode towards us, shouting greetings.

'A grand morn, sirs and lady. The name's Livingstone. Of Kilsyth. Here y'are the long last, Master Foe. It's a blithe day. Have ye found her yet?'

Defoe gaped. 'How did you get here?' Strangers looking for an objective in this part of the city generally wandered for days before returning home, bemused and poorer, without finding it.

Livingstone of Kilsyth slapped him on the shoulder. 'I asked your guidwife. She was pleased to tell me where ye'd gone.'

'*My wife?*' I understood his bewilderment; in her time Mrs Defoe has parried questions as to her husband's whereabouts from constables, bailiffs, even close relatives. Either the Highlander had tortured the information out of her or he was attractive to women.

Beside him, Floss said, 'What's under the kilt, Katy?' and really wanted to know. Attractive then. Not that Floss was choosy.

'Have ye found Bonny Anne Bard?' persisted Kilsyth.

I saw Daniel wince. Heads that had poked out of the court's upper windows to complain at the Scotsman's voice – it could have reached Cheapside – remained to stare at the Scotsman's dress, like city pigeons regarding a cockatoo.

'Bonny?' Floss picked up the name. 'That the bloss as lodged with Effie way back?'

The Scotsman turned. 'Anne Bonny? Was she called Anne?'

Defoe intervened. 'We are attracting attention,' he said, warningly, 'I suggest Mistress Floss and I repair to the local hostelry where I can question her without distraction. I shall report our progress to you later.'

No you don't, I thought. I said, 'We'll all repair to Aunt Effie's. It's my bloody house now,' I added, as Bully began his automatic 'Agin the law.' I got out the roll of parchment with dangling seals that the lawyer had given me and shoved it at him, along with Effie's keys. 'I'm legal, Bully. Open her up.'

He had to think about it, a difficult business for Bully, but eventually he agreed to unlock Aunt Effie's door and we followed him in – Daniel, reluctantly.

It was oppressive inside, always had been. Strips of sun through the drawn curtains of the front room lit some of Effie's bric-à-brac and left the rest shadowed shapes. Daniel started back as he saw the bottled embryo. Death had settled on the place as thick as the dust.

Daniel whispered, 'Was it here?'

Bully shook his head. 'Upstairs.'

Without consultation we all headed for the kitchen at the back of the house where, though its walls were blackened by years of smoke from Effie's large fireplace, there was the reassuring familiarity of pots and pans. A pile of oyster shells thrown into a corner added their contribution to the smell of old grease.

Floss was aggrieved. 'We'd be better off at the Beggar Maker's. I can't go rememb'ring without me whistle's wetted. Send out for a pint, Marty, there's a chuck.'

'Send who?' I asked her. Whatever was said, I was staying to hear it.

'Send the Bratchet.'

We looked where she was pointing and saw a dog. Effie always kept a dog to run her turnspit, which was set high up in the wall next to the fireplace, but I hadn't seen this one before. It was small, with a body too long for its head and legs. Its colour blended in with the ashes it crouched on.

'Can't send that for a jug,' I said, 'it'd slop it.'

'Not the buffer,' said Floss, 'the Bratchet. That bleached mort in the nook there.' She approached the fireplace, then drew back as the dog snapped at her. 'Come out o' there, you, Bratchet.'

Something crawled out from the inglenook which, on close inspection, turned out to be human and female. Like the dog, it was small and ash-coloured; clothes, skin and hair, all were grey.

'Where does she come from?' asked Daniel, while I was just beginning to recognize the maid who'd asked me to take her away.

'Effie got her from the poorarse years back,' explained Floss, 'She's a orphing.'

'The where?' asked the Highlander.

'The poorhouse,' translated Daniel, 'an orphan, poor child.' He spoke kindly. Among his projects was one to create an asylum for weak-witted naturals such as he obviously thought the girl to be.

'She ain't no child,' scoffed Floss. 'Effie used to give her to her lodgers to play with sometimes.'

Defoe looked less warmly on the sharp little features which showed here and there pits left by smallpox. The girl's snarl resembled the dog's.

Since nobody else reached into a pocket, I put a few coppers into Bratchet's paw and sent her off with instructions.

'At the inkwitch,' Bully said, 'the corner wondered if the Bratchet was in with Effie's killer, seeing as Effie weren't what you'd call a ideal employer, but there weren't no evidence for it.'

'I give evidence for it,' Floss said, sharply, 'She knew the fucker all right. I saw her meself out my windy, chasing after him and shouting for him to come back.'

'But if she suspected him, she would, wouldn't she?'

'That's what the corner said,' said Floss, 'but it weren't that sort of "come back".'

The Highlander was becoming restive. 'The guidwife's dead, rest her. Will we stand around like saulies at a funeral bake?' He swung a stool to the table and escorted Floss to it, bowing, and took another near it. 'Sweet soul, will ye tell me of the woman, Bonny? Yclept Anne, was she?'

Floss was won. 'Don't he talk pretty?' She caressed the Scotsman's bare knees. 'You got prime legs, dearie. Anybody tell you?'

'Leave him alone, Floss,' I said, 'Who was this Bonny?'

'Turned up four, five year ago out the blue. Mistress Bonny, we had to call her,' said Floss. Her voice went artificially high. 'Mistress Bonny wants this. Mistress Bonny wants that. Mustn't curse afore Mistress Bonny, Floss. Ooh, how Effie treacled that chit. Best vittles, best linen. Like she was royalty.'

I leaned forward and refastened Floss's wrapper across her breasts. 'High nosed, was she, this Anne Bonny?'

'High nosed? Only hired a rattler one day, din't she?'

'A coach,' Defoe interpreted for the Scotsman.

Floss was concerned we wouldn't believe her. 'Crook me elbow and wish it may never come straight. On my life, a rattler. Stood at the end of the court it did. And Will Pickens carryin' her to it 'case her stampers got shit on 'em.' Floss's voice went up another octave, 'And that Mary Read with 'er, got up like a dog in a doublet.'

'Mary Read?'

Floss turned to me. 'After your time, Mart. Effie took her on as a abby, soon after she took in Bratchet. Had a lot of lodgers then, did Eff. Scowling bitch, that Mary. And temper! Near tore my ear off once. But the Bonny bloss took to her. Thick as thieves, they was.'

Defoe asked, 'Did she ever tell you where she and Anne Bonny went in the coach?'

'Nah. Only flim-fam. Laughed when I asked her and said they'd been to London to see the Queen. Bitch, she was.'

The Scotsman wasn't interested in Mary Read. 'Good soul, will ye tell me where Mistress Bonny went after lodging here?'

'Dunno. Here one day, gone the next. Skipped it. And bloody Mary Read with her and good riddance. Where's that bloody Bratchet? She don't come soon, I'm goin' home.' Floss had become bad-tempered and slumped on the stool, hands in her lap, looking sideways down at the floor like a sulking child.

The beadle nodded portentously. 'It were four year ago. 1702, year of Her Majesty's accession. Enquiries was made. The Bratchet was in a taking and come to me saying as the women was kidnapped and I was to go to the magistrate. Accused Effie of getting rid of 'em. Acourse Effie denied it. Said why'd she want to lose a good lodger and a good maid? Enquiries was made, but nobody knew nothing.' He shrugged. 'Easy come, easy go.'

If I knew Bully, his search for two friendless females would have been even less energetic than usual. I went to the door to look for Bratchet and escape the heat of the kitchen with its smell of oysters, old cooking, sweat from the beadle's caped coat which he wore winter and summer, and Floss's stale perfume, but the aroma of Puddle Court in the sun wasn't any better.

When the maid came back with a full, chipped ewer, I stopped her on the steps. 'Remember me, Bratchet? Martin Millet, Mrs Sly's nephew. I gave you sixpence once.'

She merely stared.

'Who done it, Bratchet? You know him, don't you? There'll be no trouble for you, I swear. Just tell me.'

She knew all right. She tried to duck under my arm and kicked when I held her back. I offered her a sovereign, 'Who was it? A lover?' Her face distorted; that had amused her. I saw her little white teeth. I tried threat. 'You know I can go to the coroner and tell him you lied? Now, who was it?'

'I'm not telling you nothing, you fucker.' Her malice was extraordinary; she hated me.

'All right,' I said, 'who's Anne Bonny?'

It was a line worth pursuing; it had brought Daniel Defoe and a mad Scotsman to Puddle Court and I didn't know why. It might have nothing to do with Aunt Effie's killing, but then again it might.

This time, kicking out, she caught my bad leg and I had to let her go. By the time I limped into the kitchen, Livingstone of Kilsyth had settled down to get Floss drunk. I joined him, refilling her beaker as fast as she emptied it, which was fast. A fine fellow, I'd become; threatening poor sluts and getting others barley-capped.

Distancing himself, Defoe joined the beadle who, having filled a beaker, sat on a settle and stared contentedly at the dried herbs hanging from the rafters.

Gin turned Floss's mood against me. 'Left you all of it, did she? Never a bit for poor Floss as stood by her these years.' She flapped at me. 'You creeper. Go it, you cripple; wooden legs is cheap. Much good may it do you. Ill-gotten goods, that's what. Bring you bad luck, send you where Effie's gone. Know what your aunt was, you badger-legged bastard? A Dark Lantern an' a blacker an' a spirit . . . spirit'list, thass what she was. And give us some more of that bloody crank.'

As the Highlander steadied Floss's beaker for me to fill it again, he whispered: 'Was your aunt some form of Dissenter?'

I shook my head. 'Did she spirit Anne Bonny and Mary Read, Floss?'

Out the corner of my eye, I saw Defoe sit up. He knew what 'spiritualist' meant. Floss waved her beaker and then pressed it against the side of her nose, slopping the gin down her cheek. 'Like to know, wouldn'tcher?'

'I would,' I said. If Floss was right, Effie had been an informer and a blackmailer; more to the point, in calling her a spiritualist, Floss wasn't referring to Aunt Effie's religion but to the trade of the press boats that trawl quaysides by night, snatching unwary souls into servitude. Now it's mostly young men they take, to swell the ranks of the navy or army, but in those days women were kidnapped too, for sale to the servant-starved colonies in the West Indies and Americas. Merchants, bearing high shipping costs for vessels sent for this very purpose by plantation-owners, didn't bother to question their agents' methods in supplying them.

I turned on the beadle. 'Come on, Bully. You made enquiries. There must have been some trace of what happened to 'em.'

Bully shrugged. 'There was a pedlar told a constable he'd seen a couple of women struggling with some men on the docks. But women is always struggling with men on the docks. It's what they're for. Asides, the pedlar was full as a goat and didn't remember whether it was that night or Christmas.'

'Why did Effie do it, Floss?' I asked.

'Acause she was paid to. Why else?'

Defoe said sharply, 'There are laws against spiriting.'

Floss's head was lolling. 'Laws,' she said, 'Them as make 'em can break 'em.' She hauled herself up – 'I gotta go and puke' – and weaved an unsteady course through the back door into the yard.

'That's what happened to your Anne Bonny then, Mr Kilsyth,' I said.

'What?' he demanded, 'what's happened to her? I can't make out the woman's clack.'

'She and her friend were sold to the press crews. Shipped to the colonies somewhere.' There wasn't any other explanation for the suddenness of the two women's disappearance and the Bratchet's reaction to it.

The Highlander cried out. 'Do ye tell me so? Och now, there's the end to a great house.' He clasped his hands round his bonnet and rocked it back and forth on his head. 'What will I tell my chief? Lady Anne, Lady Anne, poor soul, poor soul, why did ye na' come home to your ane? Why put ye your trust in the Sasunnoch?'

He was still keening as Floss returned from the backyard, trembling and wiping bits of breakfast from her mouth. She'd undergone another change of mood during her absence and was soberer but frightened. 'Here,' she said, 'You got me bosky, you fuckers.'

'Who paid Aunt Effie to sell the girls, Floss?' I asked.

Livingstone of Kilsyth advanced on her. 'Will ye say if the woman of this house sold Anne Bonny to slavery, aye or no?' As she shrank away from him, he tried to put persuasion back in his voice. 'There's ten shilling for you, soul, if you'll speak.'

But silver couldn't buy Floss in the terror that had come over her. 'I never said nothing,' she shrieked, 'They ain't coming back for my neck. You tell 'em. Tell 'em I never said nothing.'

'Tell who, Floss?' I persisted.

'Nobody. Nothing. I ain't ending up like Effie.' Her eyes had fixed on something we couldn't see and she began to scream, batting her hands at it.

We got the beadle to take her home. Not all the ewer's contents had gone into Floss. We watched the two of them, leaning on each other's shoulders, legs obtruded sideways like a walking tripod, stagger across the cobbles to next door.

'Is there nae hope of finding her?' asked Livingstone of Kilsyth.

'No,' I told him, 'They could have been shipped to the West Indies, the Carolinas, New England, anywhere. And if they've not come back in four years, they ain't coming.'

'Then I'll haste me back with the tale. And sair hearts they'll be that hear it.'

Defoe intervened. 'I should stay awhile. Don't lose hope yet. I shall go to Deptford and question the skippers of the press smacks. To see if any of them took the young ladies.'

I thought, He doesn't want to lose sight of Kilsyth yet. And wondered why.

'Would any yon admit to such hellishness?'

Defoe attempted a grim smile. 'There are ways and means.'

The Highlander doubled his fists and waved them under Defoe's nose. They looked like builders' mallets. 'I've the way and here's the means. I'll gang wi' ye.'

'No,' said Defoe, quickly, 'A stranger mutes them. I shall go alone. I speak their language. However, perhaps a little monetary persuasion?' He looked hopefully at the Scotsman's sporran.

'Aye, that's the way. Tell them there'll be thirty pounds in good Scottish siller for the man that can point to Anne Bonny. Ye'll bring me word tonight?'

Promising, Defoe shut the door behind him as he left.

I looked at him. 'Did I hear you tell the gentleman in a kilt you'd talk to the press skippers? *Press* skippers? The girls are dead, Daniel. No need to join 'em.'

'They ain't dead,' came a ferocious whisper behind us.

We'd forgotten the Bratchet. Her grey figure looked insubstantial in the dim light of the hallway. The little teeth showed as she whispered again. 'They ain't dead. They ain't dead. They ain't.'

'What makes you say so?' Defoe stretched out his hand to grasp the girl's meagre shoulder. 'What do you know?'

She shrank back and rolled her eyes down with the sullenness of the half-witted. 'They ain't dead.'

'My good girl,' said Defoe, 'it's as this gentleman says. If they've not returned in four years, they won't be returning.'

'They ain't dead.'

'Better leave her to me,' I said, 'She's frightened.'

Defoe was happy to do it. He'd had his fill of hysterical fe-males, and the house had oppressed him more than it had any of us. He prides himself on being a modern man but there's parts of him where ancient superstitions lurk like harpies. He believes in ghosts. I suggested we go upstairs and look over the room where Effie Sly died to see if she'd left any papers that would help us, but horror of the place wouldn't let him. He wished me well of it and left.

I sat down on Aunt Effie's front steps to watch him out of sight. There goes another who knows more than he's telling, I thought. I owed him and his family a great deal for their kindness to me as a child, but even then Daniel Defoe had been a man with so many fingers in so many pies that those on the right hand often didn't know what the left ones were doing.

And at this moment, I'd have given a lot to know who he was acting for. It wasn't the Scotsman, I'd have taken my oath on that; he was more intent on keeping that poor hill-skipper ignorant than on informing him.

This Anne Bonny or Bard, who was she? The Scotsman, Daniel Defoe and whoever Daniel was acting for wanted to find her. But four years ago somebody had wanted to get rid of her. And had employed Aunt Effie to do it. Now Effie Sly was dead and the question was whether her murder and the Bonny/Bard affair were related.

Probably not. The simple, most likely answer was that Effie had surprised a thief. Local legend always credited her with possession of valuables. Actually, according to the letter her lawyer had sent me, Effie *did* own jewellery worth a sum that surprised me, but she'd kept it in a City bank, not in her brass-bound box.

If it had been a thief who'd killed her, I'd find him. Questions in the right place, another interrogation of Floss and the Bratchet, a modest reward – in Puddle Dock they'd sell their mothers, let alone their grandmothers, for a sovereign – and I'd find him. But the longer I sat on those steps, considering, the more the other mystery kept tapping for my attention: why, four years ago, had somebody paid Aunt Effie to spirit a couple of apparently harmless young women? The Scotsman had cried for 'Lady Anne'. Floss, in her cups, had said, 'Laws. Them as make 'em, can break 'em.' Mary Read had said, 'We've been to London to see the Queen.'

Anne Bonny Bard, I thought, who in hell *were* you?

Bard. Unusual name. I'd only ever heard of it in one connection.

When I joined the Dragoons, during my training at Hounslow, there was an old cavalryman called Bore – good name for him, too – had a cottage in the next village. He was one of those as can't let the army go; every unit tolerates an old man like him. He'd stagger over to camp each day to watch us train and tell us the Dragoons were bloody hermaphrodites who weren't fit to lick a true cavalryman's boots, that we rode like turnip sacks, and if England was going to depend on us to keep the Frogs out he'd better start learning French.

When I hadn't anything better to do, I used to escort him home and listen to his account of Civil War battles. He'd ridden with Rupert of the Rhine and, royalist though Rupert was, I was interested in a man who'd single-handedly revolutionized cavalry tactics. Bore worshipped his memory. 'Crap to Marlborough,' he used to say, 'These modern generals can't hold a bloody candle to Prince Rupert of the Rhine.'

Anyway, the point is the old trooper knew everything about Rupert: his birth in Bohemia, his dogs, his horses, his women. As Bore told it, only two women had been important to Rupert. The first was Irish, Francesca, the daughter of one of his royalist captains who'd died and left her to the wardship of his commander. 'And he done her proud,' old Bore would say, 'Set her up, took care of her, gave her a son.'

'Did her proud in more ways than one, then,' I said once.

That got the old man angry. 'You ignorant dandiprat. He was cavalry, not a bloody Dragoon; he married her. He was a gentleman, our Prince Rupert. Sort of married her, anyway, one of them morgan-thing marriages. Though it ain't generally known.'

The other woman, who'd come along afterwards, when Rupert was an old man, was an actress called Peg Hughes.

'Did he marry her, too?' I asked.

'Acourse he didn't. You don't marry actresses. But he left her all his money – her and their daughter. Called the baby Ruperta. After himself, see?'

'What'd he call his son? Rupertson?'

'He called him Dudley,' said Trooper Bore with dignity, 'And he loved him and was proud of him and sent him to Eton College with the rest of the nobs, so there. And a good boy he was till the fucking Turks killed him. Poor lad went off to fight for the Holy Roman Crusade. Led a forlorn hope against the Mohammedan bastards at Buda and got killed for it.'

And the poor lad, said Bore, took his mother's, Francesca's surname, which was Bard. Dudley Bard.

As I sat on those steps in Puddle Court, it seemed a coincidence worth following up that this Anne Bonny of Aunt Effie's had also been called Bard. I couldn't question the late Master Bard, but I could go and see his half-sister, the girl Ruperta, whom Rupert had fathered in his old age on an actress. She had married a certain Major Howe.

The odd thing was, I had business with that same Major Howe. I'd spent a large amount of time in a Dutch hospital looking forward to meeting him again. It was one of the reasons I'd come back. Coincidence, fate, whatever it was, it looked as if something was intending me to pursue the mystery of my aunt's lodger, Miss Anne Bonny Bard. I hauled myself up and set off across London to do it.

The decay of Puddle Court gave way to the more wholesome smell of fish and the manure heaps on the quays waiting to be transported upriver to the gardens of the rich. Further along came the whiff of oranges being unladen at one wharf and the pungency of raw wool from bales being craned into a cargo hold at another.

I cut off north to go through the City and out by Ludgate. There are still old men and women who mourn London as it was before the Great Fire of 1666, the London of Tudors and Plantagenets, and tell you what a wonder it was, despite the fact that the same wonder managed to kill a third of its population in the Great Plague of '65.

The City fathers put up The Monument to the fire in Pudding Lane but nothing to mark the death of the tens of thousands of men, women and children the year before. The plague merely killed people, of course; the fire killed property.

The true wonder is the new City that Wren has built. Great man, Sir Christopher. Slums like Puddle Court have re-established themselves, but mostly he's given us space and light. As I went, I could walk on fresh sand along the pedestrians' way, kept aloof from the traffic of the streets by smart little bollards. Beyond the wrought-iron gates of the houses powdered flunkeys lounged in the porches watching mulberry trees and vines flourish in the gardens.

Since I'd been away it had obviously become fashionable for every wealthy family to own a male Negro servant, the taller the better, and dress him in clothes that put even Defoe's in the shade. Junior but equally gorgeous versions of the same race trotted along behind their mistresses like pet dogs.

The walk was so pleasurable, I took a circuitous route and went by Bread Street to pause at the sign of the Spread Eagle and pay mental homage to John Milton and feel satisfaction that the author of *Paradise Lost* was a Cockney like myself, that if Bow bells had fallen from their steeple they might have crushed the infant poet in his cradle.

A few yards further along I spotted the man who'd parted from me less than an hour before. Defoe was on his way home, but he'd stopped to peer through the gates of some almshouses. The crest of their founder was pargeted above the central door and Daniel was staring at it, his hat pushed back as he scratched at the edge of his wig, like a man trying to put the name to a face he's seen somewhere before.

'It's Prince Rupert's crest,' I said, tapping him on the shoulder. 'He founded the houses for some of his veterans.'

Defoe jumped round, then fell back against the gates, patting at his heart. 'Lord, boy, don't *do* that. I thought you were a bailiff.'

'I think Rupert's the name you're searching for,' I said.

He looked from me to the almshouses and back again and his frown cleared as it came to him. 'Of *course*. I'd forgotten. Bohemia, Bard. *Bard*. I knew the name was somehow connected to that crest. I've been pursuing it for a night and a day.' His frown came back. 'But how did *you* guess?'

'Daniel, I was in the Dragoons. In the Dragoons there's two gods. One of them's the quartermaster sergeant and the other's Rupert of the Rhine. I only ever heard of but one man called Bard.'

'Ah.' Daniel nodded towards the crest. 'His son.'

'Dudley,' I agreed, 'I'm just now going to call on his sister.'

'Ah,' he said again, then after a pause, 'What for?'

'For one thing, I'm wanting to ask her if she had a relative who called herself Anne Bonny. For another, I'd like to renew an acquaintance with her husband.'

He didn't like it. 'I know that tone of yours,' he said, 'Martin, let me go and see the woman alone. This is a tangled skein and we must be careful how we unravel it. If you intend trouble to Major Howe, we'll discover nothing.'

'No trouble,' I said, 'I just want to tell him something. We'll go together.' I put my arm through his and headed him west.

To enter the Strand is to return to the Elizabethan age, with the sun lighting and shading the projections of the old palaces and the plastered gables of the shops that have filled in the spaces between, but once under the trees of Pall Mall you're in the elegant and promiscuous world of Charles II and Nell Gwynn. He'd set her up in one of the smart row of houses along this, his pell-mell course. And Prince Rupert, we knew, had owned a house in the same area which, like everything else, he'd left to his daughter. After some enquiries we found it, just off Birdcage Walk.

'Are you going to tell me what this is all about?' I asked Daniel as we paused outside its gate.

'What what's about?'

' "Person or persons unknown," ' I said.

He became over casual. 'As you saw, the Scotsman requested me to use my local knowledge to find this . . .' he flirted his hand '. . . this Mistress Bonny or Bard. I am obliging him. Like you, I think there is a possibility she was a relative of these people here and tried to contact them during her stay with your Aunt Effie.'

'And that's your only interest?'

He widened his eyes. 'What else?'

'Very well.' I rang the bell set in the gatepost.

It was hot by now. Through the gates we could see topiaried box hedges, their geometric shapes contrasting with the lolling heads of multi-petalled pink roses and phlox. The splash of water from an unseen fountain reminded us we were thirsty.

A porter appeared from a canopied chair just inside, rubbing his eyes. 'Name?'

'Master Daniel Foe,' I said, 'and friend. To see Major and Mrs Howe.'

'*De*foe,' said Defoe.

'Business?'

'Financial.' As the porter moved away, I muttered to Daniel, 'The major's got an enthusiasm for the financial.'

'How do you know him?'

'He was a major in my company.'

The porter came striding back down the brick path, selecting a key from the chatelaine at his waist. Defoe hung back, suddenly disconcerted. 'I don't know what to say,' he told me.

'I do.'

The front door was flanked with potted bay trees and stood open, allowing sunlight into a black-and-white flagged hall. I let Defoe go ahead; he looked the part, I didn't. He was swaggering because he was nervous and not just about the coming interview. The tradition in the gentry's houses is to tip practically everybody; porters and footmen make sure you do by turning fractious if you don't – but, as Defoe whispered to me, there was too little in his pocket for generosity. If he was hoping that I'd do it for him, he was unlucky. The house of Howe would get nothing from me.

We were handed over to a footman and announced into a large parlour dominated by a garden that lay beyond its open sash windows, leaving the room in shade. 'Master Daniel Defoe and Friend.'

47

Defoe swept off his hat and donned it again, though the man at a desk over on the far side didn't look up. 'A moment, gentlemen.'

He was a big man, fortyish, fattish, fairish, and wore a silk day robe with a turban-cum-nightcap of Turkish fashion in keeping with the turned-up embroidered slippers on his feet. Commanding the wall behind him was a portrait of Prince Rupert on horseback with a large black poodle at his stirrup. The painted countenance with the unmistakably Stuart cleft to its chin had more life than the formless, living face below it.

Major Howe appeared absorbed in papers which he took from a pile with hands that shook, either from nerves or a palsy. He was posing. He always did; so unsure of himself that he must appear important even to the most casual visitor. I felt Daniel relax; he could cope with Howe. The business world is full of men who use bombast to hide their lack of confidence and talent.

'Master Defoe.' Howe rose at last and swept forward to shake his hand, blaring superiority. 'Heard they had you in the pillory. Injustice. Read "The Shortest Way". Agreed with every word. Too many damn Dissenters. In government and out.'

Sighing, Defoe tried to introduce me but I kept in the shadows and Howe barked on. 'Read your "Essay on Projects". Interesting. Found one for me, have ye? Always prepared to invest in a good project. But be quick. We're expecting visitors.' He had to add, 'Colonel and Lady Cadogan. The Duke's aide de camp, don't ee know.'

'Major, we are here on a graver matter,' Defoe said. He'd decided on an authoritarian approach. 'It concerns Anne Bard also known as Bonny. We have reason to believe you are or were acquainted with her.'

I saw immediately that Daniel had hit his mark. Howe knew the name all right; there was alarm in his eyes. It hung in the balance; it was a matter of which line he would choose. If he wasn't a fool, if he denied all knowledge, we'd go away empty.

He tried a feint. 'What's your interest, may I ask?'

'Friends in the government,' Daniel said, 'are concerned by the lady's disappearance and have asked me to look into it.'

If it was a bluff, it was grandly done. I found myself wondering whether it was bluff or truth. Either way, it was good enough for Howe. He was a fool. 'Not exactly acquainted, no.' He reached for a paper on the desk to give himself time; his hand trembled more than ever.

'I beg your pardon, Major? I didn't hear.'

Howe turned round. 'Wouldn't have her in the house.' He'd decided on bluster. 'A damned female claiming kinship, doesn't mean . . . I'll not have my wife unsettled by some impostor.'

'She approached you, then. When was this?'

Howe swung his head in disgust. 'Can't remember. Years ago. Tore the letter up at once. Used it for tapers. All it warranted. Then she came to the house. Wouldn't let her in.'

'What did it say?'

'Eh?'

'What did her letter say, Major?'

'Some taradiddle that Dudley Bard had married before he died.' Howe sat himself back at his desk as if behind a barricade. He groped among his papers and attempted vagueness.

'She claimed to be his legitimate daughter – His Highness Prince Rupert's legitimate grandchild, if you'll credit it. Just arrived in the country from the old home in Bohemia. So she said. Said she had papers proving her claim.' He looked up, triumphantly. 'But they didn't transpire, did they? Never heard another word from the bitch. Called her bluff, by God. No Bohemian whore's going to flam my wife out of her inheritance.'

'Was that what she wished to do?'

Howe shrugged. 'As good as. Said her mother was dead. Wanted to contact her father's side of the family. But I could read between the lines, by God. Charlatan. A flammer. Not a word of truth in it. Sent her packing, by God.'

'Where did you send her, Major?'

A voice from outside came in with the birdsong. 'Are they here yet, George? Am I late?'

There was a fig tree in the garden. Beneath it, on a path that led from some back gate, was a woman. Young. She was in a riding habit with a white jabot at her neck. Her hat was off and her dark curls brushed her shoulders as she dusted her skirt

49

with her riding whip. The splayed green leaves of the fig formed a mottled background for her shape and the sun shone on huge eyes and a skin like pearl, a face which was the face in the Rupert portrait made exquisite.

'No, my dear.'

The change of tone was so marked that I managed to stop looking at the vision to glance at my host. Howe's expression had become raw with something so nakedly tender, a sort of passion approaching despair, that it was near indecent to witness it.

'No, my dear. These . . . fellows have come to talk business. They are about to leave.'

He got up and put his body between us and that of his wife. 'Go and change, Rupie. I'll come and tell you when our guests arrive.'

'Ba-ba's cast a shoe, George,' said the birdsong voice. 'I had to walk her home.'

'George will have it seen to, dearest. Go and change now.'

She smiled and waved her whip and went away. Our three pairs of eyes watched her take the spirit of the garden with her.

'Out.' Howe turned on us in fury. 'Out. I'll not have your sluts and impostors mentioned in my house. Out and be damned.'

'Just one more question, Major.'

'No.' He was almost screaming, shooing us towards the door. 'Out. Out.' He stopped and went pale. He'd seen me. His arms dropped to his sides. Weakly he said, 'Out.'

I stepped forward. 'Where did you send Anne Bard packing to, Major? To her death? You're good at that, Major.'

Howe winced. He plucked at his lip. 'I . . . Out.' He lurched forward, brushing past Defoe and calling for his servants. 'Put these fellows out.'

Before two footmen hustled us off, I managed to tell him what he was fit for. I'd come for that. Then we were down the path and into the street, the porter swearing at us before slamming the gates.

Defoe readjusted his coat and dignity. 'At least that solves the tipping problem. Now some refreshment, I think.'

Without consulting, we turned westwards, skirting the canal and St James's Park to enter Whitehall, heading for the anonymity of one of Westminster's taverns. It was rhubarb time, when society deserted town for the country, so the wide street was less crowded than usual, though a troop of cavalry powdered us with dust as it headed past for Horse Guards. I didn't look at it – and Daniel noticed. 'Is your leg too bad to ride any more?'

'It'll do.'

'What did that man do to you, Martin?'

'Drink first,' I said.

Once over the Tyburn Ditch and through the gatehouse, you're in the Middle Ages, a city that's grown up around a cathedral and a palace, both of them showing their age in the grime that blurs the carvings covering them until, from a distance, they look as if they're suffering from an outbreak of warts.

Or perhaps I was jaundiced that day by too many of the world's sins to appreciate beauty. Westminster's got its own sin, mind you – the alleys we wandered into had nearly as many whorehouses and taverns as the docks, but it's a higher class of sin; the cathedral chapter collects the rents.

We chose the Gabriel because it seemed quieter than most. Defoe told the tapster to bring ale but I countermanded with an order of brandy, 'On Aunt Effie.' Defoe kept trying to probe what lay between me and the major but I said it was something that'd happened at Ramillies and had nothing to do with the matter in hand, which it hadn't.

'Ramillies? You were at Ramillies? I read all the communiqués. What a victory! The news of it arrived in England like a thunderclap of joy. The seemingly omnipotent French army beaten yet again. I was unable to sleep with the glory of it.'

I'd read a few of the communiqués myself. Very accurate, too, except that they left out the mud, blood, and chaos. And quake-buttocked bastards like Major Howe.

It wasn't that he'd been an incompetent officer. You expect incompetence in officers; they'd train it into them if they trained them at all, which they don't – even Marlborough wasn't trained; he just happens to be a genius. It wasn't even just that Howe was a coward. He was incompetent, a coward *and* a liar.

There comes a point in any battle, James, when all the prevision and provision ain't worth a damn. What you need is luck. The Duke of Marlborough's not just a good general, he's a lucky general. But, Christ, he nearly ran out of it that day at Ramillies. Everything got itself whirled around. The major and my troop and some others were separated from the rest of the regiment and found ourselves fighting alongside the Dutch, with the French counter-attacking. And suddenly, there was Marlborough, the Duke himself, unhorsed, running like a rabbit in his jackboots through the mud with a handful of French cavalry riding after him for the kill.

I made for him. Somehow Captain Molesworth was there with a remount. Colonel Bringfield was hoisting the Duke on it and I was holding back the leading French and yelling for Major Howe to help. I had a quick glimpse of him galloping hell for leather back to our lines before Colonel Bringfield's head was shot away with a cannon ball.

I killed one of the enemy. Molesworth was pulling Marlborough and his horse out of the fray. The next thing I knew some frog-eater was hacking at my leg and my horse was going down. I doubt if I'd have survived if the Dutch, our dyke-digging allies, bless them, hadn't taken me along with their own casualties to a hospital they'd set up in a hamlet called Francqnée. I had to fight to stop them cutting my leg off but after that they cared for me like their own.

When, at last, I went back to my regiment, the colonel gave me my discharge. I said I could still ride even though I'd only got one good leg, but he said I couldn't. 'Your major feels that your injuries are incapacitating.' I'll bet he did.

Anyway, it was then that Paulie Hicks, a fellow sergeant, told me the Duke had enquired of the major the identity of the brave Dragoon who'd held back the French while he was trying to remount. Paulie said, 'The major told the Duke he didn't know. The major told the Duke he'd been too busy bravely holding back the French himself. The which he hadn't. But he knew all right.'

Paulie wanted me to go to the Duke and tell him. I told Paulie, 'Like I was some begging bloody gentleman-rounder? "It was me, my lord"? And have him write to Duchess Sarah and tell her to look after me, even if he believed me? Like fuck I could.'

'Pride is a sin, my boy,' Paulie said. But it was all I'd got. I was keeping it. And thanks to Aunt Effie I could now afford to.

Defoe was watching me. 'This is good Dutch brandy,' he said, 'but you're drinking it medicinally. Is the leg painful?'

To stop him dwelling on my leg, I said, 'Do we think the major done Aunt Effie in?'

He stared at me. 'Why would he do that?'

'In the letter this Bonny Anne Bard sent him she said she had papers claiming her legitimacy. There were papers in Effie's box. The major may have tried to steal them.'

We drank more brandy while we thought about it. After a while, Defoe said, 'Why wait four or five years? No, it wasn't him.'

I didn't think it was either. The major had run from the French; he'd certainly have run from Aunt Effie. 'But four years ago he might have paid her to get rid of Anne. To prevent her claiming his wife's inheritance.'

We called for more brandy and oysters and a loaf of bread to mop it up. Happily, we began setting out lineages on the table. The pot-bellied bottle became Prince Rupert of the Rhine, the Dragon Prince, scourge of the Roundhead forces.

'God bless him. Great man. I'd have been on Cromwell's side myself, but he was still great man.' We drank to him.

'So'd've I. Great man, though.'

'Now then. Did he marry Francesca Bard, or didn't he?'

'My friend Trooper Bore, grand old man . . .' We drank to Trooper Bore. '. . . he said he did. A morgan-thing marriage.'

'Morganatic. Means any children can't inherit a title but can inherit the money.' We drank to morganatic marriages and put a pepper pot to represent Francesca by the side of the bottle. 'And Rupert's sister must have . . . that's the Electress of Hanover, by the way . . .' We drank to Sophia, Electress of Hanover.

53

'*She* must have thought they were married because she received Francesca into her court at Hanover, thereby . . . thereby, paying her the honour due to a sister-in-law.'

'And they'd had a son, Dudley, poor old Dudley Bard. Died fighting the bloody Turks.' We called for another pepper pot and put it with the other one and drank to it.

'Rupert always treated him like he was l-legitimate son,' Defoe pointed out. 'Sent him to Eton.'

'Now then. The actress. What was her name?'

'Peg Hughes.' Defoe tried to frown. 'Don't approve of actresses.'

'Rupert did. Her anyway. And, God almighty, if she was anything like her daughter . . .'

'Do you think,' asked Daniel, 'do you think Anne looked anything like Ruperta?' Tears came into his eyes at the thought. 'Lovely woman like that lovely, lovely woman, lovely Anne, sent to the colonies?'

While he cried I put the second bottle down on Rupert Bottle's other side under the second pepper pot. 'Anne.' Then I put some coins on the table. 'That's Rupert's riches. Riches. And he leaves all of it to Ruperta.'

'Let's drink to Ruperta, bless her.' Daniel went outside to piss and came back with a rose to represent Ruperta. 'Now what we got?'

I studied the table. 'Two brandy bottles, two pepper pots an' a bloody rose.' We helped each other out to the pump in the backyard and poured water over our heads to sober up and came back. We set out the lineages more carefully on the table, borrowing a flagon to represent Sophia of Hanover, and studied them.

'Odd thing,' said Defoe carefully, 'Very odd thing. If Rupert loved Peg Hughes and Ruperta so much he left them all his money, why didn't he marry 'em? Peg Hughes, I mean.'

'Couldn't? Already married to Fran . . . wassname?'

'Exactly.'

'So he was *definitely* married to Francesca. Probably.'

'So if young Dudley got married before he was killed . . . How old was he when he died?'

I puzzled my memory to recall what the old cavalryman had told me of Rupert's family. 'I think he was born in the year of the Great Fire. And the siege of Buda took place in 1686. So he was twenty. Old enough to marry.'

'And have a legitimate daughter, our Anne Bard. She'd be about seventeen or eighteen herself by the time she came to England and disappeared, if it was four years ago, travelling in the name of Bonny for reasons we don't wot of . . .'

'She'd be entitled to some of these.' Defoe pushed some of the coins away from Ruperta to the Bard side of the brandy bottle. 'Maybe all of 'em. If she *was* legitimate. And had papers to prove it.'

'Not necessarily. Rupert could leave his money where he liked.'

'True. But if a legitimate grand-daughter turned up, she'd have a good case with which to contest his will,' Daniel pointed out. 'Think of the stir it would cause. Think of the lawyers' fees eating up most of the estate.'

'And do we think Major Howe, the bastard, would send the grand-daughter to her death in the colonies to protect his wife and her money from all that?'

'Wouldn't you?'

I thought of the girl under the fig tree in Howe's garden. 'I ain't him, thank God.'

We leaned back in our facing settles to recover, flushed with the fever of supposition and brandy. But, as I looked at the things on the table, I thought that from the point of view of discovering who killed Aunt Effie I was no further forward. I said so.

'Nonsense,' Defoe said, 'We've built a pretty case.' He assumed a legal voice, 'We charge you, Major Howe, that, on a certain night in 1702, you did with murderous intent don hat and cloak and make your way to Puddle Court, the address on the letter you'd received from Anne Bonny/Bard, your wife's niece, and there you did conspire with a certain Effie Sly to get rid of said Anne so that she shouldn't be a threat to your wife's inheritance.' He tapped both hands on the table in satisfaction. 'It follows that he killed your aunt. She could have been blackmailing him over it these past four years until at last his temper gave way.'

'A pretty case, I grant you,' I said, 'but he didn't do it.'

'Do what? Kill your aunt? Or get rid of Anne Bonny?'

'Either.'

Defoe was piqued. 'Of course he did. I insist on it.'

I shook my head. 'I'd like to think so, too, but he ain't that sort of man, Daniel. I know him. You get to know a man you serve under in war. You have to. He ain't got the ruthlessness. He'd shut his gates against poor Anne, right enough, refuse to believe her, leave her to starve. He's good at turning his back, is Major Howe. But make his way to Puddle Court? Conspire with Aunt Effie? Go back four years later and strangle her? He ain't got the steel.'

Daniel sulked, setting out the lineage artefacts again on the table. He wouldn't have his pretty case collapsed by what he obviously regarded as prejudice.

I had a sudden thought. 'That girl as disappeared with Anne Bonny, Effie's maid, what was her name again?'

'Mary Read.'

'Mary Read.' I was remembering. 'Funny thing, Daniel. There was a girl in the army called Mary Read.'

'A camp follower, do you mean?'

'No. A trooper. It was the talk of the regiments, this young Dragoon as marched and fought through Holland and turned out to be female. Nobody even suspected until she married a fellow trooper and set up as landlady of some Flemish inn. Her name was Mary Read.'

Defoe was shocked. 'Women in the army? What's the world come to?'

'It's not unknown,' I told him. 'There's been others.'

'But this harpy, this Mary Read, can't be *our* Mary Read. She was spirited along with Anne Bard.'

'She could have escaped. If it's the same one, she must have. She fought in the Battle of Blenheim. And that was in '04. Two years after Anne was spirited.'

'Can't be the same woman,' said Daniel vaguely, 'It's a common enough name.' He was staring at the table.

Then, abruptly, he said goodbye and, as if by accident, swept his arm through the bottles and pots on the table and hurried off, leaving me to pay and consider the detritus before me.

I began setting up the bottles and pots as they had been. Sophia. Rupert. Francesca. Ruperta. Anne. There was something there and Daniel Defoe had seen it; the manner in which he'd rushed off suggested a man struck by an idea to be acted on immediately. Who was he working for? What was it in this representation of a family group that he'd seen and I hadn't?

After a while, I called for a pint of ale, put the tankard at the head of all the other vessels and crowned it James the First of England, Rupert's grandfather. Then I saw it. It was a matter of dates.

It'll seem strange to you, James, who will have the benefit of hindsight, that when Queen Anne came to the throne she was still expected to produce an heir, despite her many pregnancies, none of which had produced a child that lived beyond the age of eleven. But at that time she was only a few days past her thirty-seventh birthday, young enough.

In case she didn't have another child, there was the Act of Settlement which was to make sure that the crown didn't pass to the Catholic Pretender but to the nearest Protestant heir, who was Anne's father's first cousin, Sophia, Electress of Hanover, the flagon.

It mattered a great deal for those with a vested interest in a Protestant succession, either that Anne produce an heir or that, when she died, we accept Sophia in her place.

And it had been at this point that a girl who'd just arrived in England, trying to contact her relatives, was mysteriously made to disappear.

Now, four years later, the situation in the country had changed. For one thing it was obvious that the Queen wasn't going to have any more children. For another, it was equally likely that her successor wouldn't be Sophia – she was an old woman – but Sophia's son, George of Hanover. Just as one element in the country didn't want a Papist like the Pretender on the throne, there was another, equally strong, that certainly didn't want George.

Mostly, the army didn't object to young German George. He showed signs of shaping up into a good soldier and his troops, the Pickel-Heads, had courage if they didn't have brains. But at home there was a growing body against him; he was proving a brave but difficult ally whose hatred of the French might prove a stumbling block if they sued for peace. He was too far away from the direct Stuart line. Queen Anne didn't like him; wouldn't even allow him to visit England. If he was crowned, there might be another civil war. Anyway, he was German. Couldn't even speak English.

And now somebody, presumably the person or persons Daniel was working for, wanted to find the girl who had been abducted four years ago.

In that Westminster tavern that summer day in 1706, I sat for a long time staring at the table in front of me and its various vessels. I wondered if Bonny Anne Bard was a Protestant, like her father and grandfather, and fancied that she must be. If she was, she fitted certain very specific requirements like a glove.

What the position of the vessels on the table showed was that her grandfather Rupert had been Sophia of Hanover's elder brother and that therefore his descendants had a better claim to the throne than any Hanoverian.

If Anne Bonny Bard was alive somewhere the Act of Succession made her, as Rupert's legitimate grand-daughter, the next rightful monarch of England.

CHAPTER TWO

It became apparent that in inheriting Aunt Effie's house I had also inherited the Bratchet.

I didn't want either; the house was up for sale, Effie's goods were being converted into cash. Along with the rest of her estate, it turned out that she had left me an astounding £2,429. 4s. 7d. By my standards, I was now a rich man and could indulge my long-held wish to buy a farm and find peace.

I offered a sizeable sum to Bratchet to secure her future for her. 'You can go back to your parents. Where d'you come from?'

'Dunno.'

'You must know.'

'Don't remember.' It was her answer to practically everything. What did the man look like she'd seen coming out of the house when Effie was murdered? Didn't remember. What sort of person had Anne Bonny been? Didn't remember. Why had she accused Effie of having Anne and Mary Read spirited? Didn't remember.

The only person who offered to take her off my hands was Floss, who said she'd find the girl a place in her establishment next door. 'Set her up as a virgin. Good trade in virgins. She looks like one even if she ain't.'

She was certainly young and small enough to tempt some of Floss's clients into thinking they were violating an innocent, but how virginal she looked under the dirt it was difficult to say.

'You sellin' me for a whore?' she asked, when Floss had gone.

'No.'

'Keepin' me for yourself?'

'*You?*'

But she was afraid enough of my supposed designs on her skinny person to run upstairs to the room I'd given to her and lock the door. The dog, Turnspit, who followed her everywhere, went with her.

'Aunt Effie,' I thought, 'you've got a lot to answer for.'

I hoped the wench was reassured by my absence at nights which, at that time, I was spending with a pleasant widow who ran a school for girls in her cottage in Chelsea. I'd met her at Chelsea Hospital when I went to visit Sergeant Smith. He'd taken a French bullet in the chest as the Third advanced across the Offuz marshes during the battle for Ramillies. You could hear it whistling when he breathed. I'd gone to see him because, two years before, he'd been in charge of the troop Mary Read served in at Blenheim.

I still doubted whether the Anne Bonny/Mary Read business

had anything to do with Aunt Effie's murder but I wasn't getting very far in my efforts to discover whether she'd been killed by a chance thief. Floss maintained her frightened silence, the Bratchet maintained hers for whatever reason she had. The offer of a reward had brought in enough information to occupy the assizes for a month, but most of it came from locals indulging in their favourite pastime of settling old scores; mothers of unhappy wives accusing their sons-in-law – or, as in one case, the other way round – neighbour accusing neighbour. One man who'd bought a short-weight loaf said the baker'd done it. The popular candidate for murderer was the area's most rapacious landlord but, since he was a wizened old man who'd have had to get up on a ladder to strangle Aunt Effie, I'd discounted him.

So it seemed worthwhile to follow another thread and try to find out whether Aunt Effie's Mary was the same one who later turned up in Flanders as a Dragoon.

As far as getting information out of Sergeant Smith was concerned, I could have saved the walk to Chelsea; he was dying by inches and too short of breath to do much talking. In any case, over the years he'd been ribbed so hard by his fellow sergeants for not recognizing that one of his troop was a female that he'd become defensive. 'Tell you ... this much,' he wheezed, 'she ... one ... best bloody troopers ever saddled a horse. And the bravest. More balls than most ... carry their courage in their cocks.'

'When did she join you?'

He thought back, gasping. 'Came out as a recruit ... in time for Bonn.'

Marlborough had taken Bonn in 1703, the year after he'd been made Captain General of the allies and begun the long fight back against France's occupation of Europe.

'Where'd she come from?'

'Never asked.'

I'd never asked any of my men either; if they'd been in happy circumstances they wouldn't have taken the queen's shilling in the first place. Unless they were dolts. Or drunk.

'What happened to her?'

'Married Trooper Johnson and took a tavern for a bit. He died, I heard. Don't know . . . where she went after that.'

'What'd she look like, Sergeant?'

But he'd run out of breath and patience. 'Think I'm a faggot . . . go looking . . . at troopers? Enough trouble . . . training the bastards.'

I saluted, gave him the tobacco I'd brought for him and left, not much wiser than when I came. In the grounds I met other old comrades, one of them being visited by his daughter, the school-teaching widow.

I'm no Belvidere, I don't rivet women's attention at first glance, but by the time I'd walked this one home to her cottage and she'd told me the pump in her backyard was broken and I'd taken off my coat to mend it for her, she was looking on me as kindly as I was on her. Her father had been an infantry quartermaster sergeant – a species that does itself well – and he'd spent some of his loot on his girl's education. She'd also followed her husband to Flanders and had a good command of French. She had an even better figure, being one of those full-breasted ladies the army calls 'crummy'.

We suited each other. I guarded her reputation by arriving at her cottage after dark and leaving before dawn. At first I made the journey on foot but its effect on my leg meant that by the time I arrived I was hard put to suit anybody, so I hired a horse from a livery stable.

I still remember those rides. Nowadays wealthier London reaches out as far as Chelsea in plain parapeted mansions. But in those days the market gardens and orchards of Westminster's suburbs gave way to meadowland which, in that long, dry summer, was passable by paths along the river and led in the distance to fields ripening barley for the London breweries.

I used to water the horse at Millbank and watch the horse-ferry go back and forth to Lambeth against the sunset, the water's surface reflecting it so exactly that it seemed to travel on an upside-down reproduction of itself in an ambered laziness. There's talk of building a bridge there now in order that the mansion-owners don't have to travel all the way to the City to cross into Kent and Surrey. The watermen and City interests have put up a fight against it, but I doubt if they'll win.

Once in Chelsea, the smell of herbs from the apothecaries' physick garden would tell me I'd nearly reached the widow's cottage. I might have offered for her, pleasant woman that she was; whether she'd have accepted, I don't know. Anyway it came to nothing because somebody began trying to murder the Bratchet.

At first, when I came home in the early hours of one day and saw a figure clambering through a downstairs window, I assumed it was a thief – theft being the area's main source of income. By the time I'd hobbled across the court, the figure had wriggled to the ground and run off. Just in case it had been leaving, rather than entering, I knocked on the Bratchet's door. Her squawk told me she'd been asleep and still suspected me of having designs on her person.

There wasn't much point in informing the Watch of the incident, though I did; night watchmen have better regard for their health than to patrol Puddle Court. I boarded up the ground floor windows from the inside and forgot the matter.

I was busy just then. The house was proving difficult to sell; well built though it was, most prospective customers lost interest when they discovered its locality. There were the arrangements for the auction of Aunt Effie's bric-à-brac, interviews with informants applying for the reward, the search for a farm – I was considering the Chelsea area – and visits to the widow.

Also, nearly every day Effie's lawyer was demanding my signature on some document or other; my aunt, it appeared, had deposited her money in not one bank but several and, though my inheritance was mounting (to near £3,000), so was the paperwork. Saving time, I took to using the Bratchet as a messenger to carry the documents back to the lawyer's office in the City once I'd considered and signed them.

Until, that is, the day when Bratchet came back bleeding from a cut on her forehead. 'Fuck of a flowerpot,' she said when I asked how it had happened. The pot had missed her by inches when it fell from a roof in Caper Alley but as it crashed on the cobbles a shard had bounced up and sliced through a bit of skin. Falling flowerpots and rusted-through shop signs take as high a toll of London pedestrians as hackney carriages – and one of those, Bratchet grumbled, had nearly run her down the day before.

She took a gloomy view of life, did the Bratchet, and assumed these near-misses as natural to her attendant bad luck. They might have been but I was uneasy, and when Floss came to tell me that Bratchet had been marked, it was obvious something had to be done. In the army and navy a mark is a target for firing practice. In underworld parley it's much the same thing, except that the target is human. Word had gone out, said Floss, that Bratchet's short life wasn't to get any longer.

'Who's marked her, Floss?' I didn't doubt the woman's information; whores know more about what's happening on the streets than any parish beadle – they're closer to them.

'The Brotherhood.'

'*Pirates?*'

It's a wide term, the Brotherhood, and takes in not only the men who seize entire ships on the high seas but Thames water rats who'll plunder a bale of taffeta from a vessel as she goes upriver. It's accurate, though. The fact that they take other people's livings, sometimes their lives, by boat makes a bond of cooperation between men who otherwise can't be trusted with their own mother's savings. Perhaps they're welded together by their mutual skill on water, or by maritime language. Whatever it is, some current informs them all. If they'd marked the Bratchet, she was as good as dead unless I took avoiding action very quickly.

'Who told you, Floss?'

She wouldn't say; there's a code even among harlots. 'Just get her away. Inland for choice.'

After she'd gone I went into the kitchen where Bratchet was preparing a meal for herself and Turnspit. She was a vile cook. I never ate at home; I wasn't even sure the dog should. 'What is it you know, Bratchet? Somebody's trying to mutton you for it.'

She pretended a gape.

'Don't act the lurk with me,' I told her, 'They done Aunt Effie and they'll do you.'

63

'Not me, they won't.' There were the little teeth again; she was absolutely sure of it.

There was so little she could be certain of in her miserable life that there was no point in frightening her, so I didn't tell her about the Brotherhood; she wouldn't have believed it in any case. I wasn't sure that I did. What threat could she be to the pirate trade?

On the other hand, Floss hadn't invented the intruder I'd seen, nor the flowerpot, nor Bratchet's near escape from a runaway hackney. 'What am I going to do with you, Bratchet?'

After consideration, I sent a letter to the Chelsea widow asking her to provide a temporary refuge for the child. She replied immediately, agreeing. The next thing was to make Bratchet fit to stay in decent company. I made her come with me to Mary Defoe, wife to Daniel, who'd been a mother to me in the absence of my own. She took one look at the Bratchet and said, 'Bath.'

As Daniel was absent I read a book in the parlour while sounds of splashing and slaughter came from the kitchen where Mrs Defoe had prepared a washtub and was forced to call on her older daughters in order to quell Bratchet's resistance against getting in it. Cleanliness, if not godliness – she was still spitting and cursing when she emerged – prevailed. Mrs Defoe led her into the parlour with the air of a tired but victorious general parading a defeated queen into Rome.

She was wearing a blue dress they'd found for her. The hair was flax. The skin, apart from slight pockmarks on the cheeks of the face, was ivory overlaid on thin bones.

'I washed the dog an' all,' said Mrs Defoe, 'She won't go nowhere without it.'

As I thanked her and said goodbye, she tapped my arm and whispered, 'Dan'l says, will you meet him tonight.'

'The Beggar Maker's,' I said, 'Late.'

After it was dark, I took Bratchet to the widow's in Chelsea and left her there. I was looking forward to a talk with Daniel Defoe. Thinking over our last one, I still couldn't see Major Howe as Aunt Effie's killer nor as the man who, four years before, had paid her to spirit Miss Bard-cum-Bonny to the colonies. There was no proof either way, of course, but my bones told me my old major, incompetent, lying coward as he was, didn't have the viciousness to kill. Besides, the discovery that the missing girl was a contender for the throne of England put the business on a different plane.

From what I could make out, Anne Bonny had stayed with Aunt Effie for a few months in the spring and summer of 1702 trying to contact her father's and grandfather's relatives. Mary Read had jibed to Floss that in that time they'd been to London to see the Queen. Suppose they had? If Anne Bonny/Bard was Rupert's grand-daughter, then Queen Anne *was* her relative. A cousin.

But if the girl had presented herself at court, she'd chosen the wrong time for her arrival. At that point England was needing every ally she possessed in the war against Louis XIV. And one of those allies, a very valuable ally, was the Electorate of Hanover from which it had been ordained the next heir to the English throne would come if Queen Anne failed to produce one of her own. An heir with a better claim, such as Anne Bonny/Bard could produce, would have been an embarrassment just then, almost a disaster. Better to have her out of the way and avoid complications.

I didn't suspect the Queen of eliminating her young cousin, but I knew enough of government, and know even more now, to believe that it can stoop to any crime in the name of what someone in it regards as patriotism.

The Beggar Maker's habitués are conservative in their taste and the tavern resembles in every particular the predecessor which stood on the site before the Great Fire, except that its roof is slate rather than thatch. Dirty oiled paper does the duty of window glass, mist from the river is rotting its timbers, and dust has eased back on to its jutting frontage to help its regulars feel at home. A potted bay bush outside, which contributed to the flames of London in 1666, has been replaced by one equally dead.

An uneasy Defoe was waiting for me outside. 'Could we not meet somewhere more private? And salubrious?' His hat was pulled down low and he'd wrapped himself to the ears in a cloak. In view of the weather – the hot summer was giving way to a hot autumn – he looked as inconspicuous as St Paul's.

'Prefer Aunt Effie's, do you?' I knew the house gave him the horrors. I didn't find it too pleasant myself and had lowered the price to be rid of it. In any case, I liked the Beggar Maker's. Inside, the great, dark, tallow-lit, elm-floored, ale-scented be-barrelled room extended the welcome of all good taverns.

Not so the regulars. As Daniel walked in, conversation ceased. Customers froze in the attitude of tigers disturbed at dinner. A stranger might be the Law, and the Beggar Maker's clientele don't enjoy legal scrutiny. But when I followed Daniel in, the atmosphere relaxed; as Effie Sly's nephew I had the right credentials.

Daniel looked round for somewhere to talk out of all earshot, but that was impossible. We sat on two stools either side of a barrel and hoped the noise would cover our conversation.

'Another line from the old author?' asked Defoe.

I declined and ordered ale – it had taken me a day to recover from our session on Westminster brandy.

'Have you decided what you will do with your life now?' he asked when it came.

'Not yet.'

He paused; he was approaching something carefully. 'I have formed an interest in this Anne Bonny creature, Martin,' he said casually. 'I wondered if I might use you while you are yet unemployed to find her, always supposing she is still alive.'

I nodded. 'I wondered if you might.'

He looked disconcerted, but pressed on. 'I am prepared to pay you one hundred pounds and any subsequent expenses if you will return to the Low Countries to locate this Mary Read you told me of.'

He waited for me to say something and, when I didn't, added, 'She may know to which ship the press boat that captured her and Mistress Bard was bound.' He cleared his throat. 'It may even be that she *is* Anne Bard.'

'How do you work that out?'

'Just consider,' he said, 'Two young women are dragged aboard a press smack. One escapes, or bribes her release, and later turns up in disguise across the Channel – as you pointed out, it is unlikely to be coincidence that another, completely different, Mary Read should appear at that time.' He leaned forward. 'Let us suppose it is Anne Bonny/Bard who escapes. Anne Bonny, who has already proved herself of adventurous spirit, is forced to yet more desperate measures. As we know, she had already found it necessary to adopt an alias, so let us suppose she now discards one that has proved useless and instead takes the identity of her unfortunate companion.'

I nodded. This was devious thinking, and I didn't think it was Daniel's. Daniel Defoe, apparently as open as a church, inquisitive about everything in order to instruct and pass on what he learns, has a deep vault to him and somebody had found it. He was carrying secrets, half appalled at them, half excited. He was a man in a romance, but he wasn't writing this one; somebody else was.

'Suppose she did,' I said, 'And let's suppose, Master Defoe, you're taking me for a clinchpoop. What's made you suddenly decide the woman that joined the Dragoons as Mary Read was one of the women who lodged at Aunt Effie's?'

He was dignified. 'I have seen her army papers, that's what. She volunteered just after the two women were reported missing.'

'Let me get this clear,' I said, 'You now believe that when the two girls were spirited, one of them escaped from the press boat. It could have been Mary Read who got away while Anne Bonny was carried off to the colonies. It could be the other way round. You believe that the girl who escaped then joined the army.' I sat back and surveyed him. 'Why? Why didn't she go hot-foot to the nearest magistrate and say that some bastard had kidnapped her friend and bloody near kidnapped her too? Why didn't she alert the authorities?'

He didn't answer.

I leaned forward and poked a finger at his gaudy waistcoat. 'I'll tell you why she didn't, Daniel, shall I? Because she had a damn good idea it was the authorities who'd done it. That's why.'

He opened his mouth to reply, but I hadn't finished: 'Incon-

67

venient, was she, this Anne Bonny/Bard? A bit too near the throne? Might cause concern for those who wanted the Hanovers to succeed to the crown?'

He became indignant. 'This is nonsense you're talking, Martin. War has hardened you. Even Mrs Defoe has noticed it. I'm sorry to say it, but you've become a cynic. Her Majesty's ministers are honourable men.'

He believed it. Daniel's older in age than me by twenty years and younger in innocence by thirty.

'Which minister are you acting for?' I asked him. 'Don't tell me you're not. Daniel, the day before I got back from Flanders you were in the pillory and facing debtors' prison. Word on the street is you got sprung by high-placed gentlemen, some *very* high-placed gentlemen. Next thing you turn up in Puddle Court asking after a girl nobody's ever heard of. Now you've suddenly got access to army papers and are offering me a hundred pounds. Daniel, you haven't *got* a hundred pounds. Whose money is it?'

He thought for a bit, then said, guardedly, 'I may be permitted to tell you that I am acting for quarters close to the throne. By finding the woman called Mary Read and learning what she knows you will be serving your country.'

'I served it,' I told him. 'And what quarters close to the throne may they be? Godolphin? Harley?' I could see I wasn't far off the mark. I went on, 'If she's Rupert's grand-daughter she's got royal blood, morganatic or not. What do they want with her? Put her on the throne? Is that it? Or keep her quiet. Is *that* it?'

Daniel said, 'Martin, I'll put the case to you as it was put to me. That into this country, in the year of 1702, arrives a young woman. She is penniless but well educated, for a female. She says her name is Anne Bard, though she travels under the pseudonym of Anne Bonny because, it appears, she has passed through Germany and been afraid of being spirited or even killed by the Hanoverians.'

Daniel acknowledged my surprise at the thought of old Electress Sophia as a killer by pouring me out another beaker of ale. 'I merely put her case, Martin. If her existence could displace Sophia of Hanover as heir to the English throne she might feel that Sophia had no reason to love her. This young woman says she has papers to prove her claim. She takes a coach to Kensington Palace and begs an audience. She is refused, naturally; Her Majesty's ministers don't wish to have Her Majesty's kindness distressed by a female who may at best be deranged, at worst a scheming impostor.'

'So they don't tell Her Majesty about the female who begs an audience.'

'No.'

'True power lies behind the throne, eh? Not on it.'

He shrugged.

'So they got rid of her, is that it?' I said, 'And now they're not sure they succeeded in getting rid of her permanently, so they want to get rid of her again. I'm not finding her for you, Daniel. Send an assassin. Cut out the middle man.'

'They did *not* get rid of her,' he shouted. To do him justice he really did believe it. He saw heads turning towards him and lowered his voice. 'They don't know who paid your aunt to spirit her. I have received assurances that Her Majesty's government now wishes to extend its aid to this most unfortunate of Her Majesty's subjects.'

I could see that they might. The situation had changed. Young George of Hanover was proving an embarrassing ally, especially to the Tories. He looked as if he might prove an equally embarrassing King of England. 'They want Anne Bard in their hand, a queen as it were, to trump any others – if the situation arises.'

He opened his mouth for the other phrases Godolphin or Harley or whoever-it-was had fed him, then shrugged again. 'Yes.'

'I see.' At least, I thought I did. 'And what's the bloody Scotsman doing in all this?'

'Livingstone of Kilsyth is related to Anne Bard through her mother. She was a Cassilis. How she met Dudley Bard, I don't know. She went abroad after some quarrel with the clan. Kilsyth is also a Jacobite, an upholder of James II's right to the crown and, now that James is dead, an upholder of his son, the Pretender.'

'I know what a Jacobite is,' I told him, shortly.

'Yes, well. Remember that not all Jacobites are Roman Catholics. Claverhouse, for instance, who led the rebellion to put James II back on the throne when England ousted him, belonged to the Scottish equivalent of the Church of England. He was an Episcopalian.'

I nodded.

'And the Episcopalian Jacobites are nearing despair at the Pretender's refusal to change his religion, knowing he has no chance of succeeding to the throne of Scotland and England if he remains a Papist.'

I squinted. 'And our Anne Bonny isn't a Papist?'

'No. It is believed she is a Protestant, like her father and grandfather. If the Pretender persists in remaining Catholic, these same Jacobites may transfer allegiance to the cause of a more suitable Stuart.'

'Anne Bonny?'

'Anne Bonny.'

It was too deep for me. If Defoe's employers wanted Anne because she was a Stuart and a Protestant, and the Scotsman's employers wanted Anne because she was a Stuart and a Protestant, why couldn't they stop spying on each other and get together over a dram? I supposed it was a matter of who controlled the girl once she was found. God save me from matters of state. I said, 'It didn't occur to them she might just have come to England because she was lonely?'

He smiled for the first time. 'No. It wouldn't.' He went off to order more ale, the tapsters having become involved in a rowdy game of shove-ha'penny which was being rivalled by a fight in the far corner and by Floss, who was lifting her skirts to dance in another, refusing to be dissuaded from it by her male companion's fists. A normal night at the Beggar Maker's.

I considered. There were good reasons for refusing Daniel. My memories of Flanders weren't such that I wanted to see it again. Anyway, I'm a man who likes to look at a horse's teeth before I buy it whereas Daniel was trying to sell me this one without, as far as I could tell, even having opened its mouth. He might be excited by being the confidant of Her Majesty's ministers and receiving their assurances, but too many soldiers have been waved off to war with government assurances only to end up begging on the streets. Or dead.

On the other hand, it looked likely that Aunt Effie was killed for the papers Anne Bonny/Bard had brought to England four years before to prove her legitimacy. While I didn't care if Bonny Anne was heir to the Great Chan of China, I cared about finding Effie's killer. If I went, it would be for that. And to oblige Daniel. Not the government or the Queen but Daniel Defoe. I owed him a great deal. And I owed Mrs Defoe more.

Every Sabbath of my early childhood that I can remember, I was held above my father's head at meetings while he led the congregation in prayer that the Lord might punish my mother for deserting me and him, her lawful husband.

'Let her carcase be as dung upon the face of the fields. Let the dogs eat her by the wall, as they did Jezebel. Scourge, we beseech thee, the whoredoms of his mother from the body and soul of this child.' And mostly, in case the Lord hadn't heard him, he'd scourge me himself when we got home.

Afterwards I'd go next door to Mrs Defoe's lap where my stripes were dressed with salve. 'It ain't so, Martin,' she'd say. 'He's a righteous man, your pa, and a powerful preacher, but it ain't so and don't thee believe it. She left, 'tis true, but she took you along with her. It was thy pa followed her and took you back.'

'I'll find her, won't I?' I always asked, 'She ain't dead, is she? When I'm grown, I'll find her, won't I?'

Mrs Defoe would wipe her tears on my head, 'In the next life if you don't in this. When you get to heaven your poor ma'll be waiting for you. The Lord loves all and forgives all, praise His name.'

Two tankards of ale were put on the barrel top in front of me. 'Do I order your passport for the Low Countries?' asked Daniel.

'Two passports,' I said, 'I'm taking Bratchet with me.' I saw his look. 'Give me credit, Daniel, for God's sake. I like 'em older. And plumper. But I'm responsible for her. No friends, no family. Leave her behind and she'll be on the streets quicker than ninepence.'

71

I didn't tell him about the Brotherhood. It was hot, I was tired and I couldn't be sure that it wasn't his employers who'd set the Brotherhood on to mark the Bratchet, afraid she could identify the agent who'd killed Aunt Effie and stolen the box containing Anne Bonny's papers. It was no more fantastic than anything else in this world of plot and counter-plot I'd stepped into.

'Besides,' I said, 'suppose I meet up with Mary Read. Who's to tell me whether she's Mary Read or Anne Bonny? There's only the Bratchet knows.'

'Floss would know, my dear boy.' He was delighted. 'But I suppose that even the Bratchet is a more suitable travelling companion than Floss. Very well. Two passports.'

'And a hundred pounds,' I said, 'and expenses.' I might be rich now, but his employers were a damn sight richer.

'You shall have it, my boy. I need expenses myself, for my jouney to Scotland.'

He bent towards me, full of importance. 'I am to employ my pen over the Pennines to persuade our Scottish brethren of the value of the proposed union of their country with England.'

'Are you taking Livingstone of Kilsyth with you?'

'Certainly not. He and his kind oppose the Union. Mine is as secret a mission as your own.'

I pointed across the room. 'What's he doing over there then?' I'd only just spotted the Highlander through the tobacco smoke that filled the air like fog; he was in a corner, as swathed in a cloak as Daniel and, with his bare legs, about as incognito. He was listening to a man who'd been sitting on a settle behind us.

Daniel, not usually a man to swear, looked where I was pointing and said, 'Oh, bugger.'

Since I wasn't prepared to go anywhere until Aunt Effie's house was sold, it was over a year before the Bratchet and I set out.

Occasionally, notes urging me to be on my way would arrive from Daniel in Scotland, but I ignored them. I could see even then that my lameness would get worse rather than better with age and I was going to make damn sure that every penny Aunt

Effie left me would be safeguarded for my return. Daniel's notes usually included suggestions that I invest in one or other of his 'projects', but I ignored those too. Love him as I did, I wasn't going to take financial advice from a man who spent as much time as he did avoiding the bum bailiffs. Here was one veteran who wouldn't end up begging on the streets.

My friend in Chelsea employed the time in teaching her new charge to read and write for which I paid her. When I thanked her for a thankless task, she said Bratchet was a more rewarding pupil than most. 'She's quick and grateful to learn.'

It wasn't a description of the Bratchet I knew. 'No,' said the widow, when I said so, 'she bears you a grudge, Martin, I don't understand why. Do you know she can speak French?'

'I'd teach her to speak English first,' I said.

'She speaks French, Martin,' said the widow patiently, 'because she *is* French. I'm sure of it. It's her native tongue.'

'Are you certain?' It seemed extraordinary.

My friend nodded. 'Her vocabulary in French is wider than mine, wider than in English.'

From what I'd heard of Bratchet's English vocabulary, I hoped it was also cleaner. I said, 'She's an orphan. Aunt Effie got her from a poorhouse.' I tried to recall the last time I'd seen Effie, which was soon after she'd acquired Bratchet. 'I think she said she got the girl cheap because she was dumb.'

'Yes. She can remember the poorhouse but little before that. There must have been some tragic mishap that stopped her mouth for a while. She may be a Huguenot. When the subject of Louis XIV came up in class the other day, she denounced him in immediate French, as if quoting her parents.' My friend pursed her lips. 'She then lapsed into English in terms which obliged me to send her from the room.'

It was possible. There had been and still were Huguenots arriving in England by the thousand to escape Louis XIV's persecution of his French Protestants.

When, at last, the widow and I bade each other goodbye, I said, 'I hope to be back in six months at most.'

She said, 'Perhaps, while you're over there in Europe, you may get some word of Bratchet's people.'

We never did, of course. Whoever they were, or had been, they were lost to Bratchet. I never saw the widow again either. By the time I was able to look for her, she'd remarried, this time to a parson, and was living with their four children in Hertford-shire. I know because I made careful enquiries, in case she'd got into any difficulty.

I hope she was happy. She was a very nice woman.

CHAPTER THREE

JAMES, I've considered for a long time whether to include in this account a journal that came into my possession on the day Queen Anne died. I think I must. It'll fill in the gaps; it gives information of events that I didn't know about at the time and are important to your story.

Incidentally, they also bear upon the history of England; there are people who'd cut off their right arm to read it if its contents were known, and even more would undergo another amputation to suppress it. I hope you'll give none of them the opportunity to do either.

The journal is confused but it roughly covers a period which stretches from the Bratchet's and my embarkation for Flanders in the autumn of 1707 to my return. It explains why we suffered the adventures we did in that time. I'll insert the appropriate pages between the leaves of my own account so that they are contemporaneous and so that what was befalling the puppets is interleaved with the words of the puppet-master – more cor-rectly, the puppet-mistress.

I hope, too, that, like me, you'll regard the woman who wrote it as mad. Insanity has excuses; wickedness has not. And ex-cuses can and should be made for this woman, though it was a long time before I could bring myself to make them; she tried to murder the Bratchet and she bloody nearly killed me.

I call the diary *The Madwoman's Journal* to remind me that I mustn't judge her. Nor should you.

Long before her journal begins, great men she'd never met had sent her to hell with no more thought than they'd give to choosing a waistcoat. I never did manage to discover their names or whether they were Whig or Tory, Hanoverian or Jacobite, but I know they were powerful and as mad as she became.

It's my considered opinion, James, that the possession of power brings on madness.

Slave owners, with absolute power over Negroes, are not only cruel, they are *unnecessarily* cruel. In their need for their slave's labour, they have taken away his right to property, decency, his own children. They refuse to educate him and then call him ignorant. They are, of course, afraid of him.

When you come to think about it, men have done much the same thing to women, and for the same reason. If I wanted to, I could legally turn my wife out of this house and refuse to let her see her children again. My sex makes the law and she has no rights under it but mine.

Sometimes, though, slaves revolt and women fight back. The revenge this woman took is terrible, but she took it because a terrible thing was done to her. I doubt if she knew who paid Aunt Effie to get rid of her any more than I do – perhaps the order was given through subordinates, perhaps it was expressed as a wish, a Henry II demanding to be rid of his turbulent priest, perhaps the culprit or culprits had already retired to an old age of comfort on a country estate, or were already dead. It didn't matter to her. She directed her vengeance on the class that had hurt her, not caring who suffered for it. And that is madness.

First Extract from *The Madwoman's Journal*

I AM DEAD who writes this account. I'd better be. If it's discovered in my lifetime I shall be dead soon after in any case. I'll be turned off, trined, invited to dance the gallows' waltz. They'll swing me, hang my pretty corpse for the tide to cover three times on Wapping wall, where they've hung so many of the Brotherhood. What a crowd I'll pull. But the record must be written. The future must know the revenge Anne Bonny and Mary Read took or it will be no revenge at all. When the account is finished I may bury it secretly for another age to dig up, perhaps under the Banqueting House where they're putting down a new floor after the Whitehall fire. I'll direct my soul, if I've got a soul, to haunt the spot so that ghostly laughter terrifies them when they find it.

I'm laughing now. Frightened and laughing. It's like running from a navy vessel on a beam reach with all sail crammed on. God, I was alive then. Born for it. The risk is dreadful. The court is an anthill of spies. Door bolted, shutters closed, I've searched the walls for spyholes. There are none. Still someone's watching me, I know it. There's a presence in the room. I think it may not be mortal. I think it's the same creature that's begun entering my dreams. It may be the Devil even. In that case, welcome, honoured Sir. May your purse and your prick never fail you, as Calico Jack used to say. You don't scare me. Hell doesn't scare me. I've been there.

Thank you for the suggestion. I'll slit open one of my menstrual pads and keep the papers in there until the account is complete. If they look for it there they are no gentlemen and I hope their nutmegs drop off.

Must I have the Bratchet killed? I know you say so, but I was fond of the slut. She was fond of me, too. I looked into her eyes as I left that hideous house and saw the admiration in them undimmed. She wouldn't betray me. Effie Sly deserved to die. The Bratchet doesn't.

Yes? Very well then. It's probably too late to stop it in any case. I've put out the word to the Brotherhood and she is already marked. She may be dead as I write. What power. I exult in it. I have come back with an army at my command, a rodent army to gnaw away at the wooden walls of England. Stamp on one of us, there's a thousand to use their teeth in its place. Nibble, nibble, London Bridge is falling down. Did you hear my squeaks, my lords, when your boot came down? Did you care? You will.

No, my sulphurous friend with the horns is perfectly correct. The Bratchet must die. She saw me and therefore could give me

76

away, even without meaning to. Nothing must risk the plan. It's already begun. The plan. I am in position at the Court of Her Majesty Queen Anne. I have taken my place in this royal anthill, unsuspected and unnoticed, just another busy insect among the hundreds that keep our fat, white queen clean and fed. Queen Ant.

It was so easy. You wouldn't believe how simple it was. I took a leaf out of Abigail Hill's book. They say she turned up one day claiming to be a long-lost relative of Sarah, Duchess of Marlborough and oh please, your ladyship, I admire you more than all women, let me serve you, I'll bow, I'll scrape, only find me a position. I can imagine it; those weasel eyes looking sideways through tears, that meek little voice. What skill. And Sarah swallowed the bait, hook and line. Pity, really. I'd have thought better of her.

Now there's a woman who's alive; Sarah. More alive than anyone at Court, more alive than Queen Ant. Given the chance, Sarah could have ruled the world. At the moment she's ruling England, tyrannizing poor Queen Ant who loves her body and soul and would give her the moon if she had a long enough ladder. But power's made Sarah drunk. After her husband won Blenheim and Ramillies, she's become a despot, being sure there were no limits to what she could do. The Court rings with her commands.

And they are obeyed. Vanbrugh is building her and the Duke the greatest palace since Hampton Court. She's going to call it after Blenheim. She wants only her fellow Whigs to be in government and tries to undermine Harley, who is a Tory. What a woman. The great and the good wait not the Queen's nod but hers.

Hubris. She speaks to the Queen as if Her Majesty were a servant. She can't see the Abigail snake she introduced to Court insinuating its way into the Queen's affection and spittling balm on the hurts her bullying causes. Everybody else can. She's away too much, writing her interminable letters, plotting to put another Whig in power, granting interviews. And all the time, our Abigail slithers her skinny body in and out of the royal closet with another little mess she's made to tempt the royal appetite. Another cushion behind our poor, dear, royal back? A draught? Affectionate Abigail will close the window and sit at cards with you, dear madam.

She's playing the hand well, I grant the little corner-creeper that much. Watch out, Sarah. And Abigail, watch out. I'm close behind, stepping on your tail. If you can supplant Sarah, I can supplant you. Then I shall look about me how to play my hand. It has stronger cards than yours.

I've had to start lower down than Abigail did, of course. She gulled a duchess for her place, using their kinship – for all I know the Hills are truly Sarah's distant relations. My gull is Cofferer of the Royal Household, a grand title for a very minor post, and we are most certainly not related.

The Negroes selected him for me. They are another brotherhood to which I am a sister, their white-skinned sister. It is strange how nobody notices them. They couldn't be more conspicuous, with their black faces under their jewelled turbans, uniformed like peacocks. Yet they are invisible as they stand behind the chairs and smile and say 'Yes'm'.

'I'm warm, Sambo, fetch me a fan.'

'Yes'm.'

'Pick up my handkerchief, Goliath.'

'Yes'm.' The fan is fetched, the handkerchief is picked up and the recipient is barely aware that it has been done. They might as well be a tapestry. Anybody who is anybody has one and everybody is used to them.

It's a mistake to ignore them, my lords and ladies, such a mistake. They hear everything and see everything. And they pass it on to me. Thanks to them and the Brotherhood I hold reins of information in my little hand that criss-cross land and sea. What power now.

As I say, the Negroes selected my gull, the Cofferer. One of his sisters had gone with her husband and children to begin a new life in Jamaica and all of them, the entire family, died of the yellow fever epidemic that swept Kingston last year and were buried in the mass grave.

'Except me, Uncle,' I told him, weeping, 'No one left to care for me and just enough money for the passage home. Oh, what shall I do?' I furnished him with the names of the family that the Negroes had given me; there had been a daughter about my age. When he asked more questions, I broke down in a fit of crying; I didn't want to remember the tragedy that had over-taken dear Mama and Papa and all my siblings, please don't ask me, Uncle. I was convincing enough on conditions in Ja-maica – who knows them better?

He was the perfect gull; he wanted to believe me. He's old, nearly sixty, and his wife's crippled with the gout and no good to him. He couldn't resist a pretty young niece who'd help to look after her. He couldn't resist kissing the pretty young niece's tears away, either, and there, there-ing, my little one, with his hand sliding down my neck. I knew then I'd landed him.

Next day I took up residence with him and his wife in his apartment at St James's. He had to ask the Duchess of Marlbor-ough for permission, of course. Officially, he's Queen Ant's ser-vant but in reality he's Sarah's creature, like everyone else in the Household, except Abigail. Sarah is Groom of the Stole, Mistress of the Robes and Keeper of the Privy Purse and has the disposal of places at Court as well as being treasurer of the Queen's personal monies.

As Cofferer, my so-called uncle is no more than one of Sarah's secretaries. Luckily, she likes him; he does what she says. He took me to be presented – to Sarah, of course, not to the Queen. Another post that Sarah holds is the Rangership of Windsor Park and it entitles her to Windsor Lodge as a residence.

'A delightful habitation, you will find, my dear,' said Uncle Cofferer on the journey down in the coach that delivers Sarah's mail, putting his hand on my knee and keeping it there.

So it is. Too small for Sarah, of course, but Rome would be too small for Sarah. The palace of Blenheim she's having built out at Woodstock in Oxfordshire is said to be a second Rome in any case. But Windsor Lodge will do for me. A double-fronted building with ivy up to the first storey where it cuts off straight. Arches in hedges so neat they might be carved from green stone. The orange trees in tubs along its frontage stand up straight as soldiers on parade. Not a weed, not a fallen leaf on the lawn. The gardeners at the royal palaces could take lessons from Sarah.

So could the royal maids. Every piece of furniture in her hall shone and its flags were treacherous with polishing. At Kensington Palace royal spiders lurk in the overlooked corners; at Windsor Lodge there's no dust to dare give them a home.

Uncle Cofferer was nervous. 'Be not afeared, now,' he told me, as we waited with other supplicants for our turn to be ushered into the Presence, 'She's formidable, but she's kindly.'

Uncle Cofferer, I have fought duels with men who'd munch your bones for breakfast. And won.

I was on edge even so, this woman could make or break the first step of the plan. Yet if Abigail Hill could gull her, I reckoned she'd be easy meat for me.

The Duchess of Marlborough was at her desk, alone in the room, except for a child Negro standing behind her chair. I kept my eyes down. She'd been writing and was rubbing her fingers with pumice to rid them of ink. She sat straight as we made our courtesies. Uncle Cofferer's bow was so low I had to help him upright.

'Master Cofferer?'

He introduced me and explained.

She's about forty-five and having trouble with the change, I'd guess. Handsome, though. Her hair's a honey colour which doesn't show grey too soon and she holds her head like the empress she thinks she is. Her eyes are deep blue and very quick. Fine skin, but the mouth has set in a line; strength has driven out grace. Her only son died of the smallpox a year or two back. He'd wanted to join the army like his father but Sarah insisted the lad be kept safe and sent him to Cambridge instead. The smallpox killed him there. They say she's never been the same since.

A hard woman to love. Yet after twenty-odd years of marriage, it appears, the Duke's still in a passion for her.

'You're old to be an unmarried niece, girl.' She'd waved Uncle Cofferer back and was stalking round me like a horse coper. 'Twenty-three? Twenty-four?'

Twenty-four. 'Twenty-three, Your Grace,' I bobbed.

'And found no husband in Jamaica?'

'Not one to love, Your Grace.'

She approved of that. I thought she would. 'Marriage is a heavy yoke without love,' she lectured, 'but where affection is grounded on good reason, it cannot be too soon. We must find you a suitable husband.'

'Yes, Your Grace. Thank you, Your Grace.' In the reign of Queen Dick, Your Grace.

'You are a comely piece. Are you a good girl?'

Bobbed again. 'I trust so, Your Grace.'

'I trust so too.' She turned to the old man. 'What is it you want for her, Master Cofferer?'

He came forward, bleating. 'Some position, however lowly, Your Grace. The royal laundress is become old and expressed a wish for an assistant. I wondered if perhaps . . .'

The Devil, I thought. Up to my elbows in bloody suds.

'Mmm,' she pondered. 'The royal linen has shown signs of yellowing of late. I made a note to talk to Mrs Peach about it. Are you competent in laundry, girl?'

'Yes, Your Grace.' Bundled the washing in a net and dragged it behind the ship, Your Grace.

'Very well.' She tacked back to her desk and scribbled a memorandum. 'Fifty pounds a year and all found. And, Master Cofferer, she must have suitable dress; her clothes are abominable. Take twenty pounds from the household account. She lives with you?'

'If you please, Your Grace, she will prove most useful in helping to nurse my dear wife who is . . .'

'How is the poor soul? Do you feed her comfrey?'

'Your Grace, I . . .'

'Comfrey, Master Cofferer. Lots of it. Tell Hawkins to bring you a bushel each week. It strengthens the bones.'

Tears of gratitude from Uncle Cofferer. Sarah waved them away. 'I think it well to give employment to those that are in so unhappy a condition as to want it. I shall inform the Queen of the appointment.'

We began to go out backwards, Uncle Cofferer bowing like a flapping jib, me bobbing like a cork.

'Master Cofferer.'

He shot up. 'Your Grace?'

She was rubbing her fingers with the pumice again. 'Her Majesty has withdrawn monies from the Privy Purse and neglected to tell me. An oversight, naturally. Do you have a notion what it was for?'

'No, your Grace. I would tell you if . . . '

'You may go.'

Returning to London in the carriage, I asked Uncle Cofferer what monies the Queen was spending that she wasn't telling Sarah about. I could see it worried him but he wouldn't tell. 'There are forces clashing at court, my dear. Antagonisms. Better not to concern your pretty little head about them.' His hand was back on my knee. 'Your loyalty now, like mine, is to the Duchess. Did I not tell you she was kindly? Formidable, but kindly?'

Kindly, perhaps. Formidable, certainly. And mad. There's obsession in her eyes. I've seen saner March hares.

What else could she be? Once, she was one of us. I can tell. She's heard the boats at anchor plunging to be free. A restless spirit that should have followed the wind where it blew. But they chained her up in closets and dulled her ears with chatter and left her to play with dolls. It's a bigger doll's house than most, I grant. But it's not big enough for Sarah and it's sent her mad.

What is the Queen keeping secret from her, I wonder. Where's the royal money going? To Abigail? I must find out. Will the post of assistant royal laundress, fifty pounds a year and all found, bring me close enough to what is going on? Ah well, it will do for now. It's a long climb to the top of the mast. Take it slowly.

I could see Uncle Cofferer expected gratitude for his exertions on my behalf. How much gratitude became apparent when I heard his slippers on the stairs coming down to the room where I sleep.

Our apartment is in one of the turrets. The brass plaque on the door says 'Cofferer to the Household'. The old fool polishes it with his sleeve entering and leaving. It leads to three rooms, each above the other on a winding stair, his and his wife's bedroom at the top. Beneath is what he calls his salon, a pleasant enough room though its furniture was new in the time of William the Conqueror. It is also his office and has a desk. Below that is the room where he stores chests of winter clothes and old tennis racquets and lumber not needed elsewhere. Here is a cupboard bed set in the wall with a fretted, sliding panel to keep out the draught, and here I sleep. It is well enough as long as the panel is open and the window too, so I can hear the seagulls following the Thames barges and imagine I am in my hammock at sea.

There is no kitchen. Uncle Cofferer and I eat in the buttery and a maid brings food to Aunt Cofferer who, being gouty, is marooned in her high bedroom and only occasionally is helped down to the salon to receive her friend, one of the housekeepers, so they can complain to each other of how much better things were when they were young, which was also in the time of the Conqueror.

I heard his slippers, I say, and then his breathing. 'Is my little niece comfy? I have come to kiss my niece goodnight.' The word 'niece' excites him, incestuous old bugger.

I let him slobber awhile, then closed the panel, saying I was tired. He stood outside panting, before he could get breath for the stairs.

Shall I let him? On reflection I think so. It will give me a hank on him. (No, my dear. No Brotherhood slang, not even when I write, or it will slip out one day when I talk and get me noticed.) It will give me a *hold* on him so that whatever happens after, he'll be too guilty to speak out. He'll be my creature then, not Sarah's. When they took away my dagger and cutlass the only weapon they left me was my body. Well, the body is the only weapon women have been allowed through the ages, and mine is in excellent condition so they tell me.

Oh, God, what have I become? I did not want this. I had such hopes to lead a good, useful, accomplished life. What ruin they brought on my soul as well as my prospects when they took us.

Shall I run down to the cool river now and let it carry me on the first ebb to the estuary? My spirit could take a transit from the North and South Foreland lights and then go westward until the current swings it home to Jamaica where my love lies.

No. Hold, steersman, hold, hold the course. They destroyed what I was, they shall endure what I have become.

I must finish. It's nearly dawn and an assistant laundress's work begins at daylight. I shall fold this paper, then unstitch a cloth and slip it inside. An excellent suggestion of your Satanic lordship's. Is it you watching me, Beelzebub? I can feel somebody's eyes.

The weak moment has passed. I am powerful again.

But I wish the Bratchet did not have to die.

CHAPTER FOUR

As I say, we didn't embark for Flanders until the autumn of 1707 and when we did it was from Harwich. Hope of leaving England without attracting attention was put paid to by the Bratchet. At her first glimpse of the boat's masts and the grey sea beyond, she began to scream.

I tried reason: 'It floats. I told you. We sit on it and it carries us over the water.' I tried threats: 'Do you want to be left behind to fend for yourself?' I tried force: 'Get on that bloody gangplank.'

Struggling, she kicked my bad leg again so that I hopped, holding on to her, while her dog nipped at my good one and passengers leaned over the packet's side to watch. I might as well have hired a farewell bloody band.

I was loomed over. A voice exclaimed, 'Laddy. Is it yourself, Master Millet? And Holland bound? Isn't that the coincidence?'

I was too busy for surprise. 'Help me get her on the boat, will you?'

'Does the maid come as well, then?' This time Livingstone of Kilsyth's voice held real astonishment.

'She does.'

'And the wee dog too?'

'Just get the slut aboard.'

The Bratchet was picked up and the dog turned its attention to the Scotsman's heels as he carried her up the gangplank.

Hawsers were slipped, the anchor raised and the packet moved with the tide along the channel that took us under the guns of Harwich's fort and out into the confluence of the Orwell and Stour.

Passengers were ordered below while the boat made sail to catch the strong easterly blow. I dragged Bratchet to the shelter of the stern to be out of the way; I'd crossed the North Sea below decks before, with most of my company packed into a transport's innards, and would rather be drenched in sea-spray than vomit.

Harwich packet masters make the crossing so regularly they've become surly, with a take-it-or-leave-it attitude that's losing them some of their trade to the passage-boats going back and forth to the Low Countries from the Thames which, though the voyage is longer, provide more comfort and considerably more courtesy.

But Daniel Defoe, or whoever Daniel was serving, had stipulated Harwich as an embarkation port less likely to be watched than London's. Since becoming an agent himself, he saw spies everywhere. He'd been afraid that every word we'd exchanged that night in the Beggar Maker's had been passed on to the Scotsman and it looked as if he was right. Kilsyth had kept watch on me and followed us from London in the hope we'd lead him to Anne Bonny.

He came after us to the stern but lost confidence as the boat hit the swell and meekly went down below with the rest.

The dull brown and green coastline was left behind and the last of Bratchet's defiance was tossed out of her. She degenerated into a shivering bundle. I clipped the dog's lead to the back of the belt round her cape to stop her falling overboard, tied her shawl more firmly around her head and extracted the sealed orders that Defoe had sent me. 'From my employers,' he'd said. I settled on a coil of rope with my back to the wind to read them. The seal had been slit. Somebody else had read them already.

The orders were bloody impossible, anyway. A general's orders: I wish it, therefore it will be. The paper was good quality but unembossed and there was no signature. Harley or Chancellor Godolphin, one of the two, I thought; I still wasn't sure who directed Defoe.

The orders said I must discover the woman calling herself Mary Read, satisfy myself whether the woman was indeed Read or the woman known as Anne Bonny. If Read, extract from her the whereabouts of said Anne Bonny. If Anne Bonny, assure her of Her Majesty's goodwill and procure her return to England. In need I was to call on Her Majesty's representative in The Hague.

'The whilst keeping in ignorance all but him of the true purpose of your journeying, nor permitting anyone access to either the said Mary Read or Anne Bonny. These instructions to be destroyed as soon as they have been mastered.'

I let the paper go to leeward and watched it flutter in the breeze until it flopped on to the waves. What the hell was I doing here? On a pitching bloody tub taking me where I didn't want to go?

Saving the Bratchet's life, I supposed. Marking time because my Puritan conscience – the only thing I'd inherited from my father – wouldn't let me rest at becoming a comparatively rich man on Effie Sly's money, uneasy at how the old harridan had acquired it. Pursuing a clue to who'd strangled her. That most of all. Nobody was going to be allowed to slaughter an aunt of Martin Millet's and get away with it. I owed her that much.

Suddenly I became aware of the Bratchet. She was staring at the sea. *She wants to go in it.* I knew it as surely as if she'd said so. I dragged her round so that she sat between my knees, facing me. 'When were you on a boat before?'

She didn't answer. With the money I'd given her, Mrs Defoe had dressed the girl in garments that answered their purpose but little else, a thick grey woollen travelling cloak under which was a thick grey dress and thick grey boots. Her eyes stared straight ahead, though not at me, while her hands gripped the dog shivering in her lap.

I'd once asked my Chelsea widow how old she thought

the girl was. 'Thirteen? Fourteen? She doesn't seem to know.'

'Oh, Martin,' she'd said, 'how unobservant you are. She's a grown woman. Seventeen at least.'

She looked a child to me, especially at that moment. 'Bratchet.' I had to pitch my voice against the wind so that it became a shout. 'Were you on a boat before this?'

She nodded.

'When?'

She shook her head; she couldn't remember when.

'What happened?' It was unsettling to see the small face convulse. I didn't think she was going to speak but a whisper of despair came out of her mouth.

'Tipped over.'

'You were tipped over? The boat tipped over?'

She nodded again. This time her lips compressed together twice. 'Mm, mm.' Tears were shooting out of her eyes. Agitated, the dog licked her face.

'Mama? Your mother?' It was like a guessing game, taking leads from her intensifications of pain.

'*Maman*,' she said, rocking back and forward, '*Maman, Maman. Va l'aider*.'

French. I knew that much. The widow was right. 'Did she drown, Bratchet?' The rocking became faster, so did the weeping.

The Huguenots had come fleeing to England in such desperation they hadn't bothered with how seaworthy the ships were that they came in. Some of them had sunk without trace, one or two within sight of Dover. The Bratchet would have had to have been very young, perhaps a sole survivor, not to have found her way to the many Huguenot communities that existed in London instead of being placed in the poorhouse in which Aunt Effie found her.

Poor little sod. 'Mine too, Bratchet,' I said, 'If it helps, I lost mine too.' I didn't think she heard me.

By evening the wind eased. The decking and rigging drummed with bare feet while reefs were let out and then quietened so that we could hear the creak of the wheel as the steersman kept his new course, watched by the master.

From a topsail arm a voice called out, 'Vessel on the starboard beam.' Everybody on deck looked into the dull sunset that put a watery yellow on to the tops of the waves. There was a shape on the horizon.

'Three-master. Raked. Flying no pennant.'

A few feet away from us, the master's voice called, 'What's she a-doing of then?'

'Keeping our course.'

'Armed?'

'Ten gun ports.'

'Keep them bloody eyes skinned up there, bor.'

'Aye, aye, Cap'n.'

The master called for his bosun and told him to order hot food for the crew; men were fed before an expected action in case there was no time later. A boat without identification was ipso facto a threat; the master was taking it seriously.

'Issue weapons. Gun crews to stand by.'

'Aye, aye, Cap'n.'

'An' quietly now, bor. No need to alarm they bloody passengers.'

A Sea Beggar? But those Dutch privateers had mostly disappeared when the Spanish were expelled from Holland, leaving only a few who'd degenerated into plain piracy. A Frenchman? Possibly, though Marlborough was driving the French out of their ports along the Flemish coast.

The steersman's and master's conversation was covering the same ground as me, and with no better result. 'And where's that bloody navy when a man needs 'em?' The master paced up and down, thinking, and his boot scuffed against the tarpaulin that covered the sleeping Bratchet, bringing a snarl from Turnspit. He stopped. 'You pay passage for that bloody dog, bor?'

'No,' I told him, 'And I'm not going to.'

The master nodded without rancour. He'd growled because he was worried.

'Could be a press boat,' I said.

There was a clatter from the hold as someone dropped a musket and the master swore. 'They're welcome to this bloody lot.' He scuffed the canvas again. 'Bloody dogs, bloody women. Never allowed on ship in the good old days. Bad bloody luck-bringers. Bloody priests next.' He returned to the wheel.

It can't be her. It was beyond belief that the ship out there was going to attack the packet because it had the Bratchet aboard. *It can't be her.* But if the Brotherhood had her marked, it could be. Damn you, Bratchet, I thought, what is it you know?

'She'll not come at us in the dark,' the master said, and I hoped the man was right.

A moon rose and bobbed above ragged clouds which every so often blotted out all view so that when they'd passed it was difficult to refocus on the dark patch that broke the darker line of sea. But it was always there. The packet changed course; the mystery ship changed course. The packet zig-zagged, the mystery ship zig-zagged. As if the packet's shadow had transferred itself to a point a mile away.

Dawn dragged up enough light to show two parallel ships on an otherwise empty sea. The master swore. It was unusual to be alone on this route; as a rule there would have been friendly craft in the offing; transports carrying soldiers to the front, a fishing fleet, naval patrols. Today, of all days, the sea was as bald as an egg.

A few passengers emerged from the hold, among them Livingstone of Kilsyth who staggered over. He was pale. 'I've not the liking for sea trips,' he said.

'So why are you making this one?'

He made no bones about it. 'It is a quest on behalf of my chief. He wishes me to find his kinswoman, Mistress Bonny, that I was asking for when we met. There is a likelihood that her friend, Mary Read, is in the Low Countries and can inform me of her whereabouts.'

'Coincidence you chose to cross on the same boat as me, then?'

'What else?' He actually winked. 'And yourself, Master Millet? For what have you ventured on the watery main?'

I kept up the game. 'Thought I'd try and rejoin my regiment.'

'Laudable. Most laudable.' He looked around and became aware of the crew's tension. 'What's afoot?'

There was a halloo from the crow's nest. 'She's changing course. She's making for us.'

The wind had altered a degree or two to the north in the unmarked ship's favour. The packet master shouted orders to cram on more sail and changed his own course, but the enemy clearly was faster and would overhaul us in an hour. All the passengers were on deck now, alerted by the kerfuffle, watching the angled brown sails of the pursuer grow bigger and more defined, a running wolf of a ship.

Whatever she was, I absolved the Scotsman in having a part in her purpose. The man's knuckles gripping the rail were as white as mine. His voice, however, was calm. 'Will she be a pressman? I have no liking to be pressed nor pirated.'

'Amen to that.' The damned Bratchet was sleeping peacefully.

'Sail on the port bow.' The call came from the lookout. 'It's the *Suffolk*. Out of Ipswich. The navy's here, lads.'

The packet ran up flags requesting assistance and a cheer went with them. The brown sails behind us were altering. 'She's going on another board,' sang the lookout. 'She don't like the cut of the fiver.' The pirate/pressman was making a run for it, not wanting to take on a five-masted warship.

'Fiddler's Green, lads,' shouted the master, joyfully. 'Stand down.'

The next evening, we sailed into the packet station while behind us, rocking on the big breakers that distinguish the rough waters outside from the rolling brown stream of the River Maas, HMS *Suffolk* stood off from The Hook of Holland, watching over us as we went in.

The last time I'd been to The Hague was with my regiment when the city had been too crowded with other forces funnelling through its gateway into Europe to see it properly. Then we'd been fighting under William of Orange to rid Holland of the French.

It was still too crowded to see it properly – this time with allied forces under the Duke of Marlborough on their way to rid Flanders of the French. Now they'd been joined by diplomats and entrepreneurs seeking newly opened markets.

As before, the solemn streets were a vast, horizontal Tower of Babel, a grandfather of a city pestered by manic, vividly dressed children. The only thing the allied regiments have in common, apart from a determination to deny control of the continent to Louis XIV, is a desire to knock the eye out of every other allied regiment. Coloured uniform provides recognition on the battlefield but it's also to spread the fame of the regimental commander whose responsibility it is to buy it. I've seen deserters flogged, cut up, hanged – frequently in that order – not just for deserting but because they'd made off in clothes costing their colonel-in-chief money. Here they all were: Prussian blue, Venetian purple, English red, Dutch orange, Swedish yellow, gold-epauletted, velvet-frogged, gabon-flashed, calf-belted, feather-hatted.

Colonels wanting to discuss strategy with generals, majors trying to be noticed, captains trying to discuss tactics with majors, quartermasters trying to arrange winter camps, sutlers trying to order fodder for men and horses, and sergeants trying to find out what the hell everybody else was doing.

All of it in an effort to defeat France, and all of it in the tongues of fifty-odd nations from the Hebrides to the Danube which had no common denominator other than, ironically, French.

The Bratchet hung on to the back of my belt with one hand and the lead of the dog with the other as we buffeted our way through pandemonium and the Gevangenpoort archway, making for a door in the Binnenhof. The autumn tints of trees lining the square stood out against a clear, washed-out evening sky.

Attachés to Her Majesty's diplomatic service are badly paid and those serving at The Hague since the beginning of the War of the Spanish Succession were overworked. Master John Laws, who received us, was both. A tall, thin young man, long on indiscretion and short on diplomacy.

'My dear,' he said, wagging a finger, 'if you're wanting a bed for the night you can bugger off. Just bugger off. I've got half the nobility of England camping out in my spare room already.'

He looked at me more closely and fluttered his eyelashes. 'Unless you want to share mine.'

'Letters of introduction,' I said, handing them over. 'And a dispatch. Secret.'

Master Laws looked wearily at the seals. 'About as secret as my arse which, my dear . . . oh, love me, another bloody flying cypher. It's *too* bad. What's the point, what's the bloody point I ask you, in sending it on to all our embassies when they'll *undoubtedly* have forgotten which cypher we're using this week and will enquire back in last week's and when dear Louis knows all our secrets *long* before we do. And all of them blaming me, the puddings.'

He turned to me. '*Puddings*, my dear, accusing *me*. Just because they can barely *grunt* in English and my French is perfect they assume I'm not a patriot. I tell you, if it weren't that the dear Duke needs me I'd go back to *tutoring*. I would.'

'We all have our problems,' I said. 'Mine's to find us somewhere for the night.' Tramping a city in which every inn had been commandeered by one army or another hadn't done my leg any good.

John Laws looked at the Bratchet. '*Chacun à son goût*, dear. Well, I suppose I can squeeze one more in, if you'll pardon the expression. But young Morgan le Fay here will have to bed down with the staff. *That* . . .' he pointed at Turnspit, 'goes in the cellar.'

'Do you know where the First Dragoons are camped?'

'Dear one, I can't tell you where *anybody's* camped. The Duke's in Flanders accepting surrenders and the rest of us are too busy persuading our glorious allies to keep on the offensive to know what the army's doing.'

Situation normal then. We were given supper, the Bratchet was sent upstairs to the servants' attic, and the rest of the reluctant attaché's guests came back for a nightcap, several nightcaps, before retiring to shared mattresses on his floor.

Four of them were younger sons of nobility acting as personal secretaries to envoys on government business. Two were merchants, one in wool, the other in wine, hoping to reestablish trade now the French were being forced back. There was a close-eyed gentleman of undetermined background who John Laws, raising his eyes, introduced as 'Mr *Smith*' and who I therefore assumed was on a government assignment as confidential as mine.

And there was Livingstone of Kilsyth.

'Extraordinary thing,' said the Hon. Andrew Partington ushering him in, 'Met this mighty Scotchman by the Mauritshuis and fell into conversation. Turns out he's related to m'aunt on m'mother's side. Nowhere to sleep, poor fellow, so brought him here. Knew you wouldn't mind, Laws. But what à coincidence, ain't it?'

Ain't it though. Coincidence seemed to be Kilsyth's middle name. And the bugger still pretended it was, uttering Scottish noises of surprise as he and I exchanged bows.

Laws did himself well, and us. He gave us tankards of what he called Cool Nantz – brandy with lemon, sugar, nutmeg and wine – to wash down a collation of cheeses, tongue, nuts and apples. The board held linen napkins and crystal fingerbowls. 'Dutch creditors crowd the wings, dears,' he said, 'just waiting to spring should Her Majesty withdraw my diplomatic immunity, so until then let us enjoy *le métier d'un ministre aux cours étrangères.*' He smiled lovingly at the incomprehension on our faces.

Jackets and tongues were unloosed, wigs discarded. The allies, it appeared, were as much trouble as the French, more.

''S always the damned same,' expostulated young Lord Carthew, 'It's "Please, good Duke, be our saviour," when they've got Louis up their arses. But the moment the Duke's kicked him out for 'em, the States General and the Margraves and the Electors and the Savoyards and all the bloody rest start arguing.'

''S a watchamaflip,' nodded the Hon. Partington, sagely. 'Happens every two years.'

When the situation was dangerous the allies gave Marlborough all the authority he needed, but after a victory they became over-confident and quarrelsome. Each battle won was followed by months wasted in argument and stagnation that prevented a quick end to the war.

'Couldn't exploit Blenheim,' complained on Lord Carthew, 'Can't exploit Ramillies. Louis'll merely withdraw, retrench and it'll be another two years before we're allowed to defeat the bastard again.'

The merchants, being Tories, disapproved of the war's continuing. 'What I say is this,' said the one in wine, 'We've as good as won. Why did we go to war? To stop Louis putting his grandson on the throne of Spain, that's why. Couldn't allow him to rule Spain as well as France. Well, Blenheim and Ramillies showed him we're not going to let him do it. So why not treat with him, eh? Stop all this prancing about in Europe that's ruining trade.' He wagged a thick finger, 'He's no fool, Louis; it's French trade as well as English, remember. He'll be glad to come to terms. And if he don't, well, we've kicked him out the Low Countries, so we just press on with war at sea. That's what I say.'

The young nobility, being Whigs, were appalled. For them it was a military solution or nothing. 'Treat with Louis? Treat with that Papist monster?' Cool Nantz was making Lord Carthew hot. 'Sir, any man who thinks there's any losution, solution, to this war than wiping Louis off, off, face of earth's no friend of mine.'

'Fight to last man,' agreed the Hon. Partington.

'*Poor* last man,' drawled John Laws, '*Think* of all the impregnating he'd have to do after to keep the race going.' Which deflected the conversation off dangerous ground and on to women.

I was starting to like John Laws.

'Talking of women,' said the man called Smith, after we'd been doing it for some time, 'got any for us tonight, have you? I've been on the road so long my prick's beginning to itch.'

'I'm afraid you'll just have to scratch it, dear,' said John Laws lightly, 'And talking of women, we haven't yet toasted our gracious Queen. Gentlemen, charge your tankards.'

The company rose obediently. 'Health to Her Majesty, Queen Anne, God bless her.'

But this time Laws's diversion didn't work.

Into the pause that succeeded the toast, Lord Carthew whispered incredulously, 'He passed his tankard over the finger-bowl.' Then louder, 'He passed his tankard over the bloody fingerbowl.' He was staring at Livingstone of Kilsyth. He shouted, 'This Scotch bastard's a Jacobite!'

'Can't be,' protested the Hon. Partington, 'He's related to m'aunt. Not a Jack, are you, Kilsyth?'

'Ask him,' shrieked Carthew, 'ask the swine which queen he was toasting, Anne or that bitch over the water, Mary of Modena.'

The Highlander had to lean down to put his face close to his lordship's. They were both red and breathing hard. 'I'll thank ye to keep a civil tongue behind your teeth.'

'Which?' demanded Lord Carthew, dancing like a terrier, 'Say it. Go on. Which queen?'

'The *rightful* queen,' roared Kilsyth, 'ye impident callant.'

'That's no answer.' His Lordship turned around and around demanding support from the company. 'Make him say which queen.'

I wondered why I was going to do what I was going to do. I suppose because I was sick of aristocratic young bastards like this one who were prepared to let other men fight to the last. Because, if I didn't, there'd be blood; hands were already hovering on sword hilts. I pushed myself between the two men. 'Leave it. He's with me.'

'He's with you?' Carthew had ignored me all night, I wasn't the right class. 'And who are *you*?'

I said: 'I've delivered dispatches to Mr Laws in which Master Kilsyth here is mentioned as being concerned with my mission on the Queen's behalf.' Quite likely it was the truth. The letter from Defoe's principal would have warned the attaché of the Scotsman's doubtful connections. 'Isn't that correct, Mr Laws?'

Laws looked at me carefully and then made up his mind. He didn't want blood on his carpet. 'Perfectly correct. Mr Kilsyth is most deeply involved.'

'Show us the letter, then,' said Carthew, but it was bluster.

'Oh, I think Her Majesty wishes her personal concerns to remain personal,' said Laws, lightly, and began bustling. 'A last nightcap, gentlemen, and then to bed. In view of your unexpected arrival, *dear* Mr Kilsyth, perhaps you won't object to sharing mine.'

Serves you right, I thought, seeing the Scotsman's alarm, you stupid great plaid.

In the night I was woken up by the Bratchet screaming. I could hear her from two floors down, even with the Hon. Partington's foot in my ear.

As I took up a guttering candle I counted my sleeping companions on the mattresses. Four, five, six. There should have been seven. The itching Mr Smith was missing.

By the time I'd hobbled up the stairs, the noise of screams had been replaced by another, a scuffling thump mixed with hissing, coming from an upper landing. I could see two figures, one of them very small, whipping around and around. Actually, it was one monstrous, untidy figure, because the smaller person's head was attached to the bigger one just below waist-level and the bigger one was trying to dislodge it by revolving even as he hammered at it.

I once saw a performance by two street acrobats in which the girl held by her teeth on to a long strap round the man's neck and was whirled bodily outwards as he rotated. It was like that.

'Get the bitch off me. For God's sake get the bitch off.' Smith's shriek was a falsetto.

As I went towards him, a large shape pushed past me, took Smith by the neck and hurled him to the floor. Livingstone of Kilsyth had come to the Bratchet's rescue. Even then we had trouble prising her teeth from the part of Smith's anatomy he had been trying to force into her mouth. We pulled. He shrieked. Eventually, with Kilsyth pinning Smith's arms and legs down, I got the Bratchet's jaws open. She was spitting and hissing. We had to hold her back from clawing at Smith's eyes.

'Do I sense something of a contretemps?' John Laws, in a fetching nightshirt, candle upraised, had come up. He ignored the shouted explanations – and the louder shouts by Smith that the slut had jumped out and attacked him while he was innocently trying to find his way to the privy – and escorted the still-snarling Bratchet back to the servants' quarters. Going with them, I glimpsed a shelved room with Dutch bodies stolidly asleep on the tiers.

The palliasse Bratchet had occupied had been dragged to the door. John Laws pushed her on to it. 'I want no more trouble from you tonight, my girl,' he said, and shut the door.

'She didn't ask the bastard to assault her,' I said.

'Of course she did, dear,' said Laws, patiently, 'She's a female.' He stalked back to where Smith stood, groaning, his hands clutched tenderly round the front of his breeches. For good measure, I knocked the man down. Bratchet was my responsibility, after all. Kilsyth, amused, patted me on the back.

John Laws shook his head. He looked weary with the ways of heterosexual men: 'I *told* him to scratch it,' he said.

The next morning, the Bratchet and I were hurried away before the other guests were up, with Livingstone of Kilsyth. John Laws had scribbled a letter of accreditation for me to 'whomsoever it may concern', but wouldn't give us breakfast.

'I don't wish to be inhospitable, dear,' he said privately to me, 'but bugger off and take your Jacobite with you. You may know what you're doing with our tartaned friend, but I've got one war on my hands already and I don't need you three starting another.' He stood at the door, waving, as we set out across the Binnenhof. '*Do* hesitate to call again.'

You three. Somehow the night had grouped us together; at least, it seemed to have bonded Kilsyth to me, and the Bratchet to Kilsyth; she kept directing mooning glances at him, like a rescued princess at the rescuing prince. Kilsyth, who was hungry, glanced resentfully over his shoulder at the still-waving John Laws. 'He could have provided some cheer for our bellies.' Sotto voce, he added, 'D'ye ken yon laddie wears *pair*fume?'

'He saved your bacon, anyway,' I told him.

'Mebbe.' He didn't rise to the bait. He clapped his arm round my shoulders. 'And where are we away?'

If you can't beat 'em, let 'em join. The bugger had the nose of a tracking dog. Wherever we went, he turned up sooner or later. If the Bratchet was going to go on attracting trouble, I decided we might as well use his company. The time to give him the slip would be when, and if, we closed in on Mary Read or Anne Bonny. Until then the best way to keep my eye on him was having him under it.

'I'm looking for my old regiment,' I told him. In fact, it was the regiment to which the woman known as Mary Read had belonged, but I wasn't going to hand over that information on a plate.

He gave my shoulder a squeeze. 'And I'm with you, laddie. I'll pursue my own enquiries as we gang.'

We breakfasted at a communal table outside an inn by the side of the Vyver, watching the passing barges. Kilsyth ordered generous amounts of ale, cold beef and hot beans and was equally generous in throwing scraps to Turnspit at his feet, producing more grateful glances from the Bratchet. When it came to pay, though, he fumbled lengthily in his sporran and produced monies exactly accounting for a third, despite the fact that the Bratchet had eaten less than a quarter.

This time I let him get away with it, but afterwards I saw to it we messed separately. Her Majesty's government wasn't paying me enough to treat a man who was its enemy. It hadn't paid me at all, come to that. What I'd received so far was some cash for expenses and a promise of the hundred pounds on my return.

The barges were disembarking some fifty English infantrymen of the Third Foot, the Buffs, on to the quayside where they were being met by a drill sergeant. They were new recruits, poor bastards. You could see the chafes on their neck from the stiff linen of their stocks. Their mitres sat shakily on their heads and their muskets sloped to all points of the compass. Pressed, duped or sentenced into joining the army, they'd have been shipped over the North Sea immediately, before the seas closed for the winter and they had time to desert. Here and there was one who looked around him with interest. The others hung their heads, like bullocks waiting their turn in the abattoir. Most were hungover, having drunk too well of the recruiting officer's liquor, and hoping against hope their enlistment under its influence was a nightmare they'd soon wake up from.

Muttering to his corporal and fife-player the where-do-they-find-'em complaint of drill sergeants everywhere, the sergeant watched them shamble into lines. He stepped forward, his voice slicing through the chill Dutch breeze like cheesewire.

'Welcome to the army, lads. Glad to be here, eh?' Encouraged by the flat of the corporal's bayonet, there was ragged agreement that they were glad to be there.

'Lucky lads, you are. The queen's shilling and eightpence a day. Now, ain't you fortunate soldiers?'

More whacks and yes they were fortunate, Sergeant.

Eightpence a damned day, James. The rate hasn't changed since the reign of Elizabeth Tudor, when the penny was worth something. And six of those eight pennies would be deducted for their keep. Jesus, the archers at Crécy were paid sixpence a day.

As a Dragoon, I'd been allowed a thrilling extra ninepence a day for the maintenance of my horse, horses being both more expensive and more valuable than men.

'And how fortunate we ain't got to the end of,' the drill sergeant was saying. 'You're goin' to fight under the finest general since Julius Caesar, you are. You got the Duke of Marlborough.' He smiled. His recruits rocked in recoil. 'And you got me. Thinks a lot of me, does the Duke. And you're going to think a lot of me, too. Ain't they, Corporal? Going to think a lot of me?'

The corporal said that indeed they were.

The drill sergeant's voice sharpened: 'For I'm going to take you bed-pissing, mustard-grinding buttercups to your nice, warm winter quarters and I'm going to make soldiers out of you. Gawd 'elp me, by the time I'm finished, you'll be more frightened o' me than the Crapos. Right, Corporal, march 'em out.'

While the recruits were formed up, I called the drill sergeant over and handed him a full blackjack. He drank it. 'Good health, sir.'

'Good health, *Sergeant*.'

The drill sergeant raised his eyebrows. 'Light bob?'

I shook my head. 'Dragoons.'

'Oh, the Filly-Fuckers,' said the sergeant. 'Still, good health.'

'Do you know where the First Dragoons are?'

The drill sergeant lifted his bonnet and wig to wipe his bald head on his sleeve. 'Winter quarters over Ghent way, I heard.' He replaced his bonnet, saluted and called out, 'Lip us a chant, fifeman.'

The Dutch at the inn's table cheered as their English allies ambled off to the tinny notes of the fife and the corporal's curses. Kilsyth shook his head in pity. 'I'm spiering how many of yon puir raws will desert before the year.'

'Six. Seven perhaps.' And more would die from disease than were killed in battle, and more would contract the pox. The rest, if they were very, very lucky, would survive the war to be thrown on the scrapheap to beg their living.

Sometimes I think England hates her standing army as much as she loves her navy. I suppose under Charles I, and again under the Protectorate, the army was used to keep her in subjection. For a while that small collection of cut-throats and plough-boys disappearing into the distance, swindled into enlistment to live and die far from home in billets that were sinks of squalor, would be greeted as the country's brave defenders until, having won her war, she'd again ignore their existence.

'The miracle is they don't all desert,' I said. But that wasn't the miracle. The miracle was the drill sergeant – there were sergeants like him at Agincourt. He'd take the scourings he'd just been given and bully, curse, terrify and nurse them into the finest fighting instrument the world had ever seen, under the greatest general. And, most amazing of all, I, Martin Millet, knowing all I knew, still wanted to stand up and cheer the bloody lot of them.

From The Hague we went by boat, using the broad, shallow, bun-shaped barges which are the home and workplace of the Netherlands' waterborne population. We hopped from one to another, going southwest towards the northern Lines of Brabant which the French army had been forced to withdraw from after Marlborough's summer campaign, and where the First Dragoons among other regiments had made their winter quarters.

Kilsyth wanted to take coaches. 'You can,' I said, 'but we're going by canal.' Canals are surer, if slower. Anyway, Dutch coaches were as expensive as in England and the roads were worse; I never liked the way their posters at coaching stations added a pious 'Deo Volante', God willing, to departure and arrival times. With the search for Mary Read likely to last the winter, I'd need to watch the pennies. Kilsyth, of course, decided on canal transport too. He wasn't going to let me or Bratchet out of his sight.

Sometimes we were charged a few pennies by the barge-master which entitled us to a bed and a share of the stewpot. Sometimes we paid our way by taking our place in the harness on the towpath – usually the boats are drawn by dogs or the masters' children – while the master leaned on his tiller, smoking his pipe, and the master's wife knitted dark, woollen stockings and smiled at Kilsyth's efforts to make the barge go faster than it ever had before.

I like the Netherlands. Between showers, there's a clarity to the air which makes the windmills with their rush thatching stand out with a distinctness that's almost alarming. I remember that journey because it was the last real peace we all shared, a time out of time between dykes which only occasionally gave glimpses of the polders in between, where white cottages stood round churches with bells clustered in their tower like a swarm of bees, chiming out, thin and clear, in a minor key.

It was on those canals that Bratchet began to change. It was like watching a sapper who'd been underground in his mine for too long suddenly emerging into daylight. She started to look about her, warily at first, in case she'd come up in enemy territory. Gradually, she stopped protecting her food bowl with her arms as she always had when we ate, in case somebody kicked it away from her. I saw her stroking the rough wool of her skirt like other women stroke satin.

Aunt Effie had a lot to answer for.

She'd have nothing to do with me. I was trying to take up where the Chelsea widow had left off and teach the girl her letters but she refused to learn, just sat and thinned her mouth as if I were forcing poison down it. I passed the job to Kilsyth who was always impatient for something to do. If she was going to be besotted with the man, she might at least gain some literacy while she was about it.

She did, though not in English. Sitting with him on the barge's deck top, she chattered away as she never had to me, and took her reading lessons from a book of fairytales by Perrault that he carried in his pack.

'The maid has a fine intelligence for a female,' he told me, accusingly, 'Her progress with *Contes de Ma Mère* is a miracle. Did ye not know she has the French?'

'I gathered.'

'Why then has she been so sorely treated?' The French and Scottish aristocracy have always had close association, and the discovery that Bratchet could speak French raised her class in Kilsyth's eyes.

'It's nothing to do with me,' I told him, 'I've only brought her along in case she got in trouble at home.'

He'd become Bratchet's champion. 'And what sort of man addresses a young lassie by the title of a dog? Has she no name?'

I called her over. 'What's your damn name, Bratchet?'

If she knew it, she wasn't going to tell me. I could see her searching for something she considered romantic enough and remembering what John Laws had christened her.

'Morgan le Fay,' she said.

CHAPTER FIVE

Second Extract from *The Madwoman's Journal*

THE BROTHERHOOD'S shots have missed their mark. Bratchet has been taken to Europe, out of the way. By Effie's nephew, Millet. With the idiot Scotsman in attendance. Looking for Anne Bonny and Mary Read. They won't find them there, but it's a blow. I didn't relish the Bratchet's death yet I fear it has become a necessity. The creature that comes into my room at nights is demanding it.

I don't think it's the Devil any more. I don't know what it is, except that it's female. She came in a nightmare. I was dreaming about the sea. I always dream about the sea, but this time dead hands pulled me down and water filled my nose and mouth. A voice kept saying something of which I could only hear the word 'Bratchet'. I felt similar panic to what I was in the night the press crew grabbed me and I managed to struggle out of the men's arms and leap overboard and my petticoats dragged me under until I tore their tapes away and swam out of them.

I woke up, gurgling, in my hot cupboard bed so drenched in sweat I thought my escape had just happened and I must run in my dripping state with the pressmen searching after me. Worse still, the creature that had been dragging me under was still with me. In the room. I could see a shape against the boxes in the corner.

'Who are you?' I whimpered.

'It's me,' said Uncle Cofferer outside the door.

I was so afraid of the thing in the corner that I let the old cuff in. He had a candle and I took it and held it up and made him search among the boxes, saying I'd heard a rat. It had been bigger than a rat. There was nothing there. For his pains I had to endure an hour of what Uncle Cofferer calls tickly-tickle but all the time I was aware eyes were watching us and through Uncle Cofferer's gasps my ears caught a repeating whisper: 'Kill the Bratchet, kill the Bratchet.'

It was remiss of the Brotherhood not to have finished her, though they swear the girl had the Devil's own luck in avoiding their attempts. One of them even tried to capture her at sea but was deflected by Her Majesty's navy.

Well, it is only a matter of time. The Devil's luck is mine, not the Bratchet's. You might think, my dear, that in going to Europe she has moved beyond my range. It is not so. My reach is long – and getting longer. I have made a new acquaintance.

It was in the buttery. This is a long refectory so old and beamed it must have belonged to the nuns who were here before King Henry made St James's his palace. It was a lazar house then. And still is. A strict order of seating keeps lepers like laundry women away from the scribes and the Pharisees.

Not knowing, I'd wandered with my platter to a table at the end furthest away from the serving hatch. There were two clerks sitting by themselves and as I passed them I heard one of them say, '. . . Anne Bard or Bonny, whoever she is . . .'

He stopped when he saw me. I was about to take a place near them but Uncle Cofferer, the old fumbler, hurried up then. 'No, no, dear child, this is for higher staff. You must sit further down.' He apologized to the men as he ushered me away. 'My niece, gentlemen. She's new to Court.'

The taller one said: 'I'm sure the Court is the happier for it.' I caught his eye; he meant it.

That night in my cupboard bed, I brought the old Cofferer to the brim quickly. I use a method known to sailors as 'boxing the Jesuit', which is messy but safe. All I have to do to reach a swift conclusion is whisper passionately 'Uncle, oh Uncle'. I let him finish, I say, then asked, 'Who were those two men at the top table today?'

William Greg and Anthony Frobisher, he told me.

'Which was the tall one?'

'William Greg, one of Harley's secretaries.'

'Will you introduce me to him, Uncle?' He began to baulk. What did I want with the man? What did I want with any man but him? You ask nicely and you get nowhere. I started to shout and cry which terrified him in case Aunt Cofferer should hear. Yes, yes, dear niece, if that's what I wished. Hush now.

As it turned out, no introduction was necessary. Next day William Greg came into the laundry court. Really, it is no place to dry linen; like most of St James's it's airless – only the royal apartments look out on to the garden near the river – and a gale must blow before wind reaches the washing lines. Officials often use it as a cut-through to the Ambassadors' Court in order to see the maids with their skirts bound up trampling in the washing tubs. I was giving the maids a lash of Brotherhood tongue, which I shouldn't do, but they are a lazy crew needing encouragement.

It has been a relief to me to discover that as assistant laundress my hands need never touch soap and water. Neither do I dry or iron; that, Mrs Peach told me, is for gofferers, starchers and such rabble. My task is to see clothes properly aired on the racks and folded carefully. When all's done I accompany one of my minions as she carries the piles to Mrs Peach's room where it is checked. Mrs Peach then accompanies another minion to the housekeeper's room who oversees its distribution by yet more minions into the royal linen presses. A process that could be accomplished by half a dozen women thereby employs twenty-eight.

I was encouraging the maids, I say. 'Stamp, you lubbery frigates. Harder, you fumble-footed sluts or I'll hang your skin on tenterhooks.' The whiteness of the linen has much improved since my arrival. The Duchess of Marlborough was pleased to comment on it.

'A nautical lady,' said a voice. William Greg was leaning against the court wall. He's tall and dresses above his station in what look like Harley's cast-offs so the coats are rich but his wrists stretch beyond the sleeves. Though very young, barely twenty-one I should guess, he affects a raillery towards inferior women, such as he regards me, and curlicues his hat in the air as he sweeps it in salute.

I bobbed. 'Your pardon, sir. My father was a seagoing man and I fear I imitate him at times.'

'No pardon necessary,' he smiled, 'I like a girl of spirit.' That address went out of date when Old Rowley died. He invited me to walk with him in Hyde Park on my next free afternoon. I set on the Negroes to watch him in the meantime. He has access to Robert Harley's papers, and is therefore worth attaching to my chatelaine.

Who is Harley, dearest? Well, he may or not be the man who had us pressed. True, he was only Speaker of the House of Commons at the time but even then, they tell me, he was keeper of most of the government's secrets. Now he virtually is the government, an octopus of a man whose tentacles extend everywhere. I shall hang him on a hook in the sun, like they do to octopus in Barbados, until he stops wriggling.

He doesn't look much; he's got the face of a cottage loaf, with about as much expression. Only his waistcoats are handsome;

you see a fine brocade waistcoat perambulating the corridors and realize there's Harley inside it.

He's a Tory. The Duchess of Marlborough, a Whig like her husband, hates him. They would not have got on even had they belonged to the same party, she's cake, he's dough; her barbs sink into him without trace, he just bows and goes on about his business – which is to get the Queen to do what he wants.

He is my equivalent, I suppose, my lawful equivalent. I have the Brotherhood and the Negroes, he has the network of government and its agents. To put my hand on the Bratchet I shall need access to official reports. So welcome aboard, William Greg.

In the meantime I have begun work on the next stage of the plan. It is to make Uncle Cofferer procure me a place as one of the Queen's bedchamber women. There is no vacancy at the moment but when there is I shall have it. It is as one of the bedchamber women that Abigail Hill began her ascendancy.

Uncle Cofferer fondled and kissed me pityingly. 'There is no hope of it, my child, so do not aspire. Only women of gentle birth are permitted to the bedchamber.'

I kept my temper and asked him innocently: 'Is Abigail Hill a gentlewoman then?'

'She is not. She is a special case put there by Duchess Sarah. In view of Mistress Hill's ingratitude since, it is doubtful if the Duchess will ever again recommend a place to someone of low birth. Will we play tickly-tickle now?'

Still I kept my temper. 'I wish to serve the Queen, Uncle.'

'You are serving her admirably already, little one.'

I didn't serve *him* that night but pushed him out and held the bed door against his pleas to get back in. If he can't be useful, he can damn well be chaste. But oh, Sarah, what a fool you are. Even at the lower end of the buttery they talk of how the Duchess is insisting on Queen Ant appointing her son-in-law, the Earl of Sunderland, as Secretary of State, though she knows the Queen abhors him. But he is a Whig and Sarah wants him, as she wants all her family, in power.

Poor Queen Ant. In her naïveté, she thinks she can choose the best men from either party to be in her ministry, and that they will work happily together for the good of the country. She'd have more success employing sharks. Her 'best men' spend their time rending each other.

Mrs Danvers told the housekeeper and the housekeeper told Mrs Peach and Mrs Peach told Aunt Cofferer that poor Queen Ant had burst out: 'Why for God's sake must I, who have no interest, no end, no thought but for the good of my country, be made so miserable as to be brought into the power of one set of men?'

Sarah, watch out. Better win a war than a battle. Even Calico Jack let a small ship go if by doing so he could have a bigger prize. You may gain Sunderland, but you will lose the Queen.

The walk with William Greg in Hyde Park was fruitful. He wanted to take me under the trees immediately but I showed him there was a boarding fee. I blew cold when he talked dalliance and hot when he spoke of politics; he soon picked up that only when he showed how important he was did I become receptive to his advances.

In no time he was boasting of knowing all that Harley knows. He says he is Harley's confidant though I doubt it, that gentleman being too secretive to have any confidant but himself.

'We are against the appointment of young Sunderland,' he said, grandly. He uses a constant 'we' when he talks of Harley. 'We do not want a party man. We are for moderation as the Queen is. Being Tory, we are closer to her liking than anyone else in the cabinet.'

It was the Devil's own work to speed him on to the more important subject; I dared not mention the names of Anne Bonny or Mary Read but with the Devil my helper I flattered him to greater and greater indiscretion until at last he whispered, 'We may even turn the succession on its head.'

At that I clasped his arm in amazed admiration and let him begin to lead me to the trees. 'But isn't it settled on the Hanovers? How can any mortal overturn that?'

'We can. We may. My lips are sealed.'

So were mine, against his, until he told me more. At last he said, 'There is a personage who may have greater right than

German George. We have set matters in train to procure her.'

It appears that Martin Millet has been designated to hunt down Mary Read who, they think, may in all likelihood be Anne Bonny herself. He is to send reports of his progress to the embassy in The Hague, who will send them on to London. And William Greg, bless his aspirations, is the man who decodes them.

As soon as I decently could, or indecently could, I terminated the dalliance for the day and made him escort me back, promising him more and better next week when he may have further information.

So they want Anne Bonny for the throne, do they? She wouldn't sit on it now for all the gold in Davy Jones's locker. I've seen how they keep their queen in a closet to make her swell bigger and bigger. When they trundle her out for occasions she's so trussed with jewels she staggers. No woman who's watched seagulls swing against a storm, or taken a helm, or boarded a ship with a knife in her teeth, can submit to chains again, not even when they're studded with diamonds.

No, my dear. If you please, instead we'll have the revenge we planned in that stinking cell in St Jago de la Vega.

Next day the Negroes reported that on his free nights William Greg goes to the Rummer tavern in Charing Cross where he gambles beyond his means. He would. They also report that he is being watched there by someone other than themselves, a man with a foreign accent, who has twice now followed him home.

Who is that, I wonder? It could be the French. Or the Jacobites. I may not be the only one who realizes Greg's wonderful possibilities. Would he spy for the enemies of his country? He might. Government clerks, even those attached to the First Minister's office, are miserably paid. If they offered enough for his information, he might.

So far, mine has cost me kisses and a bit of unlacing. My skirt shall stay in place as long as possible. Calico Jack would have called me a cock-chafer, permitting all intimacies but the greatest. My apparent primness has merely strengthened Greg's ardour and he's promised to take me to Vauxhall Gardens next, which will prove expensive to his indiscretion and his pocket.

I am ever amazed by how I attract men. It was always the case; I only have to set my sights long enough on one of them that can be useful and he falls at my feet and stays there. Certainly, I'm good-looking, but so are many women who have less success with the opposite sex. And the truth is I do not like men. I have to force myself to permit their liberties and only do it to gain advantage. Perhaps that is my secret; they sense my hidden antagonism and are driven to try and overcome it, in the same way that other men risk their own destruction by trying to conquer mountains, or the sea.

Greg has begun to call me 'Circe'. He says he sees danger in the depth of my eyes yet cannot resist their lure. Such twaddle. How easily men are led around by their gooseberries. I should be grateful for it, but where's the enjoyment?

I only escaped from the press smack because one of the kidnappers freed my bonds in order to fondle me and I took the opportunity to dive overboard and swim ashore. I am haunted that in doing so I left her, my only love, behind. But I thought the shore was nearer than it proved to be. I hoped to get help for her rescue, but she was out of reach before that could happen.

I knew one thing, though. One of the men had joked as they bundled us aboard from that quayside. 'You'll like Jamaica, girls,' he said. At least I knew where she had gone. And I swore to God or the Devil that I would find her. And after dreary years in the search, thank God, I did at the last.

Oh my dear and only love, will we be allowed into heaven? Or was it such sin we will be sent to hell? If they will guarantee we go there together, I shan't mind burning.

The thing in the corner has returned and is watching me this minute. It gains delineation each time it appears but there is weed over it so I cannot see its face. Its voice is clearer, though it still sounds like pounding waves, but I can make out all the words now. It gives me no sleep. It is saying, 'Kill the Bratchet.'

CHAPTER SIX

WITH THE waking up of the Bratchet your story, James, becomes hers as well.

But from here on, when I put down her thoughts and feelings as if I knew what they were, it's because I do. I've tried to repeat the words she used when she told them to me much later, in a time we had together just before we said goodbye in another country . . .

The realization that it was safe to come out of the hard, dark chrysalis in which Bratchet had wrapped herself was gradual. Nobody was abusing her by telling she was worthless. She and Turnspit were being given enough to eat. She had warm clothes. She wasn't required to work for any of these things.

Even stranger, after two clenched nights on the canals it became apparent that the men who shared the barge hold with her weren't going to abuse her body either.

Blond, bare-legged, blue-smocked children shouted greetings from the towpath. She watched old women with their wrinkled faces framed in strange white bonnets drive black and white cattle along the dyke tops and wave at her.

On the third day, cautiously, she lifted a hand and waved back.

She had only a vague idea of where she was, where she was going, or why. In her mind, I was the Limping Man who'd taken over her ownership and who'd possibly tried to tell her things, but she'd had difficulty hearing them through the chrysalis casing.

Dizzying reflections of sky and water confused her. The wild duck flying across the canal in chevrons of blue and green, the storks standing in their untidy nests perched on the thatch of houses, these were familiar, though she could only name them in French. They connected her with the True Time, the memory in which she had cocooned herself against hideous things.

A woman singing a *cramignon* on a Walloon barge brought

back a lullaby someone – she thought it must have been her grandmother – used to croon to her in the True Time. The smells of countryside, of cheeses and peat from the barge holds, brought whiffs of Normandy back across the stinking chasm that had been London.

So did the fairytales the Beautiful Man was teaching her to read.

She began listening to conversations. They tied up for the night and the men smoked their pipes, the bargemaster explaining in English learned from soldiers how he and his countrymen had thwarted the French in the time of William of Orange. 'Cut fokking dykes, sploosh. All land under fokking water. Drown fokking Frogs. Goot, eh?'

When he retired, the Limping Man and the Beautiful Man sat on.

'Good people, Lowlanders,' the Limping Man was saying. 'Never gave in, not to the Spanish or French. Nobody fought harder for religious freedom or paid more for it. The Spanish condemned every last Protestant to death, burning for men, burying alive for women. Alva boasted he executed 18,000 in the name of the Pope. But they won. In the end.'

It was another link with her French childhood. *We are Huguenots, little one. King Louis has gone back on his word and is trying to force us into popery. We must go to England to be free.*

To drown. To be on a shore where mouths shaped unintelligible questions. To a dreadful place. To Effie Sly.

The Beautiful Man rose and stretched, his arms black against the stars, rescuer's arms. 'I'll away to me bed. Good night to ye, Martin.'

She saw him speaking low to me and knew it was about her. I called her over. 'What's your damn name, Bratchet?'

Aimée, she thought it was. But she wasn't going to tell me; it belonged to True Time and nobody connected with Effie Sly was going to get hold of it. She latched on to a name she'd heard recently and which Anne Bonny and Mary Read had mentioned in their stories about King Arthur.

'Morgan Le Fay,' she said.

*

111

The barge that took us into Flanders was Kit Ross's. Or rather, Kit Ross commandeered it.

Clogs followed by a balloon of sturdy petticoats descended the rungs of the Fort de Plasendaal lock. 'What's your name?' the bargemaster was asked in a Dublin accent. 'Joost, is it? Then *joost* cast your eye over my commission, not that you can read it, you poor ignorant butterbox, so I'll tell whom it may concern – that's you – that Sutler Mrs Christian Ross – that's me – *est empuissé par le capitaine-général, le duc de Marlborough* – to commandeer *ce bateau* – that's this fish-kettle here – *pour le service de la reine Anne et sa grande armée* should provisioning of said *armée* require it. So open that hold, me lad, before the bloody burghers catch up with us.'

Mrs Ross was using the army *lingua franca* known as Parlary, though her Irish 't's were nearly 'h's and Bargemaster Joost responded, sighing. He knew a tidal wave when he met one.

He opened his hold and allowed a chain of soldiers to load barrels, sacks and crates of hens into it and store them to Mrs Ross's liking. A cow that put up a protest against being lowered to the deck submitted when Mrs Ross punched it between its eyes. I didn't blame it. There wasn't much of her, discounting the petticoats, but you were glad she hadn't joined the French. She could have requisitioned Europe. A scar split her upper lip, showing a tooth missing behind it. Her sleeves were rolled up and her hair was held in a scarf with a stiff, round, shiny, black hat, like a sailor's, crammed on top of it.

'Cloots,' puffed Kilsyth as we stacked barrels in the hold, 'How'd the army gain that bellows-lunged caillach?'

'She was a soldier,' I told him. Mother Ross's fame had spread through the regiments. 'Like Mary Read. Enlisted to be near her husband originally, then found she liked the life. They didn't discover she was a woman until she was wounded at Ramillies.'

'Were they sure?'

I grinned. 'The Duke appointed her official sutler. It means she must buy as much as she can and steal the rest.'

'Is the English army entire made up of women? It'd not do for the Scots. Well, maybe she can tell us of Mary Read.'

Mrs Ross was berating her helpers on deck. 'Lift, you idle buggers you. Lazy as Joe the trooper who laid down his rifle to sneeze, so y'are. A care for the apple-barrel now. Bruise 'em and ye'll have me bayonet up your backside.'

'I don't think we'll ask her just now,' I said.

'I warn you, Mrs Ross,' came a different voice from the lock head, 'When we arrive at winter quarters, I shall inform General Ingoldsby of your cursing and have you put in the whirligig.'

'You do that, Colonel Blackader, darlin'. Loves me apple dumplings, the general. As for me cursing, didn't he call for his own surgeon when I took a musket ball in me mouth to sew it up so that I could curse the rounder. And didn't he nurse me himself. Now get your arse off that bridge and on this barge before the bloody Bruges burghers come and take back me booty.'

Ambushed by alliteration, Colonel Blackader did as he was told.

Mother Ross's head appeared over the hold and gave us a gap-toothed grin. 'Thinks an army can live on prayer,' she said in what she seemed to think was a confidential whisper. 'Cameronians. More a bloody congregation than a regiment.'

'Canting conventiclers,' agreed Kilsyth. He was a true Highlander in his contempt for the Presbyterian Lowlanders that made up the Cameronian regiment.

'Wash your mouth out with you.' Mother Ross's smile disappeared. She might criticize sections of the British army but no civilian was permitted the liberty. 'You should've seen the buggers at Blenheim.'

We cast off with speed. Coming along the dyke in the distance was an untidy group of men and women waving hoes and axes, shouting. Mrs Ross ordered the Cameronians into the traces to pull. 'And bloody quick, gentlemen, if you'll be so good. Civilians don't always approve of me military methods.' The barge set off down the canal like a skimming pebble. It wasn't until the disapproving burghers had been left two miles behind that Mother Ross settled herself on a barrel top with stoop of ale to answer questions.

'Mary Read is it? A fine, pretty Dragoon, she was. I met her once, afore Blenheim. I knew she was shemale, us ladies being recognizable to one another. Nobody else did, mind. Bleared the army's eye, like me, so she did. Didn't serve as long, though. Some fucker grumbled her, poor bitch.'

Her language brought a scandalized groan from Colonel Blackader who had sat himself and his men apart to read the bible he carried in a holster at his belt.

'Cover your ears, Colonel,' Mother Ross shouted at him amiably. She lowered her voice to what she seemed to think was a whisper. 'A lemoncholy bastard, poor soul.'

'Mary Read,' I reminded her.

Mother Ross shook her head. 'Never saw her again though I heard she joined giblets with another Dragoon.'

Sotto voce from the Scotsman: 'Joined giblets?'

'Married,' I interpreted. 'What was she like?'

I know what she was like. It was dawning on the Bratchet that she hadn't been paying the world around her enough attention. She paid it now. *They're hunting Anne and Mary. They're going to track them down*. Mary and Anne, those amused, unafraid giantesses. Mary and Anne. She'd taken their names into her cocoon to repeat over and over like a spell. *Shall I be Queen of England, Bratchet? Come and be queen with me.*

They had lit up Effie Sly's dark house like flares.

First it had been Mary, who'd been taken on at a time when Effie had more lodgers than usual. What her background was, nobody knew. If somebody'd told Bratchet that Mary was the goddess Athene who had sprung into the world fully armed, she'd have accepted it.

Effie thought she was on the run: 'Mark my words, Bratchie, there's a reward out for that bloss somewheres.' The idea pleased Effie; she could threaten Mary with the law if she demanded her wages and tried to leave.

Mary didn't try to leave but she did demand her wages. And got them. It was a battle royal, Effie summoning up her forces of darkness until Bratchet could have sworn she saw lightning bolts firing from Effie's fingers and Mary deflecting them with an invisible shield – and her tongue: 'You hell hag, Effie Sly, you don't frighten me. Call the law? Call it then and see which they hang highest. What'll you grumble me *for*? Nothing. But I can grumble you.'

'You Athanasian bitch,' Effie hissed, 'I got powerful protection.'

'You're a Dark Lantern, I know it. But if I told 'em you was also a clipper, what then? You'd fry in your own grease.'

Bratchet, cowering in a corner, yelped with fear. Mary had penetrated in days the sources of Effie's wealth that would have lain hidden from the Bratchet for years. Whoever the nobs were that winked at Effie's many illegal activities, they wouldn't be powerful enough to protect her from the wrath of the Exchequer if it was discovered that she ran a coin-clipping operation. Tampering with currency was too dreadful a crime; it threatened the country's confidence at home and abroad.

Effie would kill her. She put her arms over her head and waited for the screams. Instead she heard Effie say calmly, 'What did I say your wages was?'

And Mary Read: 'Twenty-one shillings a month and all found.'

'Shall we say thirty shilling a month?'

'Twenty-one shilling will do, Mistress Sly, I thank you. I ain't a blacker.'

Bratchet looked up to see the older woman and the young one regard each other in admiration. Greek, as Mary said later, had met Greek.

Which was the peculiar thing about Mary; she spoke local patter, what she called the 'Boorish', but she had the address of a lady when she wanted to use it. She could not only read, she read for pleasure in the little spare time Effie allowed her from making beds, dusting, polishing, ironing, helping Effie to pre-pare meals, serving them and clearing away. Most of her twenty-one shillings a month went on books.

Bratchet, the scullion, chamber- and cooking-pot scourer, scrubber, step-whitener, laundry maid and candle keeper, had even less spare time, and no wages at all, but just before bedtime Mary would read her extracts from *Hakluyt's*

Voyages, Raleigh's *History of the World*, Malory's *Morte d'Arthur*, Virgil, Sir Philip Sidney, Shakespeare, opening windows that set vivid landscapes into the normal darkness of her dreams.

'How'd you know this gammon?' Bratchet had asked her.

Mary had smiled, 'A father with an estate and a conscience.'

'Why ain't you a nob then?'

'An Irish mother with no marriage lines.'

'What's that dark light thing you called Effie?'

'A Dark Lantern,' said Mary Read, 'She's an informer. You know when she puts on her best cap and shawl and goes off for the day?'

'Business, she says.'

'I followed her Wednesday. To see. She went to Gape's Coffee House in Covent Garden and talked to a man as crossed her palm with silver, or it may've been gold if she was lucky. I followed *him*. And he went to St James's. Straight through the gates. No challenge.'

'She spies for *King William*?'

'Not the king, birdwit. The government. How do you think they run the country without they know what goes on? They got spies all over. Old Eff's main business is shipping out the country them as can't go legal, ain't it? Think the government don't know what she's up to? Of course they do. No, I reckon our Effie keeps 'em sweet by throwing them the odd mackerel so's she can get the sprats through.'

Bratchet clutched at Mary's arm in terror. 'Suppose she grumbles you to 'em.'

'She's nothing on me she can grumble.' Mary took Bratchet by her shoulders and shook her gently. 'You got to stand up to her, Bratchie. She's a belswagger, that's all she is. She ain't in touch with the Devil. That's mumbo-jumbo to keep you cowed. Stand up to her. It's like Shakespeare says, cowards die many times before their death, the valiant never taste of death but once.'

'I die over and over, Mary.'

'I know you do, Bratchie. I know. But I'm here now and when

116

I go, you come with me. I feel there's wonders ahead of me, Bratch. My day's coming.'

'When?'

'When it comes.'

It came one night in February, just after King William's horse had stumbled over a mole hill in Richmond Park and thrown him to his death, delivering the crown to his sister-in-law, Anne. The weather was exceptionally cold and even the Puddle Courters had abandoned their nightly prowling to huddle in their homes, which was perhaps why the well-dressed young woman who had just disembarked in England was allowed to wander from the dockside in a search for shelter without being molested or robbed or both.

Answering the knock, Bratchet saw a white face by the lantern Effie kept lit over her door and heard a well-modulated voice, 'My name is Anne Bonny. I've missed my way. Your sign says "Lodgings". I need a bed for the night.' The neat sentences were managed before the young woman folded up like a fan in fatigue.

Effie wouldn't have let her in, her rooms were full at the time, but Mary insisted, and helped the girl up to the attic she shared with Bratchet, while Bratchet picked up the travelling case the young woman had been carrying and started to follow. Effie barred her way, holding out her hand for the case. Bratchet hung on. 'It's hers, Eff.'

Effie won, as usual. 'You give it here. Nobody enters my house without they can pay.' She took out and examined the few clothes, all finely made, a silver hairbrush and matching mirror and drinking-cup, a purse with some gold foreign coins and a small brass-bound box with the letter B embossed into its top.

Effie shook the box, which rustled as if it contained only paper, tried its catch and found it locked. She told Bratchet to put back the rest of the things and take the case to its owner. 'I'll keep the box for her till she comes round, case some bugger dubs it.'

The lock wouldn't hold long against Effie's expertise with a hairpin, nor would it show trace of being forced. She caught

Bratchet's look. 'Got to know who she is, don't I?' She nodded at the brush and mirror, 'Could be she's a clanker-napper for all I know.'

Wouldn't be the first in this house, Bratchet thought, as she lugged the case upstairs. She knew, and Effie knew, Anne Bonny wasn't a silver thief; she was quality. She wouldn't stay long.

To everybody's surprise she did. The reason was the instant friendship that sprang up between herself and Mary Read. It was as if long-lost halves were at last put together to become a whole; their inequality of class was negated by shared intelligence and daring. Even their looks were similar; both were tall, handsome and dark-haired, though Mary's eyes were blue and Anne's brown.

There were differences. Anne's kindness to Bratchet was as great as Mary's but it came less from fellow-feeling than from what Bratchet's French past told her was *noblesse oblige*, the obligation of the high-bred to put everyone at ease. There was no doubt of Anne's breeding; she had an excellence, not just in taste, dress and manners, but in the bone. With it all, she radiated gaiety, an almost febrile optimism that made even the Puddle Courters smile on her; it didn't stop them calculating the value of her eyeteeth but they wished her well while she had them. They called her 'Queen of the May', as if she'd brought springtime with her, like some Persephone strayed into the underworld.

Astonishingly, even Effie Sly seemed bewitched. Anne was given – *given* – a room of her own when one fell vacant, the best linen, the tastiest cuts of meat, beeswax candles, not tallow.

When Anne confided to Mary one night that she had royal blood and showed her the papers in her box to prove it, it came as no surprise to Bratchet worshipping almost unnoticed in a corner of the room with the dog Turnspit in her arms. The genealogy escaped her – Bratchet had never heard of Prince Rupert of the Rhine – but here, in Anne, was the apotheosis of a fairytale, a lost princess fallen on hard times awaiting the inevitable discovery that would restore her rightful degree.

Her mother, said Anne, was of the Scottish aristocracy and

her marriage to Dudley Bard had taken place in Austria shortly before his death fighting for the emperor against the Turks. She'd been the sort of woman who took as much thought for the future as a mayfly and Anne's youth had been spent with her travelling the courts and great houses of Middle Europe, trading on their kinship with them through the Stuart connection and her own. Such stability as Anne had known was provided by her father's old English nurse who'd travelled with them.

When the mother died Anne, though indigent, was no longer prepared to accept charity.

'Why didn't you go back to your mother's people?' Mary asked.

Anne gave an exaggerated shudder. 'Scotland? I went there once when I was small. It was cold. And, my dear, the *people*. Animal-skinned, bare-legged eaters of raw meat. And that was just the women.'

The only thing she'd liked about the Scots had been the way they'd called her Bonny Anne. 'I transposed the name for travelling purposes. It wouldn't have been suitable for a Bard to be seen using the sort of transport I've been forced to stoop to. In any case, we had to pass through Germany and my mother had always warned me to steer clear of Great Aunt Sophia of Hanover. She'd said the Hanoverians might be jealous of the fact that my claim to the English throne was greater than theirs.'

The old nurse had died on the journey, in Hamburg. 'I wish she could have seen England again,' said Anne. 'She used to tell me stories of the great days – she was my father's nurse as well and went with him on Prince Rupert's visits to Charles II's court. I grew up thinking England was a perpetual round of masques, lavish balls, beautiful and naughty women, theatre, hunting, outdoor feasts – all the jollities.'

Mary, looking round the dingy attic, drawled, 'Only have them in Puddle Court on Tuesdays.'

But Bratchet, as one who'd also been landed motherless and alone on the foreign shore of England, saw Anne's loneliness and was moved. 'We got to find your folks, we got to. They'll be ever so pleased,' she said.

119

'Will they? *Will* they?' Anne danced in a wild mazurka, catching up Bratchet and swinging her round. 'Shall I be Queen of England, Bratchet? Come and be queen with me.'

It was her way. She had no more plan to take the throne than to be pope, though she and Mary wove amused and amusing fantasies around the effect of the crown on her dark hair. 'There's an estate owing to me, perhaps. That's what I want, a niche, a comfortable marriage of my own choosing, my entitlement as Prince Rupert's grand-daughter. He settled here in his old age, so shall I.'

And not to be lonely any more, thought Bratchet. She herself was to share in this good fortune – housekeeper of the fantasy castle, with Mary as its major-domo. 'Effie can be pig-keeper.'

Until then, Anne had to husband what little money she had from the sale of some of her jewellery. She had already sent letters to her cousin and namesake, the Queen, to Rupert's surviving family, announcing the arrival of their long-lost relative. 'They'll not refuse me my right,' said Anne in her madness.

'Right' was a word she used often. If Mary's romantic reading was the key which loosed Bratchet's imagination, Anne's turned the world, as she had understood it, upside down. In the varied, generally decaying, often warring castles in which Anne had spent her peripatetic childhood, there had been one point of agreement – condemnation of an Englishman called John Locke who'd just expounded a new philosophy. As soon as she came across a library which contained copies of the man's writing, Anne had settled down to find out what he'd proposed that called forth such indignation from her high-born Middle European relatives. She'd found it in two books, *Treatises of Government*.

'What he said,' she told Mary and Bratchet, 'as far as I can understand it, is that government is only a contract; that while it can tax people for certain purposes, there still remains in the people the supreme power to remove the king if he breaks the law.'

'I thought we *did* that,' said Mary, 'I thought we cut off Charles I's head because of it.'

Anne nodded with deliberate grandeur. 'Locke and I agree with you. But, but, but, but, *I* go further . . .' And into Effie Sly's mean little room with its stained plaster was unloosed an idea sounding such trumpets as crumbled walls in Bratchet's mind and allowed it a breadth of freedom which nobody, not even Effie, managed to shackle again.

Anne said that if a king, the father of his country, could be disobeyed when he was wrong, so could any father. 'Is it right,' she asked, 'for a father to marry off his daughter against her will? Is it right that a woman loses all legal existence when she becomes a wife? Is it right that we have no say in the laws and government that rule us?' Then she laughed. 'Queen? How could I be a queen? I might have to rebel against myself.'

She left Bratchet breathless, but Mary caught fire. She and Anne kindled each other, their reasoning leaping higher and higher, shattering idols as it went, ridiculing the most ancient tenets of church and man until Bratchet looked at the door expecting some modern witchfinder-general to break in and drag them all off to the stake.

They lit a new perspective on everything. Who was St Paul to command women to be silent? A father of the church, so away with him and the rest of fathers. God the Father? Why not God the Mother? Might not Andromeda have rescued Perseus? Was it not St Georgina who slew the dragon? They were ridiculous, funny, splendid; nothing could withstand them.

Even when there was no answer to Anne's letters, Bratchet thought, as did Anne and Mary, that they or their answers had gone astray. When they hired a coach so that Anne could present herself to the Queen in person, Bratchet wanted to go with them and begged for what she'd never had: a day off. Almost compassionately, Effie had refused: 'Better for you to stay here.'

Bratchet persisted. How could it be better than seeing a palace, perhaps a queen, close to?

'They ain't going to see no queen,' said Effie as if she knew.

Bratchet gave in from a tiredness which, in fact, signalled the onset of smallpox. That night, when the two young women returned, she was too feeble to get up from her bed; she listened helplessly as Anne's rage and frustration shook the house: 'But how can they deny who I am? How *can* they? By God, I'll be revenged, I swear it. I'll go to the Scots. They'll be glad enough of a new Stuart for the throne.'

Anne's shouts infiltrated Bratchet's nightmares and echoed on through the delirium and pain of the following days. She heard her own hoarse voice issuing from an obstructed throat calling for Anne, then for Mary. Neither came.

It was Effie Sly who nursed her with extreme kindness, fanning her, sponging, helping her drink, oiling her skin when the itching of its pustules became intolerable. Afterwards, she liked to point out that she had saved Bratchet's life and Bratchet knew it was true, not just because of her care but because of a conversation that had taken place outside the bedroom door and had woven itself into her fever in which a voice, a well-spoken man's voice, had told Effie that the women Mary Read and Anne Bonny should be 'best sent to the colonies for their health'.

'How much you paying?' Effie's agreement started Bratchet's fight for life. She had to save them. She had to get better to warn them. She must to save her mother, who was drowning. *Va l'aider*. 'Shall I be Queen of England, Bratchet? Come and be queen with me.' *Va les aider*.

The quietness of the house when she was sensible again nearly extinguished the fluttering thing that was her will to live but she could not accept that even a colossus like Effie could have snuffed out two such spirits. Again and again she asked, 'Where've they gone? What you do to them, Eff?' refusing to accept Effie's account that they had merely departed without saying goodbye.

At last Effie said, 'Didn't want to tell you, did I, you being so flash for 'em. They're laid in the locker, dead and gone. Tap the Pedlar saw 'em struggling with a gang of Mohucks down the dock. Raped and chucked in the river, most like, if I know them Mohucks. Shame, two promising young buttercups like them.' Her eyes met Bratchet's with total calm.

'You spirited 'em,' screeched Bratchet, 'You fucker, you cannibal, you spirited 'em. I heard you. You was paid.'

Effie blinked but remained composed. 'When was this? When you was raving with the pox? Very likely. You was hearing the Last Trump and Long Lane clickers then as well.'

As soon as her legs would bear her, Bratchet went to Bully Watts, the parish beadle, and informed him that Effie Sly had been paid by an unknown nob, possibly a member of the Court or government or both, to have Mary Read and Anne Bonny sold to the colonies.

She should have known better; even if her accusation had sounded plausible, Bully was too lazy and too beholden to Effie's regular bribery to take any action. When Bratchet went to the magistrate with the same story, Bully accompanied her and undermined it to the point where the magistrate told her that she was a serpent's tooth of a maid and to get back to the mistress who deserved better than her.

She did. There was nowhere else to go. No decent employer was likely to take on a girl from Puddle Court with or without a reference, even if Effie had been prepared to give her one. There was other employment, but having watched one such employee after another succumb to disease in Floss's brothel next door, Bratchet wasn't inclined to take it. She was in misery. All that kept her going was her faith in the wit and courage of her two friends to extricate themselves from their capture.

'They're dead and gone, Bratchie, so no more of it,' Effie kept saying, but Bratchet had lit a mental beacon for Mary and Anne to come back to, and kept it burning. In the meantime she adopted a lolling outward indifference and inwardly retired to the True Time of her Huguenot childhood, speaking to herself in French and repeating its fairytales.

She was raped by one of the lodgers the following year and became pregnant. Effie, who'd begun to drink heavily, had been in too deep a stupor during the rape to hear Bratchet's screams for help, and she responded to the pregnancy with, 'Either you slip that calf, chucky, or my door's closed agin you.'

Not knowing how she could support a child on the streets, the dazed and compliant Bratchet was taken to a woman in Cable Lane, much in local demand for her skills, who aborted her twelve-week embryo with a knitting needle.

After that came another illness from which she only just recovered, to discover that menstruation had ceased. Certain she could never bear a baby again, the future closed down with the thud of a coffin lid. Somewhere beyond it, in the world of the living, her two indomitable friends walked and talked and had their being but the beacon she kept for them collapsed into embers.

On the night she'd seen Effie's body asplay on the floor, its face gorged blue, Bratchet had at once shrieked in triumph and felt bereft; Effie had bestridden her life so long she was without the volition to think for herself; she'd been turned to stone by a slow-acting gorgon.

With good food, gentler treatment and some education her body and mind regained some of their youth – she was, after all, only eighteen and more resilient than she knew. She fought the man who tried to assault her at The Hague with the ferocity not just of a woman who'd been raped before and would rather die than be raped again, but with healthy self-loving anger. How dare he? Her gratitude to the chivalrous Scotsman was doglike but in it was also an element of her first sexual stir.

Another anger galvanized her as she realized that she'd been dragged into a hunt for Anne Bonny and Mary Read.

It was Kit Ross who completed the process of bringing Bratchet back to life. The night after Mother Ross had come aboard we tied up by a bridge which led to a track lined with poplars, the nearest with their trunks deep in water. The breeze whisked bits of straw from packing cases into the thwarts, then dropped. The sky faded to a typical Flemish blue wash, outlining Mother Ross's hat as she drank and talked. The light from the poop lantern softened her face from middle-age to a young woman's.

She'd been in more battles than any of us. She spoke of gallantry and old, dead soldiers, and all of us, even Colonel Blackader, inched forward until we circled her. As she talked, she tidied us up, binding a Cameronian's torn finger, taking Kilsyth's jacket from him to sew on a button and telling him he needed a new coat. 'If a louse lost its footing on this cloth, me son, it'd break its neck.'

She inspired a comfortable, wistful lust in every man there. She was no beauty, Mother Ross, but that night she was a combination of mother, sweetheart and comrade-in-arms, the only woman who'd been where we'd been. She held a bubble of balance, attracting but keeping us at bay, giving a sheen of femininity to the masculine business of war.

And Bratchet, watching us all from outside the circle, thought, That's what I want. She longed for what Mother Ross had; for the Scotsman to regard her with the same admiration, unwilling though it was, with which he looked at this woman. Mother Ross had gained entry to the most powerful collegiate in the world and the Bratchet, with her new soul, wanted to join. *She's men's equal. She's like Anne and Mary.*

That night, when everybody had bedded down, Bratchet crawled to where Mother Ross lay wrapped in her army cloak and knocked politely on one of her clogs.

'Mrs Ross.'

'What, then?'

'Why'd you do it?'

Mother Ross didn't ask what. 'They took me husband, d'ye see, cushin. Got the bastard drunk as a fiddler's bitch and shipped him to Flanders. I went after him.'

'Did you find him?'

'I did. In the arms of another woman, God rest him.'

'But you stayed a soldier.'

There was a pause. 'Woman's life . . .' Mother Ross's voice was quiet with reflection, 'It wasn't big enough for me, girl. I wanted more.'

'Did you find it?' Bratchet thought of the scars, the loneliness of hiding one's sex, the courage.

'Men have got it, girl. And I shared it with them. Now clear off and let me sleep.'

As she crawled back to her palliasse, Bratchet understood that it wasn't so much of Mary and Anne that Mother Ross reminded her. It was Effie Sly.

In the healthiest development of all, Bratchet was beginning to put Effie into perspective; she hadn't been wholly bad, she'd been capricious. She'd shown true devotion in nursing Bratchet through illness; she'd regretted the rape on her maid and · ever after, when a lodger tried to assault Bratchet, Effie kicked his arse for him and sent him packing. She'd become a monster because the society in which she found herself was monstrous, a sewer you either drowned in or climbed out of on a ladder of other people to keep your own head above the excrement.

Kit Ross and Effie were from the same oven, but where Mother Ross had turned her energy to wholesome account – as long as you weren't one of the unfortunates she took supplies from – Effie had found outlet only in what was rotten.

As she lay in the barge hold, listening to the snores around her, Bratchet could have found it in her newly mended heart to forgive Effie Sly – if she hadn't sold Mary Read and Anne Bonny to the press boat because a gentleman had paid her a good price to do it.

They're dead and gone, Bratchet, so no more of it.

But they weren't. She knew.

CHAPTER SEVEN

Third Extract from *The Madwoman's Journal*

I AM THERE. The plan is working. My dear, you may congratulate the Queen's newest bedchamber woman.

Old Mrs Banks, who's been senile for years, was made to resign last week when she began biting people. Immediately I heard I sent Uncle Cofferer to Duchess Sarah to plead for me. Sarah is pleased with me, and nowadays she's not pleased with many. She appreciates crisp laundry. Also, she's running out of people she can trust. And Uncle Cofferer was desperate; I'd told him no more tickly-tickle until I got the post. Somehow he worked the oracle.

Then began a tussle between Sarah and Abigail Hill. Abigail had her own candidate. Sarah won; she is, after all, in charge of the bedchamber. But it was a near thing, Abigail's influence over Queen Ant being in the ascendancy and Sarah's waning fast.

I was called to Kensington Palace and waited in an antechamber, listening to the exchange between Sarah and Abigail in the room next door – the Duchess's voice sounding off like light cannon. Eventually she came sweeping out, mouth tight, colour high, asking did she have my loyalty.

I sank into a deep curtsey. 'I live to repay, Your Grace.'

And I do.

'Another once told me that,' she snapped, 'and has proved a gross traitor. Very well, I have persuaded Her Majesty to accept you. But remember whose influence raised you so high. Can I trust you to tell me what goes on behind my back? There is a viper in the bedchamber, as you will find out, and I wish to know when it is poised to strike.'

I protested my life was hers, she should know all and so on. She patted my head, raised my salary another ten pounds a year and glided off. Apart from gaining access to the heart of things, I am now also blessedly free of Uncle Cofferer, God rot him. Bedchamber women follow the Queen on her progress round the royal palaces, which means peripatetic attic accommodation at Hampton Court, Kensington, Windsor, etc. Queen Ant rarely sleeps at St James's because it was so much the home of her Papist father whom she deserted for William and Mary during the Glorious Revolution.

Oh yes, my dear, our plan progresses well. If I don't die of boredom. As a form of entertainment, the post of bedchamber woman resembles suffocation. After minute instruction, I took up my duties and meekly followed the Duchess of Somerset, known as 'Carrots' for her red hair, into the Queen's bedchamber. The duchess is a *lady* of the bedchamber while I am just its *woman*. The distinction is insisted on.

It's a grand room, very tapestried, very gilded and the bed is enormous. It needs to be. When Carrots drew back its curtains I had to blink at the size of the woman in it; a great white elephant seal with a lace cap on its head. Carrots said, 'God's grace to Your Majesty, a fine day,' – actually it was dull with

November mist – and its eyes opened and flinched, as if the thought of another day was a burden to it.

There was no sign of Prince George of Denmark – royal couples sleep apart – yet he must have frequented the bed pretty often to impregnate his wife seventeen times, though not one child has survived. In her hand, which is swollen by gout into the shape of a crab, she held a miniature of the boy who died when he was eleven.

Cooing sweet nothings, Carrots looks on while I and Mrs Darville, another mere 'woman', help Her Majesty out of bed to the chamber-pot, then assist her to the *prie dieu* in a corner for prayers. It's as well I'm strong. Queen Ant weighs a ton and is so crippled she can barely shuffle. Her extremities are white and puffy.

After prayers she is 'shifted'. I take a clean white linen shift from a press while Carrots takes off the nightrobe and cap. Not forgetting to curtsey, I hand the shift to Carrots, who puts it on Her Majesty. (These are morning rules; if she's shifted at noon I don't have to curtsey.) I then go to the door where the page of the backstairs is waiting with basin and ewer and accompany him to a side table. He bows and sets them down. Kneeling, he puts on Her Majesty's slippers, then leaves. (If she's going out, we have to call him to put on her gloves because that's not done by woman or lady.)

I kneel at the table while Her Majesty seats herself on its other side and holds out her hands. I pour water over them. Carrots watches. Next I fetch the royal fan from another table and hand it, curtseying, to Carrots who exhausts herself by handing it to the Queen.

That, virtually, is that. No, I forget the cup of chocolate. It's my job to take it from the page when he brings it and, kneeling, put it on the table. From then on I merely lurk against the tapestry to recover from the excitement.

Carrots was sent off to enquire after Prince George's health, while Mrs Garcia set the royal hair, which is thick and greying, not unpretty.

'Come here, mistress.' I was summoned to step under the royal eyes which are weak but more acute than you might expect. 'The Duchess tells me you are a worthy young woman. If you will treat me as kindly as I hope to treat you I shall be the overjoyedest creature in the world.' It was a plea. She wants everyone to love her. Her voice is her best feature; deep and musical, like a trained actress's. Adoringly, I prattled unworthiness, joy, gratitude, which went down well and I took a royal smile back with me to the tapestry.

Ladies-in-waiting and maids of honour take over when the Queen leaves the bedchamber. (A tiresome crew; proper as bollards in the royal presence; scandalous away from it. They think themselves daring to play Selling a Bargain, in which the dupe must be made to ask, 'What?' 'It's large and always asleep.' 'What?' 'Prince George.' And the what-ter pays a fine. I laughed at jokes like that in my cradle.)

But today I was fortunate and Queen Ant lingered in the chamber so that I was present for her visitors. The royal physician, Arbuthnot, came to sniff the royal chamber-pot, pronounce the royal urine too thick, administer a physick and recommend rest. Prince George lumbered in for a kiss and said woss there any yourneyings today because he had yoists to make. (He woodworks as well as drinking, eating and not thinking.) Queen Ant said: 'Just the thing, dearest. I have only an old cabinet meeting and after we can take tea together.' They seem genuinely fond.

Next Abigail Hill. The woman's incapable of a straight line; she serpentined towards her quarry, a few steps sideways here, some more there, until she stood at an angle to the Queen, holding up her hands as if awaiting the Second Coming to ask how We were today. She listened to the urine saga with whimpers of oh-my-dear-Majesty-how-bravely-you-suffer. They go down well.

She's invited to pull up a tabouret and sit near so that she and Queen Ant can whisper and giggle. They must think I'm deaf. They're planning something; there was much mention of a 'Mr Ashley', and did 'Mr Morley' approve, and oh-do-you-think-so-ma'ams.

Mr Morley is Prince George because everyone knows that during Sarah's reign the queen called herself Mrs Morley and

Sarah Mrs Freeman. I must find out who 'Mr Ashley' is. Whatever their plan, it's going to benefit Abigail; she wore the smile of a shark sighting a baby seal.

It became more sharkish as she looked at me and whispered again. I caught the words 'cuckoo in the nest' put into a question. But the Queen said out loud that she thought I would suit her very well. 'And so pretty.' The shark's smile froze a little.

They turned to politics without bothering to whisper. I stared raptly at the portrait of Queen Ant on the wall opposite – it's by Kneller and is over-kind to her figure – listening hard. Abigail was pushing the cause of Harley. It's turned out she is one of his distant relatives, as well as Sarah's. Who *isn't* the woman kin to? Secretary of State Harley is having his nose put out by the tendency of the Duke of Marlborough and Godolphin to side with government Whigs. He wants neither Tory nor Whig to hold sway; Harley's party is Harley.

'He would die for you, ma'am. I beg you, let me bring him by the backstair that he may lend strength in your stand against S.'

'S' is Sunderland, I'm sure, whom Queen Ant hates worse than poison. He's so republican he opposed the giving of a grant to Prince George. All this goes with the information William Greg gave me; Harley's trying to control the Queen through Abigail.

At that point, in came Sarah, without knocking. She looked marlinspikes at Abigail. 'I would speak to you privately, Your Majesty.' Queen Ant nodded to Abigail to go, though reluctantly. Abigail went, equally reluctant. I blended into the arras.

'Dear, dear Mrs Freeman,' says the Queen, patting the tabouret Abigail had vacated, 'how kind to come to your unfortunate Morley after this long time when she is so vexated with the gout.'

Sarah stayed standing. 'The matter of my son-in-law, Your Majesty . . .'

'Not Majesty, not Majesty,' begged Queen Ant. 'Let Morley and Freeman open their hearts to each other as once they did. Have I not given way that the Earl of Sunderland might be Minister without Portfolio?'

'It's not good enough, Your Majesty. He must have a proper

government position. My husband urges it from the field of battle where he undergoes such privation in your service, my Lord Godolphin urges it, as do all those with your welfare at heart.'

'Not all,' said Queen Ant and then blanched because Sarah was on it like a whippet.

'Who? Who does not urge it? Harley? That Tory?'

'Oh Mrs Freeman,' said the Queen, beginning to cry, 'All my desire is the liberty to employ those faithful to my service whether they are called Whig or Tory, not to be tied to one nor the other, for if I fall into the hands of either I shall be no queen but a slave.'

Sarah was unmoved. 'It seems to me, Majesty, that your dislike of party rule more often than not means Whig rule. I cannot see how anyone of sense can run so scared of the word "Whig".'

Queen Ant rallied. 'At least the Tories protect the church.'

Sarah gave a great, deliberate sigh and said: 'I see I must remove myself, since my counsel has no avail.'

'Don't leave me, dearest Mrs Freeman, or I shall be the miserablest creature alive and shall shut myself away.'

The exchange came wearily, like a sweethearts' threat-and-capitulation game they had played too often. Were they lovers once? Was that how Sarah gained her dominance? I can see it on the Queen's part, she is a woman's woman, but it wouldn't have come naturally to the Duchess.

But, oh, Sarah, you're throwing the game.

She refused to unbend. Went to the door with a last salvo: 'I wish you to reflect on the fact that the greatest misfortunes in your family were occasioned by ill advice and an obstinacy of temper.' Slam.

So much for the Stuarts. But it's unwise to shout rude things at queens, even this one. Deep within this mass of royal jelly is the pride and stubbornness of a Stuart. I saw her eyes when Sarah had gone. If she thinks she's in the right, they could keelhaul her and not alter her opinion.

Therefore, so much for Sarah. A woman as unaware of danger as she is will drag her allies down with her. No, I will

131

take care to placate Abigail, insinuate myself with Queen Ant and await my turn.

I began at once. With Sarah's departure we were alone. 'You are distressed, Your Majesty,' I said, oozing sympathy. 'My dear mother always recommended cold tea in such circumstances.'

'Cold tea?' says the Queen.

I fetched Mrs Darville to sit with her while I went to the butler's pantry and ordered brandy with a dash of water. On my return through an ante-chamber full of maids-of-honour one of them pranced up to me, trying to play Bargain and induce me to say 'what?' by carolling: 'It's white and it follows me.'

I didn't have time for games. 'Your arse,' I told her.

Queen Ant drank the brandy, giggling like a girl: 'Such a restorative, my child. I thank you.'

I fetched her another later. I noticed she didn't mention it to Abigail, who drinks hardly at all, except coffee. Cold tea is to be our little secret.

The plan is properly begun, then. But oh, God, oh, Devil, the littleness of this life before it's ended. Months, perhaps years. Stuffy rooms, that afflicted malodorous royal flesh, hand the fan, kneel, watch, plot, pettiness, I shall go insane in this miniature world of women. I can't breathe. Why didn't they kill me? We fought on, the two of us, when the others had surrendered. And still we didn't die.

We watched them hang Calico Jack. 'Had you but fought like a man you would not now be dying like a dog.' My true, my only love. No man could compete with your spirit. The best of me died with you. Only revenge keeps me upright to walk and talk. How can I bear the days?

Yet the nights are worse. The creature comes to me then, its hands feeling for my throat. The other bedchamber women let me have an attic to my own because I scream in my sleep.

Hold the course, steersman, hold, hold, hold.

As I indicated, William Greg is now my purveyor of information. I have to pay him in flesh. The only difference between him and Uncle Cofferer is that he is younger and hammers harder.

He's a fool. He thinks himself a gay blade. He spouts bad

132

poetry as he fucks and buys me trinkets he can't afford. The Negroes tell me he's been gambling with a Frenchman they suspect of being an agent for Louis XIV and to whom he owes large amounts of money. If they're right, the agent will use the age-old ploy: Spy for me or I go to your master. Harley wouldn't tolerate a gambler on his staff. Although he's a Tory he's also a Puritan. It would mean instant dismissal. What will Greg do? If I read his character correctly, he'll choose to spy. He's become used to high position and couldn't bear to lose it.

Well, if he does, he'll fall into my lap as well as the Frenchman's. I need a channel of communication to France. The latest information on the Bratchet, according to Greg who receives it via The Hague from Martin Millet, is that the search for Mary Read is taking her and the others to the winter quarters of the First Dragoons. And those winter quarters, my dear, are right opposite the French lines.

Can I tempt the Bratchet into France, I wonder? I think I can. Certainly I can tempt the Scotsman into taking her there. Or rather, if I can send a letter to France, I can persuade Francesca to do the tempting for me with the connivance of Louis XIV. She is with the rest of the Jacobites at St-Germain-en-Laye and high in Louis's favour.

Yes, I think a secret summons from Anne Bonny's very own grandmother might draw the Bratchet to France, to St-Germain-en-Laye, where she can be disposed of. While I doubt that Francesca would do the disposing herself, I know a woman who will – if the price is right. It all depends on William Greg and whether he decides to turn traitor. Persuading him to spend more on me than he can afford will assist his decision. What do I care if he betrays his country? Or if I do? England betrayed me. She's no country of mine.

But oh, she was, she was. She held my dreams in the days when my dreams were innocent. Before she turned me into an assassin.

At first I was relieved the Bratchet had made her escape, but the night I learned of it was dreadful. The shadow in the corner of my attic solidified into a lump as big as Queen Ant. Eyes bulged through the fronds of seaweed that covered its face and it lumbered towards me, its hands groping with fingers that were lobster's claws. Its wet mouth pulsed out a roaring like a tide race through the room.

I know what it is now and what it wants and I am afraid. Effie Sly has returned from hell where I sent her. I was promising her that Bratchet should die when Mrs Darville came in to wake me up, saying I was disturbing the other women with my shouts. But I hadn't been asleep.

CHAPTER EIGHT

HOSTILITIES STOP in winter for the sake of the horses, not the soldiers. Horses on active service needed grazing and there's no grass in winter, so during the war, allied and French armies would settle down for three months within a mile or two of each other on the Flemish plain to recoup, train, and, according to time-honoured custom, exchange prisoners. Experienced soldiers are hard to come by; better to have one's own men back to fight again than have to feed captives.

We found the First Dragoons in one of the usual Flanders winter camps – stretches of mud, canvas and wooden huts against a vast grey sky. In the bad old days, I saw common soldiers near starvation in camps like these, while their colonels lived like colonels on their men's food allowance. But that was before the Duke of Marlborough took over the army.

When you read this, James, you'll be in a better position than I am now to guess how history will judge the Duke. I know that in the last years of Queen Anne's reign, after his wife managed to alienate the Queen and drag him down with her, the Tories accused him of every crime in the book in order to disgrace him, including stealing funds earmarked for the army's bread.

I expect he did well out of the system – it's rotten anyway. But I can tell you this: his soldiers never starved. Part of the man's genius was his planning. He could march us a hundred miles in the time it took a French general to tie his cravat. He could do it because he'd sent provisions ahead and cached them so that men and horses could feed as they went. And because he employed sutlers like Mother Ross.

Once we arrived in camp she began regular requisitioning forays. That's what she called them. The Flemings called them pillage. Weeping burghermeisters demanded she be hanged. But they knew, and so did she, that complaints against her and other sutlers would end up with the Duke of Marlborough who'd listen patiently, as he listened to all his quarrelling allies, and do nothing about it. His army was saving these same burghermeisters from the French. It was his sutlers who provided the extras that made the Army Commissariat's basic ration of bread and ale bearable.

He wasn't going to stop them; marauders they might be, but their 'requisitioning' forestalled roaming and dangerous gangs of soldiers sacking this ally's countryside as they did an enemy's.

Mother Ross left the civilians enough to eat, but she took their surplus. She sniffed out buried grain stores, turnips in a hidden cellar, broody hens, a roaming horse. She took grappling irons with her to retrieve the valuables from the wells of empty houses where families fleeing from the French occupation had hidden their treasures and never come back for them. She'd pull up somebody's prized brass pail, pewter dishes and, occasionally, a silver spoon.

More than once her requisitioning party returned at a run, chased by Flemings who had to be held off by a volley over their heads from the Cameronians' muskets.

The First was proud of her. To my surprise, they were proud of Mary Read as well, despite the joshing they'd taken from the infantry when it was discovered she was a woman. Corporal Ortheris was typical: 'Saved my bloody life, din' she? A trooper saves your life, you don't care if there's cock or cleft in his breeches.' The sergeants' mess echoed Sergeant Smith when I'd met him at Chelsea Hospital: Read had been a good trooper, one of the best, they didn't care who knew it.

Kilsyth reported that the officers were equally admiring. One of them said: 'Bloody bitch dam' near stole this little Flemish whore I was hacking at the time. Played up to her like it was a great joke. I can see her now, grinning at me, as the hussy tried to kiss her.'

That was what came over, her joy in being accepted as one of the company. She'd fought duels, drunk glass for glass, cursed with the best. And laughed. They all remembered how she'd laughed. And they smiled as they remembered.

'Aye,' Kilsyth said to me in disapproval, 'For certain that lassie was Mary Read, not Bonny Anne. Anne would ne'er have swaggered so freakish in male attire.'

'Perhaps being press-ganged ain't conducive to femininity,' I suggested, but he wouldn't have it.

Despite journeying together, on our arrival the Highlander immediately took up residence in the officers' quarters while I messed with the sergeants. Neither of us found it odd. He didn't ignore me; he was always stumping over the mud to enquire after my health and the Bratchet's, bringing us some tidbit – a sort of unspoken thanks for my saving of him from the Whiggamores that time at The Hague. He must have realized I knew him for a Jacobite, but he never referred to it, and nor did I.

We settled down into that camp for three months. The journey home would have been too uncomfortable in winter. In any case, I still thought I could find Mary Read. After her marriage to her fellow-trooper, the couple had bought an inn in Ghent. I reckoned it was a queer town to choose to settle down in. It was right on the front line and as the war waged back and forth it had been regularly occupied and then re-occupied by either side. The French had been holding it for some time now, and still were, so nobody knew whether Mary was there or not. Unlikely, I thought, but as the Duke's spring campaign hoped to liberate the town it was worth staying on to find out.

I have to say I neglected Bratchet at first. I found her and her dog a place with a respectable enough family among the train of wives, children, mistresses, harlots, washerwomen, Jews and pawnbrokers – the usual collection which brings up the rear of any army, and forms a gimcrack town of its own on the edge of camp.

I was given a tent among the non-commissioned officers. Sergeant Enwright had requisitioned me to help him train new recruits and I was kept at it all day, relaxing at nights in the company of the sergeants' mess – apart from occasional excursions to the nearby village of Wijtschat where there was a grieving young Flemish widow who enjoyed my sympathy.

It was Kit Ross who pointed out that Bratchet was running wild. The girl had acquired a drummer boy's jacket and wore it with some style over a black skirt of Kit's. With a shako cocked over one eye and colour in her cheeks, she was attracting attention.

'Feeling her greens for the first time, so she is,' Kit warned me, 'And wagging her hips in front of yon Livingstone like laced mutton. Fortunate for her, he wouldn't notice if she jigged naked but, Dear knows, there's many as will.'

I acted at once. Word went out through Sergeant Enwright that any soldier taking advantage of 'Millet's slip' would be deprived of any further chances of fatherhood. The Bratchet suddenly found her days taken up with education: mathematics and literacy with Levi, the pawnbroker; cooking and household management with Mrs Enwright; equitation with the sergeant-of-horse. Her nights were spent under the dour eye of Sergeant Flesher, a Cameronian, and his even dourer wife.

Mrs Flesher was interesting on the subject of Mary Read; she was among the few who hadn't liked her. 'A jack whore,' she called her. 'You mark my words, Martin Millet, she never married Trooper Johnson for love of his soul nor body, she jumped the broomstick with that lad for his money.'

'He had money?'

'Enough to buy an inn, curse it for the Devil's habitation. And her insisting they buy one in Ghent. Why Ghent, Papist town that it is? Mark me, lad, there was purpose in it, and not one pleasing to the Lord.'

It was what I'd been thinking. Why Ghent? I did some more enquiring and found another curious thing: although Mary

Read had enlisted in Lord John Hay's regiment, she'd switched to the First Dragoons later.

It was too flimsy a suspicion to report to The Hague, but I wrote to Daniel Defoe, 'It seems to me that Mary Read might have been deliberately heading for the French lines all along. To enlist is as good a way of crossing the Channel without a passport as any. When Hay's company was sent into Germany, she got herself transferred to the First which was in the main advance towards France. When she was in a position to own an inn, she decided on the chancy location of Ghent which was always likely to be re-occupied by the French, as it was. What was she after? Did she think Anne Bonny had been taken to France and not the colonies? Or was she a traitor? If so, why?'

Two months went by before I received his reply; it was winter, after all, and Daniel was going back and forth to Scotland as Harley's agent, trying to persuade the Scots that union with England would be the best thing happening to them since God invented porridge. His letter, when it came, was in a code we'd worked out together before I left for Europe and was very long. It wasn't complimentary about our Scottish cousins. 'A refractory and difficult people with a weather to match,' he called them.

He said he was in Edinburgh – 'known as Auld Reekie for its reek' – writing pamphlets to explain the English to the Scots, and the Scots to the English, 'the Scots being assured all Englishmen are effeminate wastrels and the English assured the Scots still paint themselves with woad and eat roasted children.' He moaned a good deal about not being paid and that poor Mrs Defoe was as good as a penniless widow in his absence.

Reading between the lines, I gathered he wasn't spending all his time writing; he seemed to know a great deal more about what the Jacobites in the Highlands were doing than he could have gleaned from ordinary enquiry. I'd bet my boots he'd set up a system of espionage for Harley.

At long last Daniel got to the business of Mary Read. 'Your report of M. R.'s movements intrigues me. I agree with you that her purpose all along was to cross into France. If she was of a mind to pursue A. B., it might be that she needed assistance and dare not seek it in a country which she considered hostile to them both, but regarded France as more likely to be her friend. There is one in France who might indeed have befriended her – Francesca Bard, who, if you remember, we decided was the morganatic wife of Prince Rupert and therefore A. B.'s grandmother.

'My superiors [he wouldn't name Harley even in code] inform me that the old lady is in residence at St-Germain-en-Laye near Paris where our erstwhile queen, Mary of Modena, mother to the Pretender, holds court. Could it be that M. R. applied to her for help in tracing A. B.?'

I damned Daniel for leaving that bit of information to the last – it had taken me all night to decode his letter, and there was still a postscript I hadn't got to yet. I settled down at the mouth of my tent the next morning to transcribe the rest. It wasn't easy. First the Bratchet joined me, sullenly – I'd asked to see what progress she was making with her lettering – and Sergeant Enwright stopped by to rest his legs and drink my ale. Then, in the distance, I saw Livingstone of Kilsyth striding across the duckboards towards us, kilt swinging, colours blazing. The Bratchet's chalk screeched across her slate at the sight of her hero, making the dog Turnspit yelp in sympathy. 'He's coming.'

'He's not here yet. Get on.' I finished decoding and began to read Daniel's postscript. It ran: 'I have just received news from a secret source that our Highlander, Kilsyth, has written to his chieftain to say that he has been in contact with the French since 30 November and fully expects news of A. B. before the winter's out.'

'He's got a hare today,' said Bratchet.

'Good.' Kilsyth had been here, in camp, since before 30 November. I'd seen him nearly every day. How in hell had he made contact with the French?

'He's always giving you things. You don't give him anything.'

'No.' The French were close enough; by night it was possible to see the fires of their camp but the no man's land between was heavily guarded and I could swear he hadn't crossed it. 'He taught me the quadrille yesterday.' Kilsyth was giving her dancing lessons.

'Good.'

'*You* can't dance the quadrille.'

'No.'

Sergeant Enwright, coming to the tent mouth with his ale, spotted the Scotsman. 'Into t' trenches, lads. Here comes the Duke o' Limbs. I ask you, what's he look like? Bloody maypole.'

Enwright, in his scarlet uniform frogged with green and yellow, had no time for non-combatants. But even he didn't question what Kilsyth was doing there. Civilian visitors are an accepted nuisance. They come and go, to see friends or relatives, or out of curiosity, or to be able to go back home and say they've been in the front line. Often, during a battle, you can see spectators watching from a hilltop, ladies among 'em.

'Look at him,' Enwright persisted, 'Got his head in the bees, lolloping great bugger.' The Highlander was talking to himself as he came across the duckboards in the centre of camp, oblivious of the punishment victims either side of them – a woman in the whirligig and three dead deserters on the gibbet. 'Still,' Enwright went on, 'Blackader don't like him.'

It was a recommendation; Colonel Blackader didn't like anybody, and nobody liked Colonel Blackader. As Kilsyth came up, I rose as if to greet him and dropped Defoe's letter and my transcript into the fire just outside the tent.

'Would ye do me the honour of accepting this wee galloper for the pot.' Kilsyth handed over the hare he was carrying. He saluted Bratchet, who was nearly swooning from his presence and courtesy: 'And how's my bonny Goldilocks? Will we try the strathspey next? I am the best exponent of the strathspey in the Highlands.'

'Bashful with it,' muttered Enwright.

I walked back with Kilsyth through the camp. He strode ahead, then remembered my leg and fell back to keep step with me.

'Where'd you get the hare?' I asked.

'From the beldame Ross.' Mother Ross fascinated and repulsed him at the same time. 'For what do these women unsex themselves and take up with the military? Not that she's no a winning piece, like so many of the camp sluts. The one last night now . . .'

'Energetic?'

He clapped me on the shoulder. 'I tell ye, Martin, it was not at all like tumbling Janet Mathie in the cow byre back home. Sexual dexterity in the Highlands, it seems, is still in its infancy. Hooly, Hooly Tom, she was disgusting. Satisfying. But disgusting.'

He seemed to become aware for the first time of the activity in the camp. 'What for do they put out the gumphers?' They were hanging out all the standards, pennons, flags and bunting that day. The area round the barrack huts was being weeded while, inside, the lice and fleas in the bedrolls on the slatted shelves were being fumigated by burning wormwood. A shrill of fifes and the dad-dad mum-mum of practice drums from the bandsmen's quarters were answered in the distance by cavalry trumpets performing the wild and beautiful point of war.

'Duke of Marlborough's inspecting the camp tomorrow,' I reminded him.

Sacks of hay hung by their necks on the parade ground where Drill Sergeant Tusser was taking bayonet practice. 'Pre-e-e-zzent. Wait for it, wait for it. Fix bayonets.' His roar rolled over the camp like a wave of lava. 'Don't look down. Don't look down. You'd soon find the hole if there was hair round it.'

In the central square the stiff bodies of the deserters were being lowered from the scaffold, while Polly Garrett was receiving a last twirl in the whirligig before her release. We stopped to watch the slatted contraption, like a rectangular birdcage, being rotated faster and faster on its swivels by four puffing privates under the eye of Lieutenant Fortescue. When at last it came to a halt, the lieutenant helped out its occupant and held her arm as she staggered then vomited.

'You all right, Poll?' I asked.

Polly nodded.

'What he spin you for this time?'

Poll pointed to a notice strung round her neck. It read, 'Fornicatress'.

'I'm sorry, Poll,' said Lieutenant Fortescue, 'But orders is orders. See you tonight?'

Poll nodded again, balanced herself and wobbled off towards the women's camp.

'Yon Presbyterian bastard's the great man at war with lassies,' said Kilsyth of Colonel Blackader. 'Nae mair heart to him than a hen partridge.'

Colonel Blackader was against fornication. Polly was by no means the most promiscuous of the camp followers, but she was young and pretty and Colonel Blackader was also against youth and good looks in women, as he was against drinking and gambling. He was trying to carry discipline to the unheard-of lengths of stopping the men's pay if he heard them cursing. And troopers curse . . . well, like troopers. The First thought he was a pain in the arse. He was a good soldier, though.

'Talk o' the Deil and ye'll see his horns,' Kilsyth said. Colonel Blackader was marching towards us.

'Ah, Kilsyth. We're exchanging more prisoners this afternoon. I shall be glad of your services as interpreter again.'

I intervened: 'Again? Why can't Maurice interpret?'

Blackader turned his neat, gaunt head towards me. It was like being squirted by a lemon. 'If it's any of your business, laddie, *Captain* Maurice has passed the task over to *Mister* Kilsyth here, who speaks the language with more facility.' Having to ask a favour from a Highlander clipped his Lothian accent to the bone.

He turned back to Livingstone. 'I shall, of course, bring along Corporal Ortheris as a corrective. I'm told he too understands the paynim tongue.' He gave the impression that fluency in French was a weakness godfearing men like himself didn't succumb to.

Livingstone bowed, coldly, the colonel strode away to bring more light into Sodom and Gomorrah, and I took myself off to find Corporal Ortheris and came on him stacking the woodpile into the neatness necessary for inspection by Captain-General Marlborough.

'How good's your French, Sam?'

He put down some wood and wiped his face. 'Gets you off fatigues, don't it? I'm parlaring s'arternoon for old Blister Bollocks.'

'Yes, but how good is it?'

'Learned it when the Crapos captured me after Blenheim. Whole sodding year in the Frog stockade, I was.'

'Look,' I said, 'I'm not going to sing it. Just tell me. How good's your bloody French?'

Ortheris looked round to see if anybody was hiding behind the woodpile. 'Twixt you and me, the Jimmy Rounds officer, him in charge of the French 'change, he don't speak it proper. Got a funny accent.'

'So when the Scotsman's interpreting you don't understand a word he and the Frog are saying.'

'I do.' Ortheris was indignant. 'Now an' then. Course, that bloody plaid don't speak it proper neither.'

So that's how the Highlander was doing it. When Blackader went out to no man's land to conduct an exchange of prisoners with his opposite number, Kilsyth went with him, using his position as interpreter to chat with the French colonel.

You bastard. I ought to go to Blackader this minute and get you swung. And if I'd thought he was giving away vital military secrets, I'd have done it. But I didn't. For one thing, Kilsyth had about as much military acumen as a bedspread. For another, he couldn't tell the Frogs anything about our position and strength that they couldn't get for themselves by using a strong spyglass.

He was doing what Daniel Defoe suspected him of doing: trying to find his bloody Bonny Anne Bard. Strictly speaking, I should still have handed him over to Blackader, but on the way back to my tent I passed the deal coffins they'd put the deserters into, and knew I wouldn't.

I began regretting I hadn't that very evening. I was sitting by the fire outside my tent, listening to Sergeant Enwright trying to persuade me to re-enlist. 'Come on, Mart. I was one of the Duke's men at Sedgemoor when we put down Monmouth, he'll hear me. All right, you only got one good leg but you're still a better trainer of horses and men than most of Queen Anne's bad bargains.'

I was tempted, I admit. I hadn't realized how much I'd missed the army.

'And now you're a man o' means,' Enwright went on, 'he might even give you a commission.'

I shook my head. 'I belong in the sergeants' mess.'

'I should bloody hope so. What about it, Mart? Do I speak to the Old Corporal?'

'Maister Millet,' called a voice. Mrs Flesher came into the firelight, her face more disapproving than ever. 'I'd have ye know yon lassie of yours has broken curfew. Eight of the clock, I told her, and nine of the clock it is now. Sergeant Pairkins espied her in the company of yon Highlander before the chap of eight and naebody's seen her sinsyne. Shameless, shameless, I call it.'

Enwright wanted to mobilize a search for Bratchet right away but I stopped him: 'Let me look first.' If Blackader learned the stupid little bitch was cavorting with the Scotsman, she'd be in the whirligig quicker than ninepence. I began fumbling about in the dark tent for my hat, but Enwright handed me his and sent me off with a clap on the back.

As I went, I was cursing Livingstone of Kilsyth and cursing myself harder. I'd trusted the tartaned bloody hillskipper not to take advantage of the girl's infatuation, forgetting that even an amiable idiot of a Scotsman was a potential seducer. Especially when it's offered on a plate with parsley.

And then I thought, He's going to kill her. The attempts on Bratchet's life in London, the strange ship in the Channel . . . why the hell had I assumed she'd be any safer here? What is it the slut knows? I wondered. Knew. God, she could be dead this minute.

On the edge of camp I ran into Mother Ross returning from a foray with Corporal McGuffie and two large sacks that fluttered. They were all dripping water. 'Duck,' explained Mother Ross, 'Requisitioned 'em before they floated upstream to the Crapo lines.'

She shook her head when I questioned her. 'Didn't see a living soul. Hold your horses, I'll get on a dry skirt and be with you quick as a gallop. I know the ground.'

I wouldn't wait. As I set off, McGuffie muttered something and Kit Ross ran after me. 'To be sure. The dog.'

'What dog?'

'That flea trap she has with her. Didn't we hear barking and I thought it was a fox but, sure, it was a strange fox now I remember. Maybe it was her dog. What's it called? Gridiron?'

'Turnspit. Where was this?'

'Over there.' Kit Ross waved to the west with an arm that shook from cold.

'When?'

'Just now. Five minutes was it, Guffie? Will ye hold on?'

I went.

It had been threatening snow all day and cloud was blocking out the moon but light from the camp behind me threw out an aurora which was answered in the distance by the glow of the Frenchies' fires. The plain between was featureless – all the trees had been chopped down long ago for tinder.

It was cold out there. And quiet. Behind me I could hear the noise of the camp, laughter and cheering from a cock fight, the diddle-diddle of a violin, babies crying. I tried to tune my ears away from it and into the sounds of the plain. An owl screeched to my left and not far away I could hear a devout and lonely sentry repeating the Cameronian's Prayer for Outpost Duty as he stamped his feet to keep warm. 'Lord Jesus Christ, I stand here on the foremost fringe of the camp holding watch against the enemy . . .'

I could see the gleam of his musket. If he spotted me, there'd be a row – I didn't have a pass to leave camp. I waited until he'd completed his eastward turn '. . . But were thou, O Lord, no wi' us, then the watcher watcheth in vain . . .'

I hobbled at a crouch out of the line of his march and threw myself flat.

'. . . I pray Thee, cover us with Thy grace as with a shield.' The words came louder as the man went by, then diminished. '. . . and let Thy holy angels round about us . . .'

Go. I went.

The plain wasn't silent at all; it rustled with creatures about their nightly business. It wasn't featureless either but mined with rabbit-holes, fox-holes, badger-holes, hole-holes, dips full

145

of bramble, unsuspected marsh and sudden drops into the beds of streams.

I fell into most of them, trying to keep to the direction Kit Ross had given me. He'd have taken her that way, along the track that had been worn between the lines by men going to and returning from the prisoners' exchange point in the centre of this sodding no man's land. I kept myself warm with the thought of what I'd do to Kilsyth when I found him. *Shoot the fucker*. Except I hadn't a gun. *Haul him back to Colonel Blackader who'll shoot him*. And if Bratchet was alive when I found her, Blackader could shoot her too. But I wasn't going to find her. She'd gone; disappeared into the limbo that had swallowed Anne Bonny and Mary Read. And I minded. I minded a great deal.

Then I heard the dog bark. There couldn't be many dogs roaming the plain; Kit Ross would've requisitioned them. And if it was Turnspit, Bratchet wasn't far away. I stumbled on. She'd sewn a red coat for the dog, making it look more ridiculous than ever. It was easier going as I got nearer the outpost fires of the French; what had been areas of just differing shades of blackness gained definition. Crossing them was a wide, greyish line. The track. And something on it ahead. An impression of standing stones, one big, a medium and a little one.

Talking standing stones.

I dropped down and began crawling, using elbows and my one good knee to pull me along. Until my head exploded.

I came round, wishing I wasn't. Kilsyth was shouting into my brain. '*Imbécile*,' he was roaring, '*Sot*. What for did the bastard shoot him?'

The male voice answering him wasn't apologetic. '*Sal espion. Tant mieux.*'

'This is no spy, you gollop. It's . . . my servant. He must have followed me.'

The captain shrugged. '*Tant pis, donc.*'

My head was resting on a cushion – Bratchet's lap; I could hear her moaning. Something was panting worriedly into my face with an appalling breath – the dog. I tried to push it away.

146

There was a whisper from the Bratchet. 'He's alive.' She screamed. 'He's still alive.'

It was like being trepanned. I tried to tell her to shut up.

Kilsyth's voice came closer to my ear, he'd knelt down. 'There's no blood. But he shot him in the head. Where's the blood?'

I tried to tell him to shut up as well. I felt him lift off my hat carefully, as if afraid of finding raw brains inside it. I thought he might.

'Hooly Tom, will you look at this. The hat has an iron pot in it. The bullet just dented it.'

Good for old Enwright. Good old Dragoons.

Kilsyth was doing something to my hat. I heard him whisper to Bratchet: 'He comes with us or he'll be frozen before dawn.'

There wasn't any question of leaving me behind. The French officer didn't like the smell of things. He told his men, 'Emmenez-le. Il a sans doute des révélations à faire.' Two of his piau-piau took my arms and dragged me along the track towards their lines, at which I lost interest in the proceedings.

French bullets are lighter than English but they can still do damage at short range, even when stopped by an iron pot hat. I remember being jolted for hours in a coach, and vomiting – to the fury of the French captain who travelled with us and who hadn't even liked the dog coming along.

We changed horses several times. At one of the stops, Kilsyth whispered in my ear: 'I've put a white cockade in your hat, mannie. Ye're a Jacobite now, so act like one.'

'You bastard,' I told him.

Mostly, during the stops when I was conscious, I cursed the Bratchet. She kept saying she was sorry until she got tired of being sworn at, then she said, 'It's your own fault. Nobody asked you along.'

I swore some more.

'I'm not doing anything wrong,' she said. Silly bitch. 'I'm going to meet Anne Bonny.'

'Is that what the bastard told you?'

Kilsyth said, 'It's the truth. I've had word from Anne's grandmother. She wants to see the lassie here.'

I told him what he could do with grandmothers, and the lassie.

The next time I made sense of anything, we were approaching the gates of St-Germain-en-Laye. Near Paris.

CHAPTER NINE

You've got to hand it to the French – they can outbuild us.

St-Germain-en-Laye was impressive enough to make St James's and Hampton Court look like outhouses. Until you came close.

The flower beds on either side of the approach our coach drove up were full of weeds, slates were missing here and there on the roofs, panes from some of the windows.

The French captain explained us to various major-domos and eventually left us in an anteroom that could have accommodated a regiment. Very ornate. Spindly gilt furniture, marble statues, painted ceilings showing cherubs and naked ladies with wispy scarves only just saving their blushes. But the carpet had holes in it, and nobody'd changed the candles in the chandelier. Louis XIV might have been generous in giving his birthplace to Mary of Modena and her Jacobite exiles, but he surely wasn't maintaining it for 'em.

It was the first time the three of us had been able to talk without whispering since I'd had my head smacked by the French bullet.

'Will ye stop your cursing?' Kilsyth said, 'Ye're about to enter the presence of England's rightful queen. Be civil now.'

'She's no fucking queen of mine, you bastard,' I told him.

'She was and she is.'

'Are you going to tell her you're saving the throne for your Bonny bloody Anne? Not her son?' There was no point in tiptoeing around the subject now. 'That'll go down well.'

'I'm saving your life, laddie,' said Kilsyth, sternly, 'for you saved mine. A Kilsyth aye pays his debts.'

148

'Then pay 'em and send me back. And that clay-brained mop-stick with me.'

'I ain't going back, so you can stop your name-calling,' said Bratchet. 'I've come for to see my friend Anne. Think I want to stay with you? You . . . you gerry-grinder.' She looked around. 'I like it here.'

'Oh yes,' I said, 'they'll like you too. A Huguenot in a Jacobite court. They'll hand you to the French army to wipe its boots on.'

Kilsyth's enormous fist took the front of my jacket and shook me. 'They'll think she's the French lady she is, for all yon poxy aunt treated her. Oh, I know – she's told me. If you value her life, and your own, ye'll keep your tongue behind your damn teeth.'

A flunkey flung open two big doors at the end of the room. 'Her Majesty will receive you now.'

Kilsyth took Bratchet's hand and raised it as if they were going to dance. They marched forward together. The dog Turnspit trotted after them, first pausing to cock his leg against a gold and onyx table. 'Son,' I told him, 'you speak for us both,' and followed him in.

The room wasn't as grand as the antechamber, and better for it; there were flowers, and the furniture was good carved wood. Either Mary Beatrice of Modena had acquired a taste for English furniture during her reign or she'd managed to smuggle some pieces out with her into exile.

I'd never seen her when she was Queen of England and I was expecting a painted trollop, a sort of better-born Floss, which is how my father talked of her, not that he'd have known; he'd have as soon stood in the street to watch her go by as he'd have cheered the Pope. All Catholic women were harlots to him; he invariably referred to her as 'that Romish whore'.

As usual, he was wrong. Her looks were decaying now, like the château, but they must have turned heads when she first arrived in England to become James II's second wife. She was only a few years older than Queen Anne, her step-daughter, and, I had to admit, wearing considerably better.

Her voice was pleasant, just the trace of an Italian accent. 'Dear Master Kilsyth, how pleasant to meet you at last.' She raised him from his knees. 'Your father was a good friend to me and the king.'

'Aye, he was out for Your Majesties with Claverhouse. I've come to offer my sword in the same great cause.' Bloody liar.

'And this is . . .?' She turned to the Bratchet who'd sunk into an impressive curtsey – Kilsyth must have trained her.

'A kinswoman of mine, Your Majesty, and your devoted subject. Her mother was French. May I present Mistress Le Fay.'

'La Fée?' said Modena, 'How appropriate for one so fairylike and pretty. You are both most welcome to St-Germain, though I fear we are grossly overcrowded.'

She turned to me. 'And this gentleman?'

'My body servant, ma'am.'

'Ah.' Obviously body servants were a glut on the market at St-Germain.

'Though,' said Kilsyth quickly, 'he has the skilled hand with horses.'

'Ah.' Apparently there were more servants than horses. Mary Beatrice brightened. 'Can he cure the cough in a horse?'

'Ma'am,' said Kilsyth, 'he can make a dead quadruped jump fences.'

'Only,' said Modena, 'King Louis confided to us last week that his stables at Marly are much troubled by the cough.' She smiled at me. 'Perhaps he would not mind being our present to His Majesty.'

Oh, not at all. And thank you, you kilted bastard.

The audience closed with Kilsyth asking after the health of Francesca Bard, 'also my distant kinswoman'.

Modena gave another of her regretful 'Ah's. 'It is a happiness to us that we can provide comfort to the last years of such a distinguished and afflicted lady. But at the moment her maid has taken her to Polombières for the cure.'

The old girl's senile, I thought. Serve 'em right.

So there it was. Livingstone of Kilsyth and his very distant kinswoman, Mlle La Fée, stayed at the court of Mary of Modena while I was packed off to cure the Sun King's horses at the Château of Marly, some fifteen miles away.

*

The Bratchet shared a room and a bed with Mme Putti, who was seventy and snored, and Mme di Fiorenza, who was eighty-two and snored, and had an unreliable bladder. The room was windowless, an *entresol*, squeezed between Princess Louise's private apartments and the staircase known as L'Escalier du Pape, after an ancient pontiff who'd once ascended it. It was dark – they were economizing on candles – and low ceilinged. Its atmosphere gained an extra something during the nights from Mme de Fiorenza's bladder and the presence of Turnspit under the bed. In the daytime they had to evacuate it completely, spending time off duty around empty state rooms or in the gardens, to give Mrs Fitzsimmons, who attended on Her Majesty at nights, and her husband a chance of some uxorial privacy.

With care, Bratchet felt her way to the ewer and bowl on the ormolu table, washed, then groped for the clothes horse and dressed. Her companions' snores vibrated the door latch as she lifted it and went out, with Turnspit following her.

Immediately she stood, transfixed, in glory and sunlight. The landing's enormous window cast a rainbow through the coloured fleurs-de-lys in its centre on to the bust of Henri IV on a corner plinth. A broken pane let in fresh, morning air and the smell of autumn from the terraces that stepped down to the Seine. For over eight months this view had greeted her every morning, and every morning she was astounded by its grandeur. The smudge of smoke twelve miles away was Paris. There were only two metaphorical clouds on the rest of Bratchet's horizon.

The first was that Anne Bonny was not at St-Germain, and never had been. Kilsyth had immediately made enquiries – carefully; it would not have been healthy for the court of Mary of Modena to suspect that their Episcopalian supporters in Scotland, whom he represented, were losing patience with her son James and were beginning to look round for a more tractable Stuart to put on the throne when Queen Anne finally laid down her sceptre.

In fact, his circumspection wasn't necessary. The exiles at St-Germain were so fanatical in their loyalty to the Pretender it didn't occur to them that anyone calling himself a Jacobite could be less so. Most of them would not have considered a Protestant to be worthy of the crown in any case. Their dream of regaining power in England included restoring it to the Old Religion and they felt nothing but pride in young James III's refusal to abandon his Catholicism. Some of them had heard the name Anne Bard, a few had listened patiently while her grandmother talked of her, but none had ever seen her.

When this became apparent, Kilsyth dejectedly took the miserable Bratchet for a walk in the gardens – the only part of that overcrowded château where they could talk without being overheard.

'Ye'll think I misguided ye, mistress,' he apologized, 'but I was assured Bonny Anne was here.'

'Well, she ain't. Who assured you?'

'Her own grandmother. Francesca Bard as ever was.'

'Who ain't here neither,' Bratchet pointed out, 'What was she supposed to have said?'

'I'll not say but it was a chancy business, exchanging words with yon death's-headed Blackader looking on, but the French captain was clear enough. Mme Bard had received my message and, should I wish to meet again the lady known as Anne Bonny, to bring Mistress Bratchet to the track after dark.'

'She said to bring me? Must have been Anne then. But where is she?'

Kilsyth shrugged. 'It appears ye'll have to wait for the return of Francesca to discover that.'

'An' she's loony by all accounts. Mme Putti says she's *décousue* in her wits.' She suddenly caught on to what the Scotsman had said. 'What you mean *I'll* have to wait for her? Where you going?'

'Mistress, I canna batten on Her Majesty's bounty. I'm off to the wars to fight for the cause.'

'What cause? Against England you mean? Against your own country?'

'England's no country of mine.'

'It is now.'

152

News had just come through of the Scottish Parliament's agreement to union with England, throwing the entire court into fury.

'Never.' Kilsyth's shout shook a congregation of pigeons out of a nearby tree and into the air. 'Never, mistress. There'll be no end to the auld song for the Highlands, though a thousand treacherous carrion in Edinburgh sell them to the perfidious Sasunnoch.'

So he went, leaving a second cloud on Bratchet's sky.

At first she was lonely without him and without Anne Bonny, and not a little frightened. Only her adoration for them both would have tempted her to burn her boats by crossing into France. She wasn't such a fool that she didn't know she'd probably said goodbye to England for ever by doing so. But what had England ever done for her?

On the other hand, what had the France of Louis XIV done for her parents who'd had to escape it?

But then, a few days after Kilsyth's departure, Mary of Modena made her a *deuxième femme* of the bedchamber.

It was a very considerable compliment, especially to a skivvy from Puddle Court, but the previous fifteen or so months had wrought a considerable change in the Bratchet. Her manners had profited immensely from her stay with the Chelsea widow, as had her deportment from Kilsyth's dancing lessons. While her spoken English was still pure Cockney, her French was unaccented and not ungraceful.

It would have been nice to believe the exiled queen had chosen her because she thought Bratchet could ornament her personal staff. But Bratchet had accreted a hard stratum of gumption during her seven years in Puddle Court and guessed that Modena had picked her out because she was a neutral choice.

Had the queen filled the vacant post with one of the long-serving Irish exiles at St-Germain, or the Scottish, or the French, or English, or Italians, the passed-over contingents that set such store by the privileges of court, meaningless as they were, would have been thrown into fury against the others. As it was, they found common cause in despising the queen's taste in choosing the newcomer, Bratchet. Which was better than a feud and forgotten quicker.

Nevertheless, Bratchet hadn't experienced so much kindness in her life that she didn't respond to it. She kissed Mary of Modena's hand with real gratitude. And Mary Beatrice had said with the modesty which distinguished her, 'Remember, my child, we both owe our estate to God and King Louis.'

Bratchet did remember. Every morning when she looked out of the window outside her *entresol* she remembered it. A faint voice from her French childhood said: 'We are Huguenots, little one. King Louis has gone back on his word and is trying to force us into popery. We must go to England to be free.'

But every morning it grew fainter. She *was* free. She had the freedom of one of the most beautiful places on earth. For the first time in her life she had dignity, the consequence of serving a woman who was as fair and exalted as Effie Sly had been foul and low.

The exiles said there was no palace in England to compare with St-Germain-en-Laye and she believed them; it was the birthplace of the Grand Monarque, Louis XIV, and a mark of how kindly he'd regarded James II after that poor king's ejection from England that he'd given it to him, along with a pension – and allowed James's widow, Mary of Modena, to keep both.

The gratitude which suffused St-Germain for King Louis was infectious and Bratchet caught it. After all, King Louis's was the sun which radiated her every view, his the name lauded alongside God's during prayers in Mary of Modena's white and gilded chapel, he the ultimate pivot which had swung her from Puddle Court into her present, glorious estate.

It was so glorious that Bratchet began to swallow everything pertaining to it: Mary Beatrice of Modena was the real Queen of England, Anne was merely a usurper. She had less enthusiasm than everybody else about putting Mary's son on the English throne – so far she hadn't seen James, who was in the French army – but she was prepared to admit he might have a right to it.

Most of all, Bratchet was free of her past. She'd received the gift of anonymity; nobody here knew of the squalor to which her body and soul had been subjected and she was trying hard to forget it herself. *Joie-de-vivre* came first in fleeting moments, then for longer and longer periods until it was now almost her permanent state.

And with it all she was realizing she was pretty. In a court living in terror of smallpox its scars were an indemnification, a battle honour. In any case, powder and rouge were *de rigueur* for ladies in France and Bratchet had learned to use them. Awareness of her own worth, which began when she left England, had galloped into confirmation at St-Germain. Pretty La Fée she had become, dressing in St-Germain castoffs which, in turn, were castoffs from the ladies of Versailles but still a hundred times more flattering to her than anything she'd worn before.

There were no young men at St-Germain. Like Kilsyth, they were in Louis's army fighting with the young James Francis Edward against Marlborough and his allies. But there were plenty of old men to reinforce her new opinion of her looks with their compliments and backstairs attempts to kiss her. Bratchet absorbed the flattery and rebuffed the fumbles without difficulty; compared with the gallants of Puddle Court, Jacobite lechers were still in the nursery.

She swept down the staircase for the sake of sweeping down it – it was for the nobility, not their servants, but the Habsburgs, Medicis and other royalty whose portraits hung above the stairs remained impervious to her *lèse majesté*.

Her third-hand high heels clicking on marble made the only sound. St-Germain rose late. Later still it would be different. Today the palace would be in a hubbub, borrowed coaches waiting outside while the queen inspected the livery of her accompanying staff to make sure that the darns and worn patches didn't show. Then they would be off to Marly. *She* would be off to Marly. She would see the Sun King. She would also – at this her feelings became mixed – see Martin Millet.

At the bottom of the stairs she had to nip up them again through a complexity of corridors to a way out into the gardens. Turnspit, used to this daily performance, had waited for her on the landing. Before they went out, they foraged in the larder shared by the bedchamber women. Somebody had broken open the cupboard in which Mme Putti had locked the chocolate her son had sent her, and stolen it. There'd be trouble. Food was short at St-Germain. Mme Putti complained of hunger all the time and was indeed losing weight, though she had plenty to spare.

Lifting salver lids, all of them marked with a name and a '*Ne touchez pas*', Bratchet found a sausage on its last legs and gave it to Turnspit. For herself, she shaved off some pieces of cheese from the supplies and took the end of a stale baguette.

Out in the open air she made her way to the yew walk, her favourite, with views glimpsed like secrets through its arches. Turnspit lifted his leg against the surround of a fountain designed by Le Vau. It wasn't playing, its bowl was full of leaves. The yew was becoming blurred for lack of cutting and the gods and goddesses in its niches had weeds around their feet. St-Germain-en-Laye residents were too well-born to work and too poor to employ servants on the scale necessary for its upkeep but to the Bratchet its delapidation cast a fairytale element over its grandeur, making it friendly, a Sleeping Beauty castle. Dr MacLaverty, who was teaching her Latin, told her that Pan sprang down from his plinth on moonlit nights and piped life into his fellow statues, and she believed him.

She rounded a corner and almost ran into the old man – Dr MacLaverty, not Pan – hobbling towards the encroaching forest with his valet, a crossbow and a ferocious expression. 'Not a word, now, girl,' he said as he passed, 'Ye've not seen us.'

She curtseyed and winked a silent 'good luck'.

The last time he'd shot a deer he'd presented her with a collop of venison that had kept her and Mesdames Putti and di Fiorenza fed for a week, but hunting Louis XIV's deer was one of the few liberties Louis XIV did not extend to his guests; Jove had frowned, a complaint had come thundering from Versailles to St-Germain where, mortified, Mary of Modena had reproved her court, forbidding any more poaching, so the pretence went on that the game which adorned her table on high days was a gift sent express by loyal Jacobites in England.

Used to erratic hunger – the good days on which Effie had overfed her occurred between weeks of near-starvation – Bratchet found it a small price to pay for the surrounding beauty. When she'd pointed this out to Mme Putti, that lady said, '*Je meurs de faim. Merde à la beauté*,' distressing the Bratchet to whom the French of *la noblesse* was the language of manners. Her love of its elegance, like her mind, grew with her knowledge of it. She used English rarely; her English accent and vocabulary belonged to Puddle Court and came in handy only for swearing.

It distressed her, too, that St-Germainers should behave little better than Puddle Courters, but irascible gentry fought each other as often here as did men on London docksides, though they duelled with swords rather than knives or fists, while women whose aristocracy was beyond question could, and did, scream at each other like fishwives.

The behaviour of Puddle Court and St-Germain, if she'd been prepared to recognize it, came from similar causes – poverty and overcrowding. With their fortunes spent on a cause that had been in abeyance too long, bored, homesick, frightened that they would die before the rightful Stuart regained the throne of England, only stubborn courage kept the St-Germainers faithful. But it didn't stop them quarrelling.

As she went back to her room to help Mme di Fiorenza get up, Bratchet heard raised voices from along the corridor where the Irish among the exiles had formed a ghetto.

'I tell ye he gave it me.'

'You realize we shall have to ask him.'

'Ask then, and be damned. I'll not have me word questioned. Me seconds shall call on you tomorrow.'

From the darkness of the *entresol*, Bratchet heard Mme di Fiorenza's quaver: 'What is passing out there?' and went in to her.

'It's the clock again. You remember, madame, it stood on the mantelpiece in Donal Macdonnel's room and he pawned it. Mr Macdonnel swears King Louis gave it to him, but Mr Dicconson doesn't believe him and he's going to write and ask His Majesty whether he did or not. And Mr Macdonnel's just challenged him to a duel.'

Dicconson, the queen's treasurer, was as unlikely to accept the challenge as Louis XIV was to have given one of St-Germain's ormolu clocks to an indigent Irish exile, but Mme di Fiorenza was interested enough in the contretemps to permit herself to be got out of bed – usually an exercise which caused unpleasantness in which she called Bratchet a nagging, jumped-up member of the *canaille*, not fit to share a lady's bed let alone force her out of it.

Bratchet had to put up with a lot of that sort of thing – and not just from Mme di Fiorenza. There had been much resentment among the court women that a chit of a girl with unknown ancestry should have been favoured with a post in the royal bedchamber – a post that guaranteed her two meals a day, if not a salary.

But the Bratchet's obvious joy in her position was breaking down opposition, while her will to please and imperviousness to insults – they were pinpricks compared to what Effie Sly could hand out – were earning her the grudging liking of the queen's ladies.

It was difficult for them. 'Who is she?' 'Where does she come from?' 'Why is she here?' Down to the lowest scullion, everybody at St-Germain fitted into the pigeon-hole accorded by their birth. It dictated where they were placed at table, whether they sat, if they sat at all, in the royal presence, which servant carried out which duty, which hand rocked which cradle.

Bratchet escaped definition. Queen Mary had accepted her without question as Kilsyth's kinswoman. But others asked questions. Who was her father/mother? Where her birthplace? Her French was not of the *noblesse*, though, on the other hand, neither was the Italian Mary of Modena's.

Bratchet kept quiet; an orphaned Huguenot whose father had been in trade would have found no acceptance at all in this court of aristocratic Papists. She just wished Kilsyth could have prepared her with a provenance before he'd dashed off to the wars.

No word came to her from Francesca Bard, though the old lady had sent Mary of Modena a letter asking Her Majesty's permission to go into retreat for a few months at a convent in

Nantes when she'd finished tasting the waters of Polombières. Mary Beatrice had granted her permission with speed; there were too many elderly women eating their heads off at her table for her to mind sparing one of them for a while.

It meant that Bratchet had to wait before she could question Francesca about Anne, but in the hiatus she began adding two and two together. *Shall I be Queen of England, Bratchet? Come and be queen with me.* She put what she'd learned from Anne herself of Anne's place on the royal Stuart tree together with her growing knowledge of England's political situation – it was discussed ad nauseam at St-Germain – and found they fitted. Taken alongside other bits and pieces she'd picked up from me and Daniel Defoe in England, she made a crude but accurate analysis.

It came to this: Martin Millet was acting for Daniel Defoe who was acting for someone of importance in England's hierarchy. They were hunting Anne Bonny. Either to make her a pawn in some royal gambit or, by killing her, to remove her from the board. (Dr MacLaverty was teaching Bratchet to play chess.) Martin Millet had been sent to Europe to find Mary Read in order to track down Anne Bonny. He'd brought Bratchet along to identify Mary. And Anne Bonny when he found her. He was using her. He was a pig.

Livingstone of Kilsyth was also hunting Anne Bonny. His people really did want Anne on the throne and wouldn't kill her. He also was using Bratchet, but respectfully. He wasn't a pig.

Having arrived at these conclusions and decided that at the moment there was nothing to be done about them, Bratchet settled down to enjoy what she could of the situation. She was here because she was here. Puddle Court had happened to her. Much more nicely, St-Germain was happening to her. Swing low, swing high. 'In Arcadia ego' was a sentiment she'd picked up from her Latin lessons and, by God, she would enjoy Arcadia while she had it.

And today, she was going to Marly.

But even the determinedly blissful Bratchet was forced to admit that getting under way was a bugger. She had to deal with a noisy quarrel that had broken out between Countess Molza and Mme di Fiorenza.

Then there was the drama of finding that the riding habit, which the Dauphine had kindly sent over from Versailles for Princess Louise Marie to wear if King Louis invited her to go hunting during her visit to Marly, was too big. Mary of Modena was not sure she should wear it at all: 'I cannot bear that anyone should give you presents when we cannot make suitable return,' she told her daughter.

Louise Marie became desperate. 'But read what she says, maman. That she hopes Your Majesty will excuse the liberty in sending her own hunting dress for me, the time being too short to allow of my having a new one made on purpose. *C'est très gentille, ça.*' Wincing, the queen allowed the liberty and her women, titled and untitled, were pressed into altering the habit fast.

Bratchet was sorry for Louise Marie, a beautiful girl, who, as England's true Princess Royal, should have been able to take her pick of eligible princes but whose marital prospects were declining as fast as her fortune. Her mother was trying to arrange an engagement for her with the Duc de Berry, heir apparent to the throne of Spain, but the match was becoming unlikely as Louise Marie's poverty meant she could appear less and less often at the jewelled court of Versailles.

'You must shine at Marly this time, *chérie.*'

But when they were alone Mme Putti looked down her nose and told Bratchet: '*Elle ne possède pas le chic.*'

Bratchet didn't know what *chic* was but, in her view, if it wasn't to be found at St-Germain it wasn't worth having.

Then there was unpleasantness from those of the queen's women who hadn't been chosen to accompany her to Marly. They wanted to know why she'd picked Bratchet, but Mary of Modena was conforming to King Louis's known taste for seeing only the prettiest people, even servants, around him at his summer palace.

Then there was panic when one of the matching – and borrowed – carriage horses was found to be limping and a hack had to replace it in the shafts. 'We should have kept that fella who came here with you,' said Captain Davy Lloyd to Bratchet as he tried to marshal the cavalcade. 'What's his name?'

'Millet, sir,' said Bratchet reluctantly, 'Martin Millet.'

'Damned genius with the gee-gees, they tell me.'

And a pig, thought Bratchet.

Clambering into the servants' cart which was to follow the royal coaches, Bratchet wondered how she would feel when, if, she encountered the pig during her stay at Marly. She was enough of a St-Germainer by now to classify him. *Canaille?* Or, which was almost worse by St-Germain standards, a *bourgeois*? No, as nephew to Effie Sly he belonged among the rabble.

Either way, she'd risen above him. Poor soul, if he tried to persuade her to return to her old life, she would point out that she was no longer the manipulated creature he had once enlisted to help him find Anne Bonny and Mary Read for his masters, whoever they were.

The thought sweetened an already pretty journey as they trundled through forest in which the autumn birch and beech trees appeared illuminated from inside by the sun. She caught glimpses of deer browsing in dappled, tail-twitching groups among the glades.

The landscape was let down by the hamlets they went through; shoddy collections of patched cottages sheltering thin animals and people and displaying a poverty that Bratchet did not remember seeing when she and Martin Millet had journeyed across England's East Anglia on their way to the boat for Holland.

The men working in their fields straightened their backs and raised their caps to Mary of Modena's emblazoned coach going by, but the salute was made sullenly, without enthusiasm or curiosity. 'They don't seem very happy,' Bratchet remarked to her fellow *deuxième femme*, Frances Smith. It seemed extraordinary to her that the gold of this forest and its king had left its inhabitants ungilded.

Frances raised her eyebrows. 'They're peasants, dear.'

Frances was a good travelling companion; she had started in the Stuarts' service as wet nurse to the baby Prince James

Francis and shared his exile from the first, but even now she was only in her mid-thirties and had been judged still comely enough to accompany Mary of Modena on this visit to Marly, as she had on others.

'Think yourself lucky we're not having to travel with King Louis, dear. He has no regard for ladies' needs, not a bit. His coaches are never allowed to stop on the way for calls of nature, never. And the poor ladies who travel with him – he insists on giving them sweetmeats and cakes and *sirops* all the way, and they daren't refuse, just daren't. By the time they get to Marly, they're bursting. I once saw the poor Dauphine, and she was pregnant, alight from the coach and run, really run, into the nearest building to piss – and it was the chapel, dear. Think of it.'

Bratchet thought of it with alarm. 'Is he cruel, then?'

'Oh no, dear. What a thing to say. He's the kindest man ever, and polite – the times he's passed me and raised his hat as if I were Mme de Maintenon herself.'

There had been darker days for women at the French court, Frances said, but since the advent of the religious Mme de Maintenon, first the king's mistress and now his wife, propriety was the thing – even towards female servants – as the King reordered his previously lustful private life to placate his God and save his soul.

'No man has done more for the faith,' said Frances, 'Only think of the thousands of Protestant souls who were returned to the true religion when he revoked the Nantes Edict.'

King Louis has gone back on his word and is trying to force us into popery.

But the whisper barely registered. They had come up over a rise and below them was Marly. It was like looking down into a Titan's bowl of pot-pourri; contained in a surround of hills and trees was colour, all the reds in the spectrum – corals, peaches, pinks, plums and salmons. Only a great emperor could have commanded so many flowers in one place at one time. But it was the scent that staggered Bratchet's senses; roses and gillieflowers and lime responded to the sun's warmth with a perfume that permeated the air in all directions for miles.

Later, staying in it, she was to find that Marly had all the stinks common to human existence; cooking, sewage, woodsmoke, sweat, bad breath, the manure of livestock and dog dirt, but for that moment, on the hillside, Bratchet's nostrils were allowed the air that awaited saints as they entered paradise.

Marly was Louis XIV's dolls' house, a playground where the stringent rules of etiquette applied at Versailles relaxed to the extent that guests could join the king on his walks. They were even allowed to eat with him, as long as their conversations were whispered – Louis himself remaining silent during mealtimes.

The simplicity was studied. At a cost of eleven million francs, the original narrow and marshy valley had been drained and terraced. Entire woods had been transplanted into its soil from Compiègne and, where there had been indigenous woodland, the ground cleared to make a lake. The Cascade, a cataract which fell down a steep hill behind Marly, had been tamed and piped to spout its ice-clear water through the mouths of fifty fountains.

Shaded by lime trees was the royal residence, a square, two-storeyed building of white stone commanding flowered terraces which proceeded downwards from it, flanked by twelve low pavilions, the guests' quarters – six each side – representing the signs of the zodiac and connected to each other by trellised walks.

Quincunxes of more limes screened the Perspective, a larger structure which housed the kitchens, less exalted guests and, in its attics, the guests' personal servants.

'That's where we sleep,' said Frances Smith, pointing, 'and if you think we're crowded at St-Germain, wait till you've slept six-a-bed here. Even the king's brother has to give up his apartment for the guests to use as public rooms during the daytime.'

Cramped it might be but an invitation to Marly was the ambition of every aspirant to power, the final distinction. Frances had seen them, the petitioners lining Versailles' Galerie des Glaces, reminding the king of their desire with a murmured 'Sire, Marly', and Louis nodding at the favoured few and disappointing the hopes of the hundreds of others by ignoring them – though he liked them to persist in asking.

On the drive down into the valley the servants' carts turned away to go round to the Perspective by a back route while Mary of Modena's coach went on to the main gates where Louis would pay her the honour of greeting her in person and conduct her to his hall for refreshments. 'And allow her to sit in his presence,' enthused Frances, 'What a great and good man he is.'

Later, when they had settled Queen Mary into her apartment in Sagittarius pavilion, Bratchet was permitted to rove the grounds – keeping away, of course, from the areas reserved for royalty and guests. Even here every view was scented and entrancing. Bratchet, exploring an angelic sound coming from a grove, found a quartet of musicians playing airs by Lully as beech leaves fell on their music-stands. She knew she was encountering a grace of majesty that the world had never seen before and, probably, never would again.

To be a guest at Marly required stamina. There was at least one masked and one fancy-dress ball during the stay and each continued until dawn, although that did not excuse the dancers from attending mass next morning. One was tempted to snooze during the theatricals put on the next night – under Mme de Maintenon's influence such entertainments had become worthy, Molière's once-favoured comedies being dropped in favour of semi-religious pieces like *Esther* or *Athalie* – but the king's eye, though it frequently drooped on its own account, noticed any such *lèse majesté*.

The days were packed with excursions, fêtes, al fresco picnics, gondola races on the lake, boar hunts, wolf hunts, stag hunts, followed by evenings of cards or billiards. Then there were the practical jokers, frowned on at Versailles but given licence at Marly, who enjoyed placing petards under the beds of unsuspecting old ladies so that sleep was disturbed by the sound of light explosions and screams.

The king rationed his appearances, spending part of the day working in the quiet of Mme de Maintenon's apartment and often retiring early, but he kept himself informed of those attending his entertainments and noted those who did not. His solicitous enquiry to absentees, 'I hope you are not bored,' was a sentence of social death; there would be no more invitations to Marly.

Mary of Modena's large dark eyes began to show signs of fatigue; she would have infinitely preferred to be in retreat with the nuns of the convent at Chaillot where she increasingly escaped her debts and problems, but for the sake of Louise Marie's future she had to persist in displaying enjoyment until Mme de Maintenon, a kindred soul, took pity on her and invited the exiled queen to her own rooms for periods of religious contemplation which the king was not allowed to censure or disturb.

For Louise Marie the whirling programme was blissful after the privation and monotony of St-Germain and her gaiety attracted Louis's approval, but Bratchet was forced to see what Mme Putti had meant when she said the child lacked *chic*. The girl's natural looks and manner contrasted sharply with the ladies of the Sun King's court where genuineness, like marital fidelity, was unfashionable. With their white faces and startlingly red japanned cheeks, their studied wit, the artificiality of their laughter, their jewels and wonderful dresses, they provided a stage on which Louise Marie appeared a provincial.

In contrast to their mistress, Bratchet and the queen's other serving women were on holiday. For once an army of auxiliaries took off their hands the laundry, mending and cleaning. Apart from dressing the queen every morning, changing her for the various functions and helping her to bed at night, they were free to enjoy themselves.

The cavorting of the nobility was entertainment in itself. Gaping through the banisters at the masked ball, she saw the Duc de Valentinois, suddenly grown to ten feet tall and disguised as a lady, stride into the ballroom and open his cloak to allow a troupe of Italian acrobats to come tumbling out from between his stilts.

There was as much going on in the servants' hall where the valets and *femmes de chambre* aped their betters with their own theatricals and dancing. Though regarded as English rustics,

165

the St-Germain servants were permitted to join in but Bratchet found the attentions of the lackeys, known from their livery as the *garçons bleus*, very trying. 'The bastards keep goosing my bum,' she complained to Frances Smith.

Frances advised her to keep her back to the wall. 'They think we're fair game because the queen depends on Louis's charity.'

Bratchet spent as much time in the Marly kitchens as possible; the food prepared in those sweating, noisy, copper-potted shrines to haute cuisine not only gave her taste new values but was apparently limitless. The guests at Marly fed like fighting-cocks, and Louis XIV out-ate them all. Bratchet, watching a procession of salvers being carried to his room on which were four plates of different soups, a whole pheasant, a partridge, a large plate of salad, mutton *à l'ail*, two slices of ham, a selection of pastries, fruit and hard-boiled eggs, was forced to ask: '*C'est pour lui seulement?*'

The chef looked pityingly at her; Mary of Modena's skimpy appetite only confirmed her inferior status and, therefore, that of her women. '*Il mange pour la royaume.*' Even between meals, *la royaume* was followed around by trays of sweetmeats, cakes and candied fruits, all of which he emptied.

There was no check on the kitchens and Louis's serving household ate as well as their king – and so, very nearly, did his swine; vats of leftovers which could have fed the St-Germain exiles for a week were sent to the royal pigsties every day. Bratchet ate until she surfeited, padding the flesh on her bones for the first time in her life.

What she did not do was visit the stables.

But ... 'We must enquire for Master Millet,' said Mary of Modena after the first week. 'He is still of our household and we would not let our good Kilsyth think his man is forgotten. La Fée, my dear, do you go and ask after his health.'

For once Bratchet damned the queen's thoughtfulness, but she had to go. On her way through the grounds she reiterated the attitude she would take. Coolness and dignity. The tables had been turned, she was in the ascendant, he the inferior now. So she told herself, but inside her, like the first few bubbles floating to the surface of water about to boil, emotions began to rise – fury, resentment, something else, feelings she did not recognize for what they were, except that they were difficult to control.

The stables were like an abbey. From the paved road, the arches around the horses' doors gave the impression of a cloister. As she neared them she saw a man coming away. The sun was in her eyes and cast an aureole round a stout figure that walked with the deliberate step of the elderly. Only when he'd come close did she recognize him – and sank to the ground in the deepest curtsey she could manage.

Louis XIV raised his hat. Like everything else he did, the gesture was measured. It accorded in reverse courtesy to the status of the salutee and was therefore lifted to its highest for serving wenches like Bratchet: dukes received the merest tilt.

Sun and respect kept Bratchet's eyes down; she saw only his shoes with their famous red heels, like a magician's, as he passed her. Perhaps he was a magician. For sixty years he had ruled France, expanding its territory and making it so powerful that lesser nations had been forced to band together against it to stop being swallowed up. She stayed crouched on the road, watching him as he went away from her, this creator of beauty and sunlight.

The encounter increased her contempt for the insignificant mortal she was about to see, and she got up, squaring her shoulders, to show Millet how insignificant he was, to her, to everybody.

I can't say that Louis XIV's head stableman at Marly, Jacques Vardes, had welcomed having a supposed Scottish Jacobite exile imposed on his workforce. The workforce didn't give me an easy time of it either. But when I'd arrived, which was in early spring, Vardes was in trouble; nearly every horse in the stable was off-colour – and during most weekends of the coming summer his king would be bringing a crowd of guests with him from Versailles, all of them expecting to ride. Louis kept a string of saddle-horses at Marly and brought only his heavy horses with him, but even these would be at risk from infection if the resident animals didn't get better. And Louis, I gathered, wasn't a man to listen to excuses.

To begin with Vardes didn't listen to me, either. He was a first-class stableman but, like everybody else belonging to the French Court, he suspected any idea that had come in since the twelfth century.

The horses actually had sore throat, as Vardes knew, a condition which makes them cough when they try to swallow. Old Vardes was still treating them by blistering, if you'll believe it, and applying poultices. In the Dragoons, I never poulticed for throat unless it looked like the animal was developing strangles.

My French only extended to Parlary, not an easy tongue to be tactful in, and Vardes resented my suggestions. He was desperate, though. Eventually he gave me a free hand with four of the beasts. I made a hospital out of a disused stable, put a bed for myself in its hay loft and began hot water applications with a diet of linseed gruel, scalded hay and treacle.

The long and short of it was that we saved the lot, all except one whose wind had gone. Vardes was grateful and stopped the other stable lads trying to beat me up at nights. He must have mentioned me to Louis when he came because in no time the king and I were chatting old dandy every time he visited the stables.

I'll always believe that as a king Louis XIV was one of the bloodiest tyrants ever spawned. More millions died because of his dream of empire than were dispatched by Genghis Khan and all the barbarian hordes put together. But as a man he had charm, especially to those with technical skill who weren't afraid of him. I think he was more at ease with people like me and his smiths, gardeners and builders than he was with most of the aristocrats who surrounded him.

He couldn't abide sickness, though, in humans or animals. The afternoon that Bratchet came to the stables, I remember, he'd just paid one of his visits. During our talk I asked him if he'd like to see Montsaunès, one of his favourite hunters, who'd had the bats. He shook his head and said, *'Pas pendant qu'il souffre.'*

After he'd gone, I went into the hospital block and gave old Monty his linseed mash and a cheering up in English. 'Never writes, never calls does he? Neglects you, eh? That's kings for you, matey, I should turn republican if I was you.' Outside I could hear the stable lads whistling and catcalling, indicating that something female had come into the yard, but I didn't take any notice.

She'd probably been watching me for some minutes before I looked up and saw her. She stood under one of the circular, fretted windows that ran the length of the building so that the light fell on her.

There were a fair number of comings and goings between Marly and St-Germain so I'd been able to keep track of her. Still, I was relieved to see her. And there was no point bearing a grudge for the mess she'd got us in. After all, I hadn't consulted her when I'd dragged her to Flanders – I'd thought I was saving her life, but I hadn't told her that. To be honest, I hadn't thought her capable of much understanding then.

I could see she was now. She looked a different person. She was wearing the shepherdess sort of dress that was the French fashion just then. It suited her. But the greatest change was in the cock of her head, the confident set of her shoulders, most of all her eyes. She had the air of a woman who'd discovered herself, and liked what she found.

At that moment, she was also looking at me as if I was something to compost the roses with. I rolled my shirtsleeves down.

'Hello, young Bratchet,' I said, 'You look well.'

She said, 'Her Majesty, Queen Mary, sends to ask if all is well with you and if you are being treated kindly.'

'Thank Her Majesty. Tell her Louis loves me. I'm the best thing that's ever happened to his horseflesh and he's just walked over here to tell me so.'

She turned away as if to go and I had to hobble the length of the stalls to stop her. 'Come on, Bratchet. I've sent time and again to ask after your health.'

'Don't call me Bratchet,' she said, 'I'm Mademoiselle La Fée, *deuxième femme de chambre* to the rightful Queen of England. And you're . . . a common horse-feeder.'

169

Gone to *la mer*, she had, and swallowed the bloody anchor.

I said: 'I'm an exceptionally good horse-feeder.'

She looked down her nose. 'The whole of France can't produce linseed mash on a par with Master Millet's?'

'No,' I said, 'it can't. As a matter of fact, the whole of France *and* its king knows fuck-all about horses. It couldn't recognize a decent mount if one bit it in the arse. There was a nag drawing a coal cart in Paris the other day we'd have snapped up for the cavalry. A coal cart, I ask you. Bloody Frogs.'

She wasn't interested in horses. 'You're allowed to travel?'

'I tell you, Br . . . mademoiselle, Louis and I are like *that* . . .' crossing third and index fingers. ' "Louis, my man," I tell him, "I've invented a new snaffle but your blacksmith here's about as useless at engineering as tits on a bull." "Right ho, Martin," says Louis, "feel free to use Le Brun's workshops in Paris any time you need to." '

'Haven't found it necessary to escape then,' she sneered.

'Not yet.'

'My, my,' she said nastily, 'have we discovered France has its advantages?'

'France is a shit-hole,' I told her, 'ruled by a bastard. I'm not ready to go yet. But when I do you'd best come with me.'

'Back to Puddle Court? Fine one you are to talk about shit-holes.'

I took her arm and made her sit down on a straw bale and squatted in front of her. 'I've worried about you, Bratchet. I've sent a dozen times to find out if you're safe.'

'Of course I'm safe. And don't call me Bratchet.'

'Look, you ought to know this, the somebody who was meaning you no good in England has got a long reach. Remember that ship when we crossed to Flanders?'

'No.' She was being deliberately stupid.

'Going off with a bloody Scotchman,' I grumbled, 'You ought to've had more sense. Ain't done the decent thing and married you yet, has he?'

'Don't you dare, you . . . he . . .' She remembered she was dignified. 'It wasn't a question of that. He was merely escorting me to meet Anne Bonny.'

'Seen her yet?'

'No, but her grandmother lives at St-Germain.'

'Seen *her* yet?' I nodded when she didn't answer. 'There's dirty work at the crossroads, Bratchet. You watch out for yourself.'

She turned on me. 'Talking of dirty work and crossroads,' she said, 'why're you after Anne? I know who she is, oh yes. And friends of mine heard you talking to that fancy-faggot in the Beggar Maker, Deforge or whoever he was.'

'Defoe.'

'Defoe. I didn't make sense of it then but I do now. You're her enemy, you gammy bastard. They transported her and you're working for them. What d'you want with her? You leave her alone.'

'Hold on a minute,' I said. The kicker who'd come into the hospital to be cured was lashing out again. I got up to see to him and retied the bundle of gorse which he'd dislodged from the stall post so that his leg would be scratched when he kicked out again

'Got to learn the hard way, you stupid bugger,' I told him. I went back to Bratchet. 'Anne Bonny.'

'Anne Bonny,' she nodded.

'If I told you all I want is to find out who killed Aunt Effie and Anne Bonny's part of the answer, would you believe me?'

'Who killed Aunt Effie, who killed Aunt Effie,' she mimicked, 'Who cares who killed her? She deserved it.'

'Nobody deserves it. And you ask your Scotchman why *he's* hunting your friend Anne. Got plans of his own for her, he has.'

'He may have or he may not,' she said, 'but he didn't transport her like your lot and he's not invading Scotland like the other lot. So there's for you.'

'Who's invading Scotland? When?' I asked a bit sharpish which took her aback. But she shrugged. Apparently it was an open secret at St-Germain that the Pretender was planning to invade Scotland. 'The expedition's just waiting Louis's approval and troops,' she said, 'In the spring, so they say.'

'But our brave Scotsman's not going with them, eh?'

Nettled, she said, 'At least he doesn't wear an iron hat, like a coward. Livingstone says all the armour a Highlander needs when he goes to war is his targe, his claymore and his courage.'

'More fool him.'

She stood up and almost hit me. I was deliberately infuriating her but she'd infuriated me, her and her bloody targes and claymores. Her hands gripped into fists as if she were suffering. I could hear her quick breathing. She whispered, 'I hate you. You left me.'

'What?'

She began batting at me with her hands, almost screaming. 'You left me, you catso, you bleeder. I hate you.'

'What's this? There was no help for it. Modena and your bloody Scotchman got me out of the way.' Then I saw how distressed she was and I sat her back down on the straw. 'Do you want some water?'

'Not then, not then. You left me with Effie Sly.'

'Eh?'

She was sobbing. 'When you joined the army. You came to Puddle Court and said goodbye to her. I was there. I asked you to take me away. In your uniform you were, all splendid. But you wouldn't do it. You knew what she was and you left me with her.'

'Oh, Christ, I'm sorry. I'm sorry, Bratchet.' I didn't know what to do. I tried patting her head and upset her coiffure. 'I didn't realize how bad it would be. I didn't think. Don't cry, for Christ's sake.'

She sobbed on, unable to stop. I got up and fetched an iron cup, pumped water in it and held her chin with one hand, holding it to her mouth with the other. 'I couldn't have taken you to war now, could I? Be reasonable.' I was tipping water down her chin. 'I didn't think. I thought you were . . .'

'What?' She wrenched the cup away and threw it. '*What* did you think I was? Just another bloody drudge? A piece of kitchenware to be used by the lodgers?'

'No, never. But I'm sorry. I had troubles of my own just then, you see.'

'Did you?' All at once she was very calm. 'So did I. I got raped, did you know that? Effie made me slip the baby. Took

172

me to Ma Roberts in Cable Lane. I can't have no more babies now.' She looked at me, almost serene. Sometimes, not often, but sometimes some of the wounded look like that when they know they're going to die. As if they've already been to a place where nobody can follow. She said, '*On m'a volé l'avenir.*'

The kicker was lashing out again. I let him get on with it.

She stood up and smoothed her skirt, looking down at me. 'I'm better now.'

'Good.' I didn't know what else to say.

'I mean I'm better than you. I'm not Bratchet this, Bratchet that any more. I am Mademoiselle La Fée. I can speak Latin. Don't you ever call me Bratchet again.'

She went out. I heard her heels clicking on the cobbles of the yard and the catcalls from the stable lads start up once more. I got up and limped to the door to stop them but they'd fallen quiet by the time I got to the yard. Together we watched the straight, small figure walk under the arch and march through the birch trees towards the château. Into a future she'd said they'd stolen from her.

The lads went back to work but I stood there a long time looking after her. If she'd been a horse I might have cured her. But we treat women worse than horses. Anyway, there wasn't a cure for pain like hers.

CHAPTER TEN

Fourth Extract from *The Madwoman's Journal*

T HEY CAME for William Greg an hour ago. The sound of soldiers' boots and challenges and Greg's screams reached through the palace even up here, to the attics. All the women ran out of their rooms with counterpanes round them, hair anyhow, and hurried downstairs to watch. I dressed. If they arrest me as well I'm not going in my shift.

I was in time to watch him dragged off. I don't think he saw me; he was in terror. Will he tell? Lord, will he tell? The creature in the corner is roaring in triumph so that I can hardly hear anything else and have had to put my door ajar to listen for the soldiers' approach to my room. Between horror of one and dread of the other I can feel my mind going.

Hold there, steersman. Hold. Hold.

To keep sane, I sit at the table in the middle of my room and pare my pen, order my papers and write. I have lit a fire in the grate so that at the first step of boots on the stair I can burn all I have written, though it will be a great pity.

Oh, my dear love, are we to lose our plan after this long voyage towards it? Hold. Hold.

My apparent calm puts the creature out of countenance. She doesn't know what to do and mauls the air as if it were my throat. Her puzzled eyes bulge out at me through the seaweed like huge gooseberries.

Will Greg tell? Only an hour before his arrest he'd crept up here, to this room, for what he called 'loving recreation'. He was so careless. He's one of those who never think to reef till they're dismasted. Suppose somebody saw him, connects me with him?

I was a fool to use him, but I had no other method of communicating with St-Germain to make arrangements for the Bratchet's disposal. And he was a most excellent post office. Though not, it appears now, a consummate traitor.

Owing to the hours of posting, the ministry secretaries do their work here from eleven at night until four o'clock in the morning. It is drudgery, as Greg often complained to me: 'I am the most intelligent fellow in Harley's office and the only one with French,' he would say. He worked for a pittance – hence his treachery – though Harley, who appreciated him, paid him over the usual rate.

He'd been given the job of censoring French prisoners' letters home, which were then sent in a diplomatic bag to France, to Louis XIV's Minister of War. It was easy for him to copy state papers and include them among the letters – and to slip one of mine in with them.

My first letter got through, I know, because I received a reply through the same channels. I sent the woman money and the promise of more when the job was done. We had met when I eventually divested myself of Trooper Johnson and crossed into France from Ghent and made my way to St-Germain to ask for Francesca's help to get me to Jamaica. There was no one else to turn to. I dare trust nobody in England.

Francesca was enthusiastic for any attempt that would put her grand-daughter on the throne – that was how I represented the matter. Her maid, ambitious woman, was even more so, seeing investment in such a plan might repay her a thousand-fold and rescue her from a life of servitude that had no likelihood of a pension at the end of it.

My first letter to them got through, I say, but my second may have been in the batch discovered. Much good may it do them. We had established a code; reference to Bratchet's demise was 'the disposal of the goods' and the signature 'Anne Boleyn'. They'll make nothing from that.

The interesting thing was that the reply to my first letter came from the maid. Francesca has grown feeble-witted in the intervening years. The maid, however, will further the plan by seeing that Bratchet is silenced. If I read her character right, she'll enjoy it.

Will Greg tell? At least I had the sense never to be seen in public with him, knowing how rash he could be. But what if they torture him? The government likes to say that it has banned the use of the rack but there are more ways of skinning a cat than racking it, especially one which has sold state secrets to the enemy.

They've taken him to Newgate. I wonder, should I enquire of the Brotherhood if there's anyone in the dub can kill him? He'll be too well guarded, I fear. No, I must see the night out. If I maintain calm the creature will be unable to claw through my skull into my brains, which she longs to do. I shall keep writing.

The plan was proceeding well, too. Lord, let it continue. Let Greg hold his mouth. Queen Ant had learned to trust me. Carefully, gradually, I showed shock, then disapproval at the Duchess of Marlborough's treatment of her. A gasp would be drawn from me – 'Can she be thus unkind?' – followed by, 'Forgive me, Majesty. I did not mean so bold.'

Queen Ant did not mind in the least. Wounded, humiliated, she feeds on my sympathy. Abigail provides her with enough to swim in, dripping it like a barrel of oil, but she wants more. And always I suggest 'cold tea' to ease her distress. It is our private joke, cold tea, and I have been increasing the amount of brandy in it.

I could be sorry for the woman; she is anxious for her husband whose breath comes harder every day, yet she is harried by Sarah and the Whigs in her cabinet who want her to rid them of Harley. Through Abigail, she is equally harried by Harley, who wants her to rid him of all opposition so that he can be Chancellor and chief minister.

That is where the power lies now – with Abigail and Harley. If Sarah were not blind she would cease her fulminations against Abigail. The more she rants the closer Queen Ant holds to the woman and, therefore, to Harley who is Abigail's puppet-master.

How I have to fawn on that dreary Abigail with attentions and enquiries after her health! She is more difficult to attach than Sarah was, cold-hearted sow that she is, but I have done it. I resorted to an act of great daring to win her. I snubbed Sarah. A gamble, for the Duchess is still titular governor of the household, after all, and her husband England's hero – the Duke has won another battle against the French, at Oudenarde.

Yet, though Queen Ant orders public celebrations for the victory, on reading the casualty list in the bedchamber she wept and said: 'Oh Lord! Will this bloodshed never cease!'

With the wind in that direction, it was time to change course. I waited until Abigail was in the chamber when Sarah made one of her burstings-in, demanding from Queen Ant a promise that her (Sarah's) daughters should succeed to her posts as Groom of the Stole, Keeper of the Privy Purse and Ranger of Windsor Park which, between them, are worth £9,000 a year. As ever, she ordered Abigail – 'this person whom I took from a garret' – to leave the room. Gently, the Queen said, 'I beg that Mistress Hill may stay, Mrs Freeman.'

Furious, Sarah looked around her and saw me putting clothes into a press, and commanded me, as a creature still in her power, 'Fetch me a chair, girl, then bring a dish of chocolate.'

'Certainly, ma'am,' I said, 'when I have finished folding, as Mistress Hill bid me.'

I have faced abductors, gunfire, boarders, a hurricane, but never, till then, a gorgon. I swear her hair rose from her head and waved in the air. 'Is this the way of it, you ingrate?'

I was sorry for it; Sarah's is a greater heart than the shrivelled thing that ticks within Abigail's breast, but I have my own ship to sail. I was rewarded by Abigail's look of satisfaction and approval and, some days later, her accolade – I attended her wedding.

It was celebrated in secret, for fear of Sarah knowing.

Late one evening at St James's – I had been transferred to night duty – Queen Ant called to me to bring her cloak. Together, with her leaning on me, we tiptoed through the silent corridors. Tiptoed. A queen in her own palace, terrified of one female subject.

We reached the apartment of Dr Arbuthnot. He is the physician to Prince George, the consort, a snuffy, jovial Tory whose room is the resort of the coffee-house poets, wits and other idlers.

Tonight it was crowded with flowers, a parson, Mrs Arbuthnot in her best and twittering, Abigail in her best and smirking, Robert Harley in his best and impassive. And Sam Masham. Sam is Prince George's equerry, formerly his page. His function, as far as I can divine it, is to bow and smile, for he does nothing else. But a fine catch for the lowly Abigail. Harley arranged it, of course.

The ceremony was brief and hushed. The Queen kissed Abigail and blessed her. Harley did the same. Sam bowed and smiled. Dr Arbuthnot peered out of the door to see if all was clear and I heaved Queen Ant back to her chamber. All the way she pressed me to say nothing. Nor did I. But, inevitably, Sarah uncovered the truth.

It was just before the thanksgiving for Oudenarde, to be held at St Paul's. A tight-lipped Sarah, in her capacity as Keeper of the Robes, laid out the royal costume, train and ceremonial jewels and then retired to ready herself. As wife of the Great Duke, she was to accompany the Queen in the coach.

Queen Ant was miserable. The dead of Oudenarde weighed on her mind; she didn't want to celebrate the battle at all. Also, she had been nursing the Prince Consort day and night. The cures she's taken him to at Bath, Epsom and Tunbridge Wells have been in vain; she is soon to be a widow. She is beset by quarrelling ministers. Her rheumatism was flaring her legs into tree trunks and she would have to be hoisted into the carriage on the special platform-seat made for her.

'I have no heart for jewels,' she said, looking at the bed where Sarah had laid everything ready.

Abigail seized the moment. 'Majesty, why wear them?'

A naughty look came into the Queen's eye. 'Then I won't.'

I confess I gaped at that; the diamonds are magnificent and glitter like a shoal of flying fish. Calico Jack would have slavered at the sight of them, as would any pirate worth his salt, as did I.

We learned what happened afterwards in the royal coach from Carrots, who went in it with Sarah and the Queen.

'When Sarah saw the Queen had left off the jewels,' Carrots told us, 'she was so put out she kept silent all the way from Kensington to Temple Bar, after which she began to berate Her Majesty, accusing her of slighting "my lord, the hero of this hour". The poor Queen kept opening her mouth to gainsay her but the Duchess would not let her speak. Over and over she accused Abigail, "Did not Masham instigate this?" "Is not this rudeness the handiwork of Traitress Masham?"

'At last we reached St Paul's and the Queen was helped down on to the steps. There was a great crowd on them, held back by javelin men, but Sarah was yet fulminating as she descended. Her Majesty looked to say something in reply. At which . . .' here Carrots paused as if she could still not believe it, '. . . at which the Duchess, in front of them all, said, "Hold your tongue, madam."'

The trumpets sounded then, the organ and choir crashed out into the Te Deum, the Tower guns fired their salvo over the

City. Had Sarah known it, it was her requiem. The Queen has indeed held her tongue; she has not spoken to her since.

At last it is dawn. A cock has just crowed and is being answered by others farther away. On the river a bargeman has shouted a greeting to another. Even the creature has subdued her gibbering and is become the insubstantial shape she assumes in daylight. She never completely leaves me now.

I have survived the night, then. We shall see what the day brings.

What I had forgotten, in fear for myself, was that someone else has to wait out the days and pray that Greg keeps his silence – Robert Harley.

The Whigs would like nothing better than to bring Harley down. And they scent blood. They are in the ascendancy now since Parliament holds more Whigs than ever before, through the arrival into it, under the Union, of Scotch peers and members.

And here is the wretched William Greg, Harley's own secretary, under the Whigs' hand, guilty of treason. If they can but make him admit Harley knew and approved it . . . you can see their chops slaver at the thought. The Earl of Sunderland, the Marlboroughs' son-in-law, pads past Harley's door grinning, like a wolf sighting lamb.

Did Harley conspire in the treachery? The Whigs think him capable of it – 'Trickster Robin' they call him – but are careless whether he did or not as long as they can make poor Greg say he did.

The man is certainly a schemer, so devious he could wriggle up his own arse, as Calico Jack used to say. Sometimes I am almost sure it was Harley ordered our kidnapping all those years ago; he was, and is, ruthless and would not have scrupled to rid the throne of an annoying complication. But selling his country's secrets to the enemy? Greg never mentioned it to me – and if anybody would have known, Greg would.

I'll say this for the man, I draw strength from his demeanour. Disgrace, Newgate, the gallows await him but his cottage-loaf face remains as bland as ever. If anything, he is the more dignified. A committee of seven Whig lords interrogate Greg in his Newgate cell all day, every day. So far, he has withstood them and named neither Harley nor, more importantly, myself.

Today Harley came to the bedchamber to enquire of Queen Ant's health. In turn, she enquired after Greg's. It is now a month since his arrest. Harley said, with meaning, 'He still refuses to implicate those whom he knows to be innocent, ma'am. His only complaint is of his fetters which allow him neither to stand up nor to kneel down.'

The Queen clicked her tongue in sympathy. 'Such usage is hanging him over and over. I shall send Dr Arbuthnot to him with comforts and necessaries. And you, Mr Harley, how are you?'

Harley bowed. 'Ma'am, I know nothing that I can do but to confide in the providence of God.' Admirable. Calculated to win the Queen's heart.

If it was you, Harley, who organized the abduction of Anne Bonny and Mary Read, I shall open your stomach and take your living bowels and wind them round the nearest tree. In the meantime, my compliments. Both our heads are on the block, did you but know it. You, like me, know they press Greg harder every day. As I do, you retire at night and shake like a flapping jib sheet, waiting for the rap on the door. Yet in public there is no tremor of your voice or hand, as I hope there is none of mine.

I wanted to run after him. 'Ahoy, shipmate. We share the same boat in this hurricane.' He'd be surprised to know a mere bedchamber woman considers he'd make a most excellent pirate.

Three months gone by and still Greg has not confessed a word against anyone but himself. The Whigs are despairing that he will. There are hours in which even I forget he still might.

After all, why should they even question him about me? They have found one curious letter, but their main aim is to make Greg implicate Harley; they may overlook anything else. And Greg has a curious honour. He is refusing to say that Harley was involved in his treachery, though they are probably promising him his life if he does. Perhaps the same loyalty extends to me – he was undoubtedly mad for me.

Harley, I think, will go down whatever happens, not for employing a treacherous secretary but because the rest of the cabinet, now dominated by Whigs, has banded against him. Even Marlborough, egged on by Sarah, has threatened to resign if Harley is not dismissed. The Queen is loth to let him go, whom she regards as her one ally, but a Whiggish House of Commons is refusing to pass the Bill of Supply unless she does. So Harley must fall.

And I, it seems, have backed the wrong horse. Sarah, who loathes Harley, triumphs over the court, refuses to speak to me, and won't hesitate to demand my dismissal. The creature is delighted and howls taunts into my ear all night so that I lose sleep.

Harley has been dismissed and dear, dull George, the Prince Consort, is dead.

The Queen had sat with him night after night, not caring that hated Whigs were taking control of her government, but only that her husband, 'my dear companion', should draw an easy breath. That wish was denied her. We could hear his gasps through two antechambers. Then the silence. And the Queen's scream.

Sarah came hot-foot to Kensington from Windsor, virtually ramming the door of the death chamber to get in, evicting Abigail from Queen Ant's side and insisting Her Majesty leave the palace at once for St James's. Apparently, it is the custom for the royal family to vacate instantly the building in which one of their number has died.

The Queen didn't want to go, of course, but was too crushed to prevail against the Duchess. The poor thing went past us in a daze with barely time for us to bring her a hood, almost dragged by Sarah. She whispered, 'Send to Masham to come to me before I go,' but Sarah would not allow it.

So now we are in first mourning, which lasts three months. We are a court of rooks. Even the November sky has loyally made itself dark at noonday and is weeping. The only sound in the dull, silent palace is the swish of our black petticoats – bombazine for the maids of honour, lawn for bedchamber women, bought at the Queen's expense – as we creep about on our soft, black, chamois shoes.

Male courtiers and ministers have no buttons on the sleeves and pockets of their black worsted, wear black crêpe hatbands, black weepers, black buckles and swords.

Outside, St James's steps are draped with black flannel while indoors even the sconces are oxidized black. The pincushions on the dressing tables are black, with black pins.

Sarah is everywhere efficient and crisp in her official capacity, spotting a coloured handkerchief in the Earl of Pembroke's sleeve and whipping it away as if he might have been going to assassinate the Queen with it, noticing that Anne Sunderland, her own daughter, had put flounces on her bombazine and ordering them stripped off. Queen Ant provides the only colour – she wears the royal mourning purple – but she is hardly seen, shutting herself away to haunt the closet where George used to make his model ships.

Neither Sarah nor Abigail has allowed the Queen's sorrow to stop their wrangling over her. Sarah is convinced the only reason she has shut herself in the consort's closet is because it is near the back stairs to Abigail's apartment and so stays with her every possible moment, despite Queen Ant's pleas to be left alone. In fact, Sarah, who is unable to put herself in anyone else's situation, believes the Queen's tears are merely a show. Nor does Abigail respect the Queen's wish for privacy, but hops inside the closet every time Sarah is out of it.

I chose a moment when neither harpy was with her and went in, unspeaking, to kneel and proffer a glass of cold tea. The Ant downed it in a swallow – and it was a bumper. Handing back the glass, she said, 'Perhaps another, my dear, when no one is by.'

The little room smelled of varnish and raw wood and had shavings on the floor – she would not allow them cleared. A chisel lay in her lap and her hand stroked the vice attached to his workbench. If she pretends grief, as Sarah says, she does it well; her face blotched, her dress dirty and the bandages on her bad foot stained and trailing.

Even if it were not part of the plan to make her dependent upon me for her tipple, it would be charity to keep her three sheets in the wind for this period. Perhaps she did not, despite the seventeen pregnancies, love her dull old George with the passion which, even now, exists between Sarah and her Duke. Nevertheless, he became her child, the only one to survive; unthreatening, undemanding and comfortable, a refuge. Now she has none.

When I brought the second glass she said, 'You are my comfort, child.' There was an emphasis on the 'you' which suggests she will not part with me now, whoever becomes my enemy. I am saved. Indeed, with caution, I may be able to supplant Abigail altogether and begin my own reign. Sarah's is over for good. Somewhere within the Ant's flabby, sentimental corpulence is a register of what is owed to a Stuart Queen of England and Defender of the Faith. She will not forget being told to hold her tongue on the steps of her own cathedral.

Now we are in second mourning – not quite so rigorous as first, but dreary enough. Everyone takes advantage of free days to slip away and find relief in recreation of some sort. My fellows find it strange that I do so alone, but they have become used to my solitary ways and no longer question me.

From St James's it is a short walk to reach the river and hire a waterman – again, a usual practice since the Thames is a quicker and safer route than the roads. It is also easier to make sure I am not followed. I took double care, directing the waterman to the Bridge where I took another boat to Southwark where I took yet another to Wapping Steps.

It is always a tedious journey and, yesterday, very cold. The winter is turning bitter. I was glad of my two cloaks – the old, patched woollen to hide my mourning one of Norwich crêpe.

Swathes of holly and other evergreens have been hung along the waterfront houses in readiness for Christmas but already they are shrivelling in the frost. From every church comes the sounds of a choir practising Christmas anthems and bellringers running through a peal. Their holiness hurts the creature and she screamed so loud I told her to shut her mouth, which angered the waterman who thought I was addressing to him.

This is become a danger. She is increasingly insistent in her demands and so infiltrates her voice into my head that I have to clench my mouth to stop it forming an answer. I nearly did so in the bedchamber the other day and got an old-fashioned look from Carrots.

Christendom runs out at Wapping where inns outnumber churches by thirty-six to one. Indeed, there is a part of Wapping Wall where Lascar, Chinee and other heathen tongues drown out the English language altogether. But the Brotherhood holds sway in it and make sure I am never molested when I go to meet them there.

One of them, Billy, was at the Steps and escorted me safely past the other taverns to the Bladebone, an old whalers' inn, now the gathering-place for less admired marine professions. Not a pretty establishment; a whale skeleton still arches the roof, the skulls of sharks and dolphins decorate the walls and there is a distinct remembrance of blubber in the barrel-tables. I feel at ease there. Jem, the landlord, who was second mate on the *Childhood* under Captain Quelch before that gentleman had the misfortune to be executed in Boston, is always pleased to see me.

This time, however, one of his customers, a man I didn't know, objected to my presence as I stepped over the threshold and, not wanting 'no high-nosed lady's maid' overhearing his business, attempted to throw me out. I had my knife at his throat on the instant, which gave him pause and Jem time to come up and introduce me.

'Gentlemen, this is Marianne, as fine a member of the Brotherhood as ever plundered a prize. I, personal, have seen her stick an impudent rogue like a pig for saying less than you said, Bob Clew.' (Our visits to Jamaica's Port Royal being infrequent and both of us being of similar build with dark hair, we were often confused by Brothers, other than our own crew. To avoid mistake, they ran our names together, calling us both 'Mary-Anne', or 'Marianne' or 'Marion' indiscriminately.)

Master Clew apologized, I put my knife away and downed a

184

flagon with him, Jem extolling my virtues the while. 'Not a freebooter in Jamaicky as wouldn't have been proud to have her aboard. Worth the price of three, she was, and as handy with a cutlass as meself. Never gave her mates away when in prison, neither. There's not one of the Brotherhood as wouldn't take her place on the gallows.'

I winked at him to stop before he got into shoal waters and babbled too much of my history. I have given him to believe I've turned respectable and married a parson up Hertfordshire way, occasionally dabbling in illicit trade in order to augment my husband's stipend. The thought tickles him mightily.

'Have I a visitor, Jem?'

'Up aloft.' He lit me up the stairs to a private room where Captain Porritt was waiting, then fetched more ale, chatted, and finally left us together.

The Brotherhood set me on to Captain Porritt. He is one of the new pirates of this sad age. Politics rather than plunder is his concern; he runs information and Jacobites back and forth across the Channel. I know him for a rabid Papist and slavish admirer of Mary of Modena and the Pretender, yet from his look, which is stern, and clothes, which are plain, he could be taken for a Puritan.

I questioned him about the situation at St-Germain and learned that the Bratchet was still alive the last time he was there. Francesca had been away from the Court, taking some cure, but was expected back any day.

The creature insists now that not only the Bratchet but also Martin Millet and the Scotsman must be silenced. She points out that Bratchet might have confided in them who it was she saw leaving the scene of the murder. They cannot identify me, as Bratchet can, but it is true they are a risk to my position.

Hence my appointment with Porritt.

'Captain,' I told him, 'I am here to warn you. You are in danger. Your name is on a list of suspected Jacobite sympathizers who are to be arrested for their treason.'

It was the truth. It was on Harley's desk and Greg showed it to me. For such a devious man, Harley was extraordinarily reckless about leaving secret papers lying around – his carelessness enabled his enemies to point out that in this at least he had encouraged Greg's treachery, which he had.

Porritt went pale. 'How do you know?'

'I have a lover who is the Secretary of State's secretary,' I told him, 'You have been watched by government informers. I understand that at this moment the French are commissioning a ship for you so that you can harry the English navy in the West Indies.'

His increased pallor told me the information was accurate. More of England's wealth is vested in the West Indies than most people realize; by encouraging privateers to interfere with Caribbean trade, Louis XIV is helping to ruin this country's economy and reduce it to a state which will bring down the government, thereby giving the Pretender his chance.

Porritt would have rushed off there and then to board his boat and sail back to his French friends, and safety. I stopped him. 'One good turn deserves another,' I said, 'In fact, there is a good turn you can do for the Jacobite cause.'

He sat down. 'Are you one of us?'

'I am. Thanks to my information, I am able to tell you that there is a spy at St-Germain, a wench on Her Majesty Queen Mary's staff who has been spying on her and sending reports to the English government.'

'Who?' The venom with which he asked it made me think that he will dispose of Bratchet with pleasure; Mary of Modena inspires fanatical devotion in men like him, almost a lust. They see her as a wronged Queen of Heaven.

'Mlle La Fée, but you needn't concern yourself with her, she's being dealt with. However, she has friends, also spies, also at Court.'

'What do you want me to do?'

'I understand that your port of call in France is Le Havre.'

He gave a brief nod.

'And perhaps, during your stay in Le Havre, you have sometimes noticed a sizeable fishing smack, *L'Hirondelle*, put in there from time to time.'

He nodded again.

'She is an English government boat,' I told him, 'She crosses to Le Havre every two months or so to service their agents.'

Another gift from Greg. I was going to miss that man.

'She won't do it again,' promised Porritt. Not only did he have the appearance of a Puritan, he radiated the same hatred for everything that some of them do. Give a man like that a cause and he'll serve it in the hope of hurting anybody else's.

'I should be grateful if you left the boat alone for now,' I said, 'I want her watched. It may be that sooner or later two men will turn up at Le Havre, wishing to board her and return home. They have information damaging to the Jacobite cause. They must be stopped.' I gave him the names and descriptions of Millet and Kilsyth.

'Killed?'

I shrugged. 'As you please.' A happy thought struck me. 'Or press them and take them with you to the West Indies.'

'You're a cold-hearted specimen, missie.'

It takes one to know one, I thought. I could see it was gall and wormwood to him to be receiving advice and instruction from what he regarded as a chit. If he had a wife, which I doubted, he was the sort who would beat her. 'Will you do it?'

'I'll do it.'

He went off without a goodbye. Graceless man, he might have thanked me. I trusted him to do what he'd promised, though; it would give him the opportunity to make somebody unhappy.

'So there's for you, Martin Millet,' I said to myself. It might be, of course, that he'll try to return to England some other way but, as I knew from Greg, he is in touch with England's embassy at The Hague whose spies use *L'Hirondelle*, so there's a fair chance that he'll go via Le Havre when he wants to leave France. And with the Bratchet dead, he'll have no reason to stay.

Jem was kindly enough to leave his customers and walk me to where I could hire a hackney, talking all the way of the good old days in Port Royal, but I could not attend to him.

'What do you keep looking astern for?' he asked me, 'Afeared one of your husband's churchwardens follows you?' He thought it a great joke. I am amazed nobody but me can see her, or hear the clump of her boots stepping in time to mine.

'You don't hear anything?' I asked him. She was cackling with joy that the poor Bratchet is doomed.

''Tis a hyena,' he said, 'or a lion.'

True, we were passing the wild-beast shops such as abound in Ratcliffe Highway. Jem says one day he'll take me to see the menageries in which the pelicans and tigers and other animals brought by sailors are stored in ingenious ways. But I have my own wild beast. And am in the cage with it.

On the way out of the City, the hackney was delayed at Newgate where an excited crowd gathered outside the prison gates. I questioned my driver. He told me they were waiting to follow the cart taking William Greg to Tyburn 'and see his treasoning tripes cut out afore he's hanged'.

I had forgotten that this was the day. I told him to drive on.

CHAPTER ELEVEN

THE AUTUMN was so fine that Louis continued his visits to Marly until mid-October. Afterwards we had to see to all the injured animals he left behind – the French *noblesse* ride horses into the ground – so I didn't get to Paris until well into November.

Vardes thought I had a girl in Paris because, always before I went, I sent word that I was on my way to a Marie-Denise in the rue de Vieux Epiciers by one of the *garçons bleus*.

I fetched Rosinante from the pasture where grooms kept mounts for their own use. He was the horse I'd spotted between the shafts of the Parisian coal cart. He'd cost every franc in my pocket, plus the pocket – the coalman demanded my jacket as well. The stable lads jeered when I brought him back, still covered with black dust, and gave him the name of Don Quixote's nag: '*Voilà, c'est Rosinante.*'

He didn't look much, I admit, with his long neck and forehead and his colouring of monotonous brown, but he had the strongest and easiest action I've ever come across.

We crossed the Seine by the Pont de Neuilly. It was a cold, clear day. They say that when Louis came to the throne Paris was a medieval slum. Now it's a great, tree-lined, boulevarded city that is a pleasure to ride through, cleaner than London and, with 5,000 street lamps and La Reynie's ruthless police force, a damned sight safer.

But give me London any day. Parisiens might breathe purer air than Londoners, but London has more freedom – as long as you've enough money to enjoy it. The French have never put a check on their monarchs like we've put on ours. No king or queen of England can reign with the absolute power of a Louis, thank God. There's no habeas corpus to protect France's political prisoners; one of Louis's *lettres de cachet* could put a man in prison without trial and keep him there until he died, and often did.

He truly believed kings were sacred, answerable to God, not their people. That was why he made his biggest mistake and insisted on maintaining the Pretender as rightful ruler of England, instead of coming to terms with William of Orange like one sensible man with another. It brought France down in the end.

Still, he looked after his soldiers, I'll say that for him. As I crossed the river again at the Pont des Invalides I went past the dignified buildings and thirty acres where Louis housed 7,000 wounded soldiers who otherwise would have eked out a living as beggars. Chelsea Hospital can't compare with it.

Personally I liked the old bugger, but if Bratchet thought he was the Sun King she should have looked in the shade now and then. I could have shown it to her, the underbelly; the village on the far side of the hill from Marly where the peasants lived like rats. I could have told her about the tax he'd imposed on marriages and baptisms – *baptisms* for Christ's sake, in a country that called itself Christian – to pay for his wars.

What about the Edict of Nantes, I could have asked her. What about him going back on that agreement to allow freedom of worship? In a stroke, he despoiled his country of an entire class, the Protestant bourgeoisie – your own people, Bratchet – well-to-do shopkeepers, skilled workers, silk-makers, glass-blowers, valuable men and women who didn't want to be forced into Roman Catholicism.

That was his other mistake. When they went they left France an unskilled country. And they took with them tales of children being taken away to be turned into little Papists, of torture, rape and men sent to the galleys, so that Louis XIV's name became synonymous with brutality throughout Europe and banded its countries against him.

I don't think he even knew what was being done in his name. I'd had to attend mass at Marly, my father spinning in his grave I expect, and listen to old Louis honestly thank God he was instrumental in gently persuading heretics back to the true faith. That's the trouble with tyrants: they believe their own advertisements.

And the Bratchet believed it. The Scotch bastard's fault. Teaching her bloody Latin. Jacobite bloody mumbo-jumbo. But I couldn't get out of my head the look on her face. I kept hearing her: *You left me.* Jesus, I should have taken her away when she'd asked. Though as I told her, I'd had troubles of my own then. After all the years I'd spent searching for my mother, I had finally found her. It was just before I was sent to Flanders with the company. 'Sarah Millet? End bed. Dying from the pox.'

It wasn't any different from every other poorhouse ward I'd enquired at. Row of beds where women vomited or cried out or writhed or lay still. Same smells of lye and dirt. The notice at the end of her bed said 'Millet', but even then I wasn't sure. I'd kept the image of her face in my mind so long, I thought I'd recognize it. But I couldn't. I stood there a long time while her head turned to and fro on the wooden pillow. Then I fetched Mrs Defoe. When she saw her, she knelt down and wept. 'So altered, oh Sary, Sary. Kneel, Martin. Tell her you forgive her.'

She wouldn't have heard me. What would I have forgiven her for in any case? Marrying a bigoted bully? Trying to save herself and me from his beatings by running away?

'Jezebel, Martin, she was Jezebel. May her flesh be the portion of dogs.'

It looked as if it had been. London isn't kind to vulnerable women, no city is. You had to grant Aunt Effie that much; she'd won out – until somebody killed her. My mother hadn't. I sat for three days by her bed until she died, stroking her hand and talking to her, but I don't think she heard me. The look on Bratchet's face before she turned on her heel and left me in the stable was my mother's as the breath went out of her.

And the devil of it was that, like it or not, I was responsible for the woman because I'd been too late to save my mother. More than responsible. I was beginning to feel a great deal for the Bratchet.

After I'd finished in Le Brun's workshops, Rosinante and I ambled into the Bois de Boulogne, where the *haut monde* of Paris promenades itself up and down on sand paths between the trees. By the Lac des Patineurs there's a horse trough. I let Rosinante drink and sat down on a tree trunk where spectators sit in winter to watch the skating. Apart from some children floating twig boats on the far side of the lake there was no one around.

Except the man on the other end of the tree trunk.

'Afternoon, Marie-Denise,' I said.

'*Miss* Marie-Denise to you, cheeky,' said John Laws.

I swear his own mother would have passed him by. He was in plain brown cloth – not rich, not cheap – and wore an old-fashioned *perruque* wig, a typical Parisien bourgeois taking an afternoon off. He got up as if to admire Rosinante – 'What a *repulsive* animal' – and, while seeming to examine him, slipped a purse into my saddlebag. We sat down together on the tree, admiring the view.

'The Pretender's planning to invade Scotland,' I said.

'We know that, ducky.' He kept his eyes on the lake. 'The question is when?'

'Probably the spring.'

'Don't happen to know how big his force will be, do you?'

'Not sure. Talk at Marly says Louis is prepared to send 5,000 troops. They'll go from Dunkirk.'

'Mmm. Wish we had a date, though.'

'Have you got anything for me?'

'As a matter of fact, ducky, we have. We've intercepted a letter from St-Germain among a batch on its way to naughty,

191

naughty William Greg. Addressed to an Anne Boleyn, would you believe. Confirming an instruction to "dispose of the goods".'

Bratchet. 'When was this?'

'The letter? Ages ago. Beginning of the year. We've only just got round to decoding it. We're very *busy*, you know. Now don't go rushing off in a manly sweat.' I'd begun tightening Rosinante's girth. 'My spy at St-Germain reported Mlle La Fée as still chirruping happily around the place only yesterday.'

'Why in hell don't you get William Greg to talk?'

'My dear, they've been tickling his feet with feather dusters for *months*. Not a cheep from him.'

I tried to think. The letter had been sent at the beginning of the year, but nobody had yet made any attempt on Bratchet's life, and she'd been there since February. Perhaps they weren't going to. Or perhaps somebody was still waiting for an opportunity. Or perhaps they hadn't been in a position to use an opportunity when it came. I said, 'Who was at St-Germain in January and has been absent ever since?'

'My dear boy . . . ah, I see what you mean.' He was quick, Laws, I give him that. 'Well now, the Pretender has. He's been fighting for dear Louis against Marlborough – *such* a compelling way to inspire the English to love him. But unless she's spilled a lot of his mother's rouge, I don't think he'd kill a serving girl, do you? Then there's Mme Francesca, she's been in retreat or something, but I believe the . . .'

'The grandmother. It's her.'

Laws blinked. 'Really? Stab of her crochet needle in the dark? Fatal blow from a pincushion? You may be right, of course. My spy tells me she's only now returned for the winter.'

'When? When did she get back?'

'Two or three weeks ago. Do you really think it's her? Tut, tut, what *are* grandmothers coming to these days?'

I cantered off while he was still musing on it. I didn't say goodbye. I didn't thank him even. But when I hear faggots referred to as if they're cowards, I always remember John Laws who went regularly in disguise into enemy territory to help his country's agents.

*

With the return of Francesca Bard, life at St-Germain lost some of its sunniness for Bratchet. Winter returned at the same time and the exiles sat in front of fires too small for the château's enormous fireplaces and complained of the cold.

Bratchet waited for two days for a summons from Anne Bard's grandmother which did not come. At last she took the initiative and approached Francesca's maid in the household staff kitchen. 'Good morning, Mlle Beate,' she said quietly in French, 'I wondered when Mme Bard would want to see me.'

'She don't,' said Mlle Beate, and walked off.

Bratchet caught her up in a passageway. 'She sent for me.'

'You?' Bratchet received a look of such malevolence that she took a step back. 'You leave alone.' The woman hurried off, muttering. Bratchet heard exclamations like '*Sale poule!*' and '*Souillon!*' echoing back along the passage.

'She seemed to hate me,' she told Mme Putti.

'Magyar,' explained Mme Putti. 'She hate everybody.'

Beate, it appeared, was not popular. When she wasn't accompanying Francesca on her cures and retreats, she lived in her mistress's room and was seen seldom around the château, which was a relief to everybody. Squat, with a hairline that started low down on her forehead, and speaking, when she spoke at all, with an accent from darkest Middle Europe, she was known to the exiles as the 'Bête Noire'.

'Woman ugly like that ought to be polite,' Mme Putti said.

Not only was Beate rude, she possessed a temper that kept her fellow servants at a respectful distance. She had once, in a quarrel over some sausages, stabbed Mrs Collins, the laundress, in the hand so badly that Mrs Collins had been off duty for a month. Mary of Modena would have sent her away immediately if Francesca hadn't pleaded for her and stood surety for her good behaviour.

Dr MacLaverty spoke more kindly of her than did others, but he spoke kindly of everybody. 'She's frightened for the future, like the rest of us,' he told the Bratchet. 'She's devoted to Francesca, not the cause, so she'll have no place here when Francesca dies.'

But everybody else felt that the only compensation to be gained from the death of Francesca Bard – and they were fond of her – was that Mlle Beate could then flap off to whatever vampire-infested fastness she'd come from.

Bratchet was slow to resentment. For all her new-found self-regard, Effie Sly had accustomed her to being bullied. But the situation began to rankle. 'Bugger the Magyar. Francesca's the reason I'm here. She wants to see me. I want to see her.'

Francesca's room was at the top of a circular stair in one of St-Germain's turrets. Bratchet found herself facing a small, arched door decorated by a snarling gargoyle of a knocker. She rapped on it. And rapped again. There was no answer, no sound from inside, but the knocker had the same virulence with which Beate had looked at her in the kitchens. As if the woman were peering out at her through its eyes.

Bratchet lost her nerve and retired down the dark and winding steps. She didn't go back until Kilsyth returned to St-Germain in the train of young men that accompanied the Pretender, the war having stopped for the winter.

She was on duty on the day they trooped in to pay their duty to Mary of Modena. It was the first time Bratchet had seen James Francis, the young man who, she'd been told, was really England's king. She was disappointed. All the queen's women who'd had a hand in raising him told tales of his cleverness, beauty, piety, his fitness to be King of England – and here they'd drop their voices – a wiser one than his father. Bratchet expected a glorious young Caesar.

The prince was good-looking enough, like all the Stuarts, with the dark eyes of his mother, and, no doubt, possessed the virtues attributed to him. But something was missing, something his sister had and he did not; charm perhaps, the ability to thrill.

He's very neat, she thought. James's velvet coat had remained unspattered by his journey from the front, the buckles on his boots still shone. An inherited bitterness was thinning his mouth. Because he couldn't afford the equipment considered necessary to his rank he had to fight under the incognito of 'Chevalier de Saint-Georges'.

As far as Bratchet was concerned, it was Kilsyth who dominated the chamber, almost literally, spattering its carpet with mud from his boots, telling Mary of Modena of her son's prowess in the field. 'He was grand, Majesty, ye should have seen him. And the Sasunnoch soldiers refusing to charge when they recognized him. I tell ye, the Union's hated.' But for Bratchet, it was Kilsyth who was grand in his tartan. *Quel homme.* Ardent but manly. Sensitive, brave, wholehearted in everything he did.

Left to herself, the Bratchet of Puddle Court would have allowed her self-loathing after the rape to drive her into a grotesque fulfilment of sin. She'd felt tempted to join Floss and the ladies who plied their trade next door, not because rape had roused her sexuality – it had done the opposite – but in an attempt at distorted expiation: I am soiled therefore let me be more soiled.

Oddly, it had been Effie who'd saved her. She'd told Bratchet, 'You're a lady's maid and don't you forget it. Just because one gentleman ploughed his furrow it don't mean we let 'em all in the field.'

To that extent, Bratchet had been saved from the death that awaited so many maids who suffered fates worse than. But her sexuality was shrivelled before it could be said to have budded. While her contemporaries fluttered their eyelashes and their hearts, Bratchet wondered why they bothered. Love-making? Hate-making more like.

Now, late in the day, here was Livingstone of Kilsyth, who treated her with respect, who demanded nothing of her, and because he demanded nothing of her, Bratchet was experiencing a deliciously painful passion which stored up the beloved's every expression, every word referring to herself, to be recollected later in his absence, an experience she found as pleasurable as, possibly more than, his presence.

For the first time she felt the dewy irrigation of love.

She was glad she had an excuse to seek him out on the terrace later that evening to tell him that though Francesca had returned to St-Germain, her maid refused permission for a visit.

'Refused permission? What's the woman up to? We'll see to it this minute.'

Grabbing Bratchet's hand, he hurried her through the corridors and up the stairs to the turret. She thought how he was like an awakening prince; the flap of his boots on the stair, his knock, the cry, 'Wake there, my lady. Here's Livingstone of Kilsyth to see ye,' took menace and mystery from the door that had baffled Bratchet. After shuffling and mutterings behind it, it was opened by Beate.

Unusually for St-Germain on a winter night, the room they entered was warm, almost hot. It should have been a lantern, the windows on its eight sides allowing views on to gardens and roofs and letting in light, but the windows were shuttered and the walls covered by arras in front of which screens advanced to a few yards around a canopied, curtained bed facing the door, its resemblance to a catafalque increased by the corpse that occupied it. The corpse of Anne Bonny.

Bratchet's indrawn breath caused the corpse to open its eyes and Kilsyth to ask her what was the matter. The bones of the face, the set of the mouth, neck and shoulders were so like Anne's that Bratchet was shocked into the superstition of folk tales; the Little People had taken Anne to some kingdom where she'd aged ten years for everybody else's one.

'Anne,' wailed the Bratchet, completely unnerved, 'What did they do to you?' They'd shrivelled her, but even the wavy white hair grew as Anne's wavy black hair had grown.

'Anne? You know my grand-daughter?' The voice was Anne's given the quaver of old age.

'Indeed we do, ma'am,' shouted Kilsyth, 'And are here to enquire after her, if you will be so good. And yourself, ma'am, do ye prosper?'

'Beate, Beate, I'm not deaf,' moaned Anne's grandmother, 'I do not prosper.'

'You make noise, I kill you,' Beate told him, 'She very ill.'

That was evident. The old lady's skin was an almost transparent layer like thin beeswax over her skeleton and showed yellow against the linen of her pillows. She was so insubstantial that she seemed to have been sloughed by an emergent, newer self which had wriggled away somewhere else. Her breathing made irregular scratches on the silence of the room.

Nevertheless, the resemblance to her grand-daughter gave Bratchet an illogical *déjà vu* sense that Francesca must recognize her. She went to the bed and picked up one of the frail hands in hers and kissed it. 'You are so like Anne,' she said. 'She was my friend.'

'You know Anne?' Small, gapped yellow teeth showed eagerly.

'I've been searching for her. Can you tell me where she is?'

'She was here. When was it?' The old lady's eyes were concentrated on the end of the bed where Kilsyth stood, suddenly still, without seeing him. 'She *was* here. Beate, was it last month?'

Beate had sat herself on the other side of the bed and was working at a lacemaker's cushion which rested on a small table. Her thick hands whipped the bobbins in and out, under and over, creating what seemed to be a growing snowflake. She didn't answer.

'Or it may have been last year,' nodded Francesca. 'I become confused. Why do I think she was in the army?'

Bratchet looked helplessly at Kilsyth, who shrugged with equal helplessness, then boomed, 'Where has she gone, ma'am? Where did Anne go?'

Francesca became distressed again. 'Beate, he is too loud. Where did Anne go? Why do I think of the West Indies? Was it the West Indies, Beate?'

The maid was putting away the lace cushion. 'Now you go,' she said, and disappeared behind a screen lacquered with dragon patterns. They heard the clink of tin and into the room's smell of heavy cloth, perfume and aged skin, came a new odour.

Kilsyth demanded of Francesca, 'Can ye no tell us, lady, where Anne is that we can send for her?'

Watching Francesca's face for the answer, they both saw it slacken and her eyebrows rise as if somebody unexpected and unwelcome had appeared behind them.

Involuntarily, they looked back. When they turned again,

Francesca's hands were plucking at her sheets and she was moaning.

Beate looked round from behind a screen. 'Out,' she said, 'out, out, out.'

'Balm,' begged Francesca, 'balm.'

'Comink, my darlink,' the Bête's voice was soothing even as she made pushing gestures with her hands at Kilsyth and Bratchet. 'It cooks now. Comink.'

'Quick,' Francesca was saying, 'quick, quick.'

Beate appeared again; she had a dish warmer in her hands and the smell was stronger and headier. She screamed at them, 'Out. Out or I kill you.'

They retreated and closed the door behind them. Bratchet sagged with disappointment. 'Do you think Anne was ever here?'

'Who knows? Nobody else saw her.' It was the first time she'd seen him hopeless. By the time they'd reached the bottom of the stairs, he'd recovered. 'Tomorrow maybe the lady will have her wits back. *Si je puis*, the motto of the Kilsyths. If it can be done, it will be done. We'll spend every moment possible at the poor woman's bedside.' He paused. 'What hell's broth was that the dwarf was feeding her?'

Bratchet hadn't spent her time round the docks of London for nothing. 'Opium,' she said.

It was Kilsyth who asked, and gained, permission from Mary of Modena for Bratchet to have a short leave of absence from duty so that they could attend the sickbed of Francesca Bard. 'The dame's my kinswoman, ma'am and in a poor way.'

'God have mercy on her,' said Queen Mary. 'If you and my little La Fée can distract her thoughts, then it is charity to do so.'

But it was Bratchet who did the attending and distracting; the Highlander found it necessary to accompany James Francis when he went hunting, which he did nearly every day.

It was a period lasting three weeks but Bratchet remembered it as longer. Every morning she dreaded the climb up the turret stairs to a room as cluttered with keepsakes as Effie's rooms had been, though richer – silk fans, enamelled pill boxes, a pillared clock with a deadening tick, satin screens – and, everywhere, in crucifixes and paintings, horribly realistic depictions of Christ on the Cross to match the recurring bouts of agony suffered by the woman in the bed.

And, all the time, emanating across it was Beate's malevolence. When she wasn't looking after her mistress, the maid returned to her lacework so that, from that day on, the click of bobbins and the tick of a clock induced a feeling of discomfort in Bratchet that bordered on nausea. Why Beate hated her she couldn't think, but she felt there was more here than the general animosity of a disordered mind; this was personal.

Apart from the 'I kill you's every time the Bratchet did something to displease her, Beate didn't address her. Except once, when she suddenly spat out a question: 'You say your prayers?'

'Yes,' Bratchet told her, 'every night.'

Beate nodded.

The woman's devotion to Francesca, however, was absolute. The old lady was kept clean, given food with a spoon and drink from a beaker like a beloved child, while Beate crooned lullabies in her native tongue, whatever it was. The bed frothed with Beate's lace, every pillow was decorated with it, it hemmed the lovely caps that adorned Francesca's hair afresh every morning. A little tray of sweetmeats was kept within reach of the patient's hand, each one nestling in a tiny cup of lace.

With the onset of the pain, Bratchet was bundled out of the room to wait on the landing and smell the scent of opium coming from under the door. When she returned, the pupils of Francesca's eyes were tiny black dots and her expression peaceful.

In between the pain and the opium doses there was a point where she wanted to talk, but she did it in the form of a loop in which Bratchet's questions about Anne were met with the same answers: 'She was here, wasn't she? When was it, Beate? Was it last month? I become confused. Why do I think she was in the army? That is very ridiculous.'

The ghost of Anne Bard hovered in the room but Bratchet's attempts to grasp it were like trying to capture smoke.

'I think Anne did come here, but a long time ago,' she reported to Kilsyth, 'I think it must have been her who was in the

Dragoons and that she came on here from Ghent when the French captured it. She must have taken Mary's name to throw her enemies off the scent.'

Kilsyth shook his head. 'That bold harpy in the Dragoons was never Bonny Anne,' he said. 'Ye don't realize . . . I saw Anne once. Her mother brought her to Cairnvreckan to present her in the hall of my chief. The delicate wee hands of her, the holy innocence . . .'

'How old was she?' asked Bratchet.

'Six, mebbe seven. I was no much older myself.' He sighed. 'My heart and sword were hers then, and hers they've been ay since.'

'Yes, well,' said Bratchet, tartly, 'Things happen. People change.'

It was evening and they were walking through the gardens where other returned Jacobite soldiers were entertaining their ladies in the privacy of the chilly moonlight, the only privacy there was. Murmuring voices came from under the trees, and from behind the occasional bush, panting.

Kilsyth spoke low, but not really to her. 'I'm thinking how it would answer for Anne to marry James. Would the English not accept a Catholic Stuart if he were wed to a Protestant Stuart, and one so lovely? Aye, it would be the solution. She'd win their hearts as she won mine. It'd be the grand thing all ways round.'

It appeared that the Pretender had managed to fire at least Kilsyth's loyalty into wishing him back on to his father's throne. Bratchet stood her remembered Anne alongside the un-impassioned figure of James and doubted it. He hadn't fired anything in her; it wasn't likely he would fire Anne either.

She was irked by Kilsyth's idealized passion for a girl of six or seven. 'Don't want to marry her yourself, then?'

He was shocked. 'These are high matters. *Pair*sonal feelings do not come into it. For the good of Scotland I'd sacrifice all I have. What an alliance would be there. And a grand advantage for my clan.'

He's fallen in love with the Pretender just as he had with Anne, thought Bratchet. He wants to reconcile their two causes together. Alliances. Sacrifices. She didn't understand the politics, but she recognized nonsense when she heard it.

'All I can say is, you don't know Anne like I do.'

It struck her that very few people did. 'How well do you think Francesca knows her?' In all Anne's tales of her childhood travels, she had not mentioned her grandmother.

Kilsyth pondered and said with surprise: 'Mebbe not at all. Her daughter-in-law had little love for her, being Protestant and Francesca a strong Catholic. And with the war gone on so long, she'd no have had access to France for years.'

Then Francesca's conviction that she had met her granddaughter might well be the wishful thinking of a mind grown too old. Already depressed by the knowledge that Kilsyth worshipped a figure which lived only in his imagination and couldn't therefore be rivalled, Bratchet experienced a sense of desolation. 'We'll never find Anne.'

Kilsyth gave her a comradely slap on the back that made her cough. 'We must and we will. The flaming cross will burn brighter for James if he has a Highland lass for his queen. There'd be a true Union for ye. We'll find her, lassie.'

He took her back to the door of her room, kissed her hand and said goodnight. She could hear him singing in a loud baritone as he marched down L'Escalier du Pape:

> 'His heart was all on honour bent,
> He could not stoop to love,
> No lady in the land had power
> His frozen heart to move.'

So could everybody else hear him. Complaints in all the languages of Catholic Europe issued from doors along the passage where people were trying to sleep.

Glorious. The man created his own fiction and lived in it; kings, queens, the battle for thrones, questing knights and ladies, hopeless passion, sacrifice. And if he loved Anne, whom she loved, it gave a fitting bitter-sweet *tristesse* to the romance. She must be grateful he had whirled her into it. Whatever the ending might be, it would be better than Puddle Court.

There was little romance, however, to the days she spent in the turret room. Bratchet grew sorrier and sorrier for Francesca and her suffering as she gained glimpses into the old lady's past and her attempts to retrieve her dignity after Prince Rupert had put her away.

Certain stimuli, a word, would set up a remembrance. If the locket at her throat shifted when she moved, she would insist on Bratchet opening it to see the miniatures of Rupert and herself when young inside it. Then Francesca would whisper as if it were a secret, 'I was younger and prettier. He was mad for me, always. The actress was a counterfeit, to protect our son from plotters.'

Bratchet gathered that after Francesca's father's death – which had unaccountably taken place in Persia – Prince Rupert felt himself responsible for the stricken, beautiful girl, orphan of one of his officers. 'But if it was his duty, it was his desire too. Mad for me, he was. And it was a marriage as legal as any and wouldn't Father Waleska attest to it if he were here, poor man, and hadn't died bird-nesting in '82.'

When, once or twice, Turnspit trotted into the room with Bratchet, Francesca refused to let Beate turn him out and told Bratchet to feed him 'a jujube' from the little, lacy casings of sweetmeats which Beate made for her. 'Rupert had a poodle just like that who loved my jujubes.' It was a sign of how her eyes were failing her that she could equate Turnspit with the legendary black poodle which had galloped into battle by his master's stirrup – the only similarity was both dogs' liking for sweetmeats.

Bratchet gently mentioned the name of her grand-daughter a few more times then ceased to do so. Yes, Anne had been here. When was it? Had she been in the army? Had she gone to the West Indies? Why did she think so?

Whether Anne had in fact visited her grandmother after she'd been abducted from England – mention of her being in the army indicated that it was after – or whether it had been Mary Read who had come and, in talking about Anne, had confused Francesca, it was impossible to find out and to keep pressing the question was unkind.

Bratchet continued her visits because Francesca, in her pain-free moments, seemed to enjoy them, though such moments were becoming fewer. There were dreadful scenes as the moaning began and Francesca's eyes became huge and fixed on the door, giving to the helpless, watching Bratchet the impression that an invisible wild beast had entered the room to rend the body on the bed. Greater quantities of 'balm' were now necessary to bring it relief.

Then came the morning when Bratchet climbed the turret stair to find the door at the top open. Francesca lay on her bed, her arms crossed on her chest with a jewelled crucifix between her hands in her usual pose when asleep.

Looking round for Beate, Bratchet noticed that Francesca's more valuable possessions were missing, the enamelled boxes, some of the rings on Francesca's fingers. The room was silent. There was no tick from the dreadful clock, no scratching, laboured breathing.

Bratchet found herself crying. Before she went for Dr MacLaverty, she stood for a moment by the bed to say good-bye. Beate had dressed her mistress more beautifully than ever; the dead face, Anne's face, nestled in an exquisite lace shawl like a child's at its christening.

It was decided, after much discussion, that there was little point in trying to apprehend Beate. She had decamped at night with the connivance of a groom, who was also missing. Francesca hadn't left a will and, since no relatives were likely to come forward to claim them, her rings and pill-boxes would probably have gone to Beate anyway, for her years of service.

Francesca was buried in the St-Germain cemetery, with Prince James and the whole Jacobite Court in attendance, Mary of Modena in tears. Her grave wasn't the only one that had to be hacked out of the frozen earth. The winter was carrying off St-Germain's elderly; the wife of Sir William Waldegrave, the queen's doctor, the Abbé Rizzini, and Mrs Hunt, one of the maids.

To replace the runaway groom, Livingstone of Kilsyth applied to Marly for the return of his 'servant' Millet since the man had turned up at St-Germain anyway and showed no sign of being willing to go back. Permission was given; the horses at Marly were fit and well and Marly itself going into its winter hibernation until spring and the Sun King woke it up again.

To be honest, I felt a bit of a fool for insisting on coming back to discover that the grandmother was dead and had in any case been incapable of attempting Bratchet's life. Nobody else had either, a fact that she pointed out without warmth on the few occasions she had to bring a message from the queen to the stables. Even so, I reckoned it was time she and I escaped from France and there wasn't going to be a better time to do it.

Before the winter began, the allies had capitalized on their victory at Oudenarde by advancing into France and were besieging Lille, the strongest fortress in Europe. They were therefore nearer Paris than at any time since our arrival in the damned country.

I considered the matter carefully. The nearness of the allies wouldn't help us. Louis's forces were being kept in the field to prevent the besiegers' further advance and would cut off our escape in that direction. The route to Le Havre, though, might be open. And Le Havre was the port of call for a boat which, according to John Laws, would take us back to England when it became necessary.

Whether it could make the trip in winter seas was another question. On the other hand our escape would be easier in a winter like this one. The ground was becoming too hard even for hunting and allowing a relaxation in stable work in which my absence wasn't likely to be noticed for a day or two.

It would mean a difficult journey of one hundred or so miles. Fugitives would be more noticeable on empty roads, but there was the advantage that anybody likely to be curious – sentries, toll-keepers, etc. – would be staying indoors close to their fires.

I began making preparations for our departure, doing a lot of sewing – not my forte – using horsehair, and making a considerable outlay of John Laws's money on warm clothing.

The most difficult bit of the escape, I reckoned, would be in persuading the Bratchet to come with me.

Though Bratchet had put the queen's evening posset to warm

on the mantelpiece above the fire that had been kept blazing all day, lumps of ice fell into the glass as she poured it from the decanter.

Mary of Modena looked up from her writing table. 'The ink, La Fée, I want the ink, not the wine.' For her, the rebuke was sharp; the cold made people irritable.

Bratchet curtseyed and took the silver inkwell from the trivet at the edge of the fire. Through her thick mittens she could feel the heat distorting the metal. Unless ink was almost at boiling point, it froze on the pen and wrote white.

The queen said, 'We're all tired.'

It was a form of apology. Bratchet nodded, too exhausted to curtsey again. She had been on duty for sixteen hours because Mme Putti had complained of a headache and gone to bed. As she'd pointed out, she'd stood in for Bratchet while Bratchet sat in Francesca's room, now Bratchet could stand in for her.

Mme di Fiorenza was nodding in a chair by the royal bedchamber's fire so that all the fetching, carrying, trips to the kitchens and taking of messages fell on Bratchet. To move three feet out of range of the fire was to be in zero temperature. The high, unlit marble corridors beyond the bedchamber were, quite literally, icy.

The letters Mary of Modena was writing were of sympathy to Louis XIV and Mme de Maintenon on the loss of their confessor, old Père de la Chaise. He'd just died from the cold at Versailles. So had the Princesse de Soubise, one of Louis's former mistresses.

At last Mary of Modena finished her letters and Bratchet, dismissed for the night, took them to the hall table to await the postboy. She wondered if there would be a postboy to collect them; the last had arrived at the château frozen to his horse and had died shortly afterwards. She stopped wondering; she couldn't summon up enough concern; the cold was congealing compassion in her veins.

She went to the kitchen and fetched a brick heating in the ashes of the fire – one had to take precautions to warm one's bed to ensure one wasn't found dead in it – wrapped it in her skirt, lit a taper and climbed the stairs to her corridor.

The sounds coming from her room made her drop the brick and run. There was an obstruction against the other side of the door and she had to push hard to open it. She stumbled over something but managed to save the taper from going out.

The sounds were coming from Mme Putti on the bed. For a moment it seemed as if the old woman was fighting someone in it with her; the counterpane was billowing up and down. But there was no one else. The commotion was Mme Putti's legs, kicking.

'What is it? What is it?'

Mme Putti lurched on to her side. Bratchet saw her face and ran for Dr MacLaverty.

It wasn't until people brought candles that she found the obstruction against the door was the corpse of Turnspit. There was vomit trickling from his mouth which had drawn back in a rictus.

Mme Putti was still alive the next morning but her face and nails were livid and her breathing difficult. Every so often she went into a convulsion. A frightened Mary of Modena ordered every doctor in the château to examine her – Putti had been with her since her marriage.

Dr MacLaverty had said 'Poison' the moment he saw her. So did the others. So did an authoritative little man with black teeth and a stalk of rue stuck up each nostril named de Picard, who, despite the weather, was sent by King Louis and who'd gained his experience, it appeared, during the outbreak of poisoning in the 1680s, a scandal that had touched Versailles itself and discredited the then royal mistress, Mme de Montespan.

'Does she give herself enemas?' he asked.

The queen stared at him helplessly across her servant's bed and looked around for the Bratchet. 'Does she?'

Bratchet shook her head.

Dr MacLaverty reminded his royal colleague that a dog was included in the case which was not likely to have poisoned itself in a badly applied enema. De Picard examined Turnspit, still lying near the bed under a petticoat of Bratchet's. He forced the jaws open, stirred his fingers around the tongue and sniffed. 'Antimony.'

The other doctors nodded. 'Had she reason to commit *felo de se*?' asked de Picard.

Mary of Modena drew herself up. 'Monsieur, Mme Putti is as devout a Catholic as myself.'

'She has a rival for her lover's affection, perhaps?'

Had Mme Putti been conscious, she would have treasured the compliment. As Dr MacLaverty whispered to Bratchet, 'The good doctor has lived too long at Versailles.'

De Picard shrugged. 'Well, someone has poisoned her. In a *tisane*, perhaps, or a sweetmeat.'

Mary of Modena shook her head, unable to credit the idea. 'I shall have her moved to my room.'

'Certainly, Your Majesty, if you wish to kill her. The move would subject her to draughts.' He himself was wearing two fur caps and several blankets. 'Nor attempt to change her sheets. Did not the Prince d'Espinoy die from having his sheets changed, against my advice, before he was fully convalescent?'

They forced emetics down Putti's throat, purged and bled her until Bratchet thought there could be nothing left in the poor body.

It was useless. The patient went into a coma, then died.

They took the corpse to lie in the chapel, leaving Bratchet alone in the *entresol* to clear up.

She sat in the room's only chair staring at the bed lit by a solitary candle. She was in shock from the scenes she'd witnessed and grieving bitterly for her bedfellow. Putti had had her faults; she'd been bad-tempered, especially when hungry, and had frequently stolen Bratchet's food as by prior right, but she'd possessed an Italian sophistication that had revolutionized Bratchet's sense of style. Above all, she'd been one of the wittiest people in the château. She hadn't deserved to die like that. Bratchet was going to miss her badly; Putti had made her laugh.

But the desolation which descended on Bratchet was not due to the demise of Mme Putti but for Turnspit. She had never felt loneliness like this and, God knew, she had known loneliness. Always, during the bad times, there had been the hairy, smelly, bony cushion of her dog to lay her head on. Effie had acquired him soon after Bratchet's arrival at Puddle Court, to use in the turnspit wheel and to put down rats. Effie found him character-less and treated him as badly as she had Bratchet, resenting it when the two of them formed a dumb alliance against her.

To Bratchet he'd had dignity; it had distressed her to despera-tion to see him pedalling and scrabbling in the wall wheel to keep his paws away from the hot coal Effie tossed in it to make him turn faster. The picture came to her mind's eye now, and racked her.

When I flung open the *entresol* door, she was still sitting there. She looked up at me. 'Turnspit and Putti are dead.'

'I'm sorry.' If it sounded casual, it was because I still hadn't got over the relief. 'I thought it was you.' I'd returned from the blacksmith's to hear that one of the bedchamber women was poisoned.

She shook her head miserably. 'Turnspit. And Putti.'

'Yes,' I said, 'Come on. Put on something warm. We're going.' I began picking up pieces of clothing to feel their thickness. 'You'll need good boots.'

'Going?'

'Before they try again.'

'Who tries again?' Her face hardened. 'Oh, you're not still . . . I won't have you make a drama from it. This wasn't murder. It was . . . a bad piece of meat or something.'

'Doctors got it wrong, did they?'

'Yes.' St-Germain was goodness and happiness for her, per-haps the best she'd known. 'It was something else,' she said wearily, 'Putti was already ill . . . I did her duty for her because she wasn't well.'

'What about the dog, was that ill too?'

'No,' she admitted.

'Died out of sympathy did he? Sorry, vomit, dead. Mac-Laverty told me. For Christ's sake, Bratchet, think.'

She was too bereft and tired to think; too cold. 'Leave me alone,' she said, 'I'm not going with you. You're mad. I've got things to do here. The queen needs me.' Irritation was rousing her from lassitude. 'Go away and leave me alone. I've got to change the sheets.'

She got up and began tearing the fouled covers from the bed.

I took the pillows off for her and their cases. If necessary I'd carry the silly bitch to where Rosinante was waiting.

The flurry she was making as she folded the blankets suddenly stopped so that I turned to look at her. She was standing by the bed, her eyes fixed on something in it. Her hands were raised as if the cold had infiltrated her body and frozen it in mid-action.

I took up the candle and carried it nearer the bed. Lying on the sheet where the pillows had covered them were a cluster of lace casings such as women made to contain sweetmeats.

I buried Turnspit in a lawn within sight of the Le Vau fountain on which, I gathered, he had sprinkled admiration in the past. It was hard work to dig even that small grave. The moon shone like a great pale sun without rendering colour. Apart from the hit-hit of the pickaxe the gardens of St-Germain were silent. Like the dog in Bratchet's arms. Like her.

When I told her to put the dog's body in the grave, she put it in. I shovelled earth over it and tamped it down with my foot. When I led her away, she followed. Something had gone out of her with the realization that Beate had tried to murder her. It was easy to persuade her that we must leave; she no longer wanted to stay.

I'd tethered Rosinante and the pack donkey in the stableyard. They were still there. So was Livingstone of Kilsyth. He'd been to a neighbouring château for some jollification or another and was still in his regalia.

'Where are you taking the lassie?'

'Away.'

'Ye're not.'

I said, 'Francesca's maid left her poisoned chocolates. She put them in Bratchet's cupboard. Putti ate them instead and gave one to the dog.'

'Havers,' he said, 'why would any soul do such a thing?'

'Because she was paid to. Now get out of my way.'

He didn't move. 'How do ye know the chocolate was for the lassie? I'll not say the maid wasna mad. It may be she was trying to kill Mme Putti.'

209

I shook my head. 'We found them in Bratchet's cupboard. There was her initials embroidered on the casings.'

He frowned. 'But the woman's fled and gone. There's no danger to the lassie now.'

'She's been in danger ever since I've known her. Anyway, there's no point in her staying. Anne Bonny was never here, never will be. She's as dead as her grandmother. So haver off, I want to be well away before dawn.'

He appealed to Bratchet. 'Do ye go, Mlle La Fée? Do ye not stay with the cause?'

Her eyes were wide and pale and not looking at him, or anything. Shock had put her into a sort of trance, but it was still a healthier state than the trance the Scot had put her into, him and his bloody cause.

'We're going,' I said.

He still didn't move. He was thinking. It always took him time. At last he said: 'Aye, well, you may have the right of it about Bonny Anne. She's no dead, that I know, but she's not here either. And I've a wee errand or two of my own to take me back home. Wait till the morrow when I can explain myself and we'll all go. Ye'll need me to get through the French lines.'

I brought the gun out from my cloak and pointed it at him. It was an old one that the Duc d'Orléans had left in his saddle-holster and forgotten about. Like the *noblesse*, it was more ornamental than useful, but at this range it wouldn't miss. 'No explanation. You can write a note and leave it in the stables.' I didn't trust the bastard. 'You're coming now.'

'Like this?' He was in full Scottish rig – kilt, bare knees, sporran, the plaid scarf they wear over one shoulder of their jackets. How he wasn't freezing to death beat me; they breed them hardy in the Highlands. In that dress, they have to.

I covered him with the pistol while he went into the stables to gather every horse-blanket he could find, then into the stall where he kept his horse. I told him to put two of the blankets on the beast, then saddle up, then dress Bratchet in the padded cape I'd made for her. While he was doing it, I put on the other cape and got up on Rosinante. The Scotsman swung Bratchet up behind me. I told him to mount, take the pack mule's reins and lead the way.

Then we set off into the coldest winter there's ever been.

You had to have been in France to know just how bad the winter of 1708/9 was; it was terrible throughout Europe, but it gripped France especially, as if it was on the side of the allies. I think it was.

We heard later that the Paris thermometer fell to below what it could register. The Seine froze and ice snapped the mooring ropes of the barges. Water froze in wells, peasants in cottages, cattle in stalls, rabbits in their burrows. The air cut through feathers like invisible metal so that birds fell dead from the trees.

I'd reckoned it was about a hundred miles from St-Germain to Le Havre as the crow flew and hoped we'd cover about twenty a day, but the crow didn't have to cope with roads like rutted cast iron, or make detours to spare its horses' hooves, or persuade the beasts down hills when they balked at the slipperiness of the descent, or lead them up steep gradients. It was a good day if we did twelve miles.

We daren't rest until we found shelter. To stay still turned your blood sluggish in your veins and prevented you moving. On one detour we passed a man who'd stopped to rest in a field. He was still sitting there, dead as mutton, like a petrified scarecrow. Kilsyth wanted to bury him but I said no; it would take too much of our strength.

The only blessing was that it was too cold to snow. That would have finished us. We moved through a white world because the frost was so deep that every twig, every weed, had grown crystals which made it twice its size. Frost formed on the reins, on our cloaks; we looked like a trio of sparkling ghosts.

For the first two days, the Scotsman reasoned with me. 'There's no need for this flight. They don't think you an enemy. Let us go back, let me but to explain I must return to Scotland and we can make this journey in the spring in all pleasantness.'

He was probably right, but I didn't trust him. Even less I trusted whoever was marking the Bratchet – they'd proved to

211

have a long reach. They'd managed to track us wherever we went.

Once he'd done his protesting, Kilsyth held his peace. Being less warmly clad than Bratchet and me, he couldn't spare the breath. To talk involved pulling down the scarves covering the lower part of our faces, inviting air into our mouths that lanced the teeth.

By early afternoon we had to start looking for somewhere to pass the night. Even under cover it would be death without a fire, so when we found a charcoal-burner's hut or a barn, there remained the labour of gathering fuel. The donkey had to be unloaded, the horses unsaddled and unrugged, hooves had to be picked free of balled ice and pebbles, and icicles to be chipped from eaves to melt for water – it takes a lot of ice to produce a kettleful of water. By the time we'd settled and boiled the salted horsemeat I'd brought, we were too tired for conversation.

The roads were virtually empty except for the military. Kilsyth had to do the talking when we were questioned and I kept the pistol cocked under my cloak while he did it. But mostly the soldiers we encountered were returning from the front and were wearier than we were, many of them wounded, all of them sullen. For the first time, they were being beaten on their own soil.

There weren't even whistles at the Bratchet with which soldiers on the march usually compliment young women. Mind you, enveloped in the clumsy horsehair quilt and hood I'd made, she didn't exactly look an object of ardour. She didn't talk at all. Finding the Beate snake in her Garden of Eden had returned her to the miserable wretch she'd been at Aunt Effie's.

I did my best to raise her spirits, and Kilsyth did more, but she didn't respond. I wondered if she was beginning to suspect that her loyalty to the person she'd seen coming out of Aunt Effie's after the murder was misplaced.

I tried capitalizing on it. 'Do you want to tell me who killed Effie Sly?'

She looked at me as if I was the true enemy. I was the one who'd changed things, the man who'd taken her into winter away from the happy ignorance of her golden summer.

She shouted, 'Who got rid of Anne and Mary? The nobs did, din't they? And you're working for them.' She was all Puddle Court now. 'You're a lurker, you are, and I wouldn't tell you shitten-cum-shite if you was to piss gold in a bucket.'

Well, at least I'd roused her.

When I told Kilsyth we were headed for Le Havre where, I said, I might be able to bribe a fisherman to land me in England by night, he was better pleased than he had been. There he'd find some merchantman that traded with the Highlands to take him home. He gave me his *parole* that he wouldn't decamp until then, nor do anything to prevent us getting away.

I was glad of him. There might have been awkwardness if it had been only Bratchet and me to share the same bedding for sleeping – which it was vital to do for the warmth. The first night I clambered under the blankets beside her, she went stiff as if I was one of Effie's lodgers. 'Don't flatter yourself,' I told her.

But when the Scotsman came in from putting away the horses and knelt down and said his prayers and joined us, she relaxed. He was her *chevalier sans reproche* as the French call it. She could trust him, apparently, if she couldn't trust me. To be honest, both of us were too cold to be capable. With her blue, pinched face and red nose, she wasn't any houri either.

The next day, it was the sixth if I remember, or the seventh, Kilsyth began to wander in his wits. He was singing some Scottish song uncomplimentary to the English and, towards the end of the afternoon, I saw he'd thrown off his blanket and we had to go back for it.

We made for the next shelter we saw, a broken-down deserted farmstead. Bratchet and I got a fire going and left Kilsyth sitting by it – he was still singing and not noticing the cold – while we went out into the byre. The farmstead hadn't been deserted; the peasant and wife who rented it from their seigneur were hanging from a rafter above their frozen cow. I righted the sawing-horse they'd stood up on to adjust the noose of their ropes, and cut the bodies down: 'One cow,' I shouted at Bratchet, 'One bony bloody cow the difference whether they lived or died. Where's your Sun King now?'

It wasn't the time. It wasn't her fault anyway. She was as horrified as I was, though not so angry.

That night I slaughtered the donkey. I'd brought him along to feed us when the fodder he carried ran out. And Kilsyth needed nourishment. Bratchet knew that and approved it, but it didn't make her more kindly towards me. She'd allied with the donkey because, with Kilsyth and I having to care for our horses, it had fallen to her to lead the beast, pack and unpack him, feed him. He'd become Turnspit, her dumb comfort. I was taking everything away from her.

When we got back to the dwelling, Kilsyth was coming out of the door. 'Fareweel to a' our Scottish fame,' he was singing, 'Fareweel our ancient glory, Fareweel e'en to the Scottish name, Sae famed in martial story.'

We had trouble getting him back inside. 'I'll no enter under an English roof for your hireling wages.'

'It's Scottish,' Bratchet told him, quickly. She was sobbing.

'Verra well then.'

We took him up the hut's cupboard staircase to the room above containing one large wooden bed on which was a straw palliasse, but no bedclothes, and laid him on it. Bratchet wanted to cover him with everything we had. 'There's a warming pan down there. I'll put some fire in it.'

I stopped her. Kilsyth had become so cold over the last few days that he'd reached the point I'd seen in horses where, if you heat them up too quickly, they die. I wouldn't even let her feed him hot stew. 'Tepid's warm enough.'

It was a hard night. We rubbed his feet and hands to get the blood back in them and gradually increased the heat of the bed, giving him warmer and warmer drinks every hour.

The Bratchet wouldn't rest, she was frantic he was going to die. 'It's your fault,' she kept saying, 'You didn't have to bring him along. I'm going to take him back. So soon as he's better, we're going back to Court. I should never have left anyway. The queen needs me.'

I was tired. 'Court,' I said, 'Queen. James Francis'll be King of England when I'm Pope. They're dolls pretending to be real. Curtseying to a lot of playing cards you've been.

And near got yourself poisoned doing it.'

'It was still better than Puddle Court,' she said.

We couldn't go on like this. 'Bratchie, be reasonable. You had to come away. This is deep. It's deep business. Somebody near got you in England and they near got you in France. Somebody's got a long arm. Who is it? Why? Tell me.'

'It wasn't Somebody,' she insisted. 'There isn't a Somebody except in your mind. It was the Bête. She was always talking about killing people and she did. She's mad. She just hated me for no reason. She was . . .' she had to lapse into French to get over her meaning '. . . *un phénomène.*'

'Mme Putti'll find that a comfort. Wherever she is.'

She winced and I realized how Putti's death hurt her. I didn't want to hurt her any more. And I never seemed to do anything else.

We saved Kilsyth between us, but we had to stay in that farmstead for another week until he was fit enough to travel and to give time enough for Bratchet and me to sew two blankets together and stuff them with the mule's hair to keep the cold off him when we went.

By the time we set out the air that had been so clear had gained a furriness which cut down the view; a drop from one of the icicles in the eaves fell on my head as I inspected the horses' feet. 'Thaw's coming.'

It came slowly. Roads became slush by midday but turned back to ice at nights. Traffic increased – and so did questions. Kilsyth got us through. He was in fine form and, I think, grateful to us for being alive. We were good Jacobites, friends of the king, he told people. The usual French hostility thawed in the warmth of his bonhomie. Thanks to him we were able to stay at the cheaper inns with impunity. At nights he'd sit with our hosts and roar out his Scotland for ever songs at the top of his voice and make them laugh and join in.

Bratchet withdrew into her silence. A large part of the Scotsman's cheeriness was because he was going home. 'I'll be in the Highlands for the spring,' he said, 'and ye both in your London, poor souls.'

'Ye both.' No request that Bratchet go with him.

Even he fell silent as we followed the Seine into what should have been the richest earth in France, the apple-growing, cream-making Normandy, and saw withered orchards and fields where peasants were digging down to find their winter corn seed shrivelled.

As we approached Rouen we passed a *haras*. Through elaborate gates we could see up the sweep of a drive to the château-like stables around a *cour d'honneur* where liveried grooms led stallions for inspection past the officers. The fact that it was the only energy and prosperity we'd seen during the whole journey, and that it existed in a place devoted to breeding horses for Louis XIV's cavalry, pointed up the misery of the people whose taxes paid for it.

I suppose we neglected Bratchet those last days towards Le Havre. She was quiet and, anyway, spent most of her time asleep riding pillion, her head nodding against the back of one of us. We swopped her over when whichever horse she happened to be on had endured her weight long enough, and she nodded even during the changeover.

'The weaker sex,' said Kilsyth, winking at me, 'Lord bless their saucy hearts.' I winked back.

She slept, I realize now, because there was nothing else for her to do. Directions were taken, inns entered, stayed in, paid for, more directions taken, without reference to her. The journey was turning we two men into friends; our talk was horses and war. Being a woman, she had no contribution to it and, because she was a woman, we didn't expect any.

By the last but one day, we'd become so used to her silence we started comparing our past women. It was only when Kilsyth, in full flight on brothels he had known, was dismounting that we recalled her presence behind him. 'Wheesht now, Martin. Remember the lassie.'

We rode into Le Havre in late evening and found an inn. There Bratchet made a stand. 'I'm not going. Go and find your bloody boats and sail off. I'm not coming. I'm not going back to Puddle Court.'

'It won't be Puddle Court,' I said, 'It'll be . . . somewhere else.'

'Where?'

She'd floored me. I hadn't thought. 'I don't know, yet.'

'What as?' she demanded, 'What'll I be? A maid again? You can stick that, you mimpin. I've served a queen, I'm not serving nobody else now.'

'What do you want to do, lassie?' Kilsyth asked.

'I'm going to enlist. I'm going to do what Mary did and Kit Ross did and become a soldier.' She was standing up and facing us both like a rabbit making a last stand against two dogs.

'Which army are you thinking of strengthening?' I asked.

'It don't matter. French or English. Just as long as I'm quit of you two.'

I saw Kilsyth's mouth twitch. 'Ye're maybe a wee bit on the short side for a soldier. I doubt they'd take you.'

'Besides,' I said, 'you'll need money while you wait for the 'listing officer. Livingstone here ain't got any and I'm lending him what I've got for his passage.'

'Ye'd best press on to England now, lassie. There's no going back.'

'Don't call me lassie.'

'Come on now, Bratchie, join us in a drink and something to eat. You'll feel better.'

'Don't call me Bratchie.'

We left her in her room and went off to make a night of it. When we came back we looked in on her and saw she was asleep again.

We arranged that Kilsyth should go to the harbour and, while trying to find a boat for himself, make enquiries about *L'Hirondelle* on our behalf. He'd not taken back his *parole* and I was pretty sure I could trust him. It was a case of having to; my French wasn't good enough to avoid suspicion, while the Bratchet had gone into a torpor which made her useless.

He returned in high spirits that evening. 'The luck of the Kilsyths is back with me. There's a fine big boat in harbour this minute that's to set out to the Firth of Moray on the morn's tide. The master's a leal Jacobite and trades with the clans, he tells me.'

'What about *L'Hirondelle*?'

'I asked him. Casual, as ye told me. He knows her. She's late this month which he puts down to the weather, but for certain will be here within the week.'

'So you sail before we do.'

'I go aboard this night. With your permission, of course.'

I couldn't see any reason not to give it, but I was uneasy. Oddly enough, so was he. 'Och, Martin, but what will you and the lassie do without me?'

All we had to do was stay in the inn until our boat came. Bratchet could do our talking. But I was still uneasy. And I'd miss him. I told him so.

'Ye'll come and see me off? It'd be as well you accustom yourself with the harbour. The quays are a puzzle.'

We took the Bratchet with us, in case somebody stopped me on the way back with questions I couldn't answer. Unmelted blocks of ice had been swept into dirty piles along wharves where swing-bridges and cranes glistened with wet. Flotsam knocked against the sides of water-basins. A fight broke out in a tavern, spilling men out of its doors into the light thrown through its open door on to the slimy setts of the quay. Ports are the same all over the world.

I thought of the two women whose fate had sent the three of us chasing across Europe in the first place. Docks like these were the last thing they'd seen before they were overpowered and bundled aboard some scow bound for . . . where? Was it really Mary who'd escaped and become a soldier? Or Anne? And which of them had returned to England and murdered Aunt Effie?

I looked down at the Bratchet. She knew.

She was looking around her with aversion and I thought she was probably remembering her friends, like I was. *One of them's trying to kill you, Bratchet. Or she's got high-placed friends who need to kill you on her behalf. Believe it.*

She wouldn't, of course. She would, literally, rather die than believe it. So she might, unless I could stop it. It all came back to the same question. 'Tell me who killed Effie Sly, Bratchet,' I said.

In the murk her eyes looked pale as she shrank away from me and nearer to the Scotsman. He put his hand under her elbow and hurried her along.

I don't know much about boats, or I didn't then, but the *Holy Innocent* seemed overlarge for an illegal merchantman needing to avoid attention from the English navy on her trips to Jacobite Scotland. There was only a flambeau on the dockside and her own riding lights to see her by, but I got the impression of bulk looming above us in the dark. She had gun ports along one deck.

Her welcome was hearty enough. An officer standing by the gangplank with a dark lantern said, 'Captain Porritt's compliments to you, Mr Kilsyth, and welcome aboard. He asks if you and your friends would be pleased to come to his cabin and down a nightcap with him before we set sail.'

'Ye might as well, Martin,' Kilsyth muttered, 'Ye're paying for it.'

Only Kilsyth could have persuaded passage money out of a lender which would enable him to join a plot against that lender's government. More ironically, it was that same government's money – part of the purse of louis d'ors that John Laws had given me in Paris. But he'd pointed out that I hadn't given him time enough that night when we left St-Germain to go and borrow from somebody else.

So we all went aboard the *Holy Innocent* to have a drink with Captain Porritt.

Four sailors grabbed Kilsyth and me as we went through the entry port. Another one grabbed Bratchet. We heard her shouting and kicking as he carried her off. Kilsyth put up a better fight than I did, I got a sea-boot in my stomach which put me out early but he did a lot of damage before he went down. They bound our hands and feet and bumped us down companionways to somewhere black in the ship's innards. My head took punishment and the last thing I remember thinking was that Anne Bonny and Mary Read had done better than us in the same situation. At least one of them had managed to escape.

We'd been unlucky, as I found out much later. If we'd arrived in Le Havre the following week instead of when we did, the *Holy Innocent* wouldn't have been able to set out because the winter came back with a vengeance, refreezing the seas.

Behind us, wolves began prowling the forests of France and fed not just on domestic stock but human flesh; people were dropping dead from starvation. In Paris the shortage of bread produced riots and a mob of women setting out to protest to Versailles had to be stopped by the army. The *noblesse* stayed indoors rather than confront the accusing faces in the streets, black with hunger. French currency lost a third of its value; public institutions and great private financiers went bankrupt.

There was no policy like the English Poor Laws system to deal with the situation; charity in France relies more on individual generosity; in past food shortages Louis had always been rich enough to help with distributions of 'The King's Bread', but the scale of this emergency was beyond his scope; anyway the war had begun to impoverish even him.

He did what he could, imposing a tax for the hungry from which no one was exempt, making an immediate contribution himself of £1,400. He lifted all tax on transport, ordered wholemeal bread to be baked for everyone, rich and poor, and banned hoarding and speculation. As an example to his nobles, he had his own gold plate melted down to pay for food for the starving. But the food wasn't there. Crops had withered. Bracken and roots were being used to make flour. Children were seen cropping the grass in the fields like sheep.

As God's representative on earth, the Sun King was responsible for his country's suffering. He did the only thing he could; he began suing for peace.

CHAPTER TWELVE

THE BANNER stretching along the warehouse in Freeman's Yard, Cornhill, read: 'Gowns for men and women from £7 10s. to 13s. each. The Silk, Stuff and Callicoes bought at Bankrupt Sales. Ladies may be furnish'd with all kinds of Quilted Petticoats and Canvas Hoops and the newest Matted Petticoats.'

But ladies wishing to be so furnished had to use the door-knocker and listen to the withdrawing of bolts and turning of keys before they could come in. Even then, the woman who attended them had no sense of fashion, invariably had a duster in her hand, and puffed anxiously as she displayed the inadequate stock. If her customers asked her about the source of the rumbling coming from the ceiling she blinked hopefully and said, 'Mice.' She rarely made a sale.

Having conscientiously barred and locked the door behind her latest visitor, she heaved herself up the open wooden flight of steps leading to the upper storey and knocked on the hatch.

The rumbling stopped. 'What?'

'There's been a gentleman, Dan'l.'

The hatch was unbolted and Mrs Defoe was helped up into the long room above. It was lit from the north by a series of windows and had a waist-high shelf running its length underneath them, all of it covered by piles of paper, quills, sanding pots, ink bottles and wells, candles and sealing-wax. It was served by an inky chair to which castors had been attached. Blots of ink decorated the dusty floorboards and even the bales stacked in the corners, while an untidy laundry of proofs was pegged to overhead lines.

The eye went to the room's only smartness – an embroidered coat of arms hanging like a battle flag over the shelf-desk; per chevron engrailed, gules and or three griffins counterchanged declaring the owner of the warehouse to be Daniel De Foe, Gent.

Mrs Defoe went over to it, stood on stubby tiptoes and dusted it, annoying her husband by the futility of applying cloth to cloth. 'What was he? Shoulder-tapper?'

'I don't reckon so.' Mrs Defoe knew the look of creditors and bailiffs. 'Asking for Claude Guilot. That's one of your allusses, ain't it, Dan'l?'

'Aliases, woman.'

'Said to meet Mr Brown at his lodgings at eight of the clock tonight.'

Robert Harley. Defoe felt a surge of excitement, mixed with guilt. Since Harley had been dismissed from office, Defoe had been neglectful of the man, devoting himself to the winner of the political battle, Lord Godolphin.

'I said you would. Was that right, Dan'l?'

'That was right,' Defoe said reluctantly; his wife irritated him almost as much when she was right as when she made mistakes.

Mrs Defoe nodded. 'I'll be off home now then, Dan'l.'

'Lock up before you go. I'll leave the usual way.' He counted out shillings into her toughened little palm, enough for her to take a hackney to their house in Newington, kissed her and watched her go down the steps, moving at her careful, unaltering pace.

Why didn't she ask questions? Why, however fashionable the clothes he bought her, did they always look the same once they had been fitted over her short frame? He could never take her anywhere.

Except to funerals. It was a thing he'd noticed, that at times of personal crisis people wanted Mrs Defoe near them. The newly bereaved always touched her, as if absorbing a strength that tapped the roots of earth and reduced death to a phase as natural as winter, promising rebirth in the great cycle's due course.

When Henry Foe, Daniel's father, lay dying, it was his daughter-in-law he wanted by his bed. He hadn't left his son a penny, afraid it would be spent on projects. Instead he'd willed the proceeds of his tallow-chandler business to his grandchildren, ensuring that the Defoe family house in Newington with its orchards and gardens wouldn't be sold up by creditors.

There were times when Defoe recognized that his wife possessed the dull, deep benchmark of human goodness that he tried so hard to emulate. There were times when he was jealous of it. There were even times when he knew he was jealous of it.

Well, what else did she have to do but be good? Apart from keep house and seven children. And the shop. And bamboozle creditors. Anybody could be a true Christian if they weren't dragged hither and yon by the expediency of politicians.

It was he, Defoe, Gent., who provided the base for her goodness, working all the hours God sent, often putting his life at risk, to say nothing of the risk to his soul. He went back to his chair and gave a push with one of his feet, like a child on a scooter, to send it rumbling along the shelf to where his 'Essay on Public Credit' was waiting to be finished.

If I'm assassinated, will she even ask why? Since working for Godolphin he'd been writing fervent Whig propaganda in his *Review*. And the Tories didn't like it. They'd already killed that violent old Whig, John Tutchin of *Observator*, who'd been cudgelled by ruffians in a dark alley, everyone knowing the Tories had paid them. He kept to the populated areas and had his sword always at the ready. He was being followed everywhere. Yet Defoe shall not be silenced.

He shook his pen, added a full stop to Public Credit and scooted himself further down the bench to his half-finished 'Essay on South Sea Trade'. Here's a project. Here's romance. The South Seas. Colonies planted in South America. Settlers in Chile to produce rice, cocoa, wine, sugar and spice and quarry gold. Put natives to work and clothe them in English wool. It was a copper-bottomed certainty, if he only had money to invest in it. If Godolphin would only pay him what he deserved.

He didn't feel comfortable with Godolphin who used him with distaste, having a contempt for pamphleteers. Harley now – there was a man who'd appreciated the power of the press. The Union between Scotland and England had been due to the two of them.

The Exchange clock was striking. God bless us; just time to go to Wait's Coffee Shop and pick up the latest gossip before he kept his appointment with Harley. Defoe flung down his pen, put on his coat and wig, adjusted his cuffs and went to the sack-hoist, a relic from the days when the warehouse had been a corn merchant's.

Nobody in the yard at the back. He put his foot in the looped chain and attended to the difficult business of holding himself out from the wall while he locked the sack-hoist door. Then, clinging to the slack, he paid it out until he was on the ground. I'm too old for these exploits, he thought. By the age of forty-nine a man should have won the right to walk out through his own front door. And I could have been Lord Mayor.

He swaggered down Cornhill like one who'd never been in

its pillory, his nose up, eyes narrowed, hand on sword hilt, ears cocked for the sound of quickening feet behind him, instinct sniffing for danger. Such a fox I am. They'll not run down Daniel Defoe.

On the front of houses hung the black crêpe of mourning. Malplaquet. Another Marlborough victory. Yet when the French army had drawn off, defeated, they were neither demoralized nor pursued. And the list of allied dead had been dreadful, a butcher's bill. Old Sims at the 'Change had lost his son, Mistress FitzHarding hers. And for the brave Dutch, 8,000 wounded or killed. So many young men, all our sons. Defoe blinked, drew his kerchief from his sleeve and blew his nose. It has gone on too long. The war must be ended. He agreed with the Tories on that much. Mobs in the street were turning against the Whig Parliament.

Wait's smelled of coffee, new bread and perspiring men. It was the favoured meeting place for Whig writers and lawyers, a talking shop and an excellent barometer of the nation's political weather. Just now its atmosphere was depressed. The electorate had turned against the Whigs. Defoe joined a group he knew by the fire.

'Take Malplaquet,' said one, 'Four, five years ago the buggers would've greeted it as a great victory. Cheering. Hats in the air. And it *was* a great victory. Lads got killed, lads do get killed. Nature of battles. Marlborough's spoiled the bloody voters, that's the trouble. Don't want mere victories now, want bloody miracles.'

'And the Queen only giving a thanksgiving in her private chapel,' pointed out another, 'No more St Paul's.'

'That's Sarah. Dragging the poor old Duke down with her. That's what you get for involving bloody women in politics.'

An optimist said, 'Well, but we've got Louis suing for peace.'

'But we're offering him terms he can't accept.'

And there were the taxes causing the landowning Tories in their shires to yelp in pain at the continuing war, and Tory hacks egging them on to blame Marlborough for it. Tory mobs out on the streets yelling for Godolphin's blood.

There was miserable nodding. 'The war's gone on too long.

The Tories will get in for sure. Harley'll be back within the year.'

At that, Daniel Defoe left them. It would be as well not to keep Britain's next Prime Minster waiting.

'. . . and it is always, always, with regret, my lord, that I have found myself obliged by circumstances to continue in the service of those who have proved themselves your enemies.'

Defoe had been chewing on humble pie for fully ten minutes. Why doesn't he say something? Does he want me to eat more? He'd forgotten Harley's terrible silences which allowed the words you'd just uttered to resound in your own ears. What else could I do? You've been out of power, Godolphin was in. I've a wife and seven children to support. He said, wearily, 'Such as it is, my pen is at your disposal, my lord.' I'm tired. Let me sit down. I want a glass of that port.

'Lodgings' was an impoverished word for the apartment in Villiers Street which was where Harley was staying while he waited for the next election to put him back into power. It was a bachelor's hideaway, a rich bachelor's hideaway, with the cohesive dark-gold untidiness of too many books.

Harley held his glass up so that the flames from his fire glowed through it like a ruby set in crystal. 'Are you acquainted with a Dr Swift, Master Defoe?'

'Swift? Swift? I don't think I know the gentleman,' lied Defoe.

'An Irish Protestant churchman recently arrived in London and a promising writer. He has written most excellently on the misbehaviour of the Whigs. Most excellently.'

'Really?' He knew what Harley was doing, but screaming, infantile jealousy scorched through him just the same: You never called a piece of mine excellent. Swift's cleverness was being bruited through the coffee shops, as was his phrase for Defoe: 'an illiterate hack'.

Panic! I've left it too late to crawl back. Harley had found another, better apologist, one who would return him and the Tories to power by blaming Marlborough for the war's progress.

Despising himself, he said, 'By coincidence I am myself penning an essay on similar lines. I call it . . .' he thought fast

'. . . "Reasons why this Nation ought to put a Speedy End to this Expensive War".' It sounded crude even to him. But it would probably have to be.

The inclination of Harley's head indicated he might be pleased to read it. Later. When he had time. But at least he was also indicating a chair. 'How goes the Agency, Master Defoe? Do you have news of Martin Millet?'

'None, my lord.' Defoe sat down. He was worried about Martin.

'Allow me to enlighten you. He was captured and taken into France.'

'Captured?' asked Defoe in distress. 'Oh, my poor boy.'

'And taken into France,' said Harley, 'along with the girl, Bratchet, and your friend, Livingstone of Kilsyth.'

'No friend of mine, my lord, as you know. I warned Martin against him. I thought he might be heading for St-Germain to see the Bard grandmother. Did Martin follow him? Is that how he came into France?' He should have known that Harley, even out of office, would have access to government information.

Harley continued as if Defoe hadn't spoken. 'But now, I fear, all three of them have disappeared.'

'Disappeared, my lord?'

'Millet had been informed that, should it become necessary for him to escape, he must make for Le Havre and enquire for a boat called *L'Hirondelle* which would bring him back home.'

'The Swallow,' said Defoe, to show his education.

Harley ignored it. 'This he did. Unfortunately, he got on the wrong boat, so our agents discovered later. He and the girl and the Scotsman boarded one that was bound for the West Indies where, I fear, little good will befall them.'

'Oh dear Lord,' cried Defoe, 'How shall I tell Mrs Defoe? She loves Martin like another son. So do I.'

Harley got up to pour more port, and this time gave a glass to Defoe. Being out of office had improved the man. He was thinner and there was a keenness back in his eyes which, towards the end of his ministry, had been too frequently dulled by drink. He sat down again.

'Master Defoe, it became my conviction, while I was in office

– and it still is – that an element had taken a hand in the search we initiated for a certain lady at our first meeting.'

Defoe looked around him, in case there were listeners in the shadows. 'An element?'

'Someone we did not know. Someone unconnected with the usual politics. Someone who did not wish us to find the lady and was prepared to go to great lengths to stop us doing so. That conviction has now become a certainty.'

Better. Oh, how much better. He'd wager the excellent Dr Swift wasn't this deeply in Harley's confidence.

'You will remember the unhappy business of my secretary, William Greg.'

'Er, yes, my lord.' Defoe wondered if Harley felt himself to be partly responsible through the laxity with which he'd left secret papers lying around for minions to read.

'Among the information which Greg passed to France there was a letter or letters sent to St-Germain-en-Laye.'

'Where Francesca Bard is in residence.' Defoe was excited.

'No longer. She is dead. We only know of those letters' existence because among the documents sent from France to Greg, and which our agents intercepted, there was a reply.'

Defoe envied Harley's contacts. With spies like his I could rule the world. Perhaps Harley *was* ruling it. Even out of office. I need his patronage. I was wrong to neglect it.

'The reply was on St-Germain headed writing paper,' Harley went on, 'It promised that the writer would see to "the disposal of the goods". I fear that the disposal has been carried out. I fear that the "goods" were Master Millet and Miss Bratchet.'

Defoe put his head in his hands. The poor young people. After a while he said, 'But why would Greg want them disposed of?'

'I do not think he did. I believe him merely to have been the post office, as it were. I think the original letter which ordered the disposal was written by somebody else. I think that all along the writer's intended victim was the girl Bratchet. Did you not tell me that Martin Millet had said he thought somebody was trying to kill her?'

Defoe nodded.

'Then I think we can safely assume that the maid recognized the person who killed her mistress, Effie Sly. Through some distorted loyalty she kept her silence at the time. Such trulls have a natural disinclination to assist the law. However, the knowledge has proved dangerous to her. Somebody thinks it worthwhile to go to considerable trouble to make sure she never disseminates it.'

'A Jacobite plot, my lord!' Jacobites were Defoe's favourite enemy. 'They stole Anne Bonny Bard's papers from Effie Sly to ensure that she could not prove her right to the throne. Now they are eliminating anyone who can implicate them.'

'It may be. But I do not think so. In my view we are dealing not so much with plotters as with a devious, ruthless and ambitious individual with considerable resources. I think it is a woman. And I think she is at Court.'

'At *Court*?'

Harley said, 'Poor Greg was unwise enough to keep a diary. It proves that he was in thrall to some female at Court whom he refers to throughout the diary as "Circe".'

'Circe?' *And Circe changed men into swine.*

Harley's eyes twitched. 'We shall proceed faster, Master Defoe, if you do not repeat every statement I make. He refers to the woman as Circe. There are entries such as "Saw Circe today when I went to the household quarters." And "Sexual recreation with Circe". There was a particularly interesting entry which said that Circe wished him to include a letter to St-Germain among some information which he was sending to France. I must conclude that it was this letter which requested the disposal of our poor friends.'

'Who is this Circe?'

'We do not know. Obviously a woman in Her Majesty's household. Obviously the person who, all along, had been trying to dispose of the Bratchet, since it is too great a coincidence that the girl attracted the attention of two different assassins. And, since the attempts on the Bratchet's life began after Effie Sly was murdered and the papers stolen, we can safely assume that Circe is involved in the matter of Anne Bard, otherwise known as Bonny.'

Daniel, staring into the fire, saw in its blaze a pockmarked, anguished little face and heard a whisper: 'They ain't dead. They ain't.' 'Oh my God,' he said.

All at once Harley was brisk and appeared to change the subject. 'How do you read the political situation, Master Defoe?'

Defoe blinked himself into the present. 'I have no doubt the next election will bring in a Tory Parliament.'

And God help England.

'Yet if I read you aright in the *Review*, you, Master Defoe, have been doing everything in your power to urge the country to keep the Tories out.'

And God help me if I have offended this bland, terrible little man who will lead them. 'Only the extremists, my lord, the High Tories red in tooth and claw, ready to appease France merely in order to stop taxation, intolerant towards Dissenters, hating the financiers who run the City, a disaster to the country's credit.'

Harley nodded. 'We are moderate men, are we not, Master Defoe?'

I've come full circle. Here he was again, promising his soul away in order to keep in favour. 'We are, we are, my lord.'

'I shall be pleased to see you employ your *Review* to urging the cause of moderation in future.'

It was a warning. 'Yes, my lord.'

'Listen to me, Daniel.' For once Harley lost his blandness. He leaned forward with the jutting jaw of his tough, Radnorshire farming ancestors. 'The hand I shall have to play in the next few years is difficult beyond belief. The peace negotiations with King Louis will be difficult enough, yet they are as nothing to the question of the succession. The Queen is a sick woman. How much longer she'll last is anybody's guess. Already the country is beginning to divide on who should succeed her. The High Tories are not the only ones who feel that the Pretender is the rightful heir. But the Whigs will not countenance him.'

Daringly, Daniel asked, 'And which do you favour, my lord. James? Or Hanover?'

The glass in Harley's hand shook, sending a quiver over its

blood-red liquid. Afraid. The great manipulator was afraid. And suddenly Daniel Defoe was afraid too.

'It's not a question of whom I favour,' said Harley, 'It's a question of avoiding civil war.'

Like a dread, silence came over the room except for the crackling of the fire. Civil War. Not again. Daniel had been born while they were still picking up the pieces from the last one. A torn country where the graves were still settling on torn bodies. Please God, not again.

Harley leaned forward. 'I'll need to hold all the cards, Daniel, *all* of them. Especially the court cards. I'll need your pen and your soul. I shall also need your agency, that gang of rogues and villains who go everywhere and know everything. Do you understand?'

'I'm to continue the search for Anne Bonny?'

Harley sat back, his mask reinstated. 'Yes,' he said, 'You are also to conduct a very secret enquiry into the lives of the women who surround our queen. This "Circe" endangers us all. She has some design of her own. Search for her while you search for Anne Bonny. I think you may find they are one and the same person.'

That night Defoe dreamed that a succubus sat on his loins, showing long white teeth between red lips as she screamed in victory before leaning down to suck out his tongue. He woke up wet, afraid and embarrassed, and had to lie still, suppressing his gasps, in case Mrs Defoe beside him had been disturbed. She had not; she snored on.

Picking up his robe, he got up and went downstairs to the kitchen and poured himself some porter, ducking under the clothes that hung from the drying rack. Anne Bonny still inhabited Defoe's mental garden, gentle and wronged. He had difficulty crediting Harley's conviction that she had returned in the transformation of a vengeful harpy. Yet Harley was so sure, and he was once again Harley's creature.

Circe changed men into swine.

Women. What malignancy when they went to the bad. Such power for evil if they ranged free. Educate them, certainly. To a point. But contain them. What blessedness if they were all like Mrs Defoe, meek, loving helpmeets. Such white, clenching thighs the succubus had. Defoe fell on his knees and prayed that he might be delivered from lust and Woman rampant. The uneven flags of the kitchen floor hurt.

He had been hunting an elusive doe only to discover he was on the trail of a tigress – a tigress, moreover, that was lurking nearby, hidden in the gentle, English shade of his Queen's Court, its topaz eyes narrowed and watchful. Watchful for what? If he found her, would she be a queen? Or a murderess? Which was she?

In the end it didn't matter. If England could be saved from tearing herself apart by finding an heir to the throne that was neither the Pretender nor the Hanoverian, an heir that was acceptable to both Whig and Tory, she was acceptable whatever she was. It was England that mattered.

He felt the damp from the floor seeping into his bruised knees. 'Oh Lord,' he prayed, 'guide my country through its difficulties. Protect my soul. And Lord, if it is within Your power, keep Martin Millet and his Bratchet from harm.'

CHAPTER THIRTEEN

KILSYTH AND I were in the shot locker. It took us time to find that out because it was black in there. Not dark, black. No light from under the door, no filtering of daylight – it was night when we were thrown in, anyway, but dawn made no difference. There was sound; creaking timbers, the slap of water against wood by the side and below us, pattering feet and thumping above us, all coming from a distance as if we were suspended in a cocoon in the middle.

And there was smell. All ships stink below deck; in fact, the shot locker is cleaner than most, but fresh air doesn't reach it; what does is a mixture of bilge, sewage and sour wood.

When my head recovered a bit I groped about and found

Kilsyth's legs and knew they were his because they were bare. Since he'd put up the better fight, they'd treated him harder. My hands were bound but I managed to untie his feet and then tried to crawl up beside him to where his head was but his body filled the available space and I had to lie on top of him to feel where he was hurt. I loosened his jabot and patted his cheeks. He whispered something. I put my ear to his mouth. 'Get off,' he repeated.

I slid back and heard him groan as he sat up. We sat back to back and untied each other's wrists. 'What happened?'

I said, 'It looks as if your Captain Porritt wanted a couple of extra hands and didn't like to ask.'

'We've been pressed?'

'I think so.'

'And the lassie?'

I'd led her to the shambles, carefully, taking trouble over it. 'My fault,' I said, 'my grievous fault. The burden of it is intolerable. Have mercy on her, have mercy on her, most merciful Father, for thy Son our Lord Jesus Christ's sake.'

In the extreme moments you go back.

'Lift up your hearts,' said Kilsyth from the darkness.

'We lift them up unto the Lord.'

'Let us give thanks unto our Lord God.'

I couldn't say it but he went on with the litany, 'It is very meet, right, and our bounden duty, that we should at all times and in all places give thanks unto Thee, O Lord . . .'

Either I passed out or slept, I can't remember which. When I woke up the boat was under way and the Scotsman's great feet were stepping on my hair as he explored our prison.

'It's a cupboard of sorts,' he said, 'a great cupboard. There's shelving here to my right with . . . balls in it. Balls?'

'Are they iron?'

'Oh aye, cannon balls. Behind netting. The shelves are maybe ten foot wide. How deep I canna say.'

I could feel for myself that the space we were in, the gap between the shelves and the door, was about eighteen inches across. I joined his exploration, me taking the shelf side and him the other, so as not to get in each other's way.

I found four shelves. Stretching the length and depth between each of them them was strong, tarred rope netting, like a vertical hammock, to stop the shot from dislodging in the ship's movement and falling out. From what I could judge through the netting, the shots were smallish, sixteen- or seventeen-pounders, though crashing about loose in a storm they could have holed a ship as well as if they'd been fired at it.

There must have been a hundred or more on each shelf. The thought that such a mass was poised on one side of us added to the suffocation that tormented us both.

Kilsyth was excited about the door. 'It slides. Aye, they'd need wide access. Well, a sliding door's easier dealt with than a hinged. We could maybe crack it open with one of they balls, they're heavy enough.'

We were in open sea by now and the boat acted like a bucking horse, trying to throw us out of its stomach. The noise was almost as wicked as the motion. I felt for the floor and hung on to it.

Kilsyth stepped on me again. He was still exploring. 'There's something here. Glass. What for would they put a panel of glass in a wall with no aspect?'

I'd lost interest.

Kilsyth shouted, 'At least we are suffering as Bonny Anne was made to suffer, laddie. Do you not sense a holiness in that?'

I didn't. I wanted death. In an hour I was really, really, wanting it. And kept on wanting for the best part of a week. They must have brought us water because Kilsyth kept giving me sips, and a bucket because I remember being sick in one. Then I heard Kilsyth calling me. 'Will ye haste, laddie?'

The ship was still tossing and when I got up it pitched me over. I had to claw myself upright by the shelves and hang on while I felt about for him. He was standing with his front pressed against the shelves with, as far as I could tell, his arms spread out in a crucifix position.

'I've no been very clever,' he said.

While I'd been comatose he'd been spending hours gnawing away at a section of rope in the netting of the middle shelf. To

233

do it at all he must have had teeth like scissors. Now he'd managed to fray the piece until there were only strands left. Then one of the shot had rolled against his cheek as the ship pitched and he'd heard the rest shift. At that point he'd realized he'd made a hole in a dam. 'I'd an idea to use a shot against the door, do ye see, laddie. Hammer it open.'

He was holding to the netting, using his body as a brace to stop the whole bloody lot come bouncing out to crush us against the door. I hammered on the door, shouting for help.

Somebody outside hammered back and shouted something in a foreign language. I tried to tell him he was in as much danger as we were; the iron avalanche behind us would throw down the door like a wattle hurdle and flatten anything beyond it. I kept hammering and shouting but either the sod had gone away or wasn't bothering.

We tried to mend the hole, Kilsyth braced against it while I worked round him in an attempt to splice the frayed rope together. I couldn't do it. Even if we could have seen what we were about, I don't think it could have been done. The pressure on the hole took·the two gnawed ends of rope too far apart from each other.

In the end we had to take it in turns to hold on to the netting. When it was time to change places we had to wait until the ship tipped forward and sent the shifting iron away from the netting. The rumble as it turned and came back and pressed against our chests, threatening to break our ribs, is a sound that lives with me yet.

Kilsyth took longer shifts than me. He said it was because when I vomited from that position I missed the bucket. But even his strength would give out after a couple of hours and then he'd say, 'If ye don't mind, laddie . . . ' and I'd take his place until my arms began to shake and the bucketing of the ship bringing iron against the same area of bruised flesh became unbearable.

Food and water came when the oaf outside the door decided to deliver it, which he did about every two days through the nine-inch square glass window in the bulkhead on our right facing the shelves. He paid no attention to our shouts and, as he

234

brought no light with him, didn't see the predicament. He was a careless bugger who managed to slop most of the stew as he passed it through and only half-filled the leather flask of water so that thirst and hunger were added to our problems.

When we talked, which wasn't much – the one resting was usually so tired from his turn at the netting that he slept – we planned what we'd do to the oaf when we got out. It was always 'when' with Kilsyth, never 'if'. And we tried to work out what the window was for. Tapping it told us the glass was extremely thick and fastened on the other side. The second time Oaf came, a whiff wound its way from the other side of it through the stink and reminded me of battle.

'Gunpowder,' I told Kilsyth. It was his turn at the netting and I was feeding him with what stew I'd scraped up off the floor where Oaf had tipped it again. 'I think next door's the ammunition room. The magazine.' It didn't make either of us feel any better, but it helped us understand why Oaf hadn't been trusted with a lighted candle.

We lost track of time but we must have been in that hold nearly a week when a glimmer came through the glass. I was on netting duty and it was Kilsyth who hammered and shouted.

I turned my neck to the right, sweating with fear. I'd prayed for light. Now I prayed that whoever was taking a flame into the ammunition room knew what he was doing. One spark would send him, us, the entire ship, into the air in pieces.

The glass opened and somebody's hand held a thick, eight-hour candle through it. Our window, we saw, was one side of a hatch. There was a corresponding glass door on the other side and between them was a shelf. 'Here,' said somebody, 'why's that bugger kissing my cannon balls?'

'There's a hole in the damned net,' Kilsyth told him, wearily.

'Ster-rewth.' The glass on our side was closed, the candle was stuck carefully on to a spike on the shelf and the window on the other side closed on it. There were shouts and then, for the first time since it had shut on us, the sliding door opened. Kilsyth was hustled outside and men came in. I was eased back, carefully, while a giant took my place and work began fixing up

235

new netting. I was allowed to stagger out into the passage. I don't suppose it smelled of pot-pourri but it was a paradise garden compared to the hold. A stolid-looking bastard in uniform kept his musket trained on Kilsyth and me.

Our deliverer came out of the hold while the work inside it went on and looked at us, picking his teeth. 'How long's that fucker of a hole been there?'

'Days,' I told him.

'Should've said, shouldn't you?'

'The guard wouldn't listen.'

Our deliverer surveyed the stolid-looking bastard. 'He's a marine,' he said as if that explained it. 'Got no milk in his coconut. Comes from Freezy-somewhere. Talk in grunts, they do.'

'Can you get us some water?'

He turned on the marine and pointed to the musket. 'What you going to do? Shoot 'em? *In this section?* Captain'll have your bollocks for breakfast. Get 'em some water.' As the marine hesitated, he added, 'Do the poor sods look like they can scamper? Water. Get.'

The man went off and Deliverer studied us. 'You both English?'

'Scottish,' said Kilsyth, sullenly.

'Should have known from the frilly skirt. What about him?'

'London,' I told him.

'Never. Whereabouts?'

'Cornhill.'

'*Never*. Cheapside, me. Nobby Clarke.'

'Martin Millet.'

'Pleased to meet you, Mart. What you doing in the service of King Louis?'

'Wishing I wasn't.'

He grinned. 'Yeah, well. Pressed men's kept in the capperdochy for a bit. Teaches 'em to appreciate the comforts of service when they come out.'

He was a typical product of Cheapside, undersized and quick as a ferret without a ferret's good teeth. He was no advertisement for the comforts of service under Louis XIV; he wore an English sailor's jacket over galligaskins, both of them filthy. In my eyes, though, he was beautiful.

'There was a woman with us,' I said.

'Little Miss Modicum? Sorry, cocky, she's in the quarterdeck cot now. Captain's perks.' He patted my head. 'Now don't take on. At least he ain't sharing her round, mingy bastard. And she's better off up there than down here.' He peered into the shot hold and held his nose. 'Gawd save us. And I ain't usually partickler.'

'The guard won't change our bucket,' I explained, 'and he's starving us.'

'See about that,' said Nobby, 'Only thing to be said about this floating fortune, the grub's good.' He shouted into the locker, 'You buggers finished yet?'

'When do we get to Scotland?' asked Kilsyth, who'd been having trouble with Nobby's accent.

'Scotland?' Nobby asked me, 'Does he think he's going home to his haggis?'

'Where *are* we going?'

'Windies.' He shook his head at Kilsyth. 'Bloody sight better'n Scotland. Warmer.'

We were put back when the netting was mended and a change of bucket and some water came in with us, which, with the relief of not having to hold back a hundred rounds of shot, would have made it first-class accommodation in our eyes if the thought of Bratchet and our destination had been more bearable.

It took even Kilsyth half an hour to find a ridiculous shred of hope. 'Maybe the West Indies is where they took Bonny Anne,' he said, 'Maybe we're the second arrows shot to find the missing first. Maybe we'll land where she did.'

I couldn't answer him. I could hear him beginning to pound on the door, a steady, slow knocking.

'I'll not be able to stand it, Martin,' he said quietly, 'If we're pressed men, why not let us out and work us? If I'm to be kept in this stank all the way, I'll lose my reason.'

'He's keeping us to sell when we get there,' I said, 'Some rich colonial widow'll buy you as a body slave and make unreasonable demands on your person.'

But he kept on hit-hitting the door until I shouted at him to stop it.

Physically, things improved. The safety lamp, which, basically, was what our glass hatch was, was kept burning now so that we had light. We were in calmer seas and the captain ordered gunnery practice and the shot-locker and magazine were in use. The shot was found to be rusty and Kilsyth and I were set to cleaning it which required space, so the door was left open with Oaf the marine standing guard outside.

He had the brain of an ox. He'd been told to stand guard and that's what he did. Luckily, Nobby was overseeing the ammunition, coming down to the hold frequently and he would tell him to fetch us water, so he did that too.

Cleaning the shot was a labour Hercules would have blanched at. Rust can damage a gun barrel and affect the accuracy of the round and meeting Nobby's specification that he should be able to see his face in each one when it was finished wore our pewterwort cloths to rags and our fingers to the bone.

But Nobby was our lifeline, bringing us food and news. He was pleased to find a fellow-Cockney among the rag-tag of deserters and pressed men of all nations which formed a large proportion of the *Holy Innocent*'s crew. Her officers were French or Scottish and Irish Jacobites and Nobby didn't think highly of them. 'Load of dolly-worshipping, land-swabbing maltoots as couldn't sail Woolwich ferry.' As for Captain Porritt, 'A cold, meat-mongering bastard.'

Nobby's own career had been eventful, a condemned young pickpocket to whom the judge had offered alternatives of hanging, transportation or the navy. He'd chosen the navy which had suited him until he'd acquired a captain who didn't and had then jumped ship, ironically enough, in Barbados where he'd joined a pirate vessel.

When the pirate came off worse in an encounter with a French warship, he'd been captured, sailed to Le Havre and transferred with the other pirates to the Jacobite *Holy Innocent*. He was indignant about this. He didn't mind Frogs, he said, but 'Jacks' gave him the fucking pip. 'Betraying your own country, I arst you.'

He denied that his own record of loyalty was somewhat blemished: 'Couldn't help it, could I? I'd a done different given the choice. If my aunt'd been my uncle she'd have had balls under her arse but she didn't. Queen Anne ought to know that.'

His claim that in the Royal Navy, then His Majesty's, he'd been a master-gunner was unlikely, but there was no doubt he was a respected member of the *Innocent*'s gun deck and it was his orders and Cheapside oaths we heard when the cannon were run out and began firing practice.

Sensitivity wasn't his strong suit, though, and he couldn't keep his tongue away from the subject of Bratchet. Being the only woman on board she was the talk of the ship. Many of the crew, like Nobby, had been transferred after a voyage in one ship directly on to another without being allowed to set foot on land, and sexual starvation had stimulated their imagination.

The first time he began musing in our company on what Bratchet and the captain were getting up to in the quarterdeck cabin, Kilsyth went for him. He was only stopped from wringing Nobby's neck by the Oaf's musket butt landing on his own. After that 'baiting the sporran-splitter' became Nobby's pastime and I had to hold on to Kilsyth's belt to stop him leaping at the little sod again.

'Will ye take this?' he shouted at me when Nobby went, 'Will ye hear the poor lassie's name soiled by that nose-dropping?'

'You're only making him worse,' I said.

'The dirty-tongued callant, does he think women begin and end at their crotch?'

'It's probably as far as he can reach.'

Kilsyth had made Bratchet into one of his storybook females, as he had Anne Bonny, an innocent virgin in the bestial grip of a villain. How he thought anyone could stay innocent in Puddle Court I can't say. I knew that what she'd been through there probably made it worse for her now, but she was alive, she was surviving.

I began to suspect that Kilsyth would respect her more if she didn't; he liked his dreams unsullied. He was getting on my nerves. For that matter, I was getting on his; a result of being cooped up together too long with not enough food and air.

Eventually, when he said, 'Better for her if she threw herself in the sea,' I hit him and we fell to brawling.

Gradually, however, Nobby's references to Bratchet changed. Her nights were still being passed in the captain's cabin, but she'd been taken under the wing of the ship's cook, he said, and spent her days in the galley where he met her from time to time. 'You never said she was Puddle Court. Knew it well. Feisty little masterpiece, ain't she? Cusses like a Christian.' He began to bring messages from her and tidbits the cook had given her. 'Wants to come and see you, cheeky mare, but Porritt's orders is he'll flay anyone as takes her below. Means it and all, the bastard.'

Neither the captain nor Nobby had reckoned on Bratchet's powers of persuasion. Two nights later the glass on our side was opened. I heard Nobby's voice, 'An' be fucking quick about it,' and I saw Bratchet's face framed in the hatch.

'You all right?'

'Yes. Are you?'

'Yes,' she said. Her face withdrew as her hand came carefully round the candle and passed over a greasy parcel. 'Sausages.'

'Wonderful.'

Her face reappeared. 'How is he?'

'Asleep.' I stepped aside so that she could see Kilsyth where he lay, his cheek cradled on his bonnet. I gave him a nudge with my boot but he only stirred and she said, 'No, let him rest. He's terrible thin.'

So was she, though it was difficult to see her properly, the glare of the candle kept us both blinking. She said: 'I asked him to let you out but he won't.'

'That's all right,' I said, stupidly.

'He's not a nice man, Mart.'

'Isn't he?'

'He was going to give me the cat. And he said he'd throw you overboard if I didn't . . . you know.'

'I know.'

'What does he think of me?' And this time she wasn't referring to the captain.

'He thinks you're a lion.'

She nearly smiled. 'Does he?'

'So do I,' I told her.

Her hands came through the hatch and I held them until she jerked as if she was being pushed. 'Hang on, Nobby,' she said irritably.

Nobby's voice hissed, 'I'll be hanging from the yardarm if you lovebirds don't give over. And you with me.'

She leaned as close as she could, nearly singeing her hair on the candle. 'Work at the crossroads,' she said, 'We're not done yet.' She disappeared. The glass closed.

When Kilsyth woke up I told him, 'There's something up. Bratchet's got a gleam in her eye.'

He was miffed at missing her. 'But maybe she'll no want to be seen, poor soul. How did she look?' He was almost disappointed when I said she was fine; he thought that a fate worse than death should carry some mark.

'There ain't no fate worse than death,' I said, 'and she's saving you and me from the fishes.'

He shook his head: 'Better for her . . .' he began and stopped at the look in my eye.

She'd considered it.

On the night she'd been taken, she was dragged shouting and struggling to the captain's cabin, pushed inside and the door closed on her. The quarters were beautifully proportioned if she'd been in a state to appreciate them. There was a wall of leaded panes opposite her through which came the smell of sea. Behind a huge table with an ornate flange running round its top, a man was studying a chart. He raised his head and she stopped shouting instantly.

'You call yourself Mlle La Fée?' When she nodded, he said in English, 'You and your friends are enemies of King James.' He reminded her of the Pretender. Very neat, very cold. And of somebody else, she couldn't think who.

'We ain't,' she said, 'We been serving his very own mother, Queen Mary Beatrice. What you up to?'

He'd got up from the desk then, walked round it and hit her

across the face. 'I'll not have that name uttered from a mouth like yours,' he said. 'You've been spying on her. You and your paramours.'

She didn't try to deny or protest, there would be no point. She could see he didn't want to believe her anything other than an enemy. Anyway, she was too afraid. She'd remembered who he reminded her of. The man who'd raped her at Effie Sly's had eyes like this one.

'You're a whore.' He was very close to her and she felt the huff of his breath on her cheek as he said, 'A harlot. I shall have your men put in a sack and thrown overboard. I shall have you stripped and lashed until the blood runs.'

The ferocious prayer that Bratchet sent up in that moment was answered by the unlikeliest guardian angel of any, but a guardian angel nevertheless. Clear as a voice from heaven, she heard the words of Floss, the Puddle Court prostitute, talking about her most dangerous clients. 'You don't want to show 'em you're frightened,' Floss had said, and now said again into Bratchet's mind. 'Show 'em you're scared and they'll do you where Maggie wore her beads.'

'A waste,' she whispered. She took a deep breath to control her breathing, and tried again. 'Waste that is. Able-bodied fellows like them. Always useful. And me. Able-bodied too.' She had trouble getting out the last word. 'Useful.'

What appalled her then and after was that they understood each other as if he'd been buying and she'd been selling at the same stall for all their lives. 'We'll see,' he said, 'Later.'

During the laborious business of getting under way, she tried to find some corner where she wouldn't be stepped on and watched him as he strode the quarterdeck, rapping out orders to his officers. The ship dwarfed her; it seemed to have been designed for giants. Hawsers were thick as sewer pipes, cables the width of barrels, blocks as big as footstools. The anchor stock came up like a whale flipper rising from the sea, sails that rose and shook out were frightening in their immensity.

She was sick twice, though not from the motion of the sea. She kept trying to tell herself, 'He'll be too tired,' or, 'He'll forget,' or, 'I'm not here at all. This ain't happening.' Only at one point did it occur to her to question *why* it was happening, though she did think the wind of fate was blowing her back and forth across 'this sodding Channel a bit too often for my liking'. She supposed it was politics; Martin Millet had displeased the Jacobites.

It didn't occur to her at all to become angry. She was a straw caught up in a whirlwind. Her self-regard had been left behind at St-Germain-en-Laye.

She was woken up by an officer with a cane and a sneer, to find that she'd fallen asleep on a coil of rope. 'On your feet, my little lap-clap. Captain wants you.'

She went to the quarterdeck cabin.

She never told anybody what went on in there. It was perfectly understood between her and Porritt that after each encounter she must bargain again for the two men he kept down in the ship's hold. She once said she reminded herself of the sultan's slave from the *Arabian Nights* that Mary Read had read to her. Except, where Scheherezade told her master tales every night in order to save her life, Bratchet used her body and saved three lives.

But after the first week she waited until evening and then went for'ard where she couldn't be seen and climbed up on the ship's rail, clinging to the shrouds.

From up here the grey sea curling past below looked very wet. And strong. It would turn her over and over like a performing seal until the ship had gone and then fill her mouth.

She held her breath to experience what those last few minutes of suffocation would be like and ended up gasping. She wouldn't be *able* to gasp. No wind down there to take into her lungs.

Would that final inability be worse than living? It would be shorter, there was that for it. No more spiralling down to greater and greater degradation. The trouble was that Martin and Kilsyth would follow her not long afterwards.

But she couldn't go on. 'I got my troubles, they got theirs,' she thought. Perhaps, with her dead, Porritt would let them off. Anyway, what did she owe them that she must go on living through hell for their sake? She was less than nothing to them;

they'd shown that clearly enough on the winter journey from St-Germain to Le Havre. Only a means to find Anne Bonny, that's all she was to them.

She knew gossip about her filtered down to where Martin and Kilsyth had been locked in the hold. If she lived and they lived there would come the moment when she would have to meet Kilsyth's eyes and the disgust in them. She couldn't.

There wasn't a single soul to offer her comfort. The crew called her 'the captain's warming pan'. Every morning in the early hours, Porritt pushed her out of the cabin to wander the deck, occupying space but no position among the hurrying, pattering seamen, sleeping in the longboat where they kept the hens, or crouching under the shelter of the quarterdeck's overhang.

She was in no danger of attack – she was the captain's property and no more to be touched than his silver snuff box – but she wasn't allowed to go below and was therefore prey to hostility and insults. Thinking she didn't understand – word had gone out that she had been at St-Germain and was therefore 'a high-nosed French bitch' – the terms 'cunnyborough', 'Hairyfordshire', 'fly-cage', 'salt-cellar', 'scut', etc., all slang for the female pudenda, were bandied about, with ornamentation, by the grinning mouths of the English among them.

There was no comfort. Oh, God help me.

'You don' wan' do that,' said a voice.

Bratchet looked down to where the ship's cook, an enormous black man, rested a bucket of peelings on the gunwale and watched the sea, as she did. Somebody had been putting plates of food in the longboat for her; she supposed he had. It didn't interest her.

'Wednesday,' he said, 'One bad day for jumping. I jumped Wednesday once.' He waited for her to say something. She didn't. 'Davy Jones, he threw me right back. That bad luck, sure 'nough.'

'I'm tired,' she said, looking down at him. He looked back. He had the most intelligent set to his face she'd ever seen; no, not so much intelligent – knowing. They shared, and had shared, something, a condition, a history. It was strange, she thought, that two such different men, Porritt and a ship's cook, should see into her bones. But whereas Porritt was pitiless, this man understood.

'What yo' name?' he asked.

'Bratchet.' The days of Mlle La Fée were over.

He knew she wasn't going to jump now. So did she or she wouldn't have spoken to him. 'You hungry,' he said, 'you come to my galley. I got coucou make you feel like spirit boiling over.'

He threw the peelings overboard then swung her down, enveloping her in a strong smell of sweat, cooking and an alien skin that was vaguely comforting after the unscented, chill wind. 'De longer you live, de more you hear,' he said.

He made up a bed for her in a corner of the galley with some sheepskins and she slept for twelve hours through the hubbub of clashing skillets, oven lids, shouting, and chopping.

When she woke up he cleared the galley so that she could take a bath in a salting pan, found a shirt and a small pair of calico trousers which he turned up for her and a jelly-bag cap which he stuffed her hair in. 'Captain, he playing cards tonight. Won't want company.' He stood back to look at her. 'Sweetest-lookin' galley mate I ever see.' She washed her dress and he hung it to dry in a gun port and then set her to work peeling turnips.

With the acquisition of trousers and a friend, she felt a bit better. The attitude of the crew towards her ameliorated slightly; they noticed her less and treated her with more of the raillery they used on one of their own. A hard core still regarded her with enmity – she couldn't decide whether it was because they suspected her of being the captain's spy, or because she was a whore or just because she was a woman – but the cook stopped their mouths. 'Dis galley ent no swear country,' he'd tell them, and threaten them with, 'You know why Jack didn' eat he dinner? He din' get any.'

He carried weight in more ways than one. Generally, he was known as Licky – all sea-cooks were called Lick-fingers – sometimes as 'Nigger' or 'Sambo' or 'you black bugger' but with no more sting than the Lincolnshire gunner was called

'Yellow-belly', or the undersized topman 'Jack Sprat', or the rating in charge of the poultry 'The Duck-fucker', and with the respect due a man who not only provided sustenance and sewed up wounds, but could, and would, if offended, throw you into the scuppers as effortlessly as breaking an egg.

To Bratchet his protection and the unspoken understanding between them hauled her above despair and kept her afloat. He rarely talked about his past, 'Don' ask me where I been, ask me where I'm gwine,' but he made her ashamed of despairing at all since she gathered he'd survived slavery. There were scars on his wrists and ankles, and once, when he spilled hot soup on his jacket and he tore it off, she saw a back which a whip had bitten into so many times and so deeply that it looked corrugated. But he could still say, 'Even if de Devil bring it, God sen' it,' though which god he referred to she wasn't sure.

The times when Porritt sent for her after she'd taken up residence in the galley, Licky made her feel like a soldier going into battle. 'You ain' short on spirit, just height,' he said, and gave her his own form of absolution, 'Remember, "can' help" don' mean "do for purpose".'

Gradually, the greyness with which she'd surrounded herself dissolved and the ship gained focus. She began to respect the skill of men, reduced to dwarves by the enormous ship, which kept the huge, complex structure ploughing onwards by invisible propulsion. The first time the wind dropped, it gave her a moment of surprise that manpower itself wasn't enough to drive the ship forward.

The *Holy Innocent* was Dutch-built, a frigate carrying a complement of over a hundred men and eighteen guns. She'd been captured by the French who'd handed her over to the Jacobites. Thanks to Marlborough, the English fleet was making life too difficult for illegal runs across the Channel and now Porritt, with a Letter of Marque from King Louis, was taking the ship to be a thorn in the flesh of the Royal Navy in the West Indies and pick up what booty he could.

The senior officers were nearly all English or Irish Jacobites, the crew a more uneasy mixture of nationalities and creeds. Only a few of them were on board from conviction, the rest mainly criminals and deserters who'd signed on because privateering promised an easier discipline than that of the prison or navy they left behind.

In that they were mistaken. Porritt had sailed under James II when he was Duke of York and Admiral of the English Royal Navy and had absorbed not only an admiration for, but also many of the qualities of his late king. 'He fierce and he stupid,' Licky told Bratchet, 'an when the head bad the whole body bad. Look like me and some fellas miss de pier head and jump in the wharf.'

Essentially, the ship was a wooden feudal castle. The entry port through which Bratchet had been ushered on the night she boarded had a curving roof held up by cherubic caryatids as did the oak-panelled door to the quarterdeck cabin, the figurehead was a gloriously sculpted lion, the ship's lantern – in which a man could stand up – a thing of brass and glass that could have graced a mansion.

Although she was not allowed to go below, Bratchet gathered that the crews' quarters were less congenial. Above decks it was noisy; sheets could flap like pistol-shots, the wind wailed a permanent dirge through the rigging, somebody was always shouting orders or swearing at the goats which, once they'd found their sea-legs, nibbled free of their ropes and got in everybody's way, eating everything in their path from wood shavings to the log book.

On the whole, the stink of rotting water from the bilges below and the pungency of goat urine and the hog and cattle pens on deck were overwhelmed by the smell of wood and salt, although once, when she was standing in the bows near the bowsprit, admiring the knights' heads carved like crusaders' helms on the principal bow timbers, Bratchet's nostrils alerted her that she'd solved the mystery of why men disappeared from sight when they clambered forward towards the bowsprit, as if intent on an uninterrupted sea view. The cross-trees supporting the projecting timbers just below her were covered with salt-encrusted excreta, suggesting that while the crew's balance in using this form of water closet was excellent, their aim was not.

Her own needs were attended to in a brine pot with a lid and used in a cupboard near the galley Licky had given her to live in; possibly less hygienic than the heads, but safer and more private.

The galley was the ship's heart, its kindness, literally the one fire in its belly – and that only permitted in calm weather. Discounting the magazine, it was the most dangerous place on board, home to the medicine chest and surgeon's needles. An unexpected wave or trough causing the ship to lurch could misdirect a chopper and cut off a cook's fingers or spit him on one of his own gutting-knives, or pour scalding water over him, or throw open a carelessly closed fire door in the huge and hideous cast-iron stove bolted to the middle of the floor, tipping live coals on to his feet and either procuring a conflagration that could consume the ship or gaining him a flogging.

In fact, a ship's cook had to be a brave man, if only to withstand the unremitting complaints against a diet which necessarily deteriorated as the voyage went on, breeding sufficient weevils in the cheese to allow it to stagger off.

For the Bratchet the galley was sanctuary and Licky the sanctuary-keeper and she left them as little as possible. Being free of officers – stewards collected and took the cooked food to the various messes – it was also a gathering ground for the discontented.

All was not well on the *Holy Innocent*. Discipline was harsher than many of its crew had expected aboard a privateer, and getting harsher. Also, the non-Jacobite Englishmen were becoming aware that the voyage's purpose was to harry the Royal Navy and were showing a surprising distaste for the enterprise, considering that most of them had deserted from the navy in the first place.

'I got mates on HMS *Vengeful* an' the *Dreadnought*,' Nobby Clarke complained, 'Firin' on 'em if they fire on you's one thing, but I ain't blowin' 'em out the water deliberate. I got feelings.'

'You ain't got feelings and you ain't got mates,' the carpenter, Chadwell, told him, ''Less it's the goats.'

'An I ain't no fucking Papist, neither,' continued Nobby, ''F I'd a knowed that fucking Porritt was a dolly-worshipper, I never would've signed.' The high Roman Catholicism of morning prayers and the mass the ship's complement was made to attend every Sunday was causing offence to those among the crew who had suddenly remembered they were Protestant. Two topmen, a German and a Dutch Lutheran, had been particularly affronted, refused to join in and had been flogged as heretics – an unheard-of thing on a privateer where belief was usually in booty and little else.

'You cuss one more time an' this soap gwen fit in yo' niggah mouth,' said Licky, who was scouring his chopping board. The reproof reminded the off-watch group in the galley of Bratchet's presence and four heads turned distrustfully in her direction; Sam Rogers, the ship's chief helmsman, Chadwell, like Nobby a Londoner, and Pickel, one of those flogged, a Dutchman, who'd been aboard the *Holy Innocent* when she was captured by the French and had turned his coat rather than become a prisoner of war. The first three and Licky had sailed together before in circumstances they preferred to keep vague and all of them hated the ship's master, O'Rourke, an Irishman belonging to the brutality school of seamanship.

Sam Rogers, the big, quiet helmsman, was particularly singled out for humiliation; known for being a first-class navigator, he had accordingly attracted the jealousy of O'Rourke who was in charge of navigation and who was pursuing a vendetta against Sam and a young topman, Johnson, on the grounds that they were homosexuals.

Nobby bobbed a mock curtsey towards the Bratchet. 'Sorry, miss. Forgot as the cap'n's f-f-f-fancy piece was present.'

Licky intervened. 'She all right.'

' 'F you say so.' Nobby shrugged.

'An' I say so.' Bratchet found her tongue. The injustice of the crew's attitude, which refused to see she was as much a victim of the regime as they were, was now exasperating rather than depressing her; donning trousers had given her confidence to fight it.

She shouted, 'I'm fucking the bastard for if I don't my friends in the hold get chucked over the side, and me with 'em. I ain't his warming pan or his fancy-piece or any other bloody thing and if you knew anything, you monkey-headed little piece of shit, you'd see *I don't like it.*'

Licky was appalled; Nobby delighted. 'Monkey-headed piece of shit, she called me. Good Lunnon cussing, that is. Cheapside?'

'Puddle Court,' sulked the Bratchet.

'Knew it well, knew it well. Give us yer famble.'

They shook hands. Nobby was horrible; from his scabby head, his broken, Roquefort cheese teeth, his agile, stunted body and his spread bare feet there issued an indescribable aroma that was unsweetened by his affection for goats, the rumour being that he was on intimate terms with Brilliana, the prettiest of the nannies. Crew members not renowned for hygiene had been known to refuse food when Nobby was in the galley and Licky, who loved him, insisted he come no nearer than the doorway: 'Whut you smell of, I ain't cookin'.'

Like so many seamen, he was tragic; he pined for the voice of his mother and Bow bells, knowing that his desertion from the navy meant he would never be allowed to hear them again. Yet what endeared him to his friends was a humour that had survived flogging at the cart-tail when a boy, impressment, flogging on most of the ships he'd served on, shipwreck, smallpox, homesickness and toothache. Against the odds, against experience and certainly against all appearances, a divine spark flickered in Nobby. And it was through Nobby that Bratchet picked up the trail of Mary Read and Anne Bonny.

She'd begun to try and relieve the lot of the two prisoners in the shot-locker. Nobby, as a senior gunner, was one of the few men allowed down there and he brought up reports that they were short of food. 'Can't you take them some?' she begged him.

'Thank *you*,' Nobby said, 'An' spend the next week huggin' the capstan? Good night, Mary-Ellen.'

Bratchet appealed to Licky and Licky overrode Nobby's objections. 'You take 'em or you get empty belly yo'self.'

'They got enough fucking troubles without your maw-wallop,' Nobby grumbled. But he did it.

Bratchet waited for him, sitting with her legs over the

companionway. 'Are they all right?' she asked when he came back.

'They ain't crowin',' admitted Nobby, 'but they're livin'. And grateful for the junk an' dumplings. More feared for you, they was, but I told 'em me and Licky had you in charge. Poor bastards, I'll give 'em this much, the shot's never gleamed like it. Nearly finished.'

'What'll he do to them then?'

'Put 'em to work. No point throwin' good men to the sharks; we're short-handed as is.' It was another cause of complaint; the *Holy Innocent*'s complement was barely enough to man a ship of her size and the crew were being badly overworked. 'Shift your arse away from the fuckin' ladder. I got to get on watch.'

He patted her bottom appreciatively as he climbed out. 'I like women's bums in trousis, I do.'

'You keep your dirty little paw off mine.'

'Here,' he said, pausing, 'you want to get Licky t'show you how to use a cutlass. Mustard with a cutlass, our Licky. Used to chop up other sambos in the jungle, shouldn't wonder.' He persisted fondly with the tradition that the cook had been a cannibal in his youth.

'What do I want with a cutlass?'

'You could trim our cap'n's yardarm for 'im, for a start. Best famble I ever knew with a cutlass was a bloss. Mary Read, that was. Sailed with Calico Jack.'

Slowly, the Brachet turned on him. She grabbed his jacket. 'Who?'

'Lay off. Wassa matter with yer? Me body's Brilliana's.'

'*Who* did you say?'

'Mary Read.' He was backing off. 'Course, I din't know her well, not to talk to like.'

'Where was this? When?'

The ship's bell was clanging for the second watch, a tocsin nobody dared disobey.

Nobby slapped her hands away from his jacket and ran off. As she watched his dirty heels disappear his voice came back to her. 'There was two on 'em. Mary Read an' Anne Bonny.'

251

Bratchet sat at the companionway until shouldered away from it by others of the watch following Nobby. Slowly, she made her way to the galley.

They found each other. Somehow, somewhere – *where*? – Mary had caught up with Anne. Both of them had been alive – *when*? – and together. Both of them alive then. *Both*.

The thought swung her into the galley which was full of stewards demanding instant food for the men just off watch. Licky was grumbling at the invariable insults to his cooking as he and his assistant, Slushy, slopped stew and beans into the waiting buckets. 'Please and thankee don' break no bones. Get back there. Some people like horse dung, they always in de road.'

'Where you been?' he demanded of Bratchet – she had become an integral part of the short-handed galley crew, 'Han' out that cheese.'

'Hand it out, girl,' somebody shouted, 'we'm goin' to carve ninepins out 'f it.'

'Ain't as hard as yo' head. Now git.'

'Looks like somebody eaten this stew already.'

'You watch yo' mouth. You kin take the man out de pig pen, but you can' take the pig pen out de man.'

At last the galley was emptied and they could begin clearing the debris. Bratchet washed down the mammoth sideboard. 'You ever heard of a Calico Jack, Licky?'

'You ever heard've elbow grease? Calico Jack? He pirate.'

'Pirate?' They sailed with a pirate? She scrubbed on. 'Well, d'you ever hear of two women, Anne Bonny and Mary Read?'

'I heard've 'em.'

The way he said it made her turn round. He wasn't looking at her. 'What? What about them? When did you hear about them?'

He said, automatically, 'Ask no questions, yuh hear no lies; Put down molasses, cetch no flies.' Then he said, 'They dead, girl. Years back. Spanish Town.'

'They ain't dead. They're not.'

He went back to his stove. 'So I heard.'

'They were friends of mine.'

He shook his head. 'Dead. An' can' run from they coffin.'

She got tired of questioning; he merely trotted out more of his infuriating proverbs. 'Don' put yuh head where your body can' go.'

Nobby was more helpful, though equally depressing, when he stood at the galley door that night. 'Yeah, dead, poor bitches. Pleaded their bellies at their trial.'

'What trial? What do you mean "pleaded their bellies"?'

'Bunged, Bratchie. Sprouted. Pregnant. Sailed with Calico Jack, din't they? Gawd, even a cockrel got in the family way sailin' with randy Jack. Licky, didn't you once say you had a brother . . . ?' He stopped suddenly.

Bratchet looked round, but Licky was innocently stirring the next stew. Nobby became vaguer after that. Calico Jack's crew, he said, including Anne and Mary, had been overpowered in a fight with the Royal Navy, taken to St Jago in Jamaica to face a Vice-Admiralty Court where all of them had been condemned to death. The sentence had been carried out in the case of the men but suspended for the two women until they had given birth. Both had died in childbirth. When? Nobby couldn't say. 'Three, four years back.'

'What happened to the babies?'

Nobby shrugged.

Unanswered questions. Oh, Anne. Oh, Mary. All that confidence dissipated in a prison cell. She went into her cupboard and shut the door. Oh, for the babies. She ached with pity for them, for the mothers; birth took the adventure out of what they'd done and made it tragedy.

There was a knock on the door and Licky's voice: 'Skirt time, Bratchie girl.' Porritt had sent for her. She dressed in her female clothes and went to the quarterdeck. The horn lantern hanging from its roof showed the plump cheeks of the cherubs at his door and the curve of their necks. Babies. Mary and Anne had given birth to the children she'd never have.

The next day she went on asking questions about Anne Bonny and Mary Read. She discovered whom to ask; men who evaded questions about their past, mainly English, a few of the other nationals, hardly any of the French, none of the officers. The ones who'd been pirates.

There was a surprising number of them, she suspected at least seventeen, perhaps more; men who'd tumbled into what they called the Brotherhood like pebbles washed on to a beach and now, with equal helplessness, had landed on a Jacobite privateer.

And they all met in the galley.

'You were a pirate, weren't you,' she said to Licky when they were alone, 'You and your brother.'

'You wash your mout' out,' he said, 'I was ree-spec'able. Din' I ever tell you how I was de Earl of Portland's favourite niggah?'

'No.'

'Bought me special from Jamaica. Give me eddification. Went with he to France on he's embassy to King Louis. I was a fine niggah, plumed hat, lace cuffs. "You one fine dam' niggah," say Louis. "You one fine dam' king," I tell him, "if a mite hasty." Din' I ever tell you that?'

She believed him; he had amazing areas of knowledge. The use of the word 'pooped' as a synonym for exhaustion, he'd once explained to her, came from captains and masters who'd had to stay too long on the poop deck of a ship during a battle or storm.

But she still knew that either before or after the embassy to France, he had been a pirate. It was slavery which had given him the empathy which he extended to her situation, but his refusal to think that a woman on board a ship spelled bad luck came from his pirate days. It was the same with Nobby. Piracy was like the army, she thought, women with love of adventure had found a niche in the freebooting life which suited them. From what little she could gather from former members of the Brotherhood, Mary and Anne had become part of its folklore just as Kit Ross had in the army.

She could find out very little more. Ex-pirates were guarded about their past for one thing and on the *Holy Innocent* they had other things to talk about. They came to the galley to grumble about the increasing severity of life above. More and more often she could hear for herself the thwack of the bo'sun's 'starter' as it hit the seamen's posteriors and the yells of encouragement from O'Rourke. Floggings, which generally occurred at the beginning of a voyage to attract the men's attention to the penalty for indiscipline, were becoming more frequent rather than less, and for slighter reasons.

One of the sailmaker's assistants had been given six of the best for the crime of feeding the ship's cat.

Sam Rogers complained little, though his face showed the strain of O'Rourke's persecution of his friend, Johnson, which was becoming savage. A lurch of the ship during a calm morning had sent a cauldron of near-boiling water over Bratchet's toes causing her to hop with pain and Licky to go storming up on deck to complain. He came back tight-lipped. 'Dat lazaretto niggah wuss than obeah,' referring to O'Rourke. He always used 'nigger' about himself or anyone else as a form of bitterness.

O'Rourke, it appeared, had sent Johnson to the tops for no reason, waited until the man was negotiating the cross-trees some sixty feet above the deck, then grabbed the helm from Sam Rogers and sent the ship veering, nearly tipping the youngster into the sea.

'Near broached we,' said Licky, 'That one lazaretto niggah.'

Porritt had come storming out of his cabin to find out what had happened. O'Rourke had blamed Sam. 'Ogling his beloved too hard to watch the way,' he'd said, and such was the fear in which he was held that nobody, except Sam, had refuted the statement. Sam had been docked pay and privileges – as the best helmsman on board he was too valuable to flog.

Bratchet asked, 'Are he and Johnson . . .' she didn't know a polite word for it in English so she used French, with which Licky had become acquainted during his time with the Earl of Portland '. . . n'aiment-les que les hommes dovés?'

'What ain't met you don' pass you,' said Licky, from which she gathered he regarded it as none of his business. Time and again she was struck by the crew's casual attitude to what, on shore, ranked high in the list of carnal sins; the result, she supposed, of enclosing men within wooden walls for months, sometimes years, at a time.

The few animals that had so far escaped slaughtering being

reserved for the officers, the rest of the crew was now on a monotonous and scanty diet of salted beef. It had to be soaked for days before it could be cooked and then kept at simmering point in its compartment in the stove for hours before it was edible.

Coinciding with the approach into warmer weather, the galley, which had been comfortable while they were in the Bay of Biscay, was now hardly endurable. How Licky kept his temper with the complaints that were becoming increasingly nasty, though justified, Bratchet didn't know.

'Ain't the vittles,' he told her, 'it's sippers runnin' out's the trouble. Cheapsgate cap'n, he din' buy enough.' Sippers was rum; according to Licky a crew could be kept on starvation food rations and still remain content as long as they got their daily ration of rum. On the *Holy Innocent*, they weren't. The ship had been badly provisioned.

There was still ale, though that was becoming musty-tasting. Water in the barrels was turning green and acquiring the richness of pond life. Bread, known as 'biscuit', crumbled to dust in the mouth and smelled of the fish that Licky had placed on top to attract the weevils from it. So far he had averted scurvy but the herbs and salads he had grown in the jolly boat for this purpose had yesterday been tipped overboard when the boat had to be launched so that Chadwell could caulk a suspected leak near the waterline.

'What are we going to do?' Bratchet asked him. She was becoming frightened; the ship was in mid-ocean, beyond the point of no return but still with over 2,000 nautical miles to go. Some of the men were beginning to show signs of sickness, mainly from exhaustion. Nobby reported that Martin and Kilsyth were suffering from heat and foul air.

'Yuh never know de luck of a lousy cat,' Licky said, which was no help.

Nobby's opinion of his captain – 'If he's a fucking fulker we're in low tide. If he's a fucking landlubber we're on the rocks' – was general. Miserliness was one thing, but the growing suspicion that Porritt didn't know what he was about was creating fear. An incompetent captain presaged disaster.

He's frightened. It was occurring to her that Porritt had bitten off more than he could chew, and knew it. His experience of seamanship, she was beginning to suspect, was limited to small ships in the Channel. In handing him the *Innocent*, Louis had promoted him beyond his capabilities. It accounted for the harshness; terror that any relaxation in discipline would lead to behaviour he couldn't control.

A wiser captain would have provided more rum, the occasional dancing on deck to Dai Griffith's hornpipe, competitions, anything to keep the men interested and keen. The only way Porritt knew was to work them till they dropped and flog them when they did. Worse still, he allowed O'Rourke's sadism free rein and then was forced to support him, leading to injustices.

The worst case was Johnson's. It had only been a matter of time before O'Rourke found an informer – Licky called such men 'Jacks o' both sides'; Nobby had other names for them – willing to testify that he had been the subject of unwanted sexual advances by Johnson. The information was enough for O'Rourke to haul him before the captain; it was also unlikely enough to have been dismissed by a man of sense – Johnson was good-looking while the informant, Thody, had an appearance that compared unfavourably to Nobby's, without the saving grace of that gentleman's humour.

But Thody was a Roman Catholic, like Porritt, like O'Rourke. Johnson was not. The bo'sun was told to pipe all hands and Porritt announced the sentence to the assembled ship's company: 'For attempted buggery which is an abomination in the sight of God, Seaman Johnson will be seized to the shrouds this night and on the morrow will receive thirty lashes.' There was a murmur from the men which died away as O'Rourke signalled to the bo'sun to be ready with his starter.

In the galley later, as all over the ship, it was the irregularity of the sentence rather than the sentence itself on which discussion centred. A man could be seized to the shrouds or he could be flogged but rarely both; with this double sentence Johnson's night exposed to spray and wind would be given additional torment by the thought of the flogging to come, a punishment more usually carried out immediately it was pronounced.

'Ain't fuckin' seamanlike,' Nobby complained from his door-way, 'Not shroudin' *an*' a red-laced jacket. You never got 'em both in the navy. I sailed under captings'd make old Porritt look like the Archangel Gabriel, but they was always seaman-like. He's green is Porritt, green as a fucking fig. Thass what worries me.'

It seemed to worry everybody except the Bratchet who was more concerned for Johnson. 'Can he survive thirty lashes?' What little she had seen of the boy suggested he was frail.

'Thirty? Thirty's nothing,' Nobby assured her, 'Easy as piss the bed, thirty. I've had forty an' walked away whistlin'.'

'An' deserved 'em,' said Chadwell.

'Not for buggery, I din't. I ain't no boretto man.'

'Goats bein' your fancy,' said Chadwell, who adored egging on Nobby's conversation, 'Capricornico man, you are.'

'I don' like to go into battle wit' zis captain,' said Pickel, 'I end up fucking dead, I think. He no seaman.'

It seemed to Bratchet that as they complained of their cap-tain's mishandling of Johnson's punishment, his inept provi-sioning, his apparent inability to keep O'Rourke in check, they were actually talking about something else, a faraway option that they could take or reject but which, even from here, was too horrific to name.

Licky, she noticed, kept them simmering, shrugging a 'You dancin' to the music he playing,' when they looked like letting the matter drop, 'You jus' a walkin' ground for monkey parade 'pon.'

'You don't *want* them to mutiny, do you?' she asked when they were alone.

He turned on her. 'That one heavy word, girl. You watch your triside.'

'I'm sorry.' He'd never been angry with her before.

'Yeah, well, you keep a still tongue an' a fuzzy eyebrow.'

It was a night when Porritt sent for her. As she passed the mainmast shrouds, she saw Johnson, a black cruciform, spread-eagled against criss-crossed moonlight, his face to the sea. To one side of him stood a marine with musket at the slope.

Crouched against the gunwale in the shadows at Johnson's hanging feet, utterly still, was Sam Rogers. The scene reminded her of a painting that hung in Mary of Modena's salon of the soldier and the mother at the foot of the Cross.

That night she begged Porritt not to have Johnson flogged, knowing it was useless but feeling that if she didn't she would bear some of the responsibility for what happened to the boy. Then and the next morning she paid for it. When the all hands was piped, the bo'sun put his head round the galley door: 'That's you an' all, girl. On deck. Cap'n's orders.'

She trailed on deck behind him and took up a place beside Licky. The sea-cook put out his hand and she held on to it. Porritt read out offence and sentence again. Two seamen assisted Johnson to the capstan where he was shackled to one of the spars. The cat's nine knotted strings hung ready over another spar. The master-at-arms stepped forward, took hold of Johnson's collar and ripped the shirt out and down, exposing his young, very white back to the waist. Inconsequentially she thought, Why do they tear a good shirt?

The master-at-arms stepped back, took up the knotted strings by their handle and swished them through the air, getting his range. There was a name for the sound it made. Seamen had a name for everything. She couldn't remember what it was, but she remembered Nobby's phrase from last night. Red-laced jacket. They're going to give him a red-laced jacket.

She'd seen floggings before, in the Puddle Court days. They'd tied Harry the Sorner to a cart-tail for begging and whipped him from Charing Cross to Temple Bar and she and Effie had followed the nasty old bastard, jeering.

What's different? She was. It wasn't just that Johnson was young and she liked him, or that the ceremonial, the silent, ordered ranks of men, were sickening; *she* had changed. Somewhere along the line of the past years she had joined a higher humanity.

As the master-at-arms stepped forward again and raised the whip she closed her eyes and kept them closed, trying not to listen to the sounds at the capstan, trying to blank out her imagination. It's a seagull screaming. It's not Johnson.

'All over,' said Licky. But she opened her eyes too soon, while they were still unshackling. It *was* a red-laced jacket. The phrase was hideously apt. Later on in the galley she held the salve while Licky's white-fronted fingers applied it to the cuts and Sam Rogers held his friend's hand and crooned to him and then hoisted him by his armpits over his shoulder and carried him to his quarters.

Johnson's eyes had become vague. For the rest of the time she knew him, they never regained the look they'd had before. Neither did Sam Rogers's.

Two days later there was the Brilliana business.

Nobby's supposed relationship with the animal had provided her with a personality, making her the ship's pet, allowed to wander at will, given slops of ale and scrapings off the men's platters, an object of amusement, affection and the butt of their most obscene jokes. They should have seen the danger. O'Rourke ordered her to be slaughtered for the officers' table.

Licky went up to argue with him knowing that, if he didn't, Nobby's outrage would get the little gunner a flogging. Bratchet poked her head above deck and watched the cook explaining that there were still three other goats that could be killed for the officers before they need sacrifice Brilliana.

O'Rourke smiled at him, showing strong, wide-spaced teeth. 'But I want that one.' His th's, like Licky's, came out as d's.

It was a fine day with a breeze keeping the *Innocent* on a beam reach and nothing but sea as far as the horizon. Swabbers were holystoning the planks, the sailmaker, Partridge, was splicing rope, Porritt was pacing the quarterdeck and two men were working the chain pump, discharging the bilge into the wake in regular, monotonous swishes – all seemingly intent on their work. The only pair of ears that weren't straining to catch the argument taking place in the waist of the ship were Brilliana's; with a fetching little bonnet that Nobby had woven for her tied on top of her head, she was eating strands of rope discarded by the splicing party.

It was a pleasant, orderly, even cheerful scene and Bratchet had hopes of it. Having kept out of O'Rourke's way, all she knew of his character was by report. In appearance he was handsome, tall and strong, with very black hair, running somewhat to fat; his musical Irish tenor made a descant to Licky's bass West Indian rumble. The crew's assertion that he was a heavy drinker was borne out by his high colour, but he seemed in jolly mood. It was too nice a day to be anything else.

His voice rang out reasonably, 'But d'you see, cook, I want *that* one.' He went to the gunwale and picked out a belaying pin; twirling it, he walked over to the goat, swung it high and smashed it on to her head. Brilliana went down. Her legs kicked and then stilled. O'Rourke nudged the body with his foot. 'With turnips, if you please, cook.'

For a moment everybody's head turned towards the quarter-deck. Porritt was looking into the distance, his hands behind his back. Helped by one of the holystoners, Licky carried the body down the galley hatch. As he passed the sailing master, he said warningly, 'Your head ain't made only for yo' hat.' Ignoring him O'Rourke ordered sawdust. There had been an issue of blood from the goat's ears.

It was an incident that, looking back on it, Bratchet thought precipitated what happened later more than any other thing – except, possibly, the paucity of rum. It had been unnecessary. Among hardship and cruelty inherent in shipboard life, the gratuitous killing of a pet goat had introduced the unprofessional element of personal hatred for an object of affection. O'Rourke's hounding of Johnson, she realized, had been from the same cause. A wiser captain would not have allowed either. They were acts of brutish ill-will spawning discontent.

Watching it grow into mutiny was like seeing birds gathering to migrate; not so much a clear decision as a gradual, corporate, fluttering unease that could not be acted upon until enough of them felt the call.

Like migration, it was brought about by weather-change. It was becoming hot. Working on deck exposed men to a thirst which couldn't be satisfied by the one scoop of green water which was their ration. Three Frenchmen who rushed a barrel received six lashes apiece on skin already blistered by sunburn.

On the gun deck the ports were opened to allow a breeze from the ship's way to waft through the officers' quarters.

261

Elsewhere the stink wasn't helped by the early symptoms of scurvy which turned men's breath fetid. Seamen who'd once climbed the rigging like monkeys began to suffer breathlessness halfway up and clung on to recover, earning themselves a lashing at O'Rourke's orders when they came down. What little coolness there was on crew deck was in the carpenter's walk, a low, narrow passageway running round the ship's inner skin to allow repairs below the waterline; ideal for conspiracy.

The ship began to whisper. Men stopped talking if an officer passed by, swabbers muttered out of the side of their mouths to each other over their mops, topmen could be seen nodding at lookout, passwords were exchanged. The whispering spread, until it seemed to Bratchet that the whole ship was connected by a cobweb of hissing that had its centre in the galley where Licky was.

Nobby and Sam Rogers, with Pickel and Chadwell as their assistants, were the mutiny's recruiting officers and its organizers; it was they who held meetings in the carpenter's walk, probed and took soundings and came back to say: 'If' – it was always 'if' in the early stages – 'If we do it, the topmen are with us.' Or the portside gunners were with them. Or the sailmakers.

But the instigator was Licky. Bratchet wondered if the others knew how much he influenced them; she thought they didn't. A proverb here, a reminder of what this or that pirate had achieved, a display of his knowledge of the Caribbean and what they could do when they got there, memories of Port Royal in Jamaica, the freebooters' heaven, built up their confidence.

'You planned to take the ship all along, didn't you?' she said to him after they'd gone.

This time he wasn't angry. He opened his eyes wide to show white all around them and let his mouth gape. 'You t'ink a stupid ol' sea-cook nigger like me plan sometin'?'

'Stop it,' she said, 'You know I'm with you. I hate him.'

'You ain't wid anybody.' He was suddenly very serious. 'You ain't going piratin'. Very dangerous business, piratin'. *Hostis humani generis*. You better've jumped. You think I doin' this to go piratin'?'

'What for then?'

262

'Ol' Porritt, he weren't goin' where I want t'go. Now, put them beans in soak. You can' stop yo' ears from hearin' but you kin stop yo' mouth from talkin'. Won't be long now.'

'It had better be soon.' She was beginning to despair of her two men's survival. She made Nobby take them her water ration. She begged him to smuggle her down to see them. It was partly her fault that they were still confined. Early on she had made the mistake of pleading with Porritt to let them out and realized that, despite his need of extra hands, he was keeping them there to spite her.

He had a crucifix over his bed; his steward, Hopkirk, told her the captain spent half an hour on his knees before it every day. She couldn't think what he had to say to it, or how he dared listen to its reply. He was a man in a dimension all his own, wandering deeper and deeper into greyness where nobody could find or touch him.

His anger if she spoke in his presence was prompted by fear of finding her an individual instead of an object. He permitted O'Rourke's cruelty because he had no standard of decency to judge him by.

There were times when she wondered what had happened to him to make him like he was, what twisted God he worshipped to permit himself to remain so. Mostly she didn't bother. He was a lost soul and he could stay lost. The revulsion and fear she'd felt for him were being replaced by contempt; prostitutes, she imagined, survived on the same basis. But I'm no prostitute. 'Can't help ain't do for purpose.' Thanks to Licky, she was a mutineer. *Hostis humani generis*, Licky had called pirates, using the Latin of old statutes, the enemy of all humanity. But she knew a greater enemy of humanity than they were.

On Porritt's card-playing nights, she went on at Nobby to take her down to the hold. Licky got tireder even than Nobby of hearing her. 'Oh, take the woman, she wuss nagger than my first wife.' He promised Nobby an extra ration of coucou and that he would deflect Porritt's manservant if he came to take her to the quarterdeck.

She followed a nervous and irritable Nobby, holding on to his shirt as he took her along the carpenter's walk in darkness.

There was an eeriness to sound down here; men's echoing voices and, always, the reminder of the sea, the castle's besieger, only inches away, threatening to break in. An occasional chink in the inner bulkhead gave her, for the first time since coming aboard, glimpses of the part of the deck which housed commissioned officers and the guns.

She saw carved bosses and cornices as if the boat-builders had taken pride and time in creating a thing of beauty. But they'd run out of both when they got to the ordinary seamen's quarters, though even here beams and planking had the dignity belonging to plain oak and elm. It was the only dignity. These were airless burrows – if air could penetrate the ship's bulkheads so could the sea – where men scurried about their business bent double or slept in tiers, outnumbered by the rats.

She gasped in air that hadn't circulated since the voyage began, but had become more and more warm. It was like being buried and she had to stop herself telling Nobby she wanted to go back. She only knew they'd arrived when he put his hand over her mouth then swaggered up to a figure that had a lantern by its feet, a musket in its hands and appeared to be studying a blank wall with every appearance of interest. 'Me and the boy just got to count the grape boxes, Hans me old squarehead. All right?'

He unlocked a door and she slipped through while Hans was still nodding. Inside there was light from a candle set in the wall behind thick, barred glass, and a stack of barrels and boxes lashed to iron rings by rope – and nothing else.

Nobby opened the glass panel and said: 'In there. Keep your voice down an' be fucking quick about it.'

We stared at each other through the hatch. She was appalled by what she saw: two dirty, bearded, slowly dying skeletons. By becoming Porritt's warming pan, she might have saved Kilsyth and me from being thrown overboard, but she could see that in the conditions we were kept in, we wouldn't last much longer.

For that matter, she wouldn't either. Porritt was becoming increasingly violent; his climaxes dependent on whipping himself into a rage. At that moment, she was grateful that the bruises and bites were on her body, not her face; she wanted us to know that she was submitting to Porritt unwillingly, but saw no need to add to our misery by letting us see she was being tortured.

She passed over the sausages Licky had given her, desperate to give us something better, some hope, a reason to hang on. She leaned as near to me as she could: 'Work at the crossroads,' she said, willing me to understand, 'We're not done yet.'

As she followed Nobby back through the ship, she discovered that she was relieved Kilsyth had been asleep for her visit. He might have absolved her for becoming Porritt's sexual companion but she didn't want absolution; she didn't deserve it. She was as much the captain's victim as the two of us in the shot locker. What she wanted was understanding, the sort Licky had given her. Kilsyth wasn't the man to give it, he was too pure, his chivalry was too unbesmirched by life's mud. For the first time, and reluctantly, Bratchet felt resentment. He wouldn't understand. Then she softened. Why should he? But she came away reassured that at least Martin Millet not only understood but admired her. And God knows I did.

It was the start of her reassessment of our relationship. She told me later that until then she had been confused; the blame she had laid on me for not taking her away from Puddle Court had been a sort of luxury, a way of focusing all its awfulness on a scapegoat. I wasn't her scapegoat any longer. She didn't know what I was; she was just glad it had been me who faced her through the hatch.

But they're dying, both of them.

If there was to be a mutiny it had to be soon. For her to encourage it was useless; the little caucus that gathered in the galley would resent a chit urging them on to risk the terrible punishment that awaited mutineers. With desperate urgency, she watched as Licky encouraged it instead.

One day it was still 'if', the next it was 'when'. The collective mind had consolidated.

'Be you with us or against us, Miss Bratchet?' asked Sam Rogers, formally.

She was surprised she was being consulted. 'With you.'

'Because,' he went on, as if she hadn't spoken, 'we do need your aid with the captain. We don't want no upset, it's to go off quiet like if so be it accords with our plan.' He was a deliberate man, every sentence was plodded through to its end.

She became frightened then. They want me to murder him in his bed. I can't.

'He keeps two pistols in his cabin, so we'm told.'

She nodded and swallowed. 'One in his table drawer near the bed. The other's in a sort of rack behind the door.' She'd seriously thought of using one of them – either on him, or herself.

'Primed?'

'I think so.'

'An' do he always lock the door when you'm . . . in there with un?'

'Yes.' Even though there was always a marine posted outside it. And he takes the crucifix down from its place over the bed.

'Then we want you to take one of they pistols and hold him at bay, like, unlock the door and let us in. We'll tackle the marine, but if so be as we have to break the door down 'twill give un time to get a pistol and us'll have to shoot un.'

They were all looking at her, Nobby, Pickel, Chadwell, Sam and one of the Frenchmen who'd joined the group, a sardonic middle-aged man, Rosier, known as 'Rosy' and reputed to be a great gambler.

They think I'm betraying Porritt. Anger overtook her. Never mind that she was being violated by a madman; in their book the sex act conferred a duty on the woman, however unwilling. You're men. You're my friends, but you're men.

'Will ee do it?'

A minute before she might have agreed unconditionally and been swept along, perhaps to be in no better case than she had before, a woman of no substance. Now she paused. How had Anne Bonny and Mary Read earned themselves a respected place among such men? True, she wasn't the stuff of either Anne or Mary, but this was her chance to try to be.

'I'd like to know your plans,' she said.

She got angrier as they looked at Licky to see if they should tell her. Rosy muttered something about 'les poules' and she made him jump by turning on him and telling him in French to be quiet.

Licky shrugged at them. 'De same dog that bring a bone can carry one,' he said.

So they told her. It was to be the next night. Nobby, followed by Pickel, would take food down to the prisoners in the shot hold as he often did and, while he engaged the guard in conversation, Pickel would knock the man on the head. Nobby was then to unlock the small arms room and hand them out to men waiting in the carpenter's walk.

She interrupted. 'My friends must be let out first.'

Sam nodded.

A third of the officers would be on deck and were to be individually overpowered, the rest would be below in their usual condition, either drunk or asleep. They were to be presented with their captain, a pistol to his head, and given a choice: surrender or be shot.

With a new respect they watched her consider the plan. It wasn't perfect, but nothing would be. Part of her was so frightened she wanted to scream, to let everything stay as it was, but part of her knew it couldn't stay as it was if she and her men were to survive.

In any case, the putative mutineers had seen a vision of the future which destroyed their patience with the present. If they knew, and they did, as she did, that failure meant an appalling death, they could none of them go back now.

She wasn't going to go back either; if this thing succeeded she wasn't going to be returned to the passed-over, directionless and inferior being men had made her before.

'I want two things,' she said, 'I want to keep one of Porritt's pistols.' Guns were like penises, they gave you power. Since she lacked a penis, she was bloody well going to have a gun. 'And once we're in charge, I want to be ship's purser.' She had to have a role. Purser Phillips had died of an apoplexy two days out, since when the job had been carried on by everyone and no one, rendering the stores into a mess that had been the despair of Licky.

'Pusser?' squeaked Nobby, 'You want to be a fucking pusser?'

She winked at Licky who winked back. 'Take it or leave it.' Let's sweep the horizon while we have one, my God.

Sam Rogers extended his large hand. 'Done.'

She shook it.

It was too much to hope that Porritt would send for her the next night, and he didn't. She wanted to flounder and ask her fellow-mutineers what she should do but that would have put her back into subservience. The mutiny had to go ahead that night; the danger of an informer alerting the officers was too great to wait. In any case, her courage wouldn't last another day. It was up to her to initiate the action. 'I'll get in to him somehow,' she said.

The chief conspirators in the galley, Nobby, the Frenchman Rosy, Sam and Pickel, were radiating a terrible energy. Chadwell muttered prayers to himself. Only Licky looked much as usual. They helped her to the companionway as if she were an invalid, patting her, and followed her up until their heads were through the hatch and they could watch her progress by peering under the stretch of canvas that deflected the galley's smoke from the quarterdeck.

On the weather side of the quarterdeck, where the officers always stood, she could see outlines against a sky still not quite black. She heard Nobby counting their hats – in this light the feature that distinguished them from the ordinary seamen. 'Lawrence, Fortescue, Forbes. That's right. Porritt ain't there. The fucker's in his cabin, sure enough.'

Her legs waded across the deck rather than walked, dragging against unreality. This isn't me. I'm not here. I'm somewhere else. Then she thought with relief, He won't let me in. He'll be playing cards with O'Rourke. There was a silver path on the sea to starboard where the moon was coming up. The ship was going fast and smoothly, the sails' canvas creaking.

As she passed the hatch to the gun deck she heard O'Rourke's voice issuing up from below in an Irish ditty about a maiden. Hopkirk would be in there giving him his supper.

She slowed, panicking, unable to remember if Hopkirk was in the conspiracy or not.

The chandler, Sweetman, was in it. He'd chosen this moment to trim the ship's lantern and was getting sworn at for his pains by First Mate Fortescue, especially as he'd brought along an unusual number of his men to help him – and all of them watching her. Look natural, you bloody idiots.

From behind a coil of rope she heard a whisper: 'Go it, girl.' How many were there hidden on deck? Sam had told them to stay below until he gave the signal. Hopeless.

The marine outside the captain's door was Beckerman. Definitely not in it. None of the marines were. Hadn't been given the chance; to all right-minded seamen marines were neither flesh, fowl nor good red herring. He gave her his usual leer and moved aside to let her knock on the door. The cherubs were leering as well.

'Who is it?'

'It's me,' she said tonelessly. Tell me to go away. I'll go.

After a long pause, he opened the door and let her in, frowning. 'I didn't send for you.'

'No.' But he was locking the door behind her, as he always did. The sight of the punch-bag had activated the usual need to use it. He shrugged and went and sat in his chair, flexing his hands, working up hatred, waiting for her to undress.

The walk across the deck had cost too much, made her too tired. She could barely move. This won't work. Languidly, she turned to the door, took the pistol out of the rack, nearly dropped it because it was so heavy and aimed it at him. She had no idea how it worked. 'There's a little safety catch here, look,' Chadwell had said, drawing the outline of a flintlock. 'Pull it back. See . . .' dotting a line backwards, '. . . like this.'

'An' if that don't work, chuck it at the bugger,' Nobby had said.

Porritt was staring at her. 'It's not primed. What are you at?'

'Oh, I'm sorry.' She transferred it to her left hand, and brought up her knee to rest it on while she unlocked the door with her right. There was the sound of scuffling outside.

Porritt still stared at her. 'What are you at? Put it down.' The strange thing was that his tone was as lacklustre as hers, as if they were rehearsing something that was not yet to come about.

I should say something. Tell him what he is. She was too tired. The pistol, which she still pointed at him, told it all, unprimed or not. Anyway, there wasn't time. Sam Rogers rushed in, holding the marine's carbine, with some of the others behind him.

Then it became real. Porritt shouted 'Mutiny,' and 'This is mutiny,' before they fell on him. Out on deck, running towards the after hatch to go and find the shot locker, she could still hear him shouting 'This is mutiny,' over and over, as the English king he'd once served had kept shouting 'This is the standard of rebellion,' again and again, equally unable to believe his reign was ending.

CHAPTER FOURTEEN

I REMEMBER Bratchet's voice outside shouting at Oaf to put down his musket and open the fucking door before she shot his bollocks away, and hoping very hard he'd obey and thinking I would if I was him because she sounded as if she meant it.

The door slid to one side. Oaf, cowering back from a very short, nearly hysterical woman with a pistol, was made to help us along and up companionways to a place full of unoccupied hammocks. There was a lot of noise and shooting going on somewhere else, but Kilsyth and I didn't pay it attention. Whatever strength had helped us to survive purgatory abandoned us on our release from it.

Neither of us remembered much of the next day or two. Dehydration was the problem. There was confusion and a large black man who swam in and out of vision at first, giving us sips of water but refusing us as much as we wanted 'else you blow yo hides out'.

If Bratchet had been our deliverer, it was Licky who gave us back our health. We were as weak as kittens – and as ignorant of what was happening. Licky fed us on strengthening stew – we later learned it was made from the last of the goats – supported us as we made our first forays out of our hammocks and brought us up to date on the situation. And all the while, the leaders of the mutiny and the ship's new captain, Sam Rogers, came to consult him on every move.

Licky, we realized, even before Bratchet told us the whole story, was a great man. He dwelt a lot on what Bratchet had endured and the courage she'd shown. He was, I realized, lecturing us on how to treat her. 'She won the respect of this ship, sure 'nough, and she entitled.'

Bratchet wasn't often in evidence; once Licky had convinced her we'd live, she was in demand elsewhere. If she'd tried, she couldn't have found a job more onerous than that of purser on a ship enjoying – if that's the word – the transformation from privateer to pirate. The Brotherhood of the *Holy Innocent*, henceforth to be called the *Brilliana*, demanded food, rum and a change of clothing to accord with their new status.

About food the purser couldn't do much – the *Innocent* had been too badly provisioned – although she found stores of beans and flour that the old regime had secreted for its own use.

The rum was nearly finished but, again, on breaking open a padlocked door in the hold she discovered a keg of brandy, three of hollands and some casks of excellent wine.

For one fearful night the *Brilliana* wallowed while the Brotherhood celebrated its liberty, before Sam Rogers relocked the liquor cupboard and put a guard on it.

In the officers' linen store there were shirts aplenty, though not enough to meet the fervent demand which symbolized the crew's new independence, so she set the sailmaker to making more.

Hats were the problem. Every hand wanted a hat on the grounds that they were all officers now. Bratchet distributed the ones belonging to the former officers as far as they'd go – Sam had to have one, obviously, so did Nobby as the new gunnery officer, etc., but she had to promise that more would be forthcoming when the *Brilliana* took her first prize. To reinforce her own status, she co-opted the one until recently belonging to First Mate Fortescue, who'd had a small head and good taste.

What she hadn't expected was the paperwork. After their surrender, the Jacobites loyal to Porritt had been given yet another choice: Help work the ship or . . . Most officers and nearly all the men had wisely agreed – on condition they were given a certificate of exoneration to show if the *Brilliana* was captured by any of the regular navies, stating that they were pirates by *force majeure*, not choice. Reasonably, Sam concocted such a document and gave it to Bratchet to translate into French, the international language, and copy out for each of them.

Then there were the Rules of the Brotherhood to be set out in a clear hand. Despite the fact, or perhaps because of it, that nearly all the pirates were illiterate they put great faith in the written word; it gave them a sense of officialdom.

Licky wanted a complete inventory of the food store, Sam a roster of the new crew and their status. Then the louis d'ors found in Porritt's cabin chest had to be shared out on the scale that would be later accorded to each man in prize money – extra to be paid in compensation for his wound to Rosier who'd had an ear sliced off by O'Rourke in the fight to overpower him. As purser Bratchet was also the ship's paymaster.

There was no sign of O'Rourke. There was no sign of Porritt. Nor of the Jacobites, mainly the marines, who'd refused to join the mutineers.

Bratchet, busy rescuing Kilsyth and me, had seen little of the confrontation between mutineers and loyalists that night. Scuffles echoed through the ship and shouting, among it the Irish oaths of O'Rourke. Later a man had screamed and gone on screaming for some time. She feared he, too, had been O'Rourke.

In listening to all the plans for the mutiny, she hadn't enquired what would happen to the officers. Now, when she asked Nobby what had become of Porritt, he said, 'What d'you think?' She'd thought he and the others would be kept prisoner and said so. Nobby blinked at her. 'What for?'

She went to Licky for absolution, 'I didn't want him dead.'

He told her, 'If you ain't got corn, you can' keep chickens that don' lay eggs.' Porritt and the others had gone over the side. Whether they were dead when they were thrown into the sea or not, she couldn't bear to enquire. She made what count she could of the men who'd disappeared; it came to seventeen. Seventeen men for whose deaths she was partly responsible. Well – she hardened her heart – there wasn't one of them who'd shown her or the prisoners in the shot hold any pity, nor tried to ameliorate O'Rourke's treatment of the men under them. And, God have mercy on their souls, but she was a pirate purser now and had work to do.

She sat in Porritt's, now Sam Rogers's, cabin, too busy at the papers on the table to equate it with the place of her degradation. Porritt had only sent for her at night and now it was day, with the oriel window aft letting in greenish sunlight through its panes, some of them open to a gallery commanding the sea and flying fish and a frigate bird that had been following them for three days, ever since the mutiny, like a good omen.

The bed was covered with charts and logs and timepieces and Davis's quadrants and astrolabes. Between it and the deck strode Sam, trying to work out the ship's longitude, and cursing the late Master O'Rourke's slipshod navigation.

'Article the 6,' wrote Bratchet, 'That Man that shall snap his Arms or smoak Tobacco in the Hold, without a cap to his Pipe, or carry a Candle lighted without a Lanthorn, shall receive Moses's Law (that is 40 stripes lacking one) on his bare back.

'Article the 7. If any Man shall lose a Joint in time of an Engagement he shall have 400 Pieces of Eight; if a limb 800.'

'Article the 8. If at any time you meet with any Woman, that Man that offers to meddle with her, without her Consent, shall suffer present Death.'

Article 8, Bratchet was surprised to discover, was a standard injunction in most pirates' homemade law, though its more usual phrase was 'righteous woman' or 'prudent woman'. '*Any* woman,' she'd said, sternly, and that's how it had gone down.

'Well,' she heard Sam say to Licky, who'd just come in, 'far as I can tell from that bugger's log and my calculations we'm in the Tropic of Cancer but whereabout's a different matter. Dang the man, if he'd just let the trade winds take un we'd be sighting Barbados.'

'Barbados bad,' said Licky, 'Bahamas good. Bahamas's Brotherhood territory, Barbados ain't. Either way, water and men can' last much longer.'

'Aye, we'll have to take the first ship we see. We need to careen an' all. Do ee know the Bahamas waters, Licky?'

Licky held out a pink palm, 'Do I know this han'?'

'Good.'

Bratchet sprinkled sand on the Articles, let it soak up the ink and then shook it off. 'On your way out, Licky, nail this up on the mainmast.'

'Aye, aye, sir.' They winked at each other.

'And tell the crew they can start lining up.' She opened the lid of Porritt's chest on the floor beside her chair and drew towards her the list of what each man was entitled to from it. 'No purchase, no pay,' was the highest on the list of pirate articles, but in that sense the crew had already taken their first 'purchase' – the *Innocent* – and were therefore entitled to such riches as it carried. She was amazed by the democracy of piratical life as it had so far been vouchsafed to her. The knowledge of it displayed by Sam, Nobby, Licky and some of the others confirmed her assumption that they had all once been part of it.

One by one the crew began to enter to receive their pay. She checked off each one on her list and counted out the monies. There wasn't much, two hundred louis in all; King Louis's generosity to the Jacobites was nearly exhausted. According to the articles Sam, as captain, received two full shares. She'd been surprised and pleased to find that, as purser, she was entitled to one and a half shares, the same as a sailing master, while gunner and boatswain got one and a quarter.

According to calculations which had made her head ache, that left each member of the crew with the English equivalent of just under three pounds.

'Master Sweetman, your share.' She ticked him off. 'Master Chadwell, yours. Master Grimes, yours . . .'

They seemed pleased enough as she counted out the coins into their hands, though the smell of their breath as they said so reminded her that unless their diet improved soon they'd be too weak from scurvy to sail the ship.

Rosier made trouble about the amount of compensation he was getting for his ear and they exchanged sharp words in French. 'I go to the captain.'

'The captain's got nothing to do with it. This is a Brotherhood vessel and we all vote the shares. You were told,' she said, trying to be patient – she didn't like Rosier – 'when we take a prize you shall have five hundred pounds for it.'

'But the pain is here now,' he said.

'Well, the money isn't. Besides, you haven't lost the ear. Licky sewed it back on.'

'And how do I know we will take a prize? It is bad luck to have a woman on board. A woman purser, it is against nature. Also a woman purser who is a turncoat.'

She looked up sharply. 'Turncoat?' He looked ridiculous with cloth tied round his face and fastened in a bow on top, like a vicious pudding. 'Turncoat?'

'One says you were a Jacobite at St-Germain. A Jacobite in your captain's bed. Whose bed next, eh?'

I must learn how to fight. Mary and Anne would have challenged him to a duel. In the meantime she'd have to overlook it. She reverted to nautical English. 'Hold your gum and get back to work.'

She returned to putting coins in horny palms. 'Master Freeble. Master Johnson – how's the back? – Master Guienne . . .'

Two hands, one large, one medium-sized, appeared in front of her.

'Pirates Millet and Kilsyth reporting for their pay, Mistress Purser, if you please,' I said.

There had been a general assumption among the mutineers that, having been Porritt's prisoners, we should be grateful enough for our deliverance to join them. Kilsyth expressed horror at the idea, though he had the sense to do it privately to me. 'Piracy,' he said, 'a filthy word and a filthy trade.' I agreed with him but in the circumstances I didn't see what else we could do except go along with it. Neither of us fancied another term in the shot locker or, more likely, following the *Holy Innocent*'s captain into Davy Jones's.

'Aye,' he said, at last, 'it'll have to be borne for now but, losh, there's many an ancestor will be turning in his grave at the idea of a Kilsyth a pirate.' And then he grinned, 'And a few that'll not.'

Sam Rogers had come to see us and gravely welcomed us into the fraternity, saying he was entitling us to a share in the purchase.

We thanked him but he said, 'You must thank the purser.'

As soon as we were steady on our legs we went to do it. The purser sat in the quarterdeck cabin, doling out monies and frowning over the papers on her desk. I saw that she'd imitated Kit Ross's headgear by tying her hair in a bandana and topping it with a hat which she'd cocked at a piratical angle. She had a pistol in her belt.

She'd changed yet again, or rather she'd matured. The sophistication of Mlle La Fée had been replaced by something better; the suffering that had always lurked somewhere behind her eyes was deeper, but it had been accepted. It was part of her, but not the main part. She was apologizing to nobody for what she'd done or what she was. If this was Licky's work, and I thought it was, I blessed him for it.

We took her out on deck, where we could talk without being overheard. It was a beautiful day and a school of porpoises curvetted along by the ship's starboard. She sat on a coil of rope while we squatted against the taffrail.

'Well?' she asked of Kilsyth. If he was expecting the ashamed blush and lowered lids of a violated virgin, he was going to have to wait for ever. She looked him straight in the eye.

'Oh, lassie,' said Kilsyth, helplessly.

'Oh, what?' she demanded, 'Oh, I saved your bloody lives for you? Oh, I'm sorry we didn't all go over the side? Is that it?'

'Aye, well, but to join up wi' pirates . . .'

'They're better men than their captain was,' she said, 'And if that's all that's worrying you . . .' She got up and strode off to the cabin. She was wearing a pair of loose breeks that must have been made for a ship's boy. They suited her. She came back with papers in her hand and shoved one at each of us. 'This here's a disclaimer. It says you've joined under protest, so shut your gum and let me get back to work. I'm busy.'

'Did Porritt ever say why he seized us?' I asked her.

She shook her head and sat down.

'Without a doubt the rogue was waiting for us,' Kilsyth said. He and I had discussed it time and again and he'd come round to my way of thinking, that it had been another in the series of attempts to silence the Bratchet and, quite probably, us too. Somebody had told Porritt to watch out for anyone enquiring for *L'Hirondelle*; there was no other way he could have been alerted to our presence in Le Havre.

'Who killed Aunt Effie, Bratchet?' I asked. It was becoming less a question than a reminder.

'Bilge,' she said, 'The French reckoned you to be a spy and were watching the ports.'

'Well, it's verra strange how our quest for Bonny Anne is duplicating her own weary travels,' Kilsyth said. 'Somebody doesna want us to find her.'

'It's stranger than that,' Bratchet said. 'Anne became a pirate, too. Her and Mary. Some time after they was spirited. They sailed with a captain called Jack Rackham. Nobby said so. He met them in Port Royal once. There's others did too. Not pirate molls, either. Pirates.' She was partly triumphant, mostly grieving. 'They had babies, Martin,' she said. 'They were caught and tried in a place called St Jago something. They were pregnant, bless 'em.'

'I'll not believe it,' shouted Kilsyth.

'What happened to them?' I asked.

'I'm going to find out,' she said, 'If we ever get to this St Jago, I'll find out. They must be grown children now, if they survived.'

'Not the babies, Bratchie,' I said, gently, 'Anne and Mary.'

She got up and stretched, ready to get back to work. 'Nobby says they're dead.' She smiled down at us. 'But they ain't.'

With distaste, Kilsyth questioned Nobby and some of the others who claimed to have met Anne Bonny and Mary Read, and was forced to accept that gentle, royal Anne had become an admired member of the most hated and feared profession in the world.

He altered after that. I think he laid his Anne to rest in a quiet place in his mind. The Anne he heard about from Nobby and the others was somebody else to him.

I grieved for the poor cow, too, in my way; for both poor cows. I'd never believed in the proposition to make Anne a queen, probably she hadn't either, but somebody had, and somebody had destroyed her and her friend because of it.

Two days later we were overtaken by a storm.

It was like being the jack in a titanic game of bowls, flipped in one direction then another by woods that thundered down a monstrous alley while the bowlers screamed in triumph.

On deck it needed three men struggling with the helm to keep *Brilliana*'s head to the wind. The four lashed to the pumps had to be replaced every fifteen minutes before they collapsed. When a trisail's tack came loose, three men wormed along the deck to refasten it, fingers clawing into planking edges, every protuberance on deck slashing their skin, a hundredweight of water with each wave crushing the breath out of them and threatening to snap the umbilical cord of their lifeline as it poured back through the scuppers.

One of them was Bratchet's friend Pickel, a mutiny leader. He was killed when the stays holding the longboat gave way. Its keel broke his back before the rest of it smashed to pieces.

Below decks water poured in through cracks in the hatches and ports, blinding, wetting and deafening us, slamming us with bone-breaking force against bulkheads and tables every time we moved.

'Enjoying yer baptism?' Nobby shouted at me.

'Don't think much of the bloody font.'

Being a landsman, I'd never before appreciated the courage sailors need to face a storm, though even by their standards this one was exceptional. Men whose faces were already grey with fatigue and fear went wordlessly on deck to stand their watch and returned like dripping corpses.

278

Kilsyth and I'd barely had time to learn which was prow and which the stern, but we had to help out because the ship had been short-handed to start with, its complement reduced by the mutiny, and a storm of these proportions required longer watches from each man. To be honest, I was so frightened at what awaited me on deck that my legs had trouble taking me up the ladder. Give me a charging French regiment any day.

It went on and on, days and nights of being shaken like dice in a box, helpless. The Highlander was magnificent, I'll say that for him. He did two men's work not only without complaint but with exhilaration. He enjoyed it, the bugger; I'd never admired him like I did then. Nor Bratchet either. Sitting wedged with her back against the galley's sideboard, feet against the stove, she bound up broken fingers, ribs, put salve on rope burns and gashes, as if she'd been born to it.

I was one of those who helped pull Pickel's body from over the side where it hung from its lifeline. Personally, I'd have cut the rope. The poor bastard was clearly dead and the effort to retrieve his corpse at rearing, changing angles of forty-five degrees risked us joining him. But no, sailors being the queer cattle they are, we had to get him back so that later, when the storm was over, we could wrap him up in calico and push him overboard again.

We lowered the body down the galley hatch where Bratchet held its head in her lap while Licky pronounced it dead. I watched the two of them lace it into a hammock and sling the resultant roll between hooks in the meat locker where it swung like a clock pendulum.

They worked as a team, with no sign of the grief I knew they'd be feeling later – they'd become close, all those who'd planned the mutiny together. But now there was too much noise, no space in the general battering for anything other than endurance. It was an odd alliance, that huge black sea-cook and the tiny, pale-skinned young woman, but I was grateful they had it. Bratchet'd told me it had saved her life and reason.

She turned and I saw her mouth something at me.

'What?'

She held on to the stove so that she could get to where I was

279

sitting with the rest of the rescue party. She wiped some of the seawater off my face with her warm hands.

'Are. You. All. Right?' We seemed to be spending our time together asking each other that.

I nodded. Licky passed over tin mugs and she handed them out to us. Cold burgoo spiced with brandy, best thing I've ever tasted.

It was time to go back on deck. As I hauled myself through the hatch, she tapped my boot. 'Take care.'

Kilsyth was the hero of the hour when half the lateen mizzen-yard snapped off and came plummeting down, crashing Guienne who, with Sam, was at the helm, into the scuppers. For the ship to broach in that sea would have been the end of it. He heard Sam's shouts above the wind, staggered to him and helped him control the helm until Sweetman got to them. It was Kilsyth who lifted the great splinter and held it off Guienne while others chopped it free of its rigging, Kilsyth who tossed it like a caber over the side and then, somehow, got the wounded seaman below.

When we came off watch we fell into our hammocks and slept in a great swinging arc. Those who were too tired to reach the hammocks fell asleep in the galley in the middle of eating burgoo, arms hooked round the holding ropes criss-crossing the cabin, water swilling round their hocks.

Licky and Bratchet were denied even this luxury; every watch needed food and medical attention. Bratchet said later all she could think was, Stop it. Stop it. I can't go on. Every action required effort and planning to effect. Where Licky got his strength she didn't know; she said he was a colossus, a black Atlas, untiring, patient, holding her and the entire ship on his back. She would have fallen off without him. Everybody was getting to breaking point; it was as if we'd been transferred to a loop in eternity.

Then, quite suddenly, there was no more screaming wind. Ordinary sounds came back; seagulls, men talking, a hammer knocking, the pump going, brushes sweeping out water below. On deck all available rigging flew a bunting of flapping, drying clothes.

We were a bleary-eyed bunch, but we'd become a company, like men do who've gone into battle together. And Bratchet had gone in with us, into a hell no landsman could ever know, and emerged with honour. We were proud of her, of each other; she was proud of us. We'd become a Brotherhood.

I saw Kilsyth change towards her. There's nothing so infectious as other men's admiration for a woman and he caught it. Into the place he'd kept for Anne Bonny stepped the scarred little woman from Puddle Court. He watched her as she stood with her comrades while Sam read the funeral service for Pickel on the morning after the storm dropped. She was crying, so was Nobby who stood next to her.

'That's an amazing wee lassie,' he said.

'Yep.'

He turned on me. 'I'd see ye more grateful. She sacrificed her honour for your hide, and mine.'

He was getting on my nerves again. The canvas-wrapped rectangle was tipped over the side and gold and azure flying fish which arced over the bubbles of its going down probably gave more grace to its departure than had been accorded to its life.

An hour later it turned out that the storm had left us a gift.

'Vessel starboard bow,' shouted the lookout.

There was a rush to starboard, jostling at the gunwale for a view.

'What be she?' called Sam, reaching for Porritt's telescope.

'Two-decker, no telling what.'

I made out a smudge on the horizon. There hadn't been a sight of sail since the coast of Portugal disappeared behind the ship, weeks ago.

'Two-decker and a tangle,' said Sam lowering the telescope and looking about him. 'She'm dismasted. Whatever she is, she's ours, lads. Bo'sun, pipe the action.'

Bratchet came rushing over to us as the crew cheered. 'We're going into action. Oh, God, we're going into action.' She clawed at my arm. 'Tell Sam he mustn't.'

'We're pirates now,' I told her.

'But it's a big ship, a very big ship. It may have lots of guns. It might be English navy. I'm tired. It's too nice a day. Why can't we let the bloody thing go?'

Nobby came up, capering like a madman. 'Prize, prize, prize.' He disappeared below to see to his guns.

'How's your teeth, Bratchie?' I asked her.

'My teeth?'

'Mine are getting loose,' I said, 'I asked Licky about 'em. It's scurvy.'

She sucked at her teeth, so did Kilsyth. 'My gums are spongy,' she said. She had good white teeth.

'Licky says lime juice, onions and green stuff'll cure 'em lickety.'

'And I suppose yon ship is carrying all three?' said Kilsyth.

'Could be.' We all felt it, a sort of fury for acquisition, the sin of the deprived.

Bratchet made up her mind. 'If that boat's got as much as one onion on board, I'm going to get the bugger.'

I knew there was no choice. Sam had set me to calculating how much water we had left on board. Though the storm had sent down enough rain to keep the ship from thirst for a month, waves throwing themselves over the ship had infiltrated every receptacle Licky put out to catch it, rendering it undrinkable. Even rationed, there was only enough for four more days.

The breeze was in our favour but it was lackadaisical and the *Brilliana* had to goosewing her way towards her prey, wetted foresails spread out either side of her foremast to catch the current of air. The slow advance was hard on the nerves, but Sam Rogers said to think what it was doing to the crew of the helpless ship.

Licky came up and said the same. 'Reckon we look like one great angel coming at them, wings open and flapping. Is we angel of goodness? Is we angel of death? They doesn't know.' He took Bratchet down with him to prepare a hot meal before we went into action.

We were kept busy. Chadwell and his assistants took down unnecessary bulkheads so that there was less for enemy shot to shatter – splintering is as lethal as shot itself in a naval battle and causes more wounds – and got ready mauls and plugs to repair any leaks. Hammocks were strung along the sides to shield the deck crew from marksmen. Hatches, except those to the guns, were battened down, spare rigging coiled in the scuppers, boarding grapnel posted fore and aft, muskets passed out to the men.

The *Brilliana* opened her eighteen eyes as her gun port lids were raised and wedged. We heard the vibration of her cannon being run into firing position. On the gun deck, Nobby was ordering the rammers, sponges, wads, priming irons to be put into racks near each cannon and coils of slow match attached to their linstocks. Partridge, the sailmaker, searched the ship looking for black cloth with which to make a new flag.

In the galley, Licky and Bratchet boiled the last of the salt fish and the few fresh they'd managed to catch, mixed them with the last of the oats and the last of the wine because the last kegs of water had already been placed on top and gun decks.

She came up to get some air, wiping her forehead with the back of her hand. I was seeing to the small arms. 'Perhaps we could just ask nicely for the onions,' she said. She was still sucking her teeth. 'How long now?' There were about two miles of flat, sparkling water between us and the ship.

'I don't know.' I took Porritt's pistol out of her belt and primed it for her.

'What can we do?' she asked. 'Common water pads, that's us. It's the gallows if they catch us.'

'See,' I said, 'here's the safety catch. Comes up like this.'

She leaned over the starboard gunwale. 'Martin, how did we get here? I don't want to kill people. I suppose I already have. How did it happen?'

'It happened.'

She said. 'It wouldn't've if it wasn't for you. You and your bloody Aunt Effie.'

'Who killed her?'

'God almighty,' she screamed, 'why do you keep asking? It doesn't matter.' She pointed at the ship, 'Any minute they'll be killing us or we'll be killing them. That matters. Aren't you worried?'

'No,' I said, 'I'm too bloody frightened. Worry's what you do when you got choices and we ain't got no choice. Here.' I handed her the pistol. 'Did you have a choice when you pointed this at Porritt?'

She rubbed her forehead again. 'I can't remember. No.'

'There you are, then. Now, keep the bloody thing dry and aim low.'

When the cooking was done, she went round the ship with baskets on each arm. Nobby was organizing a run of powder monkeys to keep up the supply of ball, shot and powder from the hold to the gun deck. 'An get a fucking lanthorn on this fucking ladder. It's black as midnight's arsehole here. What's these?'

'Flying fish cakes, Licky says,' she told him.

He took a bite. 'Dog vomit. We'll fire 'em at the enemy, that'll make the fuckers surrender.' He was gabbling from nerves; through the telescope he'd counted the gun ports on the ship we were about to engage. She had thirty-two to the *Brilliana*'s eighteen. 'Why don't Sam put her under sweeps? We'll never get there this rate.'

'They haven't got the strength to row.'

'Tell 'em to get out and push.'

On the quarterdeck she offered her basket to Sam Rogers. He waved it away. 'Later.'

'You eat,' she said and watched him while he did. It was his seamanship which had brought us through the storm; while everyone else was sleeping off its effect, Sam had toured the ship, noting what needed repair, and now he had to take her into battle. The men put a trust in him they had never placed in Porritt and, close to, she saw how much of a burden it put on him. His eyes were bloodshot with fatigue.

'What're they feeling, Master Purser?' he asked her.

'It's the waiting, Captain.'

'Tell Dai to fetch his hornpipe. After prayers we'll test the buggers' dancing.'

The service was short and heartfelt, Sam leading the Protestants on the quarterdeck, the Catholics clustered around Rosier at the mainmast, invoking the blessing of the Sinless Being on the sin they were about to commit.

284

As the *Brilliana* clawed her way, Bratchet and I watched her tired, scurvy-ridden crew get up and dance, legs and arms akimbo, while we judges beat time on her deck until it boomed like a drum.

The undisputed winner was Livingstone of Kilsyth. There were cries of 'Go it, Sawney' as he whooped, his big feet prancing in a delicate tattoo between the crossed cutlasses on the deck, his orange hair bouncing. It wasn't bravado; whatever horror he felt for piracy, the *Brilliana* had become his during the storm and he hers.

I envied the energy he gave out that men around him could absorb. When he'd volunteered to be a member of the boarding party, they'd cheered.

Beside me, Bratchet said quietly, 'I was right to love him.'

He came towards us, sweating and grinning. 'I was ay a bonny dancer.'

She said, 'You'll take care. Please.'

He looked towards the ship. By now we could make out its crew crawling like ants over her rigging as they tried to erect a jury mast.

'She's big,' he said, 'but we'll take her.'

There was another cheer. The *Brilliana* had run up her colours; from the jackstaff flew what had once been part of her former captain's best coat – now a totally black flag.

Bratchet pointed at it. 'And what about that?'

Kilsyth shrugged. 'It's her manna we're needing, no her treasures,' he said, 'Can I take bread and water from men who'll risk their lives to win it for me without risking my own? I canna. And now . . .' He put his hands round her waist and lifted her away from the gunwale, 'Ye'll oblige me, mistress, by going below and staying there. This place will be no fit for women.'

I could have sworn that, for a second, she fluttered her eyelashes, but she said, 'Anne Bonny and Mary Read didn't go below in action. They fought alongside the men. Nobby says.'

'Maybe,' he said, 'but I'll not have you end up the same way.'

This time she did flutter her eyelashes. She went below. Her post in action was with Licky, acting as loblolly boy to his surgeon.

For another ten minutes the *Brilliana* was almost totally quiet, only the occasional flap of her goosewings breaking the silence. Suddenly there was another sound, a deep booming I'd never heard before. Sam Rogers was having the battle drum played.

And the ship ahead of us ran down her colours.

For a moment, I don't think any of us could believe she'd done it. She was huge compared to the *Brilliana*. Her sides reared up in front of us, her open gun ports black, blind holes staring down from under gilded, ornate eyelashes.

Whether the *Brilliana* had, as Licky said, seemed to be an avenging angel slowly flapping nearer and nearer, whether the sight of men dancing on her deck as she approached had unnerved the opposing watchers, whether it was the unfurling of the pirate flag, that symbol of death, whatever it was, her colours had come down and another flag was being hauled up. It was white. She'd surrendered without a fight.

She was Spanish, the *San Martine*, a barque separated from her convoy in the storm, carrying cargo from Mexico to Spain, using the favoured channel north through the Straits of Florida.

More importantly from our immediate point of view, she had made a rendezvous with the other ships of the convoy in Cuba and had taken on fresh water and supplies. Thinking herself protected, she'd been greedy and disposed of most of her guns in order to carry yet more goods home to her owners in Spain.

This, her master, Jerónimo Juan Cardozo, admitted was a mistake. He was a short, stocky, pragmatic man – oddly enough, despite the difference in height and colouring, he resembled Sam Rogers, the same impenetrable calm. He said he'd once before been captured by Caribbean pirates, on which occasion he'd learned that they were more sympathetic to one's wellbeing if one did not oppose them. His English, like everybody else's Spanish, was non-existent but his French was sufficient to allow Rosier to act as interpreter.

We clustered round as he was questioned.

How many on board? A crew of one hundred and forty.

Cargo? For the first time Señor Cardozo's eyes flickered – towards Licky. Oh, the usual.

286

'Any onions?' asked Bratchet.

He didn't blink. He was so sorry, but onions, no. However, if she wished *el cocido*, a stew, he was sure he could provide one.

Practically the entire complement of the *Brilliana* had swung themselves across to the *San Martine* and the sound of tearing wood indicated that some of them were investigating the cargo for themselves. Sam sent me to impose discipline and bring them back up.

'Haven't ee got a purser, you buggers?' Sam told them, 'Master Bratchet'll make a list. Now, get they prisoners shackled. Master Sweetman, choose a prize crew and get the rest back on board *Brilliana*. Seenhor Cardizoo, I want to see your log.'

Bowing, Señor Cardozo suggested they repair to his *alcaza*. He and Sam and Rosier disappeared into his quarters, while Bratchet, Licky and I went below, carrying the master's keys, to help her make her list.

She was excited, expecting the keys to open up mounds of pearls and gold. She was almost light-headed with relief at the speed of the capture. Licky was sober. 'That too easy,' he said to me. He was afraid the crew would be carried away into thinking every prize would surrender without a fight. 'Sometimes they do,' Licky said, 'mostly don't. We lucky that Spanisher been captured before.'

He was cheered by the sight of the *San Martine*'s stores. They'd been laid in at Havana for a voyage of several weeks. He was especially delighted with barrels of dried peppers and spices. 'Now you taste my salamagundi,' he said, 'Blow your head off.'

It was true that the *San Martine* carried no onions, but there were rows of limes on her pantry shelves, enough to reverse the scurvy. Licky put one in his mouth and gave a green grin to reassure Bratchet her teeth were safe.

The Spanish were insatiable for rum if the hundred barrels of it we found in the spirit store was anything to go by. Bratchet relocked the door after taking an inventory and carefully added 'padlock' to a list of requirements.

The gun deck was stacked mainly with barrels of cocoa.

There was a small chest of pearls in the hold, but a bigger consignment was a hundred or more pigs of a metal that at first we took to be tin. It reflected dully as Brachet held her lanthorn up to examine it.

I picked one up and my arm jerked with the weight. Licky's eyes widened and he fell on his knees and bit one. 'Marty, you tell me what I t'ink dis is.'

I nodded. 'Silver.' After Bratchet had counted it, we relocked that door as well.

'What's here?' We were in the deepest part of the hold now, in a section that on the *Brilliana* would have been the cable tier. Unusually, there was a bulkhead between it and the rest of the hold and a locked door. Bratchet chose one of the keys so far unused and tried it, tried another and opened up hell. It was like that. The smell burst out as if a genie came shrieking from its bottle.

It was the slave hold. Inside were people. They were carefully packed head to toe, so that we saw lines of heads like black poppies so closely interspersed with feet that toes brushed against ears.

It was very neat. No space was wasted between the tiers; noses almost touching the slats of the tier above. There were moans and we could hear the chink of chains but there was no movement from the heads, each neck held by an iron collar screwed to the planking, not even a rolling back of the eyes to try and see where the unaccustomed light was coming from. It made no difference to them.

To be standing upright in their presence was bad enough; to be standing next to Licky was worse. Bratchet shoved her lanthorn at me and fled, calling for Chadwell to bring chisel and mallet to break the chains.

Eventually we got them up on deck, stinking, naked, stumbling, blinking. There were women among them and a few children. Bratchet had got food and water ready for them. She held out the water dipper to a little girl of about ten who was streaked with excreta; the ordure from the tier above had dripped on her.

Rosier and Sam came out of the master's cabin, Rosier

counting as he walked along the lines. 'Sixty-one, sixty-two, sixty-three. Good specimens. We'll get a good price.'

I stopped Bratchet reaching for her pistol. 'What about the dead ones?' Chadwell and Licky were hauling out corpses. Rosier counted those as well. 'Seven. Always there is wastage.' I took my hand off Bratchet's and the man looked round into the barrel of her pistol. It was shaking. 'What passes with you, woman?'

Licky took the gun away from her. 'You don' wan' do that,' he told her, waving it carelessly so that it fired. The bullet just missed Rosier's good ear. 'Dear, dear, I is one neglectful nigger.'

In the discussion on the share-out that took place on the *Brilliana*'s deck that night, we found that more of the pirates regarded the slaves as saleable goods than didn't. Chadwell, Partridge and many others took Rosier's view: they were in business now, and business was business.

Licky was curiously neutral, a silent, apparently disinterested observer. Nobby was swayed by whichever side had just put its case.

'For the love of God,' Bratchet said, 'There's thousands' worth of silver pigs down there, more blunt than any of us ever saw. We don't have to go into the skin trade.'

'There's that,' said Nobby, nodding.

'But it'll take some selling,' Partridge said. 'We'll have to haggle with nobs, maybe get ourselves agents and such. Slaves sell anywheres. Black gold, they are.'

'There's that,' said Nobby.

'Hold your gum.' Bratchet pushed him and turned in desperation to Sam Rogers. 'What about it, Captain?'

Sam was smoking crumbled leaf from a keg of tobacco that he'd liberated from Cardozo's cabin. The boy Johnson sat beside him, his eyes blank.

Sam took his pipe from his mouth. 'I sailed with a man once. Misson, his name was. One of your breed, Rosy. Froggy, but educated. Godless bugger he was, and had a priest with un, godless as himself. But he set great store by what he called Man. He didn't believe in private property though, Dear knows, he pirated enough of it.' Sam puffed and sent up a spiral of smoke that showed white against the pink and purple Caribbean sunset. We sat still to listen to him and the only sound came in sliding squeaks from the fenders of our two grappled ships as they rubbed together.

'One day,' said Sam, 'we captured a Dutcher, the *Nieuwstadt*, out of Amsterdam, with gold dust and eighty nigger slaves on board and most of us wanted to sell 'em, as it might be you now, Master Chadwell. But Misson, he said no. He'd shaken – what was it? – the yoke of tyranny off'n his own neck and he said he weren't about to put it on any other poor bugger's. He said trade in our own species wasn't agreeable with Man's liberty nor true justice, and he weren't permitting it on any ship he captained.'

Sam took a last puff and knocked out his pipe against the top of his boot, catching its ash in his other hand. He looked up. 'And while I be captain, I ain't neither.'

It was a vote of confidence and Sam won it, though there was a sizeable minority, led by Rosier, in the show of hands against him.

We put the women, some of them pregnant, in the *San Martine*'s roundhouse with their children for the night and set a guard on their door. Bratchet raided the Spaniards' clothing store and found sufficient trousers for the men and shirts for the women and children, then returned to the *Brilliana* and went to her cabin without a word.

I'd been surprised by the closeness of the vote and I knew she'd taken it hard. In England we don't see black slavery, it's just another word for profit, a method of husbandry, part of the agriculture that sends us our sugar. You don't think of it as people.

I'd admired Sam's speech on liberty and Man and all that, but what had brought slavery home to me had been the sight of that hold on the *San Martine*. I was shaken, I admit. As for Bratchet, she'd as near as dammit shot Rosier when he'd counted the blacks as merchandise.

It was personal to her. It wasn't just that Licky had become her father and brother, but something to do with being a woman and referred to, as women are, as if she was goods,

290

disposable. The warming-pan thing. Perhaps that was the bond between her and the sea-cook, I thought. He'd been a slave, making him an honorary female. She was female, making her an honorary slave. What they had was deeper than anything she'd ever feel even for Kilsyth. It wasn't sexual, I knew. Licky only reckoned black women bedworthy; 'The blacker the woman the sweeter she be,' he'd once told me. It was familial, love between the unfree.

As for me, I didn't even see him as different any more; the further we sailed into the sun, the more his colour fitted the weather while the rest of us became patched with burned skin. For all Sam's high words, I might have looked at that cargo in the hold and seen animal stock. Because of Licky, I didn't.

Bratchet changed after that. Her pirating days were over. She'd thought she'd found a home and been willing, like Anne Bonny and Mary Read, to trade the present glory of it for its inevitable ending. The swagger went. She'd achieved what she'd envied Mother Ross for in Flanders, acceptance into the exclusive club of men under fire. No matter that most were as rough a bunch of illiterates as ever spat, it had been valuable time for her, her piping times.

Like Ma Ross she'd kept the tension between desire and respect. If there was lust in their eyes when they looked at her it was a mere glint in comradely affection. She'd been part of the Brotherhood. Without a future. Desperate living for the day, which is what piracy means. A juggling act.

It was over for her now.

I stayed on deck and listened to them discuss their plans for their prize money, a spending spree on women, clothes, gambling and drink. If it brought a hangman's rope after their next prize, or the next, so be it. From birth they'd never been able to expect anything other than an early, unpleasant death. This way death wouldn't be any less unpleasant but for a short while they'd experience what it was to be rich and free.

I wondered if Anne Bonny and Mary Read had been as happy to opt for it. When I came to think of it, there was no other outlet in this world for women with spirit like theirs.

Even they'd had to succumb to the final femininity and become pregnant.

And I knew the barren Bratchet no longer envied them their great adventure; she envied them their babies.

From Sam Rogers's point of view, the most valuable thing the *San Martine* had to offer was an accurate record of her last position. Working on a rough calculation of the speed and direction of the storm, he did some reckoning. By a vote, the *San Martine* was renamed somewhat ominously the *Beginning*. Manned by a prize crew, and together with the *Brilliana*, it took a course which brought the low green islands of the northern Bahamas on to the horizon.

We spent a night ashore on white sands under palm trees and a sky like warm blue felt. It was then that Bratchet, Kilsyth and I held our own conference and found that all of us felt the same. As soon as we reached what we regarded as civilization, we would take our leave of the *Brilliana*. We weren't cut out for the pirate life and, unlike so many others on board, we still could make the choice. We had other lives to lead.

But we agreed that there was no hurry. With a prize and treasure to be disposed of, there would be no question of attacking any more ships. And all three of us, like the *Brilliana*, needed time in which to heal.

So we sailed on from island to island, helping with the disposal of prize goods to English merchants who didn't ask questions. We landed the slaves on any island they took a fancy to, and the same with those of the *San Martine*'s crew who didn't care to join us.

As we went we became overrun with the traders of the Caribbean, nearly all of them women, who clambered on board at one anchorage and slid off at another, the higglers. They carried great baskets of fruit, vegetables and trinkets on their thick, black arms, chattering in every tongue that would sell, driving bargains that left you counting your eye-teeth.

And there was one very special higgler.

CHAPTER FIFTEEN

Fifth Extract from *The Madwoman's Journal*

I WENT TO Highgate yesterday, as I have done every month since arriving in England, but this time someone followed me.

It wasn't her. She was behind me every step, of course; she always is, ranting and frenzied, but I took no notice. I control her better since the Bratchet was disposed of. I maintain long periods without answering her, though she tries different forms to frighten me; sometimes she's a tree lumbering at me from a hedgerow on fat-ankled legs, sometimes a milestone bids me good-day and it is her.

I suppose I should be grateful; unless I had kept glancing back, I would not have noticed the man who followed. As it was, I did not see him until Parliament Hill Fields. A little man with a squashed nose, poorly dressed, apparently idling along reading a newspaper. Life at sea has made my eyes keen over long distances and I saw that the newspaper was the *Review* and that it was upside down.

It was early with few people about so that at first I thought him a foist after my purse and bent down to retie my bootlaces in order to take my knife from its strap round my leg.

I did some idling of my own. It was a fine summer's day. After buying a squirt of milk from the woman who grazes her cow on the Fields, I retraced my steps a little, picking cowslips, weaving in and out of the trees, until I had regained the track. I turned, as if to consider the view of London below me, thinking I had thrown him off but caught sight of his heels as he dodged behind a bush.

I considered seizing him and carving his throat until he told me who sent him. But it is not usual for a bedchamber woman to carry a knife; he would have thought it odd. I could have stuck him, of course, but his death would arouse even more suspicion in whoever sent him. 'Very well, Captain Queernabs,' I thought, 'let us see where the wind blows us.'

It blew me to the east side of the hill, through alleyways between the cottages there, past Dick Whittington's Stone, and upwards at spanker pace.

It's a pig of a hill and the breeze brought me sounds of his puffing breath, nevertheless he was a determined little barnacle and he stuck to me.

Who sent him? What do they know? I have been careful. It could be the Whigs, of course. They are so desperate to regain power over the Queen that they may be trying to find something to my discredit so that they can force me to spy on her. They happily stoop to blackmail. Sarah, for instance, is threatening to publish the letters Queen Ant wrote to her in their early days if Anne doesn't do what she wants.

What scandal then! I have no doubt the letters display passion that the world considers improper for one woman to feel for another. But for once the Queen is holding her course, scandal or no. While the Whigs were at the helm they treated her with such contempt she has turned to fight. She is amazing in her sternness towards them. Sunderland sent packing. Godolphin dismissed, who had been with her all her reign, in a curt note delivered by a lackey. No thanks, no kindness, no mention of friendship or guidance. Just go.

She has even faced down the great Duke of Marlborough by refusing to appoint an experienced officer as chief of Essex's regiment of Dragoons and instead has given the post to Abigail's brother, Honest Jack Hill, who is about as fitted to lead Dragoons as an embroidery lesson.

This confirms the Whigs' belief that Abigail rides Her Majesty and they are after her in full cry. In fact, did they but know it, Abigail's on the wane. You can surfeit on Abigail's cloying, insinuating sweetness and the Queen is beginning to sicken. It is in me that she confides now, over glasses of cold tea, but she keeps me secret, fearing that I will be taken up by one faction or another.

Fear not, Your Majesty, I am my own faction. Oh yes.

However, I confess to fright as I climbed Highgate Hill. Did they suspect what it was I hid at the top?

There was a haywain going up, its driver leading his horses. I feigned fatigue and begged for a ride. He was impudent, demanding a kiss, which I gave him, before clambering on to the back board where I watched Queernabs showing interest in a hedge.

As I had guessed, the hay bales proved too high to pass under the archway toll and, as is usual, the wain was taken round through a yard at the rear of the Gate House tavern where I jumped off and ran into its taproom before Queernabs could see where I went.

The tavern's drudge was sweeping out. I put my finger to my lips. The creature, of course, was shrieking to try and attract his attention, but no human woman will tell on another who is pursued by a man. As I emerged from the Gate's front entrance, I heard the drudge say no, nobody had gone through to her certain knowledge. I was free.

Highgate is a strange place. Seen from London, its windmill sails give it the appearance of a typical English hill village but perhaps because the hill is virtually impassable to traffic for five months of the year, it has become the home of many foreigners on moderate incomes, especially the Mediterranean immigrants, Portuguese, Italians, Huguenots from southern France, Jews, men who are prepared to walk the six or seven miles to their work as stockbrokers' clerks, translators and the like.

And while the well-to-do English prefer to live in London in the winter, they farm out their children to wet-nurses in the village because of its healthy air; although the Great Plague struck nearly everywhere else in England, there was not a single death from it in Highgate.

So the gardens of the thatched cottages grow alien vegetables and dark-skinned women with white babies at their breast chatter to each other over the hedges and bright, foreign flowers sprout in the window pots and the taprooms of the Gate and the Black Dog resound at nights with the tongues of Babel.

Yes, my darling, my dearest love, our secret is safe there.

Although Captain Queernabs managed to catch up with me again on my journey back, it was not until Kentish Town that he did so. He had not seen where I went.

Nevertheless, it was unsettling and I was much relieved to discover, after some cunning questioning in the buttery that night, that nearly all the women close to the Queen, from maid of honour to chamber-pot scourer, are under invigilation.

Both Danvers and Abrahall say they have been followed too; the others are too stupid to know if they have or not, though, they said, they have found things shifted in their rooms, as if they had been searched. (Thank God my papers are well hidden.)

'And I heard Carrots complain to the queen that her letters are being opened,' said Danvers, 'What can it mean?'

Sarah. Everybody blamed Sarah and I pretended to accede.

It is true that the Duchess has no love for any of us. She will not recognize that her day is over; she still grips the title of Keeper of the Stole and rushes around like a Dutchman stopping holes in his dyke. She threw a fine tantrum when Danvers, who is the daughter of a former bedchamber woman, was given her mother's post on the Queen's decision alone. Sarah, of course, had her own nominee. Then again Elizabeth Abrahall holds my old job as laundress and has been unwell, so the Queen – also without consulting Sarah – granted her the right to a bottle of wine a day. Another to-do.

As for the Duchess of Somerset's letters – Abrahall believes it may be Sarah again, trying to prove that Carrots murdered her first husband, Thomas Thynne. 'There were rumours,' she said.

'He deserved it,' said Danvers, who has all the old gossip from her mother, 'but I doubt she did. She couldn't kill pussy.'

'She'll be Mistress and Keeper if Sarah is dismissed,' said Abrahall, 'so Sarah has but to throw enough shit. Some of it will stick.'

They do not understand Sarah's spirit as I do. She should have commanded a man o' war instead of expending her energy pecking herself and others in this hen coop. She'd have swept Louis's navy from the seas. If she could keelhaul Abigail she would, but she wouldn't stoop to harassing underlings who merely do their duty.

No, someone else is in command of these drawer-openings and spyings. And not to uncover poor wenches' peccadilloes. To find me. I have slipped up. It must be the letter to Francesca's maid, the second that I sent to her through Greg. Or her reply. I had hoped its code would fool them, but Harley is quicker than I thought.

Of course, it is Harley. Who else? He is Prime Minister now. Like all of the rest, he makes his plans for when Queen Ant departs this vale of tears and Anne Bonny would fit into them nicely if he could find her.

Dear man, you have to find her first. I am here. I long to shout it. I whisper it instead. Here, Harley. Do the aspirates float along the corridors and disturb your sleep? They should. Was it you sent two innocent women to live in hell because they were inconvenient? Does the memory haunt you? It should, for we are back, our innocence gone, our little nails toughened into claws. Do you feel them griping at your liver? You will. If it *was* you, I shall tear it out and gnaw it.

We must address him as My Lord Oxford, now. Queen Ant was so pleased to have him back in Godolphin's place she could hardly wait to grant him an earldom. But he is the same arch-intriguer hiding that convoluted brain behind a face like a pie and still he consorts with riff-raff.

One of his creatures is a common scribbler, Daniel Defoe, a tarnished cockalorum like most of his kind, whom he uses to wage a wordy war against the Whigs. Indeed, Defoe has now proved so successful in Harley's games, the Brotherhood informs me, he has set up an agency of spies and employs several of their ex-pirates in his work.

I wonder if it is he who has been set on to find me. It would be ironic if the Captain Queernabs who followed me to Highgate were one of my former profession. I shall find out. Two can play at Harley's table. I have another informant now, and a better one than Greg; nobler, handsomer, cleverer, and a thousand times more unscrupulous. As for ambition, he would steal the crown if he could and set it on his own handsome head. He might yet.

Henry St John, Secretary of State, whose ancestors on his

mother's side landed with William the Conqueror to be resisted at Hastings by ancestors on his father's side. They have fought ever since. An unstable family. If I have not mentioned St John to you before, my love, it is because I did not consider him important. He kept himself back, called Harley 'Dear Master' and, anyway, could not find a seat in the old Parliament. Now, with the return of the Tories, he has vaulted on to the stage like an acrobat. He is the idol of the October Club, that pack of young Tory parliamentarians who would lop the head off every Whig, transport all Dissenters and bring back James Stuart.

I credit him with no conviction other than to gain personal power; he goes around crying, 'The church is in danger. I shall defend her.' Which is like Old Nick putting himself in charge of the angels. Where Harley drinks but does not whore or gamble, St John does all three and still has energy to do the work of four men. He is the Calico Jack of politics. Harley is already jealous of him. The Queen distrusts him, despite his every sorcery to win her, because he is unfaithful to his wife.

He would use me; his intuition has divined that I am the coming power there, though he does not scorn to court Abigail as well. Yet it is not only for my influence that he woos me. I intrigue him. Deep calls to deep, pirate to pirate. He has penetrated my primness to what lies beneath and names me Circe, which is strange since Greg used the same appellation in his excited moments. 'Come to bed, my Circe,' he says, 'let us wallow like swine.'

'La, my lord, how you do run on,' I say, or words to that effect.

But he knows. I think he is even aware of the creature as she prances behind me. 'You have haunted eyes, my little bedchamber,' he said once, 'Let me exorcize your demon with my prick.'

'I am sure it is a very pretty prick, sir,' I tell him, 'but it is not for me,' which intrigues him the more. But I haven't killed and plotted and manoeuvred to get this far only to throw the plan away on the honourable member for Cockshire.

I have begun. This very morning I took the first step in the plan's last and most difficult stage.

Queen Ant was unwell; tormented by gout, eyes sore and weeping, puffiness increasing, she is exhausted by the work put on her. Daily conferences with ministers; cabinet meetings once, sometimes twice a week; petitions and foreign news to be read. Warrants, orders, demand her signature, audiences with foreign envoys, attendance on debates in the House of Lords, badgered by Harley, Abigail, or St John to grant this or prefer that. She laments: 'I am so taken up with business, I have no time to say my prayers.'

I was on duty and she had sent Carrots on an errand so that she might have a glass or two of cold tea; she doesn't like others to know how much she is drinking. Occasionally now, for the pain, she asks me to float some toast sprinkled with laudanum in it.

These are the times she reflects on death. She longs for its peace but fears it; she is in terror of her father's reproaches. The huge, darkened bedchamber is full of demons; mine and hers. I believe James II stands at the end of her bed, his accusing finger pointed at her heart, condemning her desertion of him in the Great Revolution.

But what else could she have done, poor soul? She is and was a loyal daughter of the Church of England, sworn to uphold Protestantism. Her father a practising Roman. And, after all, her desertion was not for her gain; she helped to hand over the throne not only to William of Orange but to her own sister, Mary.

Yet fathers are not easily deserted and the price is being paid now. His ghost demands restitution for her half-brother. She will not, cannot, say she wishes young Pretender James rather than the Hanoverians to succeed her, but her soul would rest calmer with the knowledge that he would. She is not fond of the Hanovers and refused to countenance a visit to England by George or Sophia when the Whigs suggested it. 'Not in my lifetime.'

So today, to keep the demons at bay, she sipped her cold tea and talked of the Stuarts generally and in doing so mentioned her father's first cousin, Prince Rupert of the Rhine.

It was the opportunity I had prayed for. 'Such a pity, Your

Majesty,' I said lightly, 'that you should not have been able to meet his grand-daughter, Anne Bard.'

'Anne Bard?' She was truly mystified. She, at least, is absolved of the crime.

I fell on my knees by the bed in pretended panic. 'I should not have said. It escaped me. I beg Your Majesty's forgiveness. Say nothing, dear madam. Don't let them know. Let it be.'

Of course, she couldn't let it be. But I pleaded on until at last I had her promise that if I would tell they should never know from her that I did. Well enough. She keeps her promises. So I spoke what is, in one sense, the truth; I had known Anne Bard when she came to London some seven, eight years before. 'She claimed to be Dudley Bard's legitimate daughter. She said she had papers to prove it. I know that she tried to see you for she hired a coach to ride to the palace in, but on her return said she had been turned away.'

It made her angry; royalty have a terror that their ministers will act behind their back. 'Was it Godolphin?'

I shrugged. We discussed it and discussed; she loves minutiae. What did the girl look like? Tell me every word. Who was her mother? Whence came she? On and on until, at last: 'What happened to her?'

'I do not know, madam. She disappeared of a sudden.'

Carrots came back then, leaving me no time to plant the seed that her poor cousin had been spirited, but I could see the royal appetite chewing on what it had learned. She seems better. The mystery has pulled her from her depression. As I curtseyed before going off duty, I put my finger to my lips and she did the same. We share a secret. It is begun.

St John waited for me outside to escort me to my chambers – Her Majesty has been pleased to grant me a suite of rooms, not as large as Abigail's who is obliging her Sam with a child every year, but above what is usual for a bedchamber woman. We walked through the gardens while I picked jonquils and tulips for the royal sick room.

St John asked after the Queen's health casually but it is of great concern to him. If the Queen dies and Sophia or her son succeeds, Whigs will come in and Tories will go out. St John, the highest High Tory of them all, will be deprived of office, perhaps for life.

'She is better today, sir, I thank you. She has taken no medicine but spirit of millipedes and Lady Charlotte has visited her.'

I was telling him nothing he wouldn't learn tomorrow. The arrival of the royal curse, for which Lady Charlotte is a euphemism, is as good as shouted by the town crier. Dr Hamilton tells her ministers and her ministers congratulate her on it. Actually, Lady Charlotte is becoming very weak and this may be her last visit, but that I did not say; the woman's entitled to some privacy.

St John was surprised. 'Good old Lady Charlotte. There's hope for us all.' Being young – he is yet in his early thirties – he thinks any woman of forty-five to be mummified.

'None for you, sir. Not if Her Majesty hears of the latest debauchery. Brigadier Breton's wife, I am told.'

He bowed. 'I am indeed the sapper of that lady's earthworks. But . . .' he picked me a tulip, '. . . 'twas only to while away the hours besieging you. You are the beat of my heart, the breath of my nostrils. Surrender.'

'My citadel is inviolable, sir, I thank you. Though, indeed, there is a service you might perform for Her Majesty's ladies.'

'All of them?' He started backwards. 'Woman, you flatter me.'

Ignoring it, I told him of how Carrots's letters were opened, how some – I did not specify myself – were being followed, of the searched rooms. 'Who can be doing it, do you think?'

'Harley,' he said at once. 'And him such a pure old gentleman if you keep the brandy from him and him from the brandy. He has taken to sniffing ladies' unmentionables in his dotage.'

But I'd caught him, I could see. He will find out; he loves a secret – and he will tell me, for he cannot keep one. He is the most indiscreet person in the world; he boasts to me that he is already ousting Harley as the Tory hero 'for the man has all the appearance of wisdom but none of its substance'. He would love nothing more than to catch Harley bending. The wonder is not that two such dissimilar Tories begin to quarrel but that they were ever friends in the first place.

I dismissed him before we reached my stairs; I permit his foolery in public because he performs so for every human creature below the age of thirty with a cleft between its legs. Everyone knows it. But I cannot afford a scandal. Not now. Not so close.

'Then I shall be off to dinner at the Beefsteak,' he said – it is one of his drinking and whoring clubs – 'they are saving me a housemaid for the first course. But I would rather eat you.'

'Goodnight, sir,' I told him and went to my stairs with something like regret; not for his fucking but for his company, which would have kept the beast at bay for a while at least.

It *is* Harley. And it *is* me he looks for. Lord knows who St John bribed or twisted last night but he was full of it and could not wait to tell me, dragging me to the orangery the moment I came off duty.

'Have you ever heard of an Anne Bard or an Anne Bonny?'

'No, sir.'

'By God, neither had I. She is the Dark Lady of the Stuarts, my child, and Harley is the dark horse who's discovered her existence. A grand-daughter of Rupert of the Rhine, no less, plumb in the line of succession, a plum for me. Harley has reason to believe she is incognito somewhere at Court.'

He fell on his knees in the grass and raised clasped hands to the sky. 'Zeus, let me find her first. I make obeisance, I will sacrifice. Take my wife – as a matter of fact I'd be glad if you would – take my ass, take all else that is mine, but let me find her first.'

'Get up, sir, I beg you. The gardeners are looking.' I tugged the clown to his feet. 'Why do you want this person?'

'To knit my stockings,' he said, brushing them off and glancing at me from the corner of his eyes, which are long and curve round almost to his temples. 'What do you think I want her for? Consider. A Stuart, an untainted Stuart from the stable of Rupert himself, warhorse of blessed memory. Young, pretty – by God, she'd better be pretty – so timid and modest she works as a servant in the house of her exalted cousin. I'll have her on the throne so fast it'll make her eyes squint.'

I frowned. 'Why would she not make herself known?'

'How the hell should I know? What does it matter? Swift shall make up some romantic legend for her, a promise to her mother, fear of the Whigs, *something*. Don't you wrinkle your pretty brow at me, madam, get on and find her and I'll make you Chancellor of the Exchequer. If Harley thinks she's here, she's here. He's a blandiloquent old blowsabell but his information is ever good.'

'But the Act of Settlement,' I protested, trying to extract what I could while I could, 'Can that be set aside so easily?'

'My dear girl, do you think England *wants* George of Hanover? A bunion-faced *pickelhaube* who speaks no English, no French, but only a language fit for calling pigs home?' He expired. 'If James Francis would turn Protestant or merely *pretend* to turn Protestant, the people would have him back tomorrow – even the Whigs. But no. He calls it honour. I call it dementia.'

'You've been negotiating with him, then?'

'*Everybody's* negotiating with him.' He was amazed I should ask. 'Harley, Marlborough, Godolphin, the second footman and the night-soil man, I shouldn't wonder. Nobody wants the Hanovers.'

'And you would put this other Anne, this Anne Bard, on the throne instead?'

'It'll still be warm from the Queen's arse,' he promised me. 'Anybody, *anybody*, but George. I've even flirted with the Duke of Savoy. He's a relative.'

'The Duke of Savoy?' I become confused with all our allies. 'Didn't he order one of his subjects boiled in oil?'

'He was probably hungry. Apart from that, Victor Amadeus of Savoy is as godfearing a fellow as you'll find in a week of Sundays. But Anne Bard now . . . I must discover if she's Protestant. She *will* be Protestant. I'll baptize her myself.' He became very earnest. 'Find her for me, dearest one, and I promise, I *swear*, you shall have any title you wish and riches beyond your dreams. Sniff her out. Which among the palace women has the Stuart look? The strain runs strong in all of them. She will be dark, I think, like yourself, perhaps a foreign accent – she will have been born abroad . . .'

On and on it went until I promised to be his secret – secret, I ask you – and cunning agent. I'll not trust him, of course. He is clever but cannot control his cleverness. Carries too much top-sail we used to say. Besides, the plan goes well. There was no opportunity to be alone with the queen yesterday; despite feeling unwell she insisted on going to Westminster Hall and touching. Carrots says it is a terrible spectacle. 'My dear, all those swollen, scabby people, weeping and crawling round her skirts, the mothers holding up their scrofulous children, thousands of them. The *smell*, my dear.'

Myself, I incline to William of Orange who, when asked by a subject to touch him for the king's evil, wished him better health and more sense. But the Stuarts believe in the magic of kingship. So do their people. Scrofulous Jacobites even cross the Channel secretly to be touched by James Francis, refusing to accept that Anne has the power.

Today she was exhausted and kept to her chamber but she was well enough to indicate that she wished to speak to me privately and asked Carrots to take some message to Dr Hamil-ton, who keeps one talking to the last trump, and sent Danvers to the kitchens.

'I have been tormented, my dear, by what you told me of that young woman. Did she say nothing else to you?'

'Your Majesty, she disappeared so suddenly I feared for her. She feared for herself and indeed, that was why she left the box in my keeping.'

'What box is this?'

'A little one, madam, brass-bound. It meant much to her and I was to guard it until she came for it, though she never did. Indeed, when my family and I were to sail for Jamaica I was in a taking what should be done with it, so I carried it with me and brought it back again. I have it yet.'

'What is in it?'

I opened my eyes wide. 'I do not know, madam. It is padlocked.'

'And you have never broken the lock?'

'Indeed not. I had no such permission.'

'She did well to trust you, my child.' She sat up higher in bed, suddenly a little girl, an enormous little girl. 'Yet it has been so long ... do you think she would wish ... ? Should we ... ? Could we ... ?'

'I shall bring it with me tomorrow, madam,' I said.

The creature is howling her displeasure at my progress today and I have had to stuff my ears with cotton so that I can concentrate on what I write. 'It wasn't your box,' I tell her, 'you stole it.'

We opened it this morning; rather, I broke the lock and let Queen Ant take out and read its contents. I was glad to stand back – my hands were shaking.

Out came the genuine record of the marriage between Dudley Bard and Euphame Cassilis of Lochiel signed and sealed in 1680 by some Habsburg priest. Out next a torn and faded account, also genuine, in French by an admiring comrade who had seen young Bard die as he led a forlorn hope on the walls of Buda.

Then a statement, also in French, also genuine, by a Countess d'Hona, of witnessing the birth of a girl to Euphame Cassilis of Lochiel in 1681.

Queen Ant read each one carefully, holding them close to her eyes. She has acquired a macaw, the gift of some foreign potentate, which wobbles back and forth on an Indian screen near the bed. She likes it; we all hate the thing and secretly call it 'Sarah'. It gives unexpected and piercing shrieks, echoing the creature's.

After that came the forgeries. They were made by a gentleman called Fist Frank, known throughout the Brotherhood for his ability to fake anybody's hand to perfection.

The first is the record of a marriage between James Francis Edward Stuart and Anne Margaret Bard in 1704, attested on oath by a Fr Jacomo Ronchi that it was conducted by him in Paris, and witnessed by Francesca, Lady Bellamont.

Queen Ant put it down slowly, staring straight ahead. 'Not possible,' she said, 'No, no. Modena would not have allowed it.'

'What is it, Your Majesty? You are pale.'

She shook her head. 'No. It cannot be credited. Better you should not know, child.'

I curtseyed, but waited. Sure enough, she could not keep it in and after much are-you-loyal-child? and can-I-trust-you-with-a-secret? she told me. 'This says that your acquaintance, Prince Rupert's grand-daughter, was married to my half-brother, James, some six years since. It cannot be. He was a child then, a mere sixteen years old. His mother would not have allowed it.'

I gave a shake of the head. A sentimental smile. 'Impetuous young love.' I had not expected she would swallow the medicine in one gulp; that she was already referring to 'Prince Rupert's grand-daughter' was well to be going on with.

'Impetuous, indeed,' she said.

'There is more, madam,' I said, pointing to the last paper.

This is an excellent forgery, modelled closely on Francesca's manner of speech, saying that she had promoted this secret marriage between her legitimate grand-daughter and young James, knowing the passion that was between them and seeing no harm in an alliance between two true and noble descendants of James I of England, VI of Scotland. '. . . That one day it may bear fruit that will be of comfort to Her Most Excellent Christian Majesty, Queen Anne of England.' (It was vital to plant the seed that the union might bring forth a child. The word 'comfort' was a nice touch, I thought.)

I saw her lips shape the words in a desperate question. 'A child?'

It is a gamble whether she takes it well or ill. Will a woman who has borne so many dead children be jealous? Or will she takes pleasure in knowing that the Stuart line goes on.

With a 'tcha' of impatience and disbelief she packed the papers back in the box and said she would keep it a while. She will consider the matter; her brain is cautious and slow but it is thorough. I can see she is in a turmoil, not wanting to credit such evidence.

But she will. Who is pressing her to accept it? Not I. I shall not mention it again until she does, acting as if I am merely the serendipity through which she has uncovered it. Belief that it is genuine will come about through her own uneasy conscience, growing in the guilt she feels for her young half-brother's dispossession, like a nettle in an untidy corner. Then she will raise the business with me again.

And then . . . and then . . .

Such to-dos there have been. Sarah has been dismissed. It is as if the roof had blown off the palace and left us amazed and windswept in the sudden air. The great beam of Knossos has fallen and the Minotaur has rushed roaring away.

What fools the Marlboroughs are! They had England between their two pairs of hands and they squeezed her too tight. The Duke has been pressing the Queen to make him Captain-General for life. He knew the Tories were out for his blood because he refuses to make easy terms with Louis so that the war may be ended quickly. He believes that only he can bring about a lasting and honourable peace. He may be right, though, as a soldier, he thinks only in military terms and St John says there are other ways.

Indeed, St John would give Louis such terms as would allow us to trade with France when the war is finished. St John's enemies call him a Frog lover. He calls himself a European. And he has the Tory landowners behind him; they say they are being ruined to enrich army officers and keep Whigs in the City juggling their shares and reaping money where they have not sown.

Queen Ant was horrified by Marlborough's demand. She has not, I think, forgiven him for Malplaquet and its loss of lives, 'a Pyrrhic victory', she called it, whatever that is, and refused to go to the public thanksgiving in St Paul's, making her mourning her excuse, and attended her private chapel instead.

It is unlike the Duke to miscalculate so disastrously. Though Sarah has no sense of the danger, *he* has always shown tact. Now he has alienated the Queen, who thinks he wishes to make himself tyrant, and has refused him, saying she cannot make him Captain-General for life without Act of Parliament and, in any case, cannot bind her successor to such.

307

The Tory press, especially Swift, egged on by St John, sees its opportunity and is baying for the blood of the Marlboroughs, accusing him of using money which should have fed his soldiers for his own purposes, and his wife, 'that insolent woman, that plague, that fury', of purloining no less than twenty thousand a year from the Privy Purse.

I do not believe it and neither does Queen Ant: 'Everybody knows that cheating is not the Duchess of Marlborough's crime.' But she saw her opportunity. When Sarah again threatened to publish the Queen's more indiscreet letters from their youth, even hinting at dark sexual doings between Her Majesty and Abigail, the axe fell.

Marlborough came back from Europe, begging the Queen to stay her hand, bringing a letter which Sarah had written saying she was sorry she had ever displeased Her Majesty and never would again – I can see her thrashing with fury in writing it, like a snake eating its own tail.

'The key must be returned within three days,' Queen Ant said. I have never heard her colder. The gold key is the symbol of Sarah's office. The Duke pleaded; at least wait until the peace was concluded when he and his wife could retire with dignity.

'The key must be returned within three days,' the Queen said again. And so it was. In two.

The next day – we were at St James's – Abigail came bleating. 'Oh, Your Majesty, see what she is doing!'

We ran to Sarah's lodgings. And there she was, bless her, directing workmen by a chisel held in her hand, and gutting the rooms of everything but the chimneypieces. If it could be unscrewed Sarah was unscrewing it, light fittings, fingerplates, the brass locks on the doors – and beautiful locks too, by the Queen's locksmith, Josiah Key, who is the most ingenious man in Europe.

Queen Ant looked, then went away. Sarah did not so much as blink but went on ordering the men to be careful, to put this in that packing case. If we'd stood there much longer, she'd have had us boxed as well. Revenge, pure and simple. With Blenheim Palace rising like a beautiful monster out there in Oxfordshire she hardly needs door knobs. It *was* being built by a grateful nation out of public money, though it won't be finished by it. I heard Queen Ant say, 'I shall build no more houses for her when she has pulled my own to pieces.'

It was Sarah's last act. She is gone. Her posts are given to Carrots (Groom of the Stole) and Abigail (Keeper of the Privy Purse) which has disappointed them both since each expected them both. But Queen Ant has learned her lesson. She has also raised my salary.

And now Harley is stabbed nearly to death! I should like to have seen it, I should like to have *done* it. The would-be assassin is, or was, I should now say, a seedy French noble who had spied for England against his country and then, when Harley reduced his pay, spied for France against England. He was discovered, arrested and brought before a committee of the Privy Council at Whitehall for examination. Suddenly Guiscard produced a penknife and stabbed Harley in the breast.

'The villain has killed Mr Harley,' cried St John – at least, that is what he says he said – and ran his rapier through the Frenchie's body a time or two.

The penknife was broken by a brocade flower on Harley's waistcoat – it was the silver and blue with gold flowers that he'd had made for the queen's birthday – but he was badly hurt nevertheless and keeps his bed. Guiscard was dragged off to Newgate, dying.

St John is incensed. The attack has made Harley the nation's and Queen's martyr and darling, just as he, St John, was outdoing him in popularity.

'The old fart probably paid Guiscard to do it,' he grumbled to me, 'and wore that dreadful waistcoat a-purpose. Besides, who could pierce his heart? They wouldn't know where to find it.' He is having it put about that he was the intended victim, not Harley, though with little effect.

However, he is making hay while the cat's away and is courting Abigail strongly, pleasing her by putting that useless brother of hers, Jack Hill, in charge of an expedition to Canada. Behind her back he is urging me to redouble my efforts to find Anne Bard.

It is possible, he says – and so do many others – that Guiscard also threatened the Queen's life. True, she is poorly guarded so now the sentries have been doubled and the locks changed.

The danger and the attack on Harley brought on another bout of her illness. This causes such panic among those with an eye to their future that they are forming alliances, breaking them, blackmailing each other for treating with the Jacobites then treating with them themselves. I am being offered such bribes to persuade the Queen this way or the other that I could be as rich as Abigail is making herself if I wanted. I don't take them. Nevertheless, I feel the same panic.

To have come so close and be robbed of our revenge because the stupid woman insists on dying . . .

Grant me time, God.

What shall I do? The creature has a new trick. She bleeds. As I write, blood is gushing from the space that is her mouth so fast that it has begun to swill on the floor. I have drawn up my feet to keep them from being covered but still it comes, thick and bright with irregular gobbets in it, like Lady Charlotte in spate, like a haemorrhage. It is rising up the walls. Oh, God, oh, Devil, grant me time before she sends me mad.

CHAPTER SIXTEEN

IT WAS MORE difficult to stop being a pirate than to become one. Article 3 of the *Brilliana*'s code insisted on the Brotherhood's agreement to any man's – or woman's – leaving of it.

The argument began with the sun still high and we sat in pools of shadow at the foot of palm trees. It was still going on by the time the sun went down and the shadows spread over the sand in duplication of the trees.

The *Brilliana* lay in the creek, propped to one side on stays with an occasional milky green wave stroking her stern. Farther out in the small bay, where the sea was the same turquoise as the sky, the *Beginning* stood at anchor, on watch for unfriendly shipping.

In the conference on the beach, the Frenchman Rosier sat and pounded on the sand, making trouble. 'I say again, we do not let them go. Maybe they go straight to the authorities and send against us.'

I wondered where he found the energy to be angry; everybody else had given way to the lassitude of the evening, tired from a hard day's careening. Sam had kept us all at it; uneasy at having his ship out of commission. Our hands were blistered and cut from limpet shells like tiny extinct volcanoes under the weed of the ship's keel.

We'd eaten well. Licky had lifted conch from the tide edge where they lumbered along under their heavy, curious shells between blades of turtle grass and made us potfuls of what he called 'chowder'.

Kilsyth said patiently, 'Ye've got our word, mannie.' He was propped on one elbow, but he'd begun whistling a dirge he called 'The Mucking of Geordie's Byre', a sign he was losing his temper.

Rosy turned on him. 'And when some person ask how you arrive, what you say? We flew like damn bird? No, you say we come on a ship. Which ship, they say. Ship that turn pirate, you say. You tell or they put you in pokey. I say you keep with us.'

As well as dining on chowder, we'd had chicken. The chickens had sailed in that afternoon. A strange business. There'd been a signal from the *Beginning* out in the bay, 'Vessel approaching', and everybody primed their weapons while Nobby prepared two of the cannon we'd run ashore from the *Brilliana*.

The vessel proved to be a small single-masted dinghy, no more than ten feet long. Sam sent one of the men up a palm tree and he shouted down that the said craft held only one person, a female. Guns were put away, jackets brushed, hair slicked down to await this Aphrodite from the foam.

The little boat scudded up the creek, keel grounding on the sand, sail collapsing, in one expert procedure. A dozen pairs of hands pulled it up on to the beach. We could hear hens cackling in a crate tucked into the boat's fish well.

Out of the boat clambered a black woman. The willing hands

dropped nervelessly away from the gunwales. She was large, *very* large, her skirt and jacket – once of military persuasion – bounced in various directions when she moved as if covering bubbling lava. A bandana tied at the back hid her hair and on top of that was a battered, brimmed hat which had led an exciting life, again some of it military. It was crammed so far down her forehead it was difficult to see anything more of her face than that it was of indeterminate age and wasn't going to tolerate liberties. A bandolier, the sort they used in Cromwell's Model Army, hung across her chest but, instead of powder bottles, it carried two sheathed knives and a vast collection of ribboned, feathered and beaded objects – one of them a monkey skull, or what we all hoped was a monkey skull.

She said nothing, didn't even look around her, but began unloading her boat, passing the crate of chickens, baskets of fruit and vegetables and lines of fish to her staring audience, as if she'd landed at a market instead of a cay in the remoter Bahamas inhabited only by strange men.

'How did she know we were here?' I asked Licky.

He shrugged. 'She a higgler. They smell trade on de wind.' He shouted at the higgler in patois and was answered by a grunt or two. 'Yip. Higgler.' He shrugged again. 'Wutless.'

Worthless? Witless? Whatever he meant, the higgler established herself as part of the scenery within half an hour, sitting with her knees wide apart, scraping conch from their shells. Nobby tried to pinch her arse and got a cackle of laughter and a blow from a forearm that knocked him backwards.

The rest of us left her alone. Even the black men avoided her, while Licky treated her with an indifference, almost contempt, which wasn't like him. It was all very odd. I said so to Sam.

'A black witch, do ee think?' he said, making the sign of the horns, 'Her sniffed us out p'raps.'

She could have sniffed Nobby. He was the only one of us who refused to bathe in the deep-water pool we'd found in the centre of the island. But it wasn't likely.

However, the argument from the circle on the beach was heating up so I turned my attention to it and forgot the higgler, like everybody else. Rosier was saying, 'Over my corpse they

leave,' and I had to stop Kilsyth reaching for his sword to arrange it.

The crew weren't really afraid we'd betray them, they just
didn't want us to go. Kilsyth was a favourite, his bravado encouraged them, his accent made them laugh. My appeal was
considerably less, although I'd become a sort of unofficial first
lieutenant to Sam Rogers.

It was Bratchet they couldn't bear to lose; their good-luck
piece, something between sweetheart, sister and figurehead, the
spirit of the ship. They'd miss her; she'd miss them. But it was
time to go.

Earlier they'd taken a vote whether to continue with piracy
or not. Everybody had their say, some for, some against. Sam
asked what I thought, so I spoke up. 'There's two things you
can do. Give up or go on. I say, give up. Sell the *Beginning* and
her cargo in Nassau. It ain't a fortune but it's tidy, more gelt
than most of us have seen before. After all, what've you done?
Mutinied against a Jacobite bastard and taken an enemy ship.
The government's not going to come after you for that. Sail the
Brilliana on to Jamaica, bung the governor a few pearls and
we'll all go our own way. That's my advice.'

They didn't take it. Their success against the Spanish ship
had whetted their appetite for greater things; they told each
other stories of Morgan, Sawkins, of the moidores and gold to
be had for the taking in the Pacific. Sam and a few others might
welcome retirement but their home countries had warrants out
for their arrest and they would be happy nowhere else. Now
there would be another vote on whether they allowed Kilsyth,
Bratchet, Licky and me to leave the Brotherhood.

I don't think the crew realized that their reluctance to let us
all go was also because Licky had declared his wish to go with
us. 'Time I's gwine home,' he told them. And home was Jamaica. None of them knew how important their black sea-cook
was to them or how clever.

But Bratchet knew. 'He engineered the mutiny,' she told me,
'And he brought us here, all the way from Le Havre. He's the
one who's really driven the ship.'

And now he'd driven it to this island. Where a higgler had

suddenly turned up. Very odd. Licky was the only one who'd known we'd be here. He'd navigated us past bigger islands and the lights they showed which, he said, were trying to draw us on to the reefs, the inhabitants making their living by wrecking honest and dishonest sailormen alike. He'd made us pass hundreds of smaller, low, white-fringed, uninhabited islands, until we'd reached this one. He said the water was fresh here, 'a blue hole', he said.

Certainly, the lake in its centre was a wonder, worth the struggle through mangroves and thorn undergrowth to reach it. Sunlight filtered down through a canopy of leaves into its shallows where translucent shoals of tiny fish flashed silver one moment, dark the next. But I reckoned there must be blue holes on other islands we'd passed. Why had he chosen this one?

The higgler was baiting hooks on a line, a silhouette against a mother-of-pearl sky of masculine hat on feminine body. Her bare feet were the same indistinguishable colour from dust and sand as the crabs which formed a wider circle around us, hundreds of pairs of eyes on stalks, like miniature boot-buttons; they the island's only natives, watched and waited for us to go away so that they could get on with scuttling and burrowing and whatever else it was crabs did by night.

Nearby, Bratchet had curled up on the sand with Kilsyth's jacket over her. She was asleep. I jerked my thumb towards her. 'So you go on. It's your choice, you know the risk. But do you want *her* to take it? Want her on the gallows with you? Think about it.'

The silence was filled by frogs – Licky said they were frogs – with their maddening, bell-like, night-long chanting. Sam called for a vote. It was a close one again. Sam had to count twice. 'The ayes have it,' he said, heavily. 'They go.'

Officially, the Bahamas were granted to six English noblemen known as the Lords Proprietors by Charles II, though neither he nor the Lords Proprietors had bothered much about the islands, leaving them to the care of governors who, without soldiers or ships, couldn't do much to enforce English rule and gave up trying.

In effect, the islands were lawless. Those settlers who'd tried to make an honest living were harassed by French and Spanish to the point that luring ships on to their coral reefs proved not only a main source of income, but a form of national defence.

Then came the pirates, happy to find hidden inlets and cays they could sail out from against ships taking the Florida and Windward passages. Successive governors hanged the weaker ones and on the if-you-can't-beat-'em-join-'em principle cooperated with the stronger.

By the time the *Brilliana* sailed in to sell her prize and its cargo, Nassau, the natural harbour on New Providence, was one of the most thriving ports in the West Indies for the disposal of stolen goods. It was there we said goodbye. It was hard saying it to Sam Rogers, Nobby and some of the others (both Nobby and Bratchet were in tears), but most of the crew were already gone ashore, leaping into the longboats, a few diving over the side and swimming, heading for the brothels of the town like iron filings for a magnet.

We four reckoned it was wiser not to be seen in Nassau – our story was going to be that we'd been cast away – so we said our farewells on the *Brilliana* and then got into the higgler's dinghy and she sailed us across the harbour to the vessel which Licky had chosen to take us on to Jamaica.

I studied it as we approached. 'I ain't usually choosy,' I said, 'but is that the best you could do?'

Licky rolled his eyes. ''F you cast off by pirate, this de sort of boat pirate cast you off in. What you want? Arrive at Port Royal in a galleon with trumpets? Mighty noticeable. Higher the blackbird fly, de more he show he tail.'

'It's no the flying high, it's the getting there,' said Kilsyth, 'What the De'il is she?'

She was a dowdy fifty-foot schooner. The smell was her cargo – sponges that had been dragged from their beds to rot in shallow water and were now drying on every part of the lofty rigging as if the boat had been attacked by a swarm of dandelion clocks.

But there are worse sleeping surfaces than mattresses of sponge. There wasn't much space and there was less privacy but Kilsyth and I, at least, spent much of our time catching up on sleep that had been disturbed for months by work and watches. We left the sailing to the two mulattos, Christopher and Samson, who made up the crew.

By day we lazed under a canvas awning in the cockpit, drinking rum, eating meals of grits, lobster and something called 'journey cake' that Licky cooked with charcoal in the stern on a waist-high wooden box filled with sand. We watched the flying fish and, once or twice, the spout of whales playing, while the boat with its wide expanse of sail went through the water as if the sea was opening inches in front of her prow.

Behind us, in her dinghy with its painter attached to our stern, we dragged the higgler, her hat down over her eyes, fishing for green turtles.

As we hopped from island to island, other higglers came aboard with their baskets, sometimes taking a lift to the next cay. They were the nomads of the Caribbean, always women, always black and always accepted by the mulattos as if they were no more than seagulls alighting and taking off again.

They fascinated Bratchet. 'Who *are* they?' she asked Licky, 'Where do they come from?'

He shrugged. 'That last one, she one-time Bantu; this one one-time Guinea.'

'Where's Bantu? Where's Guinea?'

'Africa.'

It hadn't occurred to us until then that Africa consisted of differing peoples; it had always seemed inhabited by a genus known as 'slaves'. The higglers, even though they all seemed to be called 'Nanny', had individual histories, traditions, homes, languages. 'How did they get here?'

'Slave ship. Maybe dey's mother, maybe grandmother.'

'But how here? How'd they get free?'

'Massa got no use for them. Maybe he dead. Maybe dey give him baby an' he grateful.' His grin indicated he'd made a joke.

Bratchet pointed to the dinghy bobbing behind us. 'What about her? Where'd she come from?'

Licky's face changed. 'She Ashanti Coromantin,' he said reluctantly.

316

'And you?' I asked him, 'Where'd you come from?'

He said, 'Don' ask me where I bin, ask me where I'm gwine.'

Her name, inevitably, was Nanny. I could see why Bratchet was intrigued with the higgler. She should have seemed lonely and wasn't; there was purpose to her. I decided she was a black Kit Ross without Mother Ross's appeal. She ignored us. Every so often she chanted a three-note warble, more like a prayer than song. Licky and the mulattos paid her no attention. After a while, Kilsyth and I didn't either.

Until the water spout came.

It was the last passage of the voyage and for almost the first time we were out of sight of land. Behind us were the Caymans, ahead Jamaica, and around us nothing but sea acting strangely; catspaws of wind shivered across it and billowed the sails before letting them flap. The sun changed; it was still shining but gained the colour of copper. Christopher and Samson were nervous and chattering to each other; after a bit they began taking down the mainsail, then two of the three headsails, leaving just a foresail.

I looked around for the storm they must be expecting and saw nothing. And then I did.

'God help us,' said Kilsyth beside me.

Impossible to judge how far off it was. A thin, evil, wavering column of darkness, a snake that reared up from sea to sky, dancing by itself. It saw us; I could have sworn it saw us. It headed towards us.

Everything was darkening, I pushed Bratchet's head down but, myself, I couldn't look away. It wouldn't matter anyway. If it decided on us, we'd splatter like a squashed frog, bits of the boat and bodies exploding into splinters under the pressure.

It came on. We could hear it now, roaring, and see debris tossing in it, a mast, trees, rags. The mulattos fell down on their faces as if worshipping. I didn't blame them. The fear was not so much what it would do to us as of the thing itself; it was too big, cathedrals high, nothing I'd ever seen was so gigantic. It was naked, untamed power, it would annihilate us. And it kept bloody *twirling*.

317

Licky scrambled past me and screamed something at the higgler. The boat was bucking like a horse trying to get away. It went on bucking, and on, then less.

'Christ,' I said, 'It's going.'

And it was. Dancing off as if it found us an unsuitable partner. The wind blew us around like straw but it was a relief to feel my body solid enough to be battered; I thought it had turned liquid.

Bratchet looked up at me, keeping her eyes away from the sea and the dreadful thing still twirling across it. 'What happened?'

'She sent it away,' I said. I still didn't believe it. Kilsyth had seen it too. He was pale and looking behind, at the higgler. 'She stood,' he shouted, 'she stood up and pointed a knife at it.'

Licky was triumphant. He shouted back, 'It was de Devil's tail. She told he she cut it if he din't go.'

The higgler was standing, holding on to her rocking mast, still pointing a knife in the direction the waterspout had gone. Her hat had blown off and was fluttering in the well of the dinghy.

Later, in the evening, when the wind had become a mere sprightly breeze, the Bratchet got us to haul in on the painter so that she could step into the dinghy. From the sponge boat we couldn't hear what they said to each other. The higgler got on with cleaning fish, slitting their bellies with the knife that had threatened to cut the Devil's tail, scooping out their entrails and throwing them to hovering, screaming gulls. Bratchet sat on a thwart, facing her.

Kilsyth watched the two women, then ushered me forward to the privacy of the prow. 'I'd favour a conversation wi' ye, my man.'

'I'm listening.' We settled ourselves on the coping.

Kilsyth coughed. 'It's Mistress Bratchet. I'm seekin' your permission to approach her, you being *in loco parentis*.'

'I'm what?'

The Scotsman coughed again. 'This is verra difficult. Her having been your serving maid an' all, ye are the nearest thing to a guardian the lassie has and I would be correct. I wish to approach her. Wi' your permission.'

'You want to marry her?'

Kilsyth shook his head, unabashed. 'Tha's no possible. My chief has an arrangement that I'm to wed his cousin's daughter when the lass is old enough.'

I tried to consider. 'Let me understand. You want my permission to ask Bratchet to be your mistress. Is that it?'

Kilsyth blinked. 'Ye're an unco' bold speaker.' He stopped being ridiculous. 'Martin, I love the woman. It's been coming on me these past weeks she's the bravest, loveliest female I've aye met with. Her past is unfortunate, mebbe, but . . .'

'You're a fool,' I told him.

'I am that. But I care for her.' He became formal again. 'And I have reason to think that she'll look kindly on my addresses.'

'Yes,' I said, 'she probably will.'

'I'll ask when we arrive in Jamaica and take her straight home. She'll want for no comfort, nor affection. The puir wee thing's had little enough of both. I'll set her up in a manner that'll do her the justice she deserves. Do I have your permission?'

Jesus Christ, the man was a fool. I said, 'You don't see it, do you? How many women have we met since we started out? Haven't you learned anything? Nobody owns 'em. We think we can, but we can't. No, you bloody can't have my permission. If you want to fuck the girl, ask her, not me. She's not a bloody present. I'm not giving her to you; she ain't mine to give. Now sod off.'

Kilsyth got up. He stood for a while holding on to a halyard, looking down at me. 'I didna realize,' he said, 'I'm sorry.'

I said, 'And while we're on the subject, where *is* Kilsyth?'

'A speck north o' Glasgae. Why?'

'Glasgow. That's south, ain't it? Lowlands. You're not a bloody Highlander at all.'

'My heart's in the Highlands, along wi' my chief,' said Kilsyth, stolidly. 'D'ye want a fight over it?'

'No.'

'Will we shake hands then?'

We shook hands.

319

There was a hail from the dinghy. Bratchet was shouting: 'Pull us in. You should hear this.'

We pulled on the painter and helped the two women into the sponge boat.

Bratchet was pale. 'She knew Anne and Mary.'

Shit, I thought. Isn't there anybody those two bloody harpies didn't know? The last thing we needed was to get involved again in the search for them. It had cost us too much already.

Bratchet was shaking. She arranged her cloak on a thwart so that the higgler could sit down on it. She was treating the woman as if she were royalty, but she was also afraid – not of the higgler herself but of the aura around her. She introduced her reverently: 'This is Asantewa. You address her as Great-grandmother.'

Asantewa seated herself and stared impassively for'ard where Christopher had lit a lantern. The sun was going down with the colour of fire, washing all of us in red. Licky, I noticed, was busying himself with the stove in the stern. Kilsyth, Bratchet and I sat down opposite the higgler. Her eyes were shut against the glare of the sunset.

'Tell them, Great-grandmother,' said Bratchet.

The higgler said, 'I tell you things, girl, 'cos my forces bring you half across de worl' to fin' out. I tell these here what good for them and no more, you hear?'

Bratchet nodded.

Asantewa began. 'One time I is slave to a whitey call hisself Vinner. He run big, big plantation in foothills of Blue Mountains in Jamaica. That Vinner, he one wicked whitey.' She dragged out the word 'whitey' until it scraped nerves. 'He don' feed he niggers. They get spoon and plate disease. But they still get bull-whip for if they don' work hard. Pretty lady niggers, they get picked for his haireem, but he don' pick me 'cos I is ugly.' A faint smile crossed her face. 'Ugly women, they give you yo' meals on time. I get promoted from fiel' work to housekeeper.'

Until then the higgler had been speaking with her eyes closed. Now she opened them. The effect was extraordinary. With the last flash of the sun, they glowed blood red. I heard Kilsyth gasp.

320

The higgler smiled again. She was ugly, but the force in her overrode her outward appearance so that what you saw was power, intelligent power. I could almost have believed that the waterspout had indeed turned and fled from her. I wanted to myself.

She went on talking in what I came to know as the Creole slave accent. But as the light faded, her eyes turned from red to a deep brown which had bled in tiny veins into the yellowish white surround and they dragged us all into them, away from the boat and the sea and sky, into a place of heated, human darkness. We saw images in them produced by her words as if she was creating moving paintings.

One day, she said, Vinner brought a white girl back from the quayside auctions. She was very pretty, intelligent and extremely angry at being sold into service. Her name, she told Asantewa, was Anne Bonny. She'd been stolen from a London quayside, taken to Jamaica and sold at auction to Asantewa's owner.

'Vinner, he always puttin' he whanga where it not wanted, but Anne, she ain't havin' it. She fight so hard when he try puttin' it in her, he have to put it right back in he trousers.' The eyes moved to regard Bratchet. 'Mighty brave, that Anne,' said Asantewa. 'She whitey skinned, but she nigger in she soul. Like you. You nigger underneath.'

Anne and Asantewa had become allied in their hatred of Vinner. Anne tried running away but had been caught and brought back and an extra three years added to her indenture. The physical punishment for her escape had been visited not on Anne, but on Asantewa, her friend, for assisting her. 'He strip me to the waist, tie me to a post and give me twenty-five lashes. He make all he niggers watch so they see what happen if they disobey whitey.'

Bratchet was now sitting in the well of the boat, hugging her knees. 'A red-lace jacket,' she muttered.

The higgler shrugged. 'If it don't kill yuh, yuh ain' dead.'

Instead of discouraging, the effect of the public whipping had been to increase Asantewa's and Anne's hatred of Vinner and they'd begun to foment rebellion.

'We make they other niggers rise up one night,' Asantewa said, 'me an' Anne an' my Joshua. He my son. We burn Vinner's house and lead the niggers up into the mountains to join the Maroons.'

'What's Maroons?' I asked.

The higgler looked at me with disgust. 'Dat ignorance, fella. Seems studiation ent eddication.' But she went on to explain.

Of all England's slave colonies in the West Indies, Asantewa said, Jamaica's blacks were the most prone to rebellion. For one thing the island had more of them in proportion to the white population than anywhere else.

For another, Jamaica's white masters, 'they so stupid they can' piss straight', still allowed their slaves to die rather than fostering them in conditions that would encourage the breeding of generations used to slavery, and had to keep importing others direct from Africa who still retained an unquelled spirit.

Then there was Jamaica's geography, perhaps the most varied in the Caribbean, which contained mountains so difficult of access they remained wild and unplanted. It was here the Maroons lived, descendants of blacks who'd come to the island with the Spanish and been left behind when England finally drove the Spanish out in the last century. They had established camps, even towns, in the mountains and every expedition sent against them had been beaten back.

And there they still were. Thorns in the flesh of the colonists. Examples of freedom to every slave on the island. And Anne Bonny, Asantewa and Joshua had joined them.

'What happened to Vinner?' asked Kilsyth.

A smile flickered over the higgler's face. 'He whanga don't worry no girl no more.'

The alliance between Asantewa and Anne had been based on admiration of each other's spirit. But the next example of a she-whitey's courage had, said the higgler, 'near blowed my hat off'.

Into their camp one day had marched a Maroon with a gun held on his back. Holding it had been a white woman, threatening to blow away his spine if he didn't take her to her friend.

'She call herself Ma:y Read,' said Asantewa.

Christ almighty. Following in the steps of Mary Read had taken more than two years of our lives and bloody near ended them. It must have done no less to her, following in the steps of Anne, and she'd been alone. But when Mary had got this far she'd still had to track her friend down and follow her up into mountains and a hostile, suspicious bunch of renegades. I couldn't have done it, I tell you.

I wondered what sort of woman it was who'd enlisted in the army for the sole reason, as far as I could see, of approaching near enough to France to cross the border and get herself to St-Germain so that she could ask Francesca's help to get her to the West Indies, where Anne had been taken. And then gone there and found her.

'Christ almighty,' I said aloud.

The higgler nodded. 'That Mary, she one determin' lady. If she hol' the light for the Devil, she blow it out in he face.'

'Mary loved Anne very much,' Bratchet said.

'She must have.'

The Maroons, according to Asantewa, were not homogeneous; only their determination to stay free of whitey held them together. Their society had states within a state; there had been disagreement about the presence in it of two white women. In any case, Anne and Mary decided to leave it.

'They women wid they home always in de next port of call,' said the higgler, and added sadly, 'And my Joshua, he de same breed.'

The two white girls and the black man had made their way to Negril Bay on the westerly tip of the island in the hope of finding a ship – the bay being sufficiently remote to give shelter to the occasional pirate and allow the unloading of goods from vessels as didn't want to pay duty.

'They fin' ship all right,' said Asantewa, shaking her head. 'They fin' Calico Jack. He big, big pirate. He take them on.'

Asantewa was at the time pursuing her own career among the Maroons. We gathered it mostly involved pitting her brand of witchcraft against the indigenous variety – and winning. 'I is their *ohemmaa*,' she told us. 'It like to your queen, only big, big.'

Occasionally news came to her of Anne and Mary and Joshua. Calico Jack was causing havoc on the high seas. In a profession famous for its eccentric captains, he was gaining an especial place in its folklore because of the two wild women who boarded prizes alongside him and fought with even more ferocity than the men.

I looked at Kilsyth. He was pained, but not as distraught as he was when he'd first heard of the two women's piracy. He'd buried his Anne then. I turned back to Asantewa. 'They were caught, though.'

She nodded. 'They caught. All the crew. Calico Jack. My Joshua. Anne, Mary. They taken to St Jago. The judge, he hang Calico Jack and de rest of de men. Mary and Anne, they plead their bellies. Their hangin' delayed till the babies be born.'

'And?' I asked.

The dark eyes looked straight into Bratchet's, not mine. 'Ain't no "and". They die in prison, Mary, Anne, babies. All die.'

I waited for the Bratchet to say her usual, 'They ain't dead.'

She didn't. But as if she had, Asantewa emphasized the point, still watching her. 'Dead women don't walk from dey coffin, girl. Dey dead and dere's an end to it.'

There was silence. The sun was well gone by now and the moon hadn't yet come up. The boat's lantern might have been the only light in the universe, an insignificant pinprick in the blackness of night.

Asantewa yawned and stretched up her arms, sending out a strong smell of sweat and herbs. 'I go back now.' We helped her back into her dinghy, offered her a light of her own, which she refused. Once the painter had been paid out, she was beyond the circle cast by our lantern, bobbing along behind us somewhere in the dark of the sea.

We ate Licky's meal in silence. Even the usually talkative mulattos were quiet. It was as if the higgler had hurt us. And in some way I suppose she had. For Kilsyth and Bratchet there'd be pain that women they'd loved had been brought to such an end. As for me, I wished I felt more relief than I did. I'd chased Mary and Anne for so long I'd begun to feel the bond that is formed by the hunter with the hunted; I'd followed their spoor, only to find that somebody else had brought them down. And I was sorry. Two high-spirited creatures had deserved better. They hadn't asked to become quarry.

No, it wasn't even that which caused my unease. The higgler's story was unfulfilling. I had no reason to doubt it; in essence it was what the former pirates aboard the *Brilliana* had told us. The girls had died in prison. I just wished I could be certain that the Bratchet believed it. Before we settled down for the night, I told her I was sorry that her friends had come to such an end.

'"They dead," ' she said, quoting the higgler. '"They dead and there's an end of it." Odd, ain't it? That's what Effie used to say.'

It occurred to me later in the night that the higgler hadn't said what had happened to her son, Joshua, who'd gone pirating with the girls and Calico Jack. Presumably he'd hanged with the rest of the men. I thought it strange, though, that she hadn't mentioned it.

But then, she was a very strange woman.

Back in 1692 a great earthquake deposited half of Jamaica's Port Royal and its population into the sea. I remember my father rejoicing about it when the news came to England. 'Another Sodom has received the Lord's punishment for wickedness,' he said. As far as he was concerned, a city of buccaneers, privateers, prostitutes and gamblers had got its just deserts.

I suppose there had been plenty of sinners living in the streets and houses that were suddenly thrown into the sea; there'd also been pastrycooks, sailors and soldiers, cabinetmakers, silversmiths, buildings, shops, a merchants' exchange which was envied even in London, where grandees strolled in the shade of a colonnaded gallery, with liveried Negro servants to proffer them Madeira and canary and rum punches.

Sam Rogers had known it in its great days. He'd told me it had been a free-wheeling, crowded, turbulent, beautiful city where Catholics, Anglicans, Presbyterians, Jews and atheists had managed to live side by side without too much animosity and where buccaneers and English colonial administration had reached an uneasy accommodation.

Then came 7 June 1692. Judgement Day. Two of Port Royal's four forts, most of the bigger shops and houses, churches and the exchange went under thirty feet of water. Half the population went with them. The other half contracted the fever caused by so many floating corpses and, finally, ten years later, a fire wiped out what was left of the town. Old Port Royal had gone for ever. So had the buccaneers. They made their bases elsewhere and Jamaica was left to the one god. Sugar.

Now what faced us as we sailed into it in our sponge boat was one of the world's greatest harbours, bigger than any in England. The survivors of the earthquake had built a new town across the harbour from the one that had once stood on what was now just a sand spit, and called it Kingston.

It was as beautiful as Port Royal must have been in its way – wide, symmetrical streets in a gridiron pattern, low houses with balconies, arcaded passageways keeping the sun from pedestrians – and definitely more respectable. Regiments drafted in from England kept order, despite the fact that half the soldiers died almost immediately from yellow fever. The colonial population often resented the rule and taxes of its home government in peacetime but in wartime, as now, depended on it for protection from the French. Behind the town, piling up against the horizon to a height of seven and a half thousand feet, was a huge mountain range.

'Home,' Licky told us as we leaned over the sponge boat's gunwale. 'Them's my Blue Mountains.'

They looked purple, an effect of distance and the evening light, and imposed a sort of savagery over the ordered, busy scene below them.

Ships of all kinds were in harbour, big cargo vessels receiving huge 1,000 lb hogsheads of sugar into their hold, some having barrels of rum rolled up their gangplanks. Others were unloading goods from England – we saw a harpsichord lowered to the quay in a net, followed by a billiard table.

Then Licky, Bratchet and I smelled a stench we'd met before. It reached us from a quay on the long spit of land leading into the main harbour as we sailed by it. One ship was already unloading and two others were uncovering their hatches ready. Unlike any other vessels they had nets round their decks – to stop their cargo jumping overboard. The slaves were being lined up on the quay and a long chain that passed from one's ankle to another's clanked as they moved. A barrow was going back and forth on another gangplank, bringing down those that hadn't survived the voyage and tipping them into a heap.

Bratchet closed her eyes. 'It looked a beautiful place when we sailed in,' she said. I knew how she felt.

A white clergyman was greeting the slaves. His voice came over the water in a clear monotone. 'Give thanks, my children. You have been delivered from the dark continent to a land where you may be baptized by the pure water of Christianity.'

'Alleluia,' muttered Licky, 'They lucky niggers.'

His attention, though, was not on the slaves but the harbour. 'It gone got civilized,' he said, indignantly. 'Patrol boats. Customs. I better get ashore secret.' He turned to Bratchet. 'They'll be questions so you tell 'em. You was took an' couldn't help yusself. Tell true and shame de Devil. An' then you get de fuss boat home. Don' you stay.'

He turned to me. 'Don' let her stay, Marty. She kill her. She kill you all.'

'Who?'

'Jamaica. She got sickness you ain't even heard of. She kill you.'

'I'm going to this St Jago first,' Bratchet said.

'You ain't.'

'I am.'

Licky shook his head. 'Shoulda let you jump,' he said.

'But you didn't.' She added, 'Your Majesty.'

He looked carefully at her. 'What else she tell you?'

'That she summoned you back.' Bratchet frowned. 'How *did* she summon you back?'

'Us niggers get around,' he said.

He said his goodbyes quickly and then stepped into the dinghy with the higgler, shifted a basket of paddling, helpless green turtles, and nodded to her to row. Immediately they blended into the rowdy, busy traffic of the harbour where other higglers plied between the ships, boats carrying hogsheads of fresh water went back and forth and white customs men in smart uniforms were rowed from vessel to vessel by black men in rags.

'What was all that about?' I asked Bratchet.

'The higgler's his mother,' was all she said then. She was crying.

We daren't wave for fear of drawing attention to him but we watched the dinghy until we lost sight of it in the waterborne crowd. Kilsyth became brisk. 'He says we'll not be able to transfer ourselves to another ship without questions, so here's my plan. The governor's a Hamilton, Licky tells me, and if he's the Hamilton I ken he is he's my cousin's brother-in-law. I'll go ashore, bruit his name and satisfy their questions and book us a passage as quick as lickit.'

'I'm going to St Jago first,' Bratchet said.

Kilsyth turned on her. 'That's inland, woman. Ye'll not.'

'They were sentenced there,' she told him, 'Anne and Mary. I'm going to find out what happened.'

'We know what happened.'

'I want to find out for myself.'

'Och, we'll argy-bargy later,' he said. 'I'm off to procure us a passage.' He leaned over the side and shouted, and five or more skiffs came racing towards us, each one offering to row him ashore at a bargain price.

'Why'd you call Licky "Your Majesty"?' I asked Bratchet when he'd gone.

'Asantewa's his mother, she's Queen of the Maroons. She appoints their king. She summoned him back so that he can be the king, their *ohene*.'

'And I'm to be Queen of the May,' I told her. 'Bratchie, that higgler's a fat, crafty old woman. That's all she is. Stop talking like she's some miracle-monger.'

Bratchet shook her head. 'She sends out magic. She saved us from the waterspout thing. She summoned Licky to come to her from thousands of miles away.'

I hated to see her in thrall to superstition. It offended the Puritanism in me. Everything was explicable. The waterspout business'd had me on my heels for a while, but they're chancy things and veer where the weather takes them.

As for summoning Licky . . . as he himself had said, 'Us niggers get around.' And now I came to think of it, they do. They thread the streets of London, amiable black faces under turbans, bright livery, black hands holding a parasol over a fashionable female head, arms folded on the back of carriages. Noticeable yet unnoticed.

They'd been at Marly, little ones treated like pet monkeys, grey-haired ones polishing boots. There'd been two at St-Germain-en-Laye.

Maybe the links of the chains on the slaves shuffling along the quay back there were connected to the less-visibly fettered black servants all over the world, I thought. Maybe they were an international conduit of information, black telling black what they needed to know. A Negro secret service through which a woman had summoned her son from three thousand miles away.

But when I explained this to the Bratchet she wouldn't have it. 'She summoned me.'

'Witchdoctor stuff,' I told her, 'Licky told her you were on the trail of Anne and Mary. She happened to know them, so she made her knowledge look like magic. There's no denying it was a coincidence you met, but coincidences happen. It's a small community, piracy; if you're connected with it, you only have to arrive in the West Indies to find somebody knows somebody you know.'

Around us, the trade of the harbour was slackening as the sun set. The mulattos had gone off to a tavern and we sat looking out on a quay that was emptied of everything except sponges. I lost my patience with the Bratchet. 'If you believe everything that old ebony says, why don't you take her word that Anne and Mary are dead? Going to this St Jago place, it's madness.'

She stayed obstinate. To Bratchet, the higgler was Effie Sly come back, same physical hugeness, same certainty and aggression. And just as daunting. But Bratchet hadn't believed Effie when she'd said Anne and Mary were dead, and she wasn't going to believe the higgler either.

'I wonder where Kilsyth is,' she said, and put her head back against the coping and fell asleep.

Long after dark, Kilsyth came back with an old acquaintance. 'I'd have ye meet Johnny Faa. And a wonderful lucky case to encounter him on a Jamaican waterfront, having last met wi' him poaching woodcock in the Highlands.' He clapped the man on the shoulder. 'We're well met by moonlight, Johnny.'

'We air that, Maister Livingstone,' said Johnny Faa, 'An unco' small world it is. But it's *Maister* Faa noo.' He smiled to show he was neither giving nor taking offence.

'I've met with fortune sin syne an' am a respectable body if ye please, wi' a tidy house in Laws Street and a bonny estate out by St Andrew.' He swept off his hat. 'And the both at ye're disposal as lang as ye gang.'

He was a thin man, well dressed, and he smiled a lot. He'd obviously come up in the world. Something about his eyes and teeth gave me the impression he'd eaten whoever owned his clothes before. Still, Kilsyth seemed pleased at finding a fellow Scot and it would have been churlish to gang anywhere else after his invitation, even if we'd had anywhere else to gang.

He'd employed a black linkboy to light our way and we followed him through the streets. Kilsyth was having trouble adjusting to the ex-poacher's new status and kept addressing him as 'Johnny' and having to be reminded that it was 'Maister Faa noo'.

When we got to his house, he insisted on showing us over it, but we were too tired to notice much more than it was over-furnished and hot. A black woman led us to our rooms and beds that were covered by a tent of muslin. To ward off 'gallinippers', she said. I didn't care if they were there to ward off the French cavalry; underneath mine was the first real bed I'd seen since we were taken at Le Havre.

It came as a shock to realize that it had been more than twelve months ago. Johnny Faa had been out late in Kingston because he had been celebrating Hogmanay Night with fellow-

Scots. The year was 1710. Bratchet, Kilsyth and I had left England in the autumn of 1707.

By the time we gathered in the dining room next morning, our host had already gone out to the harbour to investigate such ships as might take us to England. We settled down over a breakfast of bacon and kidneys to flesh out the story that Kilsyth had given in brief to Johnny Faa the night before.

It was a watered-down version of the truth. The ship bringing us to Jamaica had been taken over by mutineers who turned pirate and, once arrived in the Bahamas, had cast us ashore. A passing, friendly sponge boat had brought us to Kingston.

We hoped we'd be on our way home before we had to face questioning on the pirates' names and, just as difficult to answer, what we'd been doing on the *Holy Innocent*, a ship belonging to Louis XIV, in the first place. Kilsyth and I still had Sam's certificates of exoneration and could show them if necessary. But I hoped it wouldn't be necessary.

Nor did I want to go into why we'd been in France; that could wait until I got home and met Defoe or Harley. They knew I hadn't gone over to the enemy, had sent back all the information I could, but Kilsyth was in a more irregular position.

It was Kilsyth who pointed out that, while we were here, so was the Bratchet. Johnny Faa, he said, had looked at him askance that a young woman had undergone capture and had, in any case, been travelling with two men, neither of them her husband.

'So I told him she was your sister, Martin.'

'My what?'

'Will ye wheesht? I told him the lassie here was your sister. Else he would have thought her the leman of us both. We're back in respectable society the now.'

Bratchet grinned. 'Miss Millet,' she said, 'good name. Very respaictable.'

'Oh, thank you,' I said, 'thank you very much.'

When Johnny Faa came back he reported that the only ships in port destined for England at the moment were sugar boats

and naval vessels. Sugar boats were too slow and uncomfortable, he said. 'And as for the navy . . .' he winked and tapped his
nose at Kilsyth with a beringed finger, one Jacobite to another
'. . . I spier ye'd prefer a voyage without question.'

He promised that in a week or two the *Laird o' Kirkaldy* would
be arriving to take on a cargo of his muscavady sugar. 'And
she'll tak' you back to our ane land swift as blackcock to the
heather.'

Until then, he suggested, we repair with him to his estate in
the hills – 'awa' frae the worst o' the heat. I mun go back there,
for the nigger's apt to be negligent if I'm no there to tickle him
up. And I'll no part wi' ye yet. Na, na, I dinna meet such friends
as you in Jamaiky every night.'

Bratchet said, 'Is your estate near St Jago something or other,
Master Faa?'

'St Jago de la Vega,' he supplied. 'A step, Mistress Millet, if
ane's fresh and sober, though we call it Spanish Town the now.'

'Then I am sure that Master Livingstone, my brother and
myself would be delighted.'

Our delight was nothing to his, which was effusive. 'In the
meantime, mistress, ye'll mebbe wish to trick yesel' wi' a new
gown or two an' I'm thinkin' the gentlemen'll want to avail
thesselves of a fresh collar.'

We realized what we looked like to outsiders. Even our
patches were salt-stained. Kilsyth had lain aside his kilt for
breeks while aboard ship – to the disappointment of Nobby
who'd wanted to see him go up rigging in it – but, donned
again, it still looked as if it had known suffering.

The irony was that, while our prize shares had put our
finances in good order, they weren't in negotiable form. 'We'll
discuss the matter,' said Kilsyth with grandeur and added, after
a wait, 'With your permission, Master Faa.'

'Oh. Weel then,' said Johnny Faa reluctantly, 'I'll leave ye the
whiles.'

When he'd gone I said, 'Catch me offering a shopkeeper
pearls and a silver pig. We'd get new collars all right, a bloody
rope.'

'Aye, we need a banker.'

'Same applies. What's the use of us telling the authorities we're poor victims of piracy if we're walking around with pirate loot?'

'We'll hae to confide in Johnny Faa. He's a leal Jacobite like myself. He'll no betray us.'

'Well, I don't trust the bugger.'

Bratchet breathed out in relief. 'I don't, either.'

Kilsyth wouldn't have it, though, that Johnny was anything but 'leal' and, since there was little alternative, we had to let him call the man back and explain the situation.

'Weel, weel,' said Johnny, craftily, 'Ye fell in wi' kindlier pirates than the usual shake-rags, I'm thinking. I'd no mention pearls and siller to the magister when ye face him. Still and all, the governor will mebbe swallow its witters, him bein' a cousin and no long in office.'

He advanced us money, promising to exchange pearls and pig with his own banker who was 'unco' discreet'.

Then we went shopping. Bratchet, I realized, had never done any. By God, did she take to it. She was a humming bird in a nectar forest, a hen-raised duckling sliding into water. She wanted to buy everything. And Kingston was the place to do it. We went down shaded arcades where fair-skinned ladies tempted her into shops in soft, Creole voices. Black boys wafted her with a feathered fan while the ladies opened louvred cupboard doors as if they were parting the Red Sea to let her through to the Promised Land.

Her fellow shoppers were as exotic as the merchandise and as multi-coloured; beautiful, slim and very young black girls under the command of white gentlemen ordering gowns cut low; yellow and equally beautiful young women with a sneer and elaborate top-knots; anxious red-faced English matrons wondering what to wear for the governor's ball.

Bratchet was all for lemon bombazine, but I'd been making a survey of the female clientele's dress sense in the better emporia and worked out a compromise between over-warm respectability (the English wives) and the outrageous (the others). So I steered her towards pastel sprigged muslin and Indian cottons and suggested lace be sewn over what the shop ladies called 'fashionable décolletage'. (How Kingston women don't get sunburned muffins beats me.)

'But I *must* have a hat like this,' Bratchet protested, 'Look at hers,' pointing at a flat straw plate tilted almost to its wearer's very pretty nose.

'We're avoiding the pirate moll look this year. We've got to report to the authorities this afternoon, for God's sake. What about this one? Keeps the sun off and won't scare the horses.' This was a cartwheel with nice ribbons but Bratchet clung mutinously to the plate. 'We want to look like somebody's sister, not somebody's kept woman.'

But it was the plate we went out with.

'We don't want to look like Mrs Defoe, either,' she said.

I left my own attire to Kilsyth who was showing an unsuspected enthusiasm for clothes-buying generally and ruffled shirts in particular, but who needed keeping an eye on.

'What's he at now?' I asked, as Bratchet and I waited outside yet another outfitter's. Bratchet looked at the name on the warehouse sign and saw a Mac in it. 'Oh my God, a kilt. He's trying to find another kilt.'

We sprinted inside, took an arm each and marched Kilsyth off; he was shouting over his shoulder, 'Call yeself a Scotsman and ye've nae philibegs in your stock?' To us, he complained, 'The manny bare spoke English, let alone the Gaelic.'

'Creole,' explained Johnny Faa when we joined him at an inn on Harbour Street, 'MacGregor was born here to braw Scots but he's no their tongue, mair's the pity. An' I doot there's a kilt this side o' the Grampians.'

'I hope there ain't,' I said to Kilsyth, 'Look at your legs. Bloody near need careening.'

It was true. Kilsyth hadn't yet got round to buying shoes or stockings and his bare legs were covered in lumps topped by weeping craters. He regarded them dolefully. 'They're powerful midges here, worse nor Scotland's.'

'Tha's no midges,' Faa said, 'Tha's gallinippers, Jamaican special. It's to be hoped ye no wandered west in your travels afore I found ye last nicht. That's swampland where niggers live wi' foul vapours and an unchancy breed of insect.'

Kilsyth didn't know where he'd wandered. He was persuaded, however, that trews were *de rigueur* for the tropics and, having drunk a glass or two of Madeira, which Faa assured us was a specific against the heat, we went to find them.

It had been pleasant on the verandah of the inn, which overlooked a quay where ferrymen took passengers and barrels of fresh water to other parts of the immense harbour. There was a breeze from the sea – Johnny Faa said it was healthy and known as 'The Doctor', as opposed to the hot wind that came down from the hills in the evening which was called 'The Undertaker'. Changes of sentries were rowed out to the forts that guarded its entrances. Skiffs came in carrying smart officers from the naval vessels.

Best of all was the unofficial market just below the verandah where black women hustled passers-by to baskets full of yams, eddoes, corn, fruits and berries. Most of the women had a baby strapped to their hip and laughed and chaffed with each other.

Bratchet pointed at them. 'Are they slaves?' she asked Faa.

'Oh aye. Frae the estates. An' content to be so as your ee can tell.'

It wasn't so pleasant in the streets now. Despite the breeze and Madeira, the heat was wearing. My leg was aching and I could see Bratchet being more bothered by things that had escaped her notice in the thrill of shopping.

Outside one warehouse which we entered in the search for Kilsyth's trews was a large billboard stuck with notices. '£2 is Offered for the lodgement in the cages of the negro wench Phibba. She speaks Good English and may pass as Free. Guilty of petit maroonage before and carries stripes on breast and back.'

Another asked for the return to the Newton Estate of 'the runaway Assey, a yellow skin girl about 16 years old, with a Negro freckle under one of her eyes and an Aperture in her top front Teeth. Being a good seamstress. 10s. reward for her recapture.'

There were a few advertisements . . . 'James Evans who made shoes for the Fashionable of St James's in England now plies his Trade in King Street, next to Beeston House . . .' etc., but most of the notices demanded the return of escaped slaves.

'Not all content, then,' Bratchet said. Faa didn't answer.

There was a contrast between the story of servitude told by the notices, by Licky and the higgler, by what we'd seen with our own eyes, and the democracy of the culture that had been built on it. There was nowhere in Britain, and certainly not in France, where someone with a background like Johnny Faa's, a herd from the Highlands, could have been accepted by the nobs as he was here, however many acres he owned – and we later discovered that he owned none, being merely the manager of an absentee landlord's estate.

However, we had to keep pausing in the street to be introduced by him to Master Graham, 'third son to Sir William of Dalrymple, ye ken', or to Master Ferrars, 'second cousin to Lord Plunkett', or to Captain Courteen, 'one of our biggest lairds'.

Everybody knew Johnny Faa – as he was pleased to point out all the time, with sidelong what-about-that glances at Kilsyth. Nobility entertained him in their houses, as he did them in his, and welcomed us, his guests, to their society. Invitations to 'breakfast' on various estates were given, and accepted – even from a gentleman Johnny Faa introduced as 'Master Teague Macdoe', whose Irish name was belied by his dark complexion, flat nose and crinkled hair.

'Aye, a mulatto,' said Faa as we left this last encounter, 'A dingy Christian wi' black blood only a generation back but the acres in Guanaboa Vale his father left him are fair enough.'

This was still a frontier society, poised over an outnumbering and potentially threatening black population; obviously, it was unwise to despise a neighbour who might have to help you keep it down.

'And noo,' said Johnny Faa, 'ye must be explaining yesselves to Magister Thomas. I've done well for ye and told him ye're kin to the governor and were took agin' your will by scaff-raffs, for the rest ye must stand by your ane.'

I decided to leave that to Kilsyth who was more likely to impress than I was. Bratchet was beginning to sag in the heat. I said I'd escort her back to Faa's house, with her permission and his.

We could have done without Johnny Faa accompanying us, and his questions; how long had we known Maister Livingstone, why had he come here when he had been 'so blythe in his ane land', etc. I gave him vague answers, saying I'd come to seek a fortune in the colonies. 'You'll be no the worse of it,' Faa assured me. 'A man can live like a laird here, foreby he works hard.'

We found out what the 'cages' were that Phibba, the runaway, was to be lodged in when she was caught. We passed them in a marketplace, and Johnny Faa paused to peer in 'to see if any o' my ane blackbirds are singin' within'. They were Kingston's central repository for recaptured slaves, large hen coops, not tall enough for a person to stand up in, made of rectangular hardwood bars within which, in their own ordure, crouched a few black men and women.

'The trick's to leave them here a nicht or three to teach them they're no worse at hame,' Faa said.

He was disappointed at not finding his own two runaways, a man and a woman, who'd been missing for several weeks. 'It might be so they're wi' the Maroons by noo, the De'il be in them,' he said disgustedly. 'Aweel, aweel, the branding iron'll be kept heated for their return.' He was quick to see that Bratchet had gone pale. 'Dinna ye fash yersel', mistress. Ladies are tender for the ebonies when they first come oot here, but ye'll soon see the sense o' grindin' the wasters.'

I saw her look up to the Blue Mountains which dominated Kingston's skyline and knew she was wondering whether Licky and his mother had got to them safely. She pleaded a headache – a condition taken seriously in Jamaica – went to bed as soon as she got back and stayed there.

Kilsyth returned to say that Magistrate Thomas had been impressed sufficiently by his connections to swallow our story. 'But he says we've to be examined by a Vice-Admiralty Court judge when we get to Spanish Town. A formality, he says. But the Vice-Admiralty'll want to know the names of Sam Rogers and the others.'

'Bugger.'

'Martin, what else can we do?'

It was true. We had to explain our presence in Jamaica. A Vice-Admiralty Court would have all shipping lists; we couldn't make up a non-existent ship. They'd check.

'Och, it'll all come right somehow, no doubt,' Kilsyth said, 'Let's cross that bridge when we meet it.'

He'd caught up on the news at home while he'd been out. The Pretender, it appeared, had tried his invasion of Scotland soon after our departure from France and hadn't even managed to land, but had been chased back home by the English navy.

We spent the evening drowning Scotland's sorrows in rum. At least, Kilsyth and Faa did. I had other sorrows to drown. By the end of it they got maudlin, bewailing their country's union with England.

''Tis the end of an auld song, an auld, auld song,' Kilsyth was shouting. They began to sing it:

> 'For Scotland's Royal, Loyal, Joyal,
> Jemmy's our joy, the Whigs we defy all,
> We mighted him, righted him
> When England flighted him.
> Tan ta ra ra ra, boys, now we'll delight him.'

'Go down well in a Vice-Admiralty Court that will,' I said and staggered off to bed. Brachet hadn't left hers.

Her headache had gone next morning but Kilsyth, not surprisingly, had gained one. As he and I mounted the horses waiting in the street to take us inland, he was unusually silent. Johnny Faa appeared unaffected and handed Bratchet into a smart equipage with a fringed calico roof to keep the sun off, and settled himself into the driver's seat beside her. Our boxes of new clothes were loaded into a cart by a Negro servant who followed us with it through the town, heading west into the Liguanea Plain.

We travelled in our own personal dust-cloud thrown up by the horses' hooves. But from what I could glimpse of it, the view was worth seeing. There were always hills and mountains on our right and a breeze from the sea coming from our left. We crossed bridges over fast-running streams, once on a causeway through a mangrove swamp where, Johnny Faa said, there were alligators, along ridges where orchids grew under enormous cottonwood trees, back to the plain and palms, into shade so deep and out again into sun so bright that our eyes watered with the constant adjustment.

We met mule trains pulling long carts loaded with sugar hogsheads and the occasional overseer on a horse, but the most constant traffic was black women heading for the markets with estate produce, one arm up to support the burden on their head, a crate of chickens, a basket of vegetables, with the other arm crooked round a piglet or a turkey.

The younger women walked with long equable strides, the older limped along on legs that were bandy from malnutrition, some with flies clustered on their sores. Once or twice we came across a gaggle of them sitting down to rest under a mango tree. Johnny Faa flicked his horsewhip at them and told them to move on. 'There's nae good comes of their clack,' he said, 'just idleness and plotting.'

That was the trouble with the place. It looked like paradise, but you caught the fear. The women might have been discussing the weather, but, though they obeyed the crack of the whip docilely enough, their togetherness disturbed Johnny.

It even disturbed me. It was the way they looked at us. Suddenly I was a representative of a dominant race being weighed and found wanting by underdogs. For a straw, I'd have got down and explained, 'We're not with him.'

But we were. We were well dressed, well fed and white, therefore the enemy. No wonder Johnny Faa talked about the blacks like a bee-keeper afraid of a swarm. He kept shouting his methods at us as we rode along beside the trap. 'Keep 'em mixed of origin, d'ye see? Ye don't want all Coromantins who are strong but unco' proud and rebellious. They're better diluted by Papaws who're docile and agreeable, or Ibos who're timorous an' despondent.'

We had to listen to his pride in his dogs who were trained to hunt runaways and attack. 'They fear neathing wi' a black skin on't. Aye, they're fell chields at the ebonies.'

I heard Bratchet change the subject. 'Did you ever hear of two

339

white women pirates who stood trial at St Jago de la Vega a few years back?'

He hadn't. 'But it might be so and there'd have been a need to keep the thing verra quiet. Lord save us, she-niggers are beldams enough wi'out such a white example afore their eyes.'

This wasn't a country that'd want to publicize two women like Anne and Mary. Theirs was a dangerous example anywhere, here it was incendiary. Besides, Johnny said, he'd only been in Jamaica a year or two. Nor did he intend to stay – 'The fient a bit o' that. I'll fill my pot o' gold and it's back to my ane country in amber silk, wi' my ane piper marchin' before me. Aye, they'll fear Johnny Faa then.' Jamaica was a piece of meat he'd sunk his teeth into. He was going to eat his bit of it and go home.

We crossed a sizeable body of water which cascaded down rapids to swirl in pools at the bottom, and sent up wafts of cool air which unstuck our clothes from the sweat of our bodies. 'Rio Cobre,' Johnny called out. We were nearing Spanish Town, which had been St Jago de la Vega when Spain became Jamaica's first conqueror.

It still retained its Spanishness in a cathedral and buildings that had an elegance Kingston lacked. The courthouse, House of Assembly and governor's residence, were of coral limestone and stood in a square round a plaza shaded by feathery tamarinds. Parapets kept the sun off verandahs, while rattan jalousies at the windows were propped up a few inches to allow air into the dark interiors.

'Which is the courthouse?' Bratchet asked at once. Johnny pointed to the most Spanish and impressive of all the buildings.

It had an exterior stone staircase fourteen feet long leading to a portico and great mahogany doors. I'd imagined Anne and Mary standing trial in some dingy dock; as it was, they'd made their last public appearance in surroundings of some magnificence.

Johnny Faa watched Bratchet as she stared at it. 'Ye're rare interested in the fate o' two trollops, mistress. Weel, yon's the cells tha' would have held 'em.' He nodded to the arches of the courthouse's lower storey, an arcade of wooden gates hiding whatever lay inside.

Johnny wanted to show off his acquaintanceship with a laird of Kilsyth to the governor, and his acquaintanceship with the governor to a laird of Kilsyth. So, at his insistence, we were received at the residency by Lord Archibald Hamilton, a former naval captain.

He greeted Kilsyth with the enthusiasm of a kinsman and offered us sympathy at being taken by pirates. 'We'll catch them, never fear. When we've swept the seas of Froggies and Dagos, the navy'll have at those debauched rogues.'

We got another breakfast, though it was well past noon, a meal consisting of various roast meats swimming in oil. They like breakfast big and often, do the Jamaicans.

Considering that we needed every friend of Lord Archibald's class, it was a pity Kilsyth wasn't on top form. Hamilton wanted to discuss mutual friends and relations with him but, for once, our Livingstone was reticent. I put it down to hangover.

Bratchet and I made the conversational running and, of course, she had to ask if he'd heard of the women pirates who'd once stood trial in the courthouse opposite. She was disappointed again. 'Can't say I have, m'dear, though it'd not surprise me, times being topsy-turvy as they are. May I ask your interest, mistress?'

I struck in. I didn't want her becoming allied in these people's minds with pirates. I made a shot at an upper-class accent. 'My sister enquires on my account, my lord. Thought of writing a monograph. Wonderful encounters on me travels, sort of thing.'

'You've had strange and wonderful encounters enough, I'd have thought, Master Millet, without advertising a couple of unnatural hussies. It's best left, best left. The gentle sex don't need encouraging to put on trousers. Look at the Court back home; bedchamber women runnin' the country like appointed ministers.' However, he promised that he would ask among his staff, 'though the longest-serving of 'em haven't been here above a few years'.

341

'Nobody seems to have been here above a few years,' complained Bratchet.

'How right y'are, m'dear.' The governor tapped the back of her hand in approval at her perspicacity. 'That's Jamaica for ye. Quick fortunes, quick deaths. Grab and get out, that's the policy. Have ye seen aged patriarchs since your arrival? Nor will you. By fifty-five Jamaica has 'em in their graves. I tell ye, we have assistant judges that are minors. *Minors*. A boy here jumps off his hobby horse straightway to colonel of a troop.' He lowered his voice. 'Is Master Kilsyth unwell?'

'An over-indulgence in rum,' I said.

Lord Archibald shook his head. 'Keep him off it, that's my advice. Young blades grow thirsty in this climate and play the good fellow, but too much liquor aggravates choler. Only last week one of our young planters expired after downing eight quarts of Madeira in a night.'

The governor was the healthiest looking man we'd seen since arriving in Jamaica; his advice was worth having. It occurred to me that Kilsyth's despondency was lasting longer than the usual hangover.

Lord Archibald accompanied us to the residency steps. 'By the way, Faa. The churchwarden will be wanting y'hounds. The parish has decided to go after the Maroons again and I'm sendin' a troop with 'em. There's been too many runaways to the hills.' He turned to us. 'Principle of gamekeeping, m'dears. Hang a few blackbirds along the route to warn the others.'

He gave us an invitation to the ball he was giving in a week or two's time, and said our interrogation would have to await the Vice-Admiralty judges' return from Barbados where they'd been assisting at the trial of 'a parcel of scurvy pirates'.

I made Kilsyth join Bratchet and Faa in the trap rather than ride any further in the sun. Ominously, he didn't protest. He admitted to a headache that was affecting his ability to see.

'We'll have ye to bed in the minute,' said Johnny Faa and touched the horses into a trot.

It was a long bloody minute – nearly as far again as the thirteen miles we'd already travelled from Kingston to Spanish Town. And it was dreary. For the first time we saw no variety.

Here was what the English planters were making of the Jamaican plain, a rolling, treeless, unchanging, monotone of sugar cane, like a sea but without a sea's horizon. Even with the advantage of height given by horseback, my eye was stopped from seeing anything but a blazing white sky and the canes themselves, acres, miles of them, hemming in the track ahead like an advancing army of mutant grass.

Where there were trees, black men with saws and mules in traces were chopping them down and dragging them off to make way for the bent-backed black women planting seedlings so that the grove could become as featureless as everywhere else. Not a face looked up to see us go by.

Johnny Faa waved his whip. 'Here's my land noo.'

How in hell do you know? There wasn't a hedge, no fence, nothing to demarcate one hot, unmoving stretch from another. He began expounding on acreage and prices, but Bratchet stopped him. 'Can't you go faster?' Kilsyth had begun to shiver. A little further along the trap had to pull up while he vomited.

'God save us, I dread it may be the yellow fever,' Faa said.

I leaned down and felt his head. It was burning. He focused on me. 'I'm dying, Martin.' It was the first and only time I ever saw him afraid.

'You're not,' I told him and wished I was sure. Bratchet put her arms round him to save him from being shaken about as Johnny Faa whipped up the horses.

It seemed to take for ever, but at last we arrived at a large house with peacocks on the lawn in front of it. Faa drove round the side of it to a long, low, one-storey building surrounded by a verandah.

'Ye'll understand,' he said to me, 'it'd no be wise to have him in the Big House. He'll be well enough here.'

A couple of black servants helped me carry him inside and put him on a bed. Bratchet and I undressed him while they fetched a bowl of water and a cloth to bathe his face and neck. His colour was terrible. For that matter, so was Bratchet's. 'Don't let him die, Martin,' she kept saying, 'Don't let him die.'

A doctor came that evening and peered at Kilsyth without

touching him. He took me outside the room. 'Yellowjack, right enough. He'll be dead within the week.'

The building was the manager's house and Johnny Faa had lived in it while the estate owner was still in residence at the Big House before he returned to England. It was clean enough, pine-panelled and devoid of all but essential furniture. There was a master bedroom, which became the sickroom, then a large sitting room, and, at the end of the passage, a smaller bedroom.

Johnny Faa only came near it in the mornings, to stand outside the living-room window and enquire for the patient and our wants. He urged us to leave Kilsyth's care to the servants but we did the nursing ourselves. One of them always stayed outside in the garden within call, but all of them refused to come into the house itself and Faa didn't insist, I suppose because he was afraid they'd carry the infection. I couldn't blame any of 'em. Yellowjack carried off as large a proportion of Jamaica's population as the Great Plague had London's.

That first day we stayed on either side of his bed for twenty-four hours. He wanted his bonnet and when we put the thing in his hands he smiled and carried it to his cheek. Its feather had been reduced to skeleton spines on the stump of a quill.

Later that night in the height of the fever he gabbled about Scotland. He tried to sing 'Royal, Loyal, Joyal', and shouted 'Fareweel to a' our Scottish fame.' But he was too weak to be martial; mostly he seemed to have returned to his childhood, muttering comfort to himself. 'The brow of the brae at Both Bridge', 'Barley mills', 'Ivy on the mullions'; on and on about his home until, sitting either side of his bed in the stifling night, Bratchet and I could almost see the moorland streams where shiny-headed otter swam after salmon.

Once that night, he clung to her in panic. 'You'll not let them take me. I love ye so. Keep me back.'

'They'll never take you away,' she said.

He went unconscious.

She wrung out a cloth in water and bathed his head, sobbing. 'Now's a bloody fine time to tell me you love me.'

'He told me,' I said.

'Did he?' She bathed and sobbed some more. 'Ain't it good of him? I don't deserve it.'

His need for her seemed to be a revelation that brought something like guilt with it. She was indebted to him for loving her; his helplessness merely increased her gratitude, like receiving the unsought love of a child.

Later, when she'd left the room to fetch more water, he was aware of her absence. When she came back, he felt for her hand and said, 'It's an ill day for me, Mother, when you're away.'

Johnny Faa had called in his neighbour, Dr Hopkins, a typical bloody quack, all rant and liquor. If the patient lived it was the doctor's cure, if the patient died it was his own damn fault. I never saw him sober. Bratchet was in thrall to the old tope and would have poured all his remedies down Kilsyth's throat, disgusting as they were.

I ordered him not to bleed his patient, at least, though he tried to do it when my back was turned. I came into the room and caught him. I yanked the snuffy fingers from Kilsyth's arm and chucked his box of leeches out of the window. 'You touch the poor bugger again and you follow the fucking leeches,' I promised him.

He swore at me and staggered out, with Bratchet pleading for him to come back. I took her shoulders and turned her round. 'Look at him, will you? Does he look like he can afford to lose blood?'

Kilsyth's eyes were sightless. His face was yellow-white.

'They sent the Twenty-third to the West Indies five years ago,' I told her. 'Half the poor sods never came back, but the ones that did knew a hell of a lot about yellowjack. We don't bleed him, we've got to make him piss.'

'You're so crude,' she shrieked, 'You want him to die.'

'I'm not going to *let* him die. Now tell 'em to bring water from the well. Crude or not, we're going to make him piss.'

For the rest of that night we took turns forcing water into Kilsyth. When it dribbled back, we wiped the drips from his mouth and forced in more.

'I'm sorry,' she said suddenly. 'I'm so frightened.'

345

'I know.'

'I owe him, you see.'

She puzzled me. In the last years the lives of the three of us had become so intertwined that it was no longer a matter of who owed who what. If it was a question of that, both Kilsyth and I owed Bratchet more than we could repay. But all of us had rescued each other from one situation or another; the bond between us went too deep for any of us to keep score.

We organized ourselves, twelve hours on, twelve hours off. While Bratchet was on duty in the sickroom, I slept in one of the cots in the small bedroom at the end of the corridor with the door open in case she called. When it was my turn on duty, she went into the little bedroom's other cot.

We agreed he'd be in a worse case if exhaustion brought either of us down, but she'd have attended Kilsyth all the time if she could. Gradually I realized what it was she thought she owed him. Deep beneath the mature woman was still the raped girl from Puddle Court whom nobody had loved. Or, for that matter, needed. She was grateful, overflowing with gratitude that the love she'd nurtured for this admirable man was returned. Because she loved him, the little skivvy from Puddle Court was under an obligation to him for loving her back.

But I needed her too, dammit. And loved her a bloody sight more. How much I loved her was a revelation. I suppose I'd tamped down what I felt, knowing it was Kilsyth she was attracted to. But, Christ, I wished I'd told her. Here's Martin Millet, Bratchie, a common soldier with a limp. A poor catch. As an object of romance, pitiful. But he happens to think you're the sun and the moon and the stars. He just wants you to know that. No obligation.

It would have spoiled things, of course. I was her best friend, we were closer in understanding than she was with Kilsyth. But it was Kilsyth she loved. She'd never be comfortable with me again.

And I still wished I'd told her.

Too late now. You don't make declarations of love over the bed of a dying man.

We made him drink, cleaned him up, rubbed him down,

346

fanned him until the one that was coming off duty staggered past the one going on without a word and fell asleep, though in the off-duty hours we had to fetch meals from the Big House's kitchens, scour the pot, answer Faa's enquiries, take and collect the laundry, pound and seethe the herbs we put in the patient's drinks.

The Vice-Admiralty judges came back from Barbados and sent for us, but Johnny Faa went into Spanish Town to explain the situation and get us an adjournment until another sitting.

I don't remember how long it lasted, probably not more than a week, but it seemed endless. The days' heat gave way to nights so humid you woke up sweating and gasping. And the damn peacocks in the gardens didn't sleep and kept up that eerie cry they have so that you couldn't, either. I was tempted to twist their necks for them.

It ended on the night when I went to take over from Bratchet to find she'd fallen asleep in her chair, her head on the edge of the bed. She was breathing regularly. And so was Kilsyth. I touched his hand, then his face. He was cool.

I shook Bratchet's shoulder. 'I think we've done it.'

She started up. 'Is he worse?' She put her hand on Kilsyth's forehead. 'Oh God. Thank you, God.'

'Go and get some rest, now.' She stayed where she was, looking at him, so I raised her up and took her outside to the verandah into the cool. There was a Negro asleep on the steps. I woke him and asked him to fetch some brandy and two glasses. When he came back with them, I told him to go to bed. Yawning, he stumbled off towards the slaves' quarters.

I poured us both brandy. She kept glancing towards the sickroom. I propped the door open so that we could hear if the patient woke up. He was still asleep, breathing lightly.

Bratchet was holding on to the verandah post like a woman who'd fall down if she didn't. I put a glass of brandy in her hand. 'Here's to Scotland,' I said, 'We did it.'

We drank.

'You did it,' she said.

'We both did it.'

'No,' she said, 'it was you.'

347

Moths fluttered across the verandah and into the sickroom to singe themselves on the candle by Kilsyth's bed. The night smelled of raffia and jasmine and chimed with frogs. A huge Jamaican moon was up, casting shadows across the garden. In the slaves' quarters a woman was chanting. I slid down against the post opposite Bratchet and sat on the steps, looking out over the gardens, sipping the brandy.

'I'm grateful, Martin,' she said.

'For God's sake,' I said irritably, 'what was I going to do? Sit back and eat grapes? He's my friend. Stop being so bloody grateful to everybody – me, him. You don't have to be grateful to a living soul. You're one of the wonders of the modern world, Bratchie. Of course he damn well loves you. So do I. Now go to bed.'

I hadn't meant to say it. I was tired. Anyway, the record had to be set straight. Sod it, I thought.

She didn't move. 'It's always been you, hasn't it?' she said. 'I was safe the moment you came back to Puddle Court. I knew it. I was . . . warmer. I thought it was him for a long while. But it wasn't, it was you.'

I got up. She was looking away from me, towards the Big House with its walls white in the moonlight and its shutters dark. She'd tied her hair into a top-knot, damp strands of it had fallen down against her neck and cheeks and stuck to them.

She said, 'I couldn't have borne it if he'd died. For not loving him when he needed me. That's why I'm grateful.'

We stood opposite each other, my shirt plastered to my body, her dress sticking to hers. She turned to look at me. I'd waited a long time for that look, a long time.

Her hands groped like a blind woman's to touch my face. 'It was always you,' she said.

I picked her up and took her to bed.

The yellow fever left Kilsyth but something else came in its wake and affected his joints, which became inflamed and swollen. He bore it cheerfully enough though sometimes he was in agony. We poulticed his knees and hands and fed him bone marrow but, after two desperate nights, Johnny Faa rode over to Hopkins's place and bought laudanum so that the patient could get some sleep.

I wondered if Bratchet would show some sort of guilt that virtually every minute we weren't attending on Kilsyth we were making love. She didn't, which should have warned me. But, to be honest, I couldn't think of much else except when I could next get her back in my bed.

The first time, after we'd surfaced, she said, 'You might have told me earlier, you oyster.'

'It may have escaped your notice, but we've been surrounded by people these last two years. Pirates, royalty, riff-raff like that. There wasn't room to go down on one knee.'

'At least I'd have known,' she said.

'I didn't think you saw me.'

'I'm seeing you now.' It was a small, uncomfortable bed that one, but we didn't notice. 'When did *you* know?'

'I suppose it was on the boat crossing the Channel,' I said, 'It was Mrs Defoe's grey woollen that did it.'

'Fetching, weren't it? I remember. I called for my mother, and you said you'd lost yours too. "If it helps, Bratchet, I lost mine too," you said.'

I hadn't thought she'd remember.

'It did help,' she said, 'You always helped.'

'No, I didn't. I should never've left you at Effie's.' I held her close, rubbing my cheek against her ear. 'I'm sorry, Bratchie, I'm so sorry. I'd cut off my arm to have that time again.'

I felt her pat my bare back. 'You're better off with two.'

With the scare of yellow fever gone, we were able to call on one of Faa's servants to sit with Kilsyth at night now and then so that we could take some air. We used to walk in the garden until the strain of not touching each other drove us back to bed.

We did most of our talking in those times under a Jamaican moon like a pumpkin, with the peacocks trailing their tails and crying under the trees. I told her about my father, the search for my mother and finding her, the Dragoons, how scared I'd been before a battle, things I'd never told anybody.

'Know what I regret, Bratchie?'

'Not taking me away from Effie Sly.'

'Rosinante. What a horse. That bloody innkeeper at Le Havre better look after him.'

'Sensitive, was he?'

'Easily hurt,' I said, 'Mouth like a bloody angel.' As I hadn't kissed hers for a bit, we went back to bed.

In those times in the garden I hoped she'd tell me what she knew about Effie Sly's death. She wouldn't.

'A higher loyalty than to me?' I grumbled.

'Not higher. Different.' She looked up at me. 'You hate Anne and Mary, don't you?'

'I don't hate them,' I told her, 'I never met 'em. But it's been like tracking cats through a forest, watching them get wilder and wilder. Seeing where they made their kill.'

She sighed. 'Sometimes I think they'd never've fitted in. Even if they hadn't been kidnapped. They were too . . . I don't know . . . the way they saw things was too wide. It's like Kit Ross said, women's world is too small. Men want all women to be Mrs Defoes. And they ain't. Look at Effie Sly. What she could have done if they'd given her enough slack, if she hadn't gone into the trade. Ruled the world most like.'

She was right. I hadn't thought about it before. I said, 'She didn't start out a monster. Father threw her on to the streets like a good righteous brother when she was seventeen because he caught her kissing the apprentice. Perhaps she survived the only way she knew how.'

Sadly she said again, 'They'd like us all to be Mrs Defoes.'

Another night she asked, 'Do you still think I'm in danger?'

I considered it. 'Maybe not. You've been got out of the way. The danger'll start when we get back. One thing, I'll be with you day and night. When are we going to tell him, Bratchie?'

'We'll see about all that when he's well,' she said.

Kilsyth wasn't getting well. He was improving; the burning in his joints eased. But his hands and knees remained swollen and he experienced difficulty moving. He refused to let me help him walk and it was painful to watch his first foray out into the gardens and see what had become of the old, big, noisy Kilsyth.

He was the sweetest-tempered invalid I've ever come across. He made me chase after one of Johnny Faa's peacocks to pull a feather to replace the one in his bonnet – 'A symbol that I'll be striding the Highland braes afore Yuletide.' But, looking back, I think it was then he made up his mind not to see Scotland again.

His face lit up whenever Bratchet walked into the room. He said to both of us, 'It was yon woman who'd not let me go down. She said she'd keep me back from hell. And she did. And she shall.' He assumed from the first that there was a contract between them. He never suspected.

'For Christ's sake tell him,' I said when we were alone.

'When he's better.'

What haunted me, for him, for us, was that he wouldn't ever get better. There was a desperation to Bratchet's lovemaking now. We didn't laugh any more.

We planned Kilsyth's first excursion to Spanish Town, where Bratchet wanted to make enquiries about Anne and Mary at the courthouse, but when the morning came he didn't feel up to it, though he insisted that we go. 'Ye've been grand nurses and deserve a day in the fleshpots. No, no, you're looking peakit, lassie. Where'll I be if you break down?'

We borrowed Faa's trap. The Bratchet was unusually quiet on the drive in. I put it down to uneasiness at what she'd find. A note to the governor from Kilsyth and a note from the governor to the courthouse gave us the services of a young clerk who, like all the court staff, was recently out from England and, judging from his sulkiness, wished he wasn't.

'I'll need the date of the trial,' he said.

I told him we didn't know it. Mary had still been in Europe in 1703. Some time after that she'd made for St-Germain and been given money by Francesca Bard for her rescue of Anne. Then she'd had to find her way to Jamaica, discover Anne's where-abouts, make her way into the country of the Maroons, become a pirate . . . 'Try 1705,' I told him. The trial couldn't have been before then.

It had been a good year for trials, had 1705. The clerk un-rolled what seemed like a thousand transcripts, then allowed them to whirr themselves back over their wooden roller with a carelessness that began to get on my nerves. The Bratchet stood at the window, staring down into Spanish Town's square, unmoving.

The clerk's puffing and sighing got louder as he went through 1705's August's transcripts, then September's, then October's. November's whirred themselves up. The room smelled of parchment mouldering in the humidity.

'Ain't here,' the clerk said.

'Start on 1706.'

I was being chopped up at Ramillies in the May of 1706. In the July Aunt Effie was being murdered. Defoe stood in the pillory later the same month. The attempts began on Bratchet's life. I walked over to join her at the window. 'I bet the only one came out of that year the same as he went in was old Daniel Defoe.' She didn't answer.

'Here it is,' said the clerk, disgustedly.

Somehow I hadn't expected it to be found. Anne Bonny and Mary Read belonged in people's heads, not on paper. But there it was: 6 January 1706.

I snatched it from the clerk's hand and took it to the window and read it out loud to the Brachet. The two women had been formally accused of 'evil designs in that they did, off the coast of Haiti, piratically, feloniously and in a hostile manner, attack, engage and take two merchant Sloops along with Apparel and Tackle valued at £1,000'. Later the same month they took a schooner, owner Thomas Spenlow near Harbour Bay and a merchant sloop of which Thomas Dillon was master.

Specimen charges. From what we'd learned from other pirates and the higgler, they'd done a damn sight more pirating than that. Like Rackham and the others had done, Anne and Mary pleaded not guilty, but the evidence against them was damning.

Thomas Spenlow swore that when he was taken, the women were aboard Rackham's sloop. Two Frenchmen who'd been impressed into Rackham's service said the women were 'very active on board' and that when Rackham gave chase or attacked, Bonny and Read wore 'men's cloaths, and at other Times they wore Women's Cloaths'. Thomas Dillon stated that, when Rackham's crew boarded his vessel, Anne Bonny 'had a Gun in her Hand. That they were both very profligate, cursing and swearing much, and very ready and willing to do any Thing on Board.'

It was a bare account and the two women's voices were silent in it. I put my arm round Bratchet's shoulder for a moment, then turned to the clerk. 'There's no record of the defence.'

He was leaning against a wall, arms folded, eyes closed. He yawned. 'If the whores said anything they'd have said it at their interrogation before the trial.'

'Very well. Where's the record of the interrogation?'

He shrugged. 'Missing.'

I made him look through the rest of January and, for good measure, February, but he was right.

Bratchet nudged me. 'You haven't finished reading the trial.'

'It's the sentence.'

'Read it.'

I read it. 'You, Mary Read, and Anne Bonny, are to go from hence to the Place from whence you came, and from thence to the Place of Execution; where you shall be severally hang'd by the Neck till you are severally Dead. And God of His infinite Mercy be merciful to both of your Souls.'

'Merciful,' said Bratchet, 'Merciful. Oh, God. They were pregnant.'

'"After Judgement was pronounced, as aforesaid, both the Prisoners informed the Court that they were both quick with Child, one by Jack Rackham and the other by his First Mate, and prayed that Execution of the Sentence might be stayed. Whereupon the Court ordered that Execution of the said Sentence should be respited, and that an Inspection should be made."'

I finished reading and turned to the clerk. 'Was it?'

'I don't know.'

'For God's sake, there must be a record of what happened to them.'

'No, there ain't,' snapped the clerk, 'or it would've been put on the bottom of the transcript.'

I told him to find me the trial of Calico Jack. He opened his mouth to protest, then looked at me, shut it and turned back to the cupboard.

The trial of Anne's and Mary's captain had taken place ten days before their own. He and his crew had been executed the following day. There were ten of them: Captain John Rackham, known as Calico Jack, George Fetherton, Richard Corner, Noah Harwood, James Dobbin . . . The names of the crew could have been found in any country English parish register. Nobody'd asked how or why they came to be pirates on a sloop in the West Indies. I noticed that Joshua, the higgler's son, wasn't among them.

The young clerk had shown no interest even as I'd read out the transcript of the women's trial, as if English girls turned pirate every day. I wondered if finding himself in this bizarre country left him with no amazement to spare for anything else.

Bratchet said desperately, 'There must be some record somewhere.'

The clerk said, 'Ask the gaoler.'

He showed us a flight of stairs but didn't follow us down. We descended from a hallway smelling of beeswax polish and pomanders down flights so steep we had to spread our hands against the wall to keep our balance – and found them sticky.

At the bottom we came into a stench caused by too many bodies kept too long without sanitation in too small a space. Further along the passage there was a high-pitched screaming coming from cells and I had to shout over it for the gaoler. He turned up with a lantern and a friendlier welcome than the clerk upstairs. 'Don't see many gentry down here.'

He was another newcomer to Jamaica, a sailor whose naval days had ended with a musket ball in the leg during the Battle of Vigo Bay. 'Luckier than most poor canvas-climbers, I was,' he told me, 'Recommended to the Vice-Admiralty for duties by Hoppson hissel.' He seemed happy enough in his job; when it came to darkness, stink and overcrowding there isn't much difference between prison cells and below decks on a man o'war. He took us to his 'locker', a cubby-hole where a small, barred window let in the sun, fetched down a ledger, turning back its pages until he found the reference. 'Here we are, lady and gentleman. "Paid to Daisy the midwife . . ."' Now I remember *her*, beamy old besom and black as coal. Used to attend all the births, ". . . 2*s*. for the lying-in of two female pirates." Don't get many of *them* to the dozen.'

'What happened to the babies?' asked Bratchet.

The gaoler scanned the page and shook his head. 'Mostly they go to the midwife till they're old enough for the orphanage.'

Christ, how many children had been born here? I said, 'What happened to the women pirates? Upstairs they can't find any record.'

'Can't they now, can't they? What was their names again? Let's see.' He leafed through more pages; he didn't seem to hear the screams coming from the passage. 'Well, here's one of 'em dead. "For the interment of the female pirate, Mary Read . . . 6*s*."'

It was Mary who was dead then. 'And the other? Anne Bonny?'

More leafing. Another shake of the head. 'Ain't here. Could be she died like her shipmate, could be she didn't. Mind you, they didn't keep records ship-shape till I come. Anyways, female or no, pirates is accounted along o' bilgewater round here, and serve 'em right.'

I suggested there might be graves, which amused him. He led us into a bare, hot courtyard. Half its ground was baked concrete by the sun, the other half was dug-over earth. 'Less'n they hang in chains, that's where they go.' He pointed to the disturbed section, 'Quicklime.'

Bratchet stood there a long time. Maybe she still clung to the belief that Anne and Mary were alive. She knew more than I did.

If she didn't, if she was saying goodbye, she'd come thousands of miles to find nothing to say goodbye to. No tree – quicklime would kill it – no plaque. There wasn't a flowering weed, any weed – our tidy gaoler had whitewashed the stones of the walls – not a butterfly, not a bird, no scent except sour earth; a space of sun-bleached nothing.

She said quietly, 'Shall I be Queen of England, Bratchet?' She turned on the gaoler. 'I want to meet this midwife, Daisy.'

'Dead, miss. Died two year ago. We use another un now.'

'Then I want to see where they had their babies.'

He was pleased, 'Got a special cell for trollops' lying-in. Big, see, and plenty of straw and a course I keeps it clean.'

The passage narrowed as it passed between the cell fronts of open bars. Black-skinned and white-skinned hands stretched out as we went by, not so much to touch us as salute the passing of the gaoler's lantern, the only light. The madman redoubled his screams and kicked his bars. Bratchet kept her eyes straight ahead. From one cell a woman's voice shouted for water. Not unkindly, the gaoler called, 'Dipper's hoisted, chuck. Give you some tonight.' He explained to us, 'Water's rationed.'

The birthing cell was at the end, double the size of the others. It was empty just now; only a taper and a grizzle-headed Negro sweeping out by the light of it, ready for the next delivery. I wondered why he bothered to keep it clean, the smell from the other cells was enough to snuff out new life the moment it took breath.

I asked the old black man his name. It was the gaoler who answered. 'That's Pompey. He's the one to ask about your pirates. Been here years, ain't you, Pompey?'

Pompey said nothing.

'Do you remember an Anne Bonny and Mary Read who gave birth in this place?' I got a grunt for an answer. The gaoler spun a finger round his temple to indicate idiocy.

Bratchet stayed where she was. 'I'd like to talk to you sometime,' she said, quietly, to Pompey. 'What's your address?'

His amusement told us slaves didn't have addresses and that this one wasn't an idiot.

'He sleeps in an empty cell, when he can find it,' said the gaoler. 'He don't have to. The magistrates freed un, but he duddn' have nowhere else to go.'

Outside in the glare of the plaza, I said, 'I wonder which of them had Rackham's baby and which had the First Mate's.'

Bratchet said nothing. She looked very small.

'It's over, Bratchie,' I said. 'Time to go home.'

On the way back, I had to rein in the horses and hold her for a long time while she cried. I didn't know then that some of the grief was for her and me.

We told Kilsyth what we'd discovered. 'So she's dead,' he said to Bratchet, reaching for her hand. 'The Lady Anne is dead. They couldna even bother to record it.'

'Yes.'

'Thrown in a hole like a clout into a stank.'

'Yes.'

He nodded. 'Better she'd died long since, with the piper playing a piobaireachd for her and the wind fluttering the ribands on his drones and the women clapping their hands and crying the coronach.'

That night was our last in the little, uncomfortable bed. The next day, when we walked in the garden, she told me Kilsyth had asked her to marry him.

I stood still.

'And I'm going to, Martin.'

After a while, I said, 'What for?'

She put her arm through mine and led me under a fig tree where we couldn't be seen, then she stood back, took a deep breath and folded her hands, like a child trying to remember its catechism.

'He's lost everything,' she said, 'All this long way and he dreamed he'd find Anne at the end of it. All he's found is she wasn't the woman he dreamed about. It's wrecked him. The yellowjack, this thing in his bones, they're grief really. He'll never be the same again. He knows it. He won't go back to Scotland, he says he couldn't bear his folk to see him like he is now. He hasn't got anything left.'

'That's no bloody reason why he should have you,' I said.

'Exactly why he should have me. I can be useful to him.'

'You're not a fucking walking stick,' I shouted, 'I'm-feeling-a-bit-shaky-today-will-you-marry-me? These last years ain't been a bed of roses for any of us. All right, he was disappointed in his Anne. So what? He hasn't seen her since she was a child.'

'Don't get cross.'

'I'm bloody furious. You're not a damn consolation prize.'

And then she said what I'd been afraid of all along. She said, 'I can't give you any children.'

'You can't give him any, either.' Cruel maybe, but I was desperate.

'There's got to be some use for a barren life. A purpose. He needs me, you don't.'

'Wrong again,' I told her.

The irritating thing was, she was calm. 'Martin,' she said, 'I love you like I didn't think was possible. Till the end of my days I'll wish I was in bed with you. But you're complete. You get things right. You're the one who guards people's backs. You even take care when you're tying your shoelaces. I want you to find somebody who's whole, like you are, and marry them. Have complete children. I'd waste you. I owe you my life, but I'm giving it to somebody who needs it more. I'm Kilsyth's woman.'

'I can't stand it, Bratchie,' I said.

'You can stand anything.'

'Fuck you.'

She tried smiling. 'You did. But I'm still Kilsyth's woman.'

I can see her now, stood under that fig tree. Odd it was a fig. A long time ago, at the beginning, Daniel Defoe and I saw a woman under a fig tree, higher-class than mine, perhaps more beautiful. But the one in Jamaica was all I wanted, and couldn't get.

Kilsyth and I attended the Vice-Admiralty Court together before I went. We told the judge we'd originally been journeying from The Hague to England in a Dutch boat. (We reckoned the Vice-Admiralty might have the English shipping list but they wouldn't have the Hollanders'.)

We said we'd been captured in the Channel by the *Holy Innocent*, taken on board and kept prisoner, freed by mutiny and forced to assist the crew, had witnessed the taking of the Spanish cargo ship and eventually been set free in the Bahamas. Easy as kiss my hand. It was no skin off the Vice-Admiral's nose if some loyal English lads liberated Spanish cargo. Not as long as they didn't start liberating anybody else's on their own account.

The judge questioned us closely on the mutineer/pirates' names. As it was inconceivable we'd spent time in their company without learning them, we had to tell him and hope to Christ the lads stayed clear of capture. I don't think the judge would have been as understanding if Kilsyth hadn't been related to the governor. As it was, both he and I left the court with handshakes and no stain on our characters.

After that, Johnny Faa's coachman drove me and Kilsyth and the Bratchet to Bridgetown harbour where the *Laird o' Kirkaldy* was waiting to set sail for Bristol.

Kilsyth spent most of the way begging me at least to stay for the wedding the following day in Spanish Town cathedral. 'Who has the better right to stand up for me than you have, my lad? It'll be sad festivity without ye.'

I said the tide waited for no man. 'And you can stand up for yourself now.'

He was better, though his hands had become clawed. Bratchet held them between hers as she leaned over the trap side to give my cheek a brief kiss. She wanted to leave immediately but Kilsyth insisted the trap stay on the quayside until we cast off. He was crying.

I'd spent nights wondering whether they'd be safe without me to look after them, and decided they would. There weren't likely to be more questions from the Vice-Admiral. And whoever'd killed Aunt Effie had achieved their purpose and sent Bratchet to where she could do no harm, so there'd be no trouble from that quarter.

They'll be all right, I thought, me and my shoelaces, as the gap of water between the quay and the ship widened, and the two figures in the trap grew smaller.

At the last moment, Bratchet waved.

I didn't wave back.

CHAPTER SEVENTEEN

Sixth Extract from *The Madwoman's Journal*

I RECEIVED a note yesterday which sent me chasing to Wapping and the Bladebone. I shook Jem by his greasy jacket. 'Is it true?'

'Aye, seems so. Did thee know Hempen Moffatt from the old days? Sailed with Jennings? Took to whaling in Bahamas waters and found hisself a boulder of amber grease . . .'

I shook him again. 'I'll close your dead lights, you maggot. Just tell me.'

'Aye,' he said, 'poor Captain Porritt. Drinking in Davy Jones's tavern now, it do seem. Old Moffatt he sailed in Monday, fresh from the Windies to spend his fortune, the which he is doing to his loss and my profit, and he told me. He'd met up with the *Holy Innocent* in the Bahamas, only she's called the *Brilliana* now. Crew'd mutinied, d'ye see, and turned pirate. No sign of Porritt nor the officers.'

'And the Mark?'

He nodded. 'She was there. Couldn't be no one else. Only female aboard. Small, fair and pocks on her cheeks.' He poured me a tot and I drank it.

'They'd made her purser, the mutineers. She's another such as you was, I reckon. Ah, there's more lady pirates on the account these days than you can shake a stick at.' He squinnied at me. 'Makes it awkward, like. Her being one of the Brotherhood now. Do ee still want her marked?'

I drank another tot while I thought about it, then told him no. I think I was right. Where's the point? Dangle that girl in shit and she'll come up coated in sugar. She's far enough away, in any case. And besides, if she's joined the Brotherhood she's put herself out of court. Who'd take the evidence of a woman pirate against a woman of the royal bedchamber? She can live.

I don't remember getting home, though, and it wasn't the rum. I was only conscious of *her*. She was visible, I swear; the alleys shook with her screams at being thwarted yet again. She still wants the Bratchet dead.

The creature's new device of bleeding affects my eyes so that sometimes I can see nothing but blood. By day, it drips out of Carrots' hair and spurts out of Queen Ant's feet as I rub them. Abigail's slippers send wavelets of it against the skirting board of the room.

It must be the atmosphere around town that affects her; the air is full of violence. Yet, officially, we are at peace. At last. On Good Friday, about two o'clock in the afternoon a post-chaise came rattling down Whitehall and stopped at the Cockpit. Out jumped St John's half-brother, George, with the Treaty of Utrecht in his hand. The peace with France and Spain had finally been ratified. Queen Ant fell on her knees in thankfulness.

But if there is peace between countries there is none between men. Everyone is trying to murder everyone else. With the Tories in control, the Whigs are become desperate. Before he could be replaced, our Whig ambassador in Paris, the Earl of Stair, engaged men to assassinate the Pretender. He failed, but it shows the lengths to which Whigs will go to try and ensure the accession of George I.

Indeed, Harley uncovered a plot by the more desperate Whigs to draw their swords in the House of Commons itself and fall upon such ministers as oppose the Hanovers. That too was nipped in the bud.

It is said that the Mohocks who terrorize the streets by night are really Whigs in disguise seeking to devour Tories. By day the streets are nearly as violent as by night; men and women quarrel over the tracts pouring off the presses, Tory and Whig, attacking the other's cause. The writers of them hire gangs to protect themselves and these rowdies fight when they meet. Even the Court women go armed and avoid dark alleys.

The Duke of Hamilton, a Jacobite Tory, was to be sent to Paris to replace Stair as British ambassador, but before he could go, he was challenged to a duel in Hyde Park by the Whig Earl of Mohun. Each fool managed to kill the other.

The only one who stops the country from ripping apart is our fat, humdrum Queen. Without the respect both Whigs and Tories have for her there would be civil war. There *will* be civil war when she dies. Everyone knows it. And she is increasingly unwell.

She could be better if her ministers were not trying to tear her in two. The jealousy between Robert Harley and St John sickens her. She had to grant St John a title because he has been the author of the peace between herself and King Louis. She didn't want to do it; St John is flagrantly unfaithful to his wife and Queen Ant disapproves. So she created him merely Viscount Bolingbroke where she had made Harley Earl of Oxford.

St John fell into a rage with mortification. 'The people lionize me, even the French lionize me – and instead of rewarding, the great mare has punished me.'

He is not lionized by our Dutch allies; the treaty he made with Louis as good as throws them to the wolves. In this, I think, he has been short-sighted, for the Hanoverians have been great friends to the Dutch and they to the Hanoverians. The peace has placed George of Hanover firmly in the camp of the Whigs. The Tories, he feels, have betrayed him. If St John, therefore, is to continue his rise to power under the next reign, he must see to it that it is the reign of James III and not George I.

The one person missing from all this is the Duke of Marlborough, the man who brought Louis to his knees in the first place. The Tories vilified him to Queen Ant until you might have thought he was responsible for every crime since the Gunpowder Plot. Had Sarah not offended Her Majesty past bearing, he might have survived politically. As it was, Queen Ant dismissed her former friend and greatest general with a letter so curt that he is said to have thrown it into the fire. Sarah has joined her husband in his exile and the court is quieter, but poorer, for her absence.

I think it has all broken the Queen's heart. She was taken so ill at Windsor this Christmas she nearly *did* die and I feared you and I, my darling, had lost our race. It was a violent ague followed by gout of the stomach. We are still at Windsor, waiting for her recovery. It is obvious that her time – and ours – grows short.

Undoubtedly she could halt at least some of the mayhem if she named which, out of James Stuart and George of Hanover, she wishes to succeed her, but she won't. She is a democratic queen. Parliament took steps at the beginning of the reign to safeguard the succession for a Protestant heir and she had set herself to abide by that. But she is still haunted by her father for her defection in the Glorious Revolution, demanding that she pay for that betrayal by bringing back his son. I know he does, because last night she saw him; she was overtaken by a horror, sat up, rigid, eyes staring. Perhaps, like the creature, the phantom bled.

The macaw could see it and shrieked continually. Danvers ran for the doctors, while Carrots and I soothed her. It was a long night and by the time the morning came we were all four exhausted.

The creature had set herself up on a curtain with the cord round her neck so that her head hung askew. Blood gushed from her mouth like rain out of a gargoyle's. The dawn light from the window came through its fall, tainting furniture and women with scarlet. I proffered the chocolate to a queen that was massacred.

Abigail came in, all solicitude. 'My poor, dear Majesty, why did you not call me? What ails that bird? Let me take it away.'

Her Majesty didn't call Abigail, nor would she allow her to remove the macaw, because she is displeased with her for being seduced by St John. (When I say 'seduced' I talk of the mind only; even St John wouldn't bed with that broomstick.) Undaunted, the woman who used to press Harley's cause now presses St John's in a monotone. It is no wonder the screams of a fowl are preferable. At last she finished droning, and went.

The Queen indicated I draw the curtain and I lifted the pot out of the close stool but she waved it away and instead produced the box from under her pillows. I pressed my nails harder into my hands to keep sensible a while longer. Hold, hold.

'I am haunted, my dear. I cannot rest for thinking that there may be another Stuart in need ... my mind would be settled about this poor girl before I die.'

Despite the shouts of the macaw and the creature, I pretended to think. 'I wonder, madam, Anne Bard had a close friend called Mary Read ... I remember that before she disappeared she went away on a visit to Mary Read's parents. They might have some knowledge of the matter.'

'Oh, excellent,' she said. 'But can they be found?'

I tapped my hand on my lips, amazed she could not see the blood from it flow down my chin. Hold, steersman. Hold. Hold. Not long now. 'I think they were country folk. Mary once mentioned they lived Suffolk way. Ipswich, was it?'

She huffed with determination and I smelled the cold tea which is now an open secret she drinks so much of it. 'Go you to Ipswich, my dear. Find them. The sea air will revive you; you are pale. You are too devoted and I have been remiss in working you over hard.' She told Carrots to bring the purse and gave me thirty pounds out of it. I kissed her hand a dozen times and waded out of the room.

I did not, of course, go to Ipswich, nor even to Highgate, but, in disguise and making sure I was not followed, to a certain house in Southwark where I collapsed. Rachel took away my knife and locked me in a room while I kicked and frothed.

An interesting woman, Rachel. A negress who was brought to England by her master, Lord Gosse. When he tired of her, he gave her passage money to return to Africa. Instead, she set up in business. She did so well out of those white men who are attracted to black women and their arts that she now owns one of the largest brothels in Southwark. She specializes in the orgy trade and has had built a Greek temple in her back garden beneath the trees for her girls and clients to cavort in the nude with grapes, but there are rooms for other tastes and my shouts and swearing went unremarked for being regarded as coming from one of those.

Like Asantewa in Jamaica, Rachel is an Ashanti and practises obeah. When the worst of the fits was over, she unlocked the door and began the magic to rid me of the creature. She cannot do the dances because she has become immensely fat – indeed, were it not for her colour she would closely resemble Her Majesty – but has trained one of her girls to perform them while she attends to the rattles and chanting and the sacrifice of the cockerels.

At first the creature merely giggled. I nearly did myself. However, as the night wore on she became afraid as, again, so did I. Remember Nannytown, my dear? Of course you do. It was like that.

Into the little London room came the scent of orchids and rotting plants and palm thatch and the sweat off black skin. The walls expanded to become mountains where cataracts fell down the ravines like twirling white ribbon. I was walking again through moonlight to the flat rock where no men are allowed and where there is the cauldron that bubbles without fire and where women are possessed by the sacred insanity and where you and I swore to the Great Mother to take our revenge, and Asantewa's, on English enslavers. We owed it to Asantewa for our rescue. We owed it to ourselves. It was like that.

After I don't know how many hours, the dancer fell down, the rattles and chanting became a whisper and Jamaica faded into a small, Southwark room.

It cannot be said the creature had been exorcized, but she was cowered in a corner, a third of the size she had been. She had stopped bleeding. I slept for two days without waking or dreaming. When I got up I gave Rachel twenty-five of the thirty pounds and went back to the palace, ready for the last stage of the plan.

Though the creature does not like it, I am proud of Bratchet. Proud and envious. She has known it, then; felt the tilt of the deck under her feet, shared that comradeship, seen the Caribbean dawn, watched the turquoise flash of its sunset splinter across the sea. Whatever they do to you, Bratchet, whatever *she* forces me to do to you, you have shared the doomed, wild freedom that we knew, forbidden to all women but the bravest.

Live on it, Bratchet. You will pay for it. They will take it away from you. Remember.

CHAPTER EIGHTEEN

FOUR MONTHS after her marriage to Kilsyth, Bratchet discovered she was putting on weight.

The ladies of the circle she now moved in thought she was too, and began to hint. Mrs Chantry did more than hint. 'Here, Bratchie,' she said, 'We going to hear the patter of little Scotsmen?'

Bratchet explained that she couldn't have children. 'I don't have flows, Judy. I'm barren.'

Mrs Chantry, who was expecting her own baby, guffawed. 'Don't look like it to me. Must've fallen immediate.'

By the fifth month it didn't look like it to Bratchet, either.

She went to the parish church when it was empty and sang her own, qualified form of magnificat. God had fooled her into making the greatest sacrifice of her life by letting her think she was barren. On the other hand, if she *hadn't* made it He might not have given her this gift of fertility. She went home and told Kilsyth they were to have a child.

Home was Coppleston's, the house which Sir Timothy Coppleston, the absentee owner of the estate, had built when he first came to the West Indies, before he'd made his fortune and moved into what was known as the Big House where Johnny Faa now lived.

By the time Sir Timothy had built the Big House he'd learned a thing or two about how to survive the Jamaican climate; he modelled his building on the Spanish haciendas then still to be seen in St Jago de la Vega. He gave its rooms low ceilings and a wide door at both ends to encourage a through draught, verandahs around its three storeys encircling a cool, central courtyard.

He'd learned his mistakes from Coppleston's, his first home in Jamaica when, like most emigrants, he'd been homesick and built a house as much like an English manor as he could. He'd made it in brick with a high hall, a parlour and a carved mahogany Jacobean staircase. He'd put in large windows and glazed them. Even more disastrously, he'd distrusted ventilation as unhealthy and had shielded himself from the night air, especially the sea breeze, by putting no windows at all in the east side.

Then he'd decorated his parlour with hangings and snuggled up at nights in a curtained bed with three successive wives and, after their successive deaths, if the stories were true, with several black mistresses. Bratchet, living there, wondered not so much at his prowess with women as his stamina. The place was a sweat-house. Johnny Faa charged them a high rent for it, but Bratchet was so grateful to get away from the Big House that she'd have paid more for a mud hut.

Johnny's attitude towards them had altered since Kilsyth's fever, as if illness had reduced the necessity to show off to a man who had once commanded his envy and now deserved little more than contempt. It had been displayed in little things. The slim and beautiful mulatto girl whom Faa called his housekeeper began to sit at table opposite him, a position formerly given to Bratchet when they all dined together. There were no more meals concocted to tempt Kilsyth's appetite back. If they borrowed the trap, no one was supplied to drive it which meant that, to save Kilsyth's hands, an inept Bratchet had to take the reins.

They couldn't complain; Johnny Faa had provided a very necessary port in their storm. These were not unreasonable straws, but the wind which blew them had a cutting edge and the couple had taken their warning.

At Coppleston's, Bratchet disposed of the hangings, which were anyway mildewed, took out the glazed windows and replaced them with jalousies. Against all advice, she and Kilsyth made a window with shutters in the east wall and let the sea breeze do its worst. It was still a sticky place to live in but the alterations made it bearable, while its height – it was a mile into the hills from the Big House – commanded pleasant views downwards to the south, east and west.

The north was a different matter. A cellar that had once stocked sugar hogsheads extended out from beneath the house, its wooden trapdoor now covered with leaves and mosses.

Here, shaded by a giant cottonwood tree, the parlour window and that of the bedroom above looked out on to a rise on which Coppleston had built his first sugar mill.

Bratchet had taken against cane the first day she saw it and nothing about turning it into sugar – a process that took place a hundred yards from her tiny garden – altered her dislike. Human suffering marked every stage, from planting between October and December to harvesting sixteen months later, between January and May.

She and Kilsyth took up residence in May when gangs of slaves, females with babies on their back among them, cut the cane with curved knives called bills, removed the outer leaves, bundled the stalks and carted them to the mill for grinding. The mill was a horror, an open contraption consisting of three vertical rollers, turned by plodding teams of oxen, into which a slave millman fed the canes to be crushed so that their dark brown juice could flow down the rollers into a trough which led through pipes to the boiling house.

Just before the newlyweds moved into Coppleston's, a slave unwarily feeding the mill had got his fingers caught in the rollers and the rest of his body had been drawn in. Hearing about it, Bratchet learned that it wasn't an isolated incident. 'Oh that happens,' her nearest white, female neighbour, Mrs Sewell, said, sighing, 'They *never* get the oxen to stop in time. We lost two men like that and one of them was really valuable.'

Then there was the boiling house, adjacent to the mill. Ever after, when she heard mention of hell, into Bratchet's mind's eye came a picture of the Coppleston boiling house, literally a furnace on which the cane juice was boiled in successively smaller vats, the largest holding 180 gallons, gradually skimmed, evaporated and poured into the smaller vats until it became a thick, dark brown, ropy syrup.

A mistake by the slave in charge of pouring the bubbling syrup into its cooling cistern could – and had – resulted in agony to himself and anybody too close. It stuck to the flesh and couldn't be got off.

At nights The Undertaker, blowing down from the hills, filled her rooms with the sweet smell of boiled sugar, combining it with the aroma of molasses from the distilling house on the other side of the mill to give the air a viscosity thick enough to chew.

As for rum itself, she and Kilsyth forswore it on the day they watched Johnny Faa publicly pour the contents of his chamber pot into the distillery's vat of fermenting alcohol. Catching sight of their faces, he explained, 'Stops the niggers frae drinking the brew.'

Walking back with her to the house, Kilsyth said, 'Will ye credit the man exports the stuff? Lord be thanked Scotland drinks whisky.'

He himself was beginning to drink brandy fairly heavily. It dulled the pain that was distorting his feet and the knuckles of his hands. With Madeira, it was the accepted drink of the richer planter society they moved in, which regarded rum as fit only for fuddling slaves and poor whites.

Bratchet didn't blame him. The effort he was making to alter his idea of himself from a young warrior racing into battle with his clan to raise the Stuart banner over the green moors of Scotland to that of a man old before his time, crippled in exile in a country he didn't really like, was titanic and reduced her almost to tears. Several times she suggested they sail home, but he was adamant to stay.

'My pride'll not tolerate going back without I can offer my sword to my chief,' he said, and held out his hand to her, showing it could no longer wield one.

As she kissed it, she thought that never before had she seen someone who imposed the rules of Christianity on himself rather than on other people. Until now she'd not realized that faith was anything other than a word brayed by marketplace preachers. Even Mary of Modena's gentle Catholicism had accorded with her nature.

But for her husband to accept his loss of strength with the patience he did put up a good argument for both him and his god. Like Job, he believed he was being punished for a purpose; 'I'll mebbe be called on to perform a deed or two yet,' he said, 'We'll see, we'll see.'

If brandy helped him, then Bratchet was content to see him swig it – while they could afford it. But she worried about their finances, the only one of them who did. Kilsyth had no idea about money; he came from a grand, threadbare tradition. If the larder was empty you went out and shot a deer. You forgave a tenant an unpaid rent when he paid you with a salmon poached from your own stream, you kept a rabble of retainers, your personal piper doubled as a gardener, you flung your purse at a deserving cause, trusting the Lord to make up the difference. Greatest of all the commandments, you repaid hospitality. Which, Bratchet decided, was all very well and she was prepared to go along with it. Until she found she was pregnant.

Suddenly she was overwhelmed by a ferocious responsibility. She'd cheat, she'd kill if necessary, but here was one baby that would never experience Puddle Court or its like. So far their pirate loot was holding out but sooner, not later, they would have to find an income. She took advantage of Kilsyth's euphoria at the news that he was to become a father and said, 'Wouldn't it be better, Livingstone, if we didn't accept all these invitations? We only have to have the buggers back.' A request for the pleasure of their company at a ball or dinner arrived every day.

He winked at her, 'We'll accept the feasts. But we'll cut out the balls, as Martin Millet would say.' He referred to his friend frequently. Bratchet wished he wouldn't.

Kilsyth was a social animal. Since he now couldn't sit astride a horse comfortably long enough to indulge his favourite Scottish pastime of hunting – anyway, the planters were not great hunters, except of runaway slaves – he responded to the sirens of billiards, shuffle-board, the local 'clack', eating and drinking.

Despite Bratchet's protests, he bought a billiard table at a Spanish Town sale of bankrupt stock and installed it into the hall at Coppleston's where, with the dining table, it took up most of the room. He didn't mind that it was worn and scratched; it enabled him to give a return match to Sewell, Waller, Featherstone, Chantry, Faa and the others with whom he'd enjoyed 'the grand game' as he called it. This was his attitude to everything. That his house was shabby didn't worry him; he wasn't out to keep up appearances, but the food, drink and entertainment he offered must be as good and as plentiful as he'd received. And this was expensive.

The trouble was that the planters were nostalgic feeders: beer, bread and the beef of Old England was what they wanted. The local substitute for bread – cassava, corn or even plantain – wasn't to their taste so they imported flour from Pennsylvania, salt beef and pork from Ireland and England, both at enormous cost, and drank canary, brandy or Madeira like ale.

Roasting herself and huge meat joints in the outside cabin which served as her kitchen, Bratchet used Puddle Court expressions as she totted up what entertaining her neighbours to breakfast – the main meal of the day was always 'breakfast' – was costing.

'Hope it bloody chokes 'em,' she'd say. Nearly every male guest in her hall, even the youngest, was bloated with overeating, while his complexion suggested that one more swallow, one more mouthful, would tip him into apoplexy.

'And I wish it would,' she'd shout through the steam at Sarcy the cook, a former slave she now employed. That 'breakfast' was begun at midday, the hottest time there was, contributed to her bad temper though, wonderfully, it never diminished her guests' appetite.

'No wonder the bastards don't live to old age. If fever don't put 'em in their coffins, their diet and brandy will.'

When they weren't entertaining, she and Kilsyth ate lightly, partly from economy, but also from choice, buying corn, fruit, vegetables, salads and eggs from the estate's slaves, who kept their own gardens and hen runs, with the occasional supplement of island turkey or duck which Kilsyth could shoot with his recently acquired, second-hand fowling pieces from Coppleston's windows.

The staff – Sarcy – was inadequate for entertaining on any scale, pitiful at any time by planters' standards, and the other wives offered to lend her their house servants to help with the dinners. Bratchet refused; she couldn't bear to use slaves. She'd given forty-two-year-old Sarcy her freedom the moment she'd bought her at auction. Yet more help was needed.

She drove herself shakily in the ancient trap they'd bought, along with an equally ancient horse, to Spanish Town. When she came back Pompey, the elderly sweeper-out from the court-house, was at the reins. He wasn't a much better driver than she was.

'He can help out in ever so many ways,' she told Kilsyth.

'Are ye sure?' he asked, doubtfully. 'Will he carry against a breeze?'

In fact Pompey's health responded well to good food and a bed in the outhouse and his spirits even better to his few shillings a week salary, the first he'd ever had. He was never going to rival the tall, stately black butlers owned by the other planters but his slave-hood had been varied and he proved useful at odd jobs and serving at table.

From Bratchet's point of view his real usefulness lay in what information he could give her about Anne and Mary and their babies, though she left the business of questioning until later, when she'd won his trust.

As the Kilsyths continued to give and receive hospitality, what irritated Bratchet as much as the expense was the boredom. Theirs was a small society; part of their welcome into it was because they were new blood to relieve the familiarity of the old.

Queen Anne's war hardly interested the planters, except to wish it over so that freight and insurance rates could be reduced and they could recommence trading with Spain. The French had attempted an invasion of Jamaica in '94, which had laid waste the eastern parishes, but it had been beaten back and the island heavily garrisoned. Since then France had left them alone.

So the planters talked sugar; sugar's processing, sugar's extracts, sugar's export, sugar's price, and when they got to the stage of salacious jokes, which would at least have made a change, the cloth was drawn, and the ladies had to withdraw. The gentlemen settled down to put their backs into drinking, with a trencher of pipes and tobacco and a bowl of brandy laced with sugar on the table, while the ladies sat over coffee and Madeira in the parlour.

The ladies were as boring as their husbands, all except Bratchet's particular friend, Mrs Chantry, who was a Cockney like her husband. They'd come to Jamaica in 1707 and done so well their estate now covered 1,500 cane-growing acres of the Liguanea Plain.

Mrs Chantry was fat, friendly, unpretentious, interested in everything, interesting about everything; she could lecture on the smallest detail of household management and make it fascinating – it was thanks to her that Bratchet, an unlearned housekeeper, became adept at buying, stocking, preserving and cleaning in the Jamaican climate.

Best of all, Mrs Chantry was a gossip. She knew which planter slept with which slave, who was whose legitimate child and who wasn't, that Lady Hamilton wore a wig and didn't like the island, that Mrs Green, the cooper's wife in Halfway Tree, could afford silver lace for her daughter's wedding – a battery of information delivered with an uncensoriousness that was refreshing and caused Bratchet to wish Mrs Chantry had been in Jamaica for Anne's and Mary's trial.

It was a sad day when, owing to the late stages of pregnancy, Mrs Chantry had to stop visiting and being visited. 'An' Gawd help this one be a sticker, ducky,' she said as Bratchet wished her good luck, 'An' yours likewise.' Of the four babies she'd borne since arriving on the island only one survived.

Jamaica was hard on women and children. Males outnumbered females because women faced the hazard of childbirth on top of the usual tropical diseases like malaria and yellow fever. When a wife died a replacement was hard to find; often the widower didn't try too hard, contenting himself with a bedmate from among his slaves. So Mrs Chantry's departure from the social scene left Bratchet to spend breakfast afternoons – which usually lasted into the night – with a small core usually consisting of Mrs Sewell, Mrs Riley and Miss Waller.

Mrs Sewell could have won cups for boring; once she'd gained the conversational ball she ran with it and couldn't be stopped. Mrs Riley, presumably the sufferer of a secret sorrow, was a woman of such uncharitableness that her remarks, even when they referred to people not present, invariably left Bratchet feeling emotionally sore.

Miss Waller didn't talk at all. She was very young, a pallid fifteen-year-old, either too shy, too stupid or too nervous to say even so much as 'thank you'. Helyar Waller introduced her as his niece and proclaimed loudly on every occasion that he was out to find her a good husband but so far had discovered nobody good enough.

Like everybody else, Bratchet had found the girl irritating until the day that Mrs Chantry privately told her it was suspected in the community that Mary Waller was, in fact, not Helyar's niece but his daughter by one of his slaves. 'But she's white,' protested Bratchet.

'Happens,' said Mrs Chantry, shrugging, 'I seen babies fair as you born to ebonies black as coal. Take after their pa, see.'

'And what about the babies *they*'ll have? Are they white?'

'Can be,' Mrs Chantry had said, 'but sooner or later an ebony'll pop out into the family an' have to be smuggled out in a Moses basket.' She gestured Bratchet to come nearer. 'If she's who I think she is, Mary's ma's that house nigger of Waller's. The one called Juno. Never says a word to Mary in public; makes out she's no relation. Gives Mary a chance, see. Danger is if Mary *do* get a white husband she'll bear a sooty baby. Throwback. Funny old business.'

It seemed a tragic old business to Bratchet. She lost her irritation with Mary after that and tried to think more kindly of Waller himself than she had, but it wasn't easy. He was the richest planter in the area and owned over a hundred slaves, was a member of the council, a magistrate and a colonel of the militia, a large man with a head of white-gold curls that contrasted with the brutality of his face to give him the appearance of an overfed angel gone to the bad. His manners were gross, as if success absolved him from politeness. It was his voice which could be heard coming from the room where men smoked and drank, proffering advice on the proper treatment of slaves, usually 'starve 'em and flog 'em'.

In the parlour, discussion also centred on slaves, as in the richer households of England mistresses talked of the servant problem. There were no servants in Jamaica; it had been Anne Bonny's misfortune that she was among the last white women to be impressed for service in an island where it was being realized that slaves were cheaper and that, while there were laws protecting the feeding, clothing and treatment of white servants, there were virtually no legal responsibilities towards slaves.

A master could be fined as much as twenty-five pounds if he wantonly killed his slave – it was more for killing somebody else's – but since he could, and usually did, plead that the death had occurred in the course of a punishment for a misdemeanour and he hadn't meant to do it, his sentence was rarely more than nominal, even if he was found guilty, which was rarer still.

'The trouble with you, madam, is you're still thinking home,' said Mrs Riley to Bratchet, who'd expressed disapproval of a planter out at Wag Water for flogging one of his field hands to death. 'Time you saw 'em for what they are, animals that the good Lord saw fit to make human-like only in shape and speech.'

'True,' sighed Mrs Sewell, 'look at the way they dance on feast days, all that Alla Alla. Like monkeys. Why, the other day . . .'

Mrs Riley brought her down with a sliding verbal tackle: 'And you're no better, Sophie Sewell. I'd never let that Doll speak to me the way she talks to you, never. Dress your hair nice she may, but I'd stripe her for it, that I would.'

She returned to Bratchet's education. 'It's no good thinking home. They don't respond to kindness, I can tell you now, they're like savage dogs.'

Home-thinking was bad, the misdirected sentimentality of non-combatants who had no idea of what it was like at the front line where brave planters fought to keep them in sugar. 'Ain't you noticed their smell? You can smell a nigger a mile off.'

On and on it went, with Mary Waller sitting silent beside them, looking through the parlour window to where gleaming semi-naked bodies laboured beyond the cottonwood and, in

375

Bratchet's view, smelled somewhat fresher than the colonists' flesh in their perspiration-soaked worsteds and drugget.

They're afraid, she realized. Outnumbered eight to one, the whites of Jamaica had to deny humanity to the blacks, not only to keep their economy from breaking down, but to prevent their own annihilation. Slaves had to labour from dawn until dark, had to be underfed to break their resistance; any other treatment would be dangerous.

At least Waller was honest enough to admit it. What Bratchet found so offensive about Mrs Riley, Mrs Sewell and their like was that they blamed the blacks for being what their husbands made them. Denying them Christian education, any education, they jeered at the blacks for clinging to their tribal beliefs and customs and called them stupid when the mind-numbing monotony of the slaves' tasks was designed to stultify their intelligence.

And if it hadn't been for Licky, she might have believed them. It was so easy to get drawn in, to begin to fear the sullen faces that she could see from her window, to find the limited vocabulary amusing, the childishness irresponsible, the promiscuity reprehensible.

'And we don't like you giving Pompey and Sarcy their freedom.' Mrs Riley's voice recalled Bratchet's wandering mind to the present, like lemon spurting into the eye. 'Sets a bad example. We expect loyalty from our neighbours.'

'It was the courthouse freed Pompey,' Bratchet said, 'He was getting too old. They wanted rid of him.'

Mrs Riley pursed her lips. 'Sarcy, then. You shouldn't have done that.'

'Waller wanted rid of her. He put her up for auction. She was getting too old as well.'

By thirty-five, a slave was past his or her usefulness as a field hand, which was what Sarcy had been, and was given less arduous tasks, like driving the piccaninny gangs which did the weeding. Waller, with too many older females among his slaves, had exulted in selling the surplus Sarcy, openly telling Bratchet she'd got a bad bargain.

'He was going to throw her out to starve.' Bratchet remembered that Waller's 'niece' was in the room and glanced at her, but the girl Mary was staring out of the window as usual, and showed no sign of either approval or offence. She added, 'I thought she'd work better for having her freedom.' Why'd I say that? That's not why I did it. It's none of the bitch's business.

'Seems like it,' said Mrs Riley, with sarcasm, looking around at the partially dusted furniture, 'You can't train a field nigger to the house.'

'True,' said Mrs Sewell, 'I remember when . . .' She was up and running and this time nobody stopped her.

It was undeniable that Sarcy's vocation was not housework. Bratchet, needing help, had bought her because she was cheaper than a trained domestic, not understanding that Sarcy had never lived in anything but a hut and was as unfamiliar with the concept of dusting, polishing and cooking as a palm tree.

'But you must have peeled a pineapple before,' she'd said, after Sarcy's first experience with a paring knife, as she held Sarcy's bleeding hand under the pump.

'Bella Moll, she the peeler for niggers,' Sarcy had explained. Cooking communally for the *gunyahs*, the slave huts, was left to old women who had time for it.

Giving Sarcy her freedom had also proved more charitable than advantageous, to Bratchet's chagrin, because she couldn't bear the Riley woman to suppose she was right. It had taken time for Sarcy, born to slavery, to realize that she was entitled to a wage, minuscule as it was, and could walk out on the Kilsyths if she wanted. 'Where I go?' she'd asked suspiciously.

'I don't know, but you can go there if you want.'

Once the realization of her new condition had sunk in, Sarcy had become desperate to gain similar freedom for her daughter and grandchild, left behind on the Waller estate. 'You buy 'em, missy. Dey work for you free.'

'I can't afford it, Sarcy. He's asking more for her than we've got.' Sarcy's daughter, Dinnah, was a second-gang driver and therefore valuable. Her baby, only a month old, had been born with a club foot and Sarcy was terrified that Waller would sell the child away from its mother.

Fired by the previously undreamed-of possibility of happiness, Sarcy became a nagger, continually begging Bratchet to buy, or even steal, her family away from the feared Waller. Bratchet had become omniscient in Sarcy's eyes and it was difficult to explain to somebody who had never slept in a bed before that somebody who possessed three was short of money.

Gradually, however, the household settled down. As Bratchet's pregnancy went on she thought more and more about the two women who'd had their babies in the Spanish Town prison cell. She began to question Pompey. Getting answers was difficult, partly because his Jamaican accent was at first almost incomprehensible, secondly because the slave's law of not volunteering anything to whitey was ingrained in him.

At first he said he didn't remember.

'Yes you do,' Bratchet said, 'There ain't that many white women get thrown into Spanish Town gaol for piracy. Pompey, they were friends of mine. Tell me. I won't tell nobody else.'

She was sitting on the steps of Coppleston's, watching him curry one of the horses. They'd now acquired two. The old man was making a great business of it, his back towards her, bridle in one hand, comb in the other, hissing with effort at each long pass over the animal's hindquarters. She wondered if he'd heard her.

'Pompey, tell me,' she said again.

'Dey dead, missy. Bad births. Bubbas, ladies, all dead.'

She got herself up from the steps and swung him round by his shirt to look at her. 'Don't try that on me,' she said, 'They didn't all die. I *know*. Now tell me.'

He looked blank, his lower lip protruding like a child attempting to sulk, eyes rolling.

'Stop that I'm-a-loony-old-nigger-as-don't-know-nuffin' look,' Bratchet said, 'because you ain't. You're smart. You're the oldest nigger I know so you *must* be smart. You wouldn't have survived else.'

If life expectancy was short among whites, it was shorter among blacks. The number of grey-haired slaves she'd seen since taking up residence at Coppleston's she could count on one hand. Pompey's white frizzled cap was a badge of honour.

His lip pulled in and he smiled at her, showing fine, gapped teeth. 'I ain't drop down out a hollow tree,' he said. 'You say they friends, missy?'

'Yes. Good friends. What happened?'

'One die.'

'Ah.' Bratchet sat herself back on the steps.

When she looked up she saw Pompey staring at her. 'I call massa, missy?'

'No. Don't fuss. What happened to the other one?'

'The other one she escape. Don' ask which. Whitey ladies look the same an' dark night can' see cheese from chalk.'

Two dark-haired white women in the throes of childbirth in a badly lit cell. It would have been difficult for their mothers to tell them apart.

'How did she escape?'

He turned back to the horse, shrugging. 'Pompey don't know.'

'Yes Pompey does. Did she fly? Did the fairies dig a tunnel from outside? How?'

His shoulders hunched up and down and she realized he was giggling. 'Fairies,' she heard him say.

She dragged him round again. 'How?'

He wouldn't look at her, but stared at the sky. 'Dat one careless gaoler. He forget bolt de cell door an' de outside gate one time. De magistrate, he very cross with that careless old gaoler.'

She considered him carefully. 'It wasn't a careless old cell-sweeper who unbolted the door and the gate, was it?'

His glance at her was so sharp she knew she'd been a fool ever to patronize him. 'Cell-sweepers ain't careless, missy, or they get whuppin' make their skin fly.'

It had been him, she was sure of it. But the penalty for helping an escape, even one that had taken place years ago, would be so severe if the authorities discovered who the real culprit was that Pompey would never admit it.

She was amazed he'd been prepared to do it at all, if it *was* him. Whoever had unbolted the prison doors must have had a hellishly big incentive. Or bribe. She said, 'But even when she

379

got out there were sentries, guards. It's the centre of bloody Spanish Town.'

'They say they was riders outside waiting. She get up on one horse and they all git like the Devil ridin' after.'

A planned escape, then. The Brotherhood? 'The men with the horses,' she asked, 'were they pirates?'

'Pirates?' He seemed surprised, then shook his head. 'Pompey expec' they just the fairies.' He'd taken to that joke.

'What happened to the babies?'

The old face softened. She wondered if he'd watched the births. 'One dead when it pop out,' he said.

'And the other?'

'Midwife, she take it right away an' give it to de wet nurse up river by Li'l Occa's *gunyah*. But I hear later that bubby escape too.'

One baby, one mother, free. Which baby of which mother, he wouldn't know. Perhaps even the mother hadn't known. There'd have had to be some days, perhaps weeks, between the births and the escape, and a baby could change in that time so that the woman who'd borne it in a dark prison cell wouldn't know if it was hers. Or care that much; the love between Anne and Mary would cherish whichever child survived.

Although she tried, Bratchet could get no more out of the old man. Eventually she gave up. As she hauled herself up the steps to go to her room, she heard him chuckle as he started grooming the horse again. 'Fairies,' she heard him say, 'More like obeah.'

Shaken and tired, she lay on the double bed in the main bedroom and listened to the rattle and swish of the sugar mill as it pressed juice from the cane. It was hot. She felt the kicks of the baby in her stomach like the explosion of bubbles. 'Anne,' she said, 'Mary.'

She dozed. The grief-stricken dream revolved around fairies and galloping dark figures and waterspouts. 'Asantewa,' she heard herself saying and woke herself up to say it again. 'Asantewa.' She got up from the bed, went downstairs and out into the hot afternoon. Pompey was putting the horse in the lean-to that served for a stable.

She tapped him on the shoulder. 'It wasn't pirates waiting outside the gaol,' she said, 'it was Maroons.'

She watched his hand as it paused on the latch of the half-door. It had white patches on it. 'I don' hear you, missy,' he said.

She went back to the house, knowing she was right. It had come too late for one of them, but in their extreme need, Anne and Mary had called on the help of a fellow woman, their old friend the Queen of the Maroons.

She didn't tell Kilsyth. He wouldn't want to know. His Anne was long dead.

The news that peace had been signed with France came into Kingston on a naval cutter and was brought to the governor in Spanish Town, disseminating through the island by gallopers.

Privately, Lord Archibald told Kilsyth he was uncomfortable with its terms. 'England has made her separate peace with Louis and deserted the Dutch, the greatest of her allies. Marlborough, her greatest general, has been forced into exile by slanders and persecution. And a Bourbon still sits on the throne of Spain. Where's the glory in that?'

But the planters didn't care if England had made peace with Old Nick; the trade routes were open again and Britain had gained the valuable *asiento* monopoly to the slave trade in Spanish America.

Helyar Waller held the breakfast of all breakfasts to celebrate, and treated half the Liguanea Plain to fourteen types of beef, eight of fowl, three of pork, three of goat, suckling pig, mutton and veal with accompanying puddings of potato, bacon, oysters, caviare, anchovies, olives, custards, cheesecakes, syllabubs, creams, puffs and fruit and a dozen varieties of liquor to wash it all down.

Gathering his guests before the meal, he made them a speech to which Bratchet didn't bother to listen. He made another afterwards, more privately, away from listening black ears, to the male guests. The ladies could hear loud cheers coming from the direction of the house, as they rested in hammocks under the trees from the heat. They exchanged indulgent, sometimes nervous, smiles. The men were getting drunk again.

'What was all that in the billiard room?' asked Bratchet as Pompey drove her and Kilsyth back home up into the hills in the trap.

He roused himself, focusing with difficulty. 'Ach, they're after attacking the Maroons.'

'What?'

'Before the troops are called home. Now there's peace the troops'll be called home.'

'Yes,' she said, impatiently.

'Before they go, there's to be an all-out attack on the Maroons. Cannon, a' the rest of it. Wipe them out, Waller says. Once for aye.'

'Licky,' she said.

He flapped his hand warningly on her knee. 'I liked him fine, too. But ye'll admit he's been unco' pestf . . . pestiferous these last weeks.' He waved away a fly. 'I'll mebbe close my eyes a wee while.'

Licky.

The Maroons had been a thorn in the planters' flesh lately. The attack on them by armed planters and their dogs in reprisal for sheltering runaway slaves had resulted in little more than two deaths on either side, but it had brought the Maroons out of their mountain fastnesses angrily buzzing like disturbed bees, raiding outlying estates, driving off cattle, burning cane stores.

Colly Atkinson out at Kellitts had been killed defending his coffee crop. The bounty for the capture of any of the rebels had been doubled, but the difficulty of chasing them through mountains they knew like the palm of their hand prevented anyone claiming it.

Waller was right; only an all-out assault by infantry and artillery could inflict serious damage. Bratchet shook her husband's elbow. 'Where?'

'Whassit?'

'Where are the soldiers going to attack?'

'Wha's heathen name of it? Nannytown.'

Licky. What the planters called Nannytown was Licky's fortress in the Blue Mountains. Licky, who'd been brought back by his mother, the *ohemmaa*, the Queen of the Windward Maroons, to be their king, their *ohene*, because only she, the Rainmaker, who had the care of their gods, had the right of royal appointment.

Licky, whom Bratchet wouldn't exchange for all the planters on the Plain if they were gilded and came with trumpets.

She didn't even consider. She waited until they were back at Coppleston's and Kilsyth had been helped indoors to his bed. Then she followed Pompey out as he went to unharness the horse.

'Did you hear that?'

'What dat, missy?'

'Don't "what dat" me. You heard. You hear everything. Send the *ohene* a message. Warn him they're going to attack Nannytown with artillery.'

He put on his idiot look, head lolling, eyes blank, lower lip pendulous. 'What dat?'

Bratchet took hold of his jacket – it was his best, one of Kilsyth's – and slowly tugged it back and forth. 'Pompey, you're in touch with the Maroons, I know you are. Somebody took a message to the Maroons when Anne and Mary were in prison and it was you, it couldn't have been nobody else. Now are you going to warn the *ohene* or am I going to send you to the jumper for a whipping?'

'Yuh can'. I is a free nigger.'

'Pity,' she said. They both smiled. Such teeth as he had left were amazingly white. She unhooked her fingers from his jacket.

She still wasn't sure he was the right man, or whether he could send a message if he was. But later, as she lay in bed, worrying, watching an enormous moon silver the hanging parasite vines on the cottonwood, the night suddenly acquired sound, like a bud bursting into spreading flower. The air reverberated with a thrumming roar.

'Lord save us!' Kilsyth, usually a heavy sleeper, was out of bed and reaching into the cupboard where he kept his fowling pieces. 'They've risen!'

The sound was savage, sending out an impulse to run, waking race memories of blood sacrifice. It changed rhythm and became the cough of a tiger. It was a sound to reach across jungle and swampland. It was taken up by other drums farther away until the Bratchet, standing at the window with Kilsyth's arm round her, could hear its echo spreading across the Plain, skipping up into the hills to the mountains, a reminder to puny white figures in their beds that the tigers outnumbered them.

She'd been told about drums; the colonists had forbidden them. And no wonder. She'd had no idea that hands slapping on hollowed-out logs and stretched skins could fill the universe.

It stopped. The ordinary, creaking and chiming denizens of the night took back their occupation of it. She and Kilsyth stood for a long time at the window until it was clear that no feathered spears were massing behind the hill.

'And what d'ye think *that* was?'

'I think someone was telling somebody something.'

The attack on Nannytown took place a week afterwards and was a failure. Having hauled cannon over the ravines and along goat paths into the heights of the Blue Mountains, soldiers and planters were annoyed to find that their objective had moved. Where Nannytown should have been was a large space spiked with holes that showed the roof trees of many huts had once stood there but didn't any more.

Two weeks later the night of the drums was still a topic of edgy discussion in Spanish Town when Bratchet went in with Pompey to the market to buy vegetables. Sitting in her trap, pointing out the best buys to her housekeeper, Mrs Riley said, 'We've got a beacon ready to signal the militia if the niggers attack and I advise you to have the same. And don't buy those guavas, the higgler's asking too much.'

She watched Bratchet finish her purchases and mount up on the horse behind Pompey. 'It's not decent to ride pillion with an ebony.' Her attention was caught elsewhere, 'Here, Quashee. Who are you?'

A large black man had wandered into the square, leading a

bristle-backed boar by a rope through the ring in its nose. He knuckled his forehead and approached the Riley trap to stand docilely under Mrs Riley's inspection. 'I haven't seen you before, have I? Who do you belong to?'

Dumbly the man pointed to his locked iron collar which all slaves wore and which carried the name of his owner and parish. Mrs Riley tried to read it against the glint of the sun. 'Where are you taking that boar?'

'Massa send he service de she-hogses over Slaney Penn.'

'Then stop ambling about here and get on to the Slaneys'.'

Bratchet drew a deep breath to intervene, 'Here, Quashee.'

'Sambo, missy.'

'Sambo, then. You can bring the boar up to Coppleston's. I'll send your master the service fee.'

Mrs Riley didn't like it. 'I didn't know Kilsyth had hogs.'

Bratchet forced her mouth into a comic mask's smile and wiped her sweating hands on Pompey's back. 'Didn't you?'

Kilsyth had taken their only other horse over to the Big House's smithy, and Coppleston's was empty, apart from Sarcy who was doing something ineffectual with a duster and the shutters. Bratchet told her to go over to the slaves' *gunyahs* and buy guavas.

Sarcy pointed to Bratchet's basket. 'Yuh got dem already.'

'Well, I bloody want some more.' She watched Sarcy walk off up the hill. There was nobody at the mill. It was planting time. From far off, towards the southern fields, she could hear the drivers shouting at the gangs. She went into the house and prepared some lemonade, then came back on to the porch and sat awhile. Then she went back into the house and poured a glassful of brandy into the lemonade jug, then she went out on to the porch again and watched the track.

The man came wandering up the track with the slave's lack of haste that was an offence in itself. Once or twice, he stopped to pull some switch grass and feed it to the boar. *I'll kill him.* She watched him tether the hog to the ring in the mounting block at the foot of the steps, looked around, led him into the house and hugged him. 'You bugger. You shouldn't have done it. You frightened me to death.'

'Dat no way to talk to de king,' Licky told her. 'Dat a baby in yo' belly?'

She patted it. 'It is.'

He patted it as well. She handed him a glass of lemonade but he took the jug and drank every drop. There was a change in him; he looked as if he'd been honed harsher and thinner. 'You got the message then,' she said.

'Yep. One thing with cane-trash huts, you can put 'em up somewhere else. No point peltin' at de boilin' house to hit de mill wall.'

He hadn't changed that much then. It was lovely to see him, but she was terrified for him and kept going to the window to look out. 'Sit,' he told her, 'You like game cock runnin' roun' de pit.'

When she sat down he squatted opposite her. 'What you doin' here? Din' I tell you Jamaica kill you? One message deserve another an' I come tell you to git.'

'Git where? Kilsyth's poorly and won't go home.'

''F you don' hear, bye-'n-bye you gine feel. The army plannin' to capture me, but de navy plannin' to capture Sam Rogers. He bin piratin' plenty an' the Admiral don' like it.'

'How do you know?'

She gathered there wasn't much happened on the island that he didn't know. Nannytown as good as overlooked the Port of Antonio on the east coast and the Maroons were kept informed of shipping movements and plans through their network of slave spies. It had been passed on to the people in the Blue Mountains that the *Brilliana* was attacking too many vessels and the navy was out to capture her.

'Even if Sam is caught, what would happen? Livingstone told the Vice-Admiral judge we were helpless victims of mutiny and piracy. Sam wouldn't say different.'

Licky wasn't convinced. 'There was canvas-climbers on dat boat woul'n't be so particular. Where dat Martin?'

'He's gone back to England.'

Licky looked at Bratchet sideways. 'Yuh ent got sense to shelter yuh out de rain.'

Bridling, she said, 'We can manage without him.'

'Like a chicken manage de mongoose,' he said.

She changed the subject. 'How's your mother?' It sounded bizarre even to her; tea-party politeness to the most wanted man in Jamaica.

Licky rolled his eyes. 'That Great-grandma, she one trouble-some woman. She wanted Nannytown to stay put so she can catch de cannon balls in her teet' and spit 'em back at de army.'

'She probably could. And how many wives have you got now?'

Nervousness was stultifying her conversation; the iron collar round his neck kept catching her eye and making her self-conscious of her race. She kept thinking of what would happen to him if he was caught. 'I wish you'd go now,' she told him after a while, 'and don't come again.'

'Worrit, worrit. You worry for yo'self, girl. 'F you don' git, Jamaica kill you.'

'I wish we could all go. You, me, Livingstone. You away from those damn Maroons, us away from these damn planters.'

He wished they could; she could see it in his face as he put an arm round her shoulders; the attrition of constant vigilance and fear, discomfort, responsibility for a people of no homogeneity apart from their colour and dependence on him, their leader. But he said, 'Ain't nowhere to git.'

He became urgent. 'You *gotta* git. The whiteys don' like you, girl. You differen' and whitey don' like differen'.'

She said, 'Anyway, I'd never leave here without I knew what happened to Anne's and Mary's baby.' The closer she got to her own delivery, the more she thought about the prison cell in Spanish Town. She was obsessed by the idea that the surviving baby was not with its mother, but still living with the Maroons in the Blue Mountains. At nights she heard it crying.

'Who?' he asked. He'd forgotten.

She reminded him of who Anne and Mary were and she told him what Pompey had told her. 'Asantewa knows what happened to that child. I think it was her took it.'

He frowned. ''Fore my time, girl. I was playin' de good nigger in Europe then.'

'I know. But you could ask Asantewa.'

387

'An' I could marry Queen Anne if I ask her.' He cupped her chin between his forefinger and thumb. 'You git if she tell you?'

She lied to him for the first time. 'Yes.' As he went on looking at her, she said, 'That's how come I'm here. Trying to find out about Anne and Mary.'

'An' look what it got you.' He sniffed. 'We'll see. What I always tell you? Ask no questions, yuh hear no lies.'

'De longer you live, de more you hear,' Bratchet said.

She went out first to make sure the coast was clear and then said goodbye.

He was going down the steps when he turned and came back. 'You promise me now. Iffen I sweeten that old Great-grandma into tellin', you'll git?' he said.

'I'll git.' He untethered the boar, kicking its rump to make it move, and marched off down the track. Through tears she watched him go. Before he disappeared from sight, she saw his gait change to the rolling, insulting amble of a slave.

Licky had warned her. 'Whitey don' like differen',' he'd said. She was incapable of seeing the danger. She'd been brought up in a country that was ostensibly one nation but consisted of uneven incomes, differing ambitions and opposing politics. Even if she'd told Kilsyth what Licky had said, which she didn't, he couldn't have seen it either. In Scotland, as in England, the 'different' could usually fit in somewhere.

But the planters of the Liguanea Plain were suspended in one stratum that was totally in agreement with itself. There was no poverty among them; their politics and their ambition were directed towards one object: to see that nothing interfered with their uniformity. Eccentricity was a threat, a leak in their dam. It couldn't be tolerated. Their communication was more subtle than slave drums; like rooks they could smell a stranger in the nest and, like rooks, knew the necessity to turn and kill it. Bratchet didn't laugh at the right jokes, her attitude to the slaves was wrong, she didn't respond to advice from the other wives. She was, however, just a wife.

Ironically, it was Kilsyth who made the rooks uneasy. Unlike Bratchet, he had no conviction that slavery was wrong; he accepted it as part of the local scenery, a factor of sugar-growing. He didn't approve of her meddling – which was why she hadn't told him she'd warned Licky of the danger to the Maroons.

On learning that the planters were upset that she'd given Pompey and Sarcy their freedom – manumission was usually only granted to very favoured slaves in one's will – he'd reproved her and they'd had their first quarrel. 'We'll abide by the custom, Bratchie.'

'How can we? These are Licky's people. *Licky's*.'

'Licky's no' a slave.' He saw only individuals.

But because he saw only individuals, he took Pompey and Sarcy with him and Bratchet to the cathedral on Easter Sunday and didn't notice when the entire congregation fell silent as they entered, though Bratchet did. He couldn't even see what he'd done wrong when the officiating priest took him aside afterwards to chastise him.

'These are souls under my roof,' he said.

'They have had no Christian instruction, Mr Kilsyth. They are savages.'

'Then gi'e 'em Christian instruction, man. It's what ye're here for.'

But, although Pompey and Sarcy were now free, although the Jamaican Assembly had reversed its earlier decision and now allowed for slave masters to instruct and baptize 'all such as they can make sensible of a Deity and the Christian faith', the planters knew that doing it would spring another leak in the dam – and the planters' tithes paid the priest's stipend.

Efforts were made to bring Kilsyth into the fold. 'Helyar's offering to set me up as a planter,' he told Bratchet, returning from a game of billiards at Waller's house. 'There's grand sugar acres going beggin' over by Charing Cross so he says, and I'll no need to start paying him back till after the second crop.'

'You can't!' She couldn't bear that he should become one of them. 'Anyway, you haven't the health for it.' Which was true; he'd recently had a bout of fever that had advanced the pain and swelling of his joints.

'What d'ye suggest I do then?' he shouted at her. 'I'll not

spend the rest of my days sittin' rocking like an auld wife. We've not the siller if I would.'

'Pickles,' she said, 'I been thinking. Pickles. And preserves. Sophie Sewell drones on about her wonderful candied sweetmeats. And they're good. You had some of her ginger and pickled peppers the other night. I could do that. We could make a commerce out of it. The island's lousy with limes, mangoes, everything. Most of all, it's got sugar. We could export them to England, we could . . .'

'That's trade, woman.' He was appalled. 'I'll not become a bloody tradesman.'

'You're prepared to be a bloody planter.'

'That's, tha's . . . gentlemanly occupation. D'ye not see the difference?'

She didn't. She hadn't been well enough brought up.

He went to bed muttering. 'A Livingstone of Kilsyth a picklemaker. The woman'd have me a bloody grocer.'

He'd come round to it. It was a fine scheme. He'd be miserable at first, perhaps, but he was miserable now, although he tried to hide it from her.

I shouldn't've married him. I'm not his class. But she knew he'd have been worse without her. And if she'd given him nothing else, she was presenting him with a child which gave him something to live for, something for them both to live for. And work for. This baby wasn't going to grow up in the Jamaican equivalent of Puddle Court. It wasn't going to grow up to be a slave owner either.

There was nothing for it. They'd have to go into the pickle business.

CHAPTER NINETEEN

Laird o' Kirkaldy was a slow boat and an unlucky boat. One of her many mishaps, which I won't bore you with, James, nearly drowned me. I almost welcomed it. However, one way and another, the *Laird* and I didn't arrive in England until late in 1711. Like I always had when I'd taken a beating, I went straight to Mrs Defoe.

'So thin, Martin,' she said, 'so brown. Sit and rest thy poor leg. I'll heat up some white soup this minute.'

The children were all in bed, there was a kettle rattling gently on the fire and ironing airing from a string across the mantelpiece. She sat opposite me with her elbows on the table as I ate, not letting me talk until I'd finished two bowls of white soup and a loaf of home-made bread. I did my best with a syllabub but was defeated.

'You eat that all up, Martin Millet. Good English food, that is, got nutmeg in it. You can't thrive on foreign fare with all them spices. I was feared for you when I heard thy travels. A reg'lar Usselees, Dan'l says you been.'

'Usselees had a Penelope like you,' I said. 'I've yet to find one.'

'Bratchet not returned with thee, then?'

She's no fool is Mrs Defoe.

'She married somebody else. In Jamaica.'

Mrs Defoe squeezed my hand. 'I'm that sorry, Martin. Funny little thing she was, but she had the makings of a rare woman.'

She brought me up to date with the essential news. The boys were growing up, young Daniel showing signs of a good business head – the first one in the family, I thought – young Norton was so clever at his reading and writing he might follow his father's steps into journalism, Maria, Hannah, Henrietta and Sophia were all good girls and spoke their catechism very pretty.

'But the poor Queen, Martin. Failing they say and no wonder with assassins jumping out on us from every corner. What'll come of it all, I don't know. Civil war, they do say.'

Daniel himself was as gloomy when he came home. He wasn't surprised to see me. A report of our doings had been sent from Jamaica by Lord Archibald to Robert Harley who was now Earl of Oxford and the Queen's First Minister. 'And I think I can trust you, Martin, to know that I am perhaps the earl's greatest confidant.'

He didn't seem the richer for it, or happier. When he took me into his study so that we could talk privately, he flew into a rage to find it strewn with washing and threw the clothes out into the passage and muttered something about a man called Swift not having to write in a laundry.

'We can offer you but poor hospitality, Martin,' he said, 'but I beg you will stay here until you are settled. I wish to hear of your encounter with the pirates.' His eyes gleamed at the prospect. He loved a good rogue, did Daniel.

I thanked him and told him truthfully that I never felt more at home than I did in that house in Newington.

'But first to *nos moutons*, as the French say.' He looked at me. 'They *do* say that, do they?'

I said they did.

'And did you really meet Louis face to face at Marly? Our reports from John Laws indicated the monster actually talked to you.'

When I started telling him, he held up a hand. 'No, no. I must deny myself these pleasures until later. Harl . . . my Lord Oxford is in a fever to know of the quest for Anne Bonny.'

I told him most, not all, of what had happened in Jamaica.

He sat back. 'Let me clarify. There is a record of Mary Read's death but the gaoler at Spanish Town said the records were carelessly kept and believes *both* women did not survive imprisonment.'

'I think one of 'em's dead,' I said, 'I'm not sure which.'

'Hmm.' He got up and began striding about. His wig was still unfashionably long and he was wearing the same sage-green velvet coat and satin waistcoat in which he'd first come to Puddle Court. Mrs Defoe had done a good job in keeping them brushed and away from the bailiffs, but the lace cuffs were more frayed than ever.

'I must tell you, Martin, that Lord Oxford tends to your opinion. He has become near fanatical in his belief that someone, a woman, has infiltrated the very Court of our Queen and is out for mischief.' He brought me up to date with the Greg business. 'But I should also tell you that he is not well. Those who witnessed the assassination attempt on him claim he remained the calmest person in the room, yet it has undoubtedly affected him. And his colleague Bolingbroke is worse than an enemy.'

Daniel leaned forward as if to impart a state secret. I suppose it was. 'He looks too much on the wine when it is raging. While he kept his bed, I glimpsed empty port bottles beneath the counterpane.'

God help England, I thought. A drunk for a First Minister and an invalid Queen.

But I wasn't disposed to discount Harley's obession that there was a madwoman at Court. Whoever had tried to rid the world of Bratchet had known virtually every move we made.

Daniel drew himself up. 'I am empowered to co-opt you into the search for this woman, Martin. We propose to find you some position in the Queen's household.'

I shook my head. 'I'm done, Daniel. It's me for the quiet life. I'm going to buy myself a little farm and settle down on it. I've lost too much in the quest for Anne Bonny. If there's a female Guy Fawkes at Court, she can bloody well stay there for all I care.'

'For your country, Martin.'

'Sod my country.'

He was angry with me and became eloquent. Didn't I realize we were on the edge of civil war? 'The succession question is the plague come again. Men are glancing at each other for signs of infection. Is that a Stuart bubo bulging under an armpit; is that a Jacobite sneeze? Has this one breathed in so much tainted incense that he would tolerate a Catholic for a king? I tell you, Martin, the disease has spread to parlour, counting house, even kitchen. Only yesterday, in my own warehouse, I found my apprentices lined up on different sides of the floor, throwing High Church and Low Church at each other like battledore and shuttlecock.'

He shook me, I admit it. I'd no idea the split between supporters of Hanover and Stuart went so deep. In Jamaica they hardly cared who the monarch of England was as long as he took sugar.

'We shall see civil war again,' he kept saying. His lovely,

prospering England, all his wonderful projects, to be swilled away in the blood of a butcher's yard. 'God knows I have no personal affection for George of Hanover, but I will take up arms again, as I did in the Monmouth rebellion, to protect my land from the Catholics.'

'Come on, Daniel,' I said, 'there won't be popery back.'

'I have your assurance do I?' he shouted, 'The word of a man not in the country for years that the Pretender will be a good little king? We thought his father would be a good little king, until every Protestant in office began to be replaced by Papists.'

He banged the table. 'It's happening already. Bolingbroke is playing for the soul of the High Tories. He is to bring in a bill which will take the education of their children away from Dissenters and put it in the hands of teachers accredited only by the Church of England.'

Suddenly he was calm. And crafty. 'This does not affect our weary Master Millet, does it? He will buy his farm and go to sleep and wake up to find someone else telling him where he may send his children to school. But . . .' He leaned so close his nose practically touched mine. '. . . whose money will buy that farm for him?'

I sighed. 'Aunt Effie's.'

'And do we know yet who killed Aunt Effie?'

'But what's the good of it?' I pleaded, 'Unless this woman wears a notice saying: "I intend to wreak havoc", I'm not likely to recognize her.'

'You've been sniffing the trail from Puddle Court to Jamaica,' he pointed out, 'You know her scent. There'll be *something*, some word, a reference, a look.'

'All right, Daniel,' I said, 'but I ain't dressing up in livery and standing behind chairs with chalk in my hair.'

'No,' he said, looking me up and down, 'I don't see you as a footman. We'll have to find something more . . . appropriate.'

I became a royal gardener.

I knew nothing of horticulture. At home we'd not possessed even a window-box. My father hadn't liked flowers; he suspected their relationship with bees wasn't all it should be. As for the army, if they catch you standing around sniffing petunias, they put you on a charge.

I explained this to Mr Henry Wise, the Queen's gardener, at our first meeting, but he said it didn't matter as his instructions from the Earl of Oxford were that my post was to be nominal, no more than an excuse for my presence around the royal grounds.

A great man, Henry Wise. One of the few people who, when he gets to heaven, can look St Peter in the eye and say he left the world sweeter-smelling than he found it. He made the sunken garden from a chalk pit at Kensington, the rides at Windsor, the lime-bordered canals at Hampton Court and the Maestricht Garden near the Thames.

Queen Anne loved him. I'd see them together often, her very fat, him very thin, considering a flower bed like a couple of generals surveying the placement of troops. It's said she discussed state secrets with him. If she did, he never passed them on.

Actually, my employment wasn't as daft as it sounds. I saw a lot of the female royal household. The Queen's hunting days were over and she spent more and more time in her gardens, which meant that the maids of honour did too. Her other women were sent to gather flowers for the bedchamber and took their exercise around the grounds. Few of them lurked behind bushes, however, unless it was to meet a man, or in any way acted suspiciously as far as I could see.

As it turned out, I was useful to Mr Wise in organizing the transport of young plants – what he called 'the greens' – from his partner's nursery at Brompton to the grounds of the various palaces. I built him a sort of covered wain which had double roof and sides, to insulate delicate trees like myrtles and or-anges from both heat and cold. It was immensely heavy and needed a team of eight to pull it, but it worked.

There was a field which lay fallow at the back of the Brompton Nurseries and I persuaded George London, Wise's partner, to let me use it for an experiment. It was an idea that'd come to me in France, seeing the way its wine-growers planted their vines in neat rows. Piracy and other things had put it out of my mind, but the sugar planters' method of making lines of trenches for their cane cuttings to sprout in brought it back.

Why, I wondered, couldn't this tidiness be applied to corn? Broadcasting seed by hand is wasteful; too many seeds here, too few there so that wheat and barley grow up in patches. I devised a drill – Christ, I was only too happy to occupy my mind with something – which would make channels in the soil, sow the seed and cover the rows, all in one operation.

It took me a long time; composing the seed box was a bugger and when I'd finished it looked a crazy contraption and wasn't as efficient as it should have been – a man called Tull has since invented a better one – but it worked well enough for George London to praise the result to Mr Wise who, in turn, praised it to the Queen, who came to see it in action.

The night after her inspection, Defoe hurried into my grace-and-favour cottage, one of a row in Kensington village.

'Well?' he asked.

'Well what?'

'Dammit,' he said, 'the Queen brought practically every woman in the household to see that blasted drill of yours. Are you no further?'

'No. The red-headed one said what a dear little plough it was, a dark one asked why I didn't paint it pink and the others wanted to play the "What?" game.'

He fell into a chair. 'This is hopeless.' Then he sat up. 'You know which is the only way to solve this?'

'How?'

'Go to Jamaica and fetch the Bratchet back.'

'No.' He blinked and I realized I'd shouted. I sat down opposite him. 'Leave her alone, Daniel. She's safe out there.'

'Very well, my dear boy. Don't upset yourself. But Lord Oxford is becoming impatient. Time grows short. As you saw today, the Queen's not at all well.' He added wistfully, 'Anne Bonny would still prove the ideal solution to the crisis if we could find her. She would be the candidate on which both sides could compromise.'

'They're not compromising with Bratchet,' I told him.

He produced a sheaf of papers from his pocket. 'Now, then,

my agency has been gathering information on the various women in the household.'

I took the papers from him and looked them over.

Daniel's agents – better known to the London magistracy as rogues, pickpockets and tricksters – had been thorough. They'd uncovered quite a number of miniature skeletons rattling in the closets of the female household. What was surprising was the number of women whose childhoods couldn't be accounted for. If the parents were dead, or if the woman herself came from a far-flung part of the country or colony, it was virtually impossible to confirm her as the person she claimed to be.

Her Majesty's hairdresser, for example, was a supposed Huguenot refugee. But was she? And why was she enjoying a dubious relationship with a gambler who was suspected of Jacobite tendencies?

There was a bedchamber woman who'd been recommended by the late Earl of Nottingham but whose family had emigrated to Massachusetts, leaving nobody who could go bail for her background. A laundress's cousin was in the Clink for debt. There'd been the unaccountable death of a housemaid's brother.

Another bedchamber woman took mysterious trips to Highgate and had nightmares, a maid of honour was rumoured to have an illegitimate son, another maid of honour had been seen in a low tavern.

I handed him back the papers. 'What did you do in the war, Uncle Daniel?'

'Pried into the private lives of serving women, Nephew. I know, I know. It seems shameful, but these are desperate times.'

He was looking desperate himself. He'd got too many eggs in Harley's basket. If Harley fell he'd be friendless, not to say destitute. The Tories didn't trust him because he had been too great a Whig; the Whigs were disgusted with him for taking too Tory a line in his news sheet.

He took off his wig and ran his fingers through his thinning hair. 'Will we find a murderess or a queen, Martin? Put her on the throne or in the Tower? Or merely suppress all record of her existence in order to leave the way clear for the Hanovers?' He looked up. 'Or the Stuarts?'

'You don't even trust Harley, do you?'

Daniel let his hands drop. 'I'm frightened, Martin. I asked him straight out the other day. "We *are* holding to the Protestant succession, are we not, my lord?" I said.'

'What did he say?'

'He said, "We are holding to prudence, Master Defoe." There are rumours that even *he* is flirting with the Pretender.'

They were like turkeys in a pen when a fox gets in; more of them trampling themselves through panic than the fox could kill. I saw them every day, Harley, Bolingbroke and the others rushing into Kensington Palace to hector the poor bloody Queen into supporting this cause or the other. Why the hell couldn't they leave the woman in peace? A good woman, too. It'd taken her time to understand what the Millet Drill was about, but once she did she'd asked intelligent questions. She reminded me of Mrs Defoe.

Daniel got up to go. He struck a tragic attitude. 'Well, when the Pope and his minions rule England, one of the first cast on to the bonfire will be Daniel Defoe, Gentleman.'

The thought cheered him up. He made a brisk attempt to persuade me to invest any money I gained from the Millet Drill in a South Seas project he was peddling, then went.

I should have known that desperate men will do anything. The next week, when I took Mrs Defoe her usual bunch of flowers, she said Daniel had gone to Jamaica.

Harley had sent him to bring back the Bratchet.

CHAPTER TWENTY

Seventh Extract from *The Madwoman's Journal*

Here, James, the journal loses its thread as, I think, did its writer. There are some papers which are so blotched with blood and ink that they can only be deciphered here and there. They cover the years in which I came home and took up my post as royal gardener. I imagine

the Madwoman was struggling to show rationality while in public.
The condition of the papers indicates that she was losing the battle
when she was alone. I have done my best to render them coherent and
continuous.

WE ARE nearly there, my love.

After my exorcism by Rachel at Southwark, I returned to tell
the Queen that my journey to Ipswich had been successful. Not
only had I found Mary Read's relatives, I said, but I had discovered the child born to Anne Bard after her marriage to the
Pretender.

'A child?'

I nodded. 'Your Majesty, it appears that Anne Bard was carrying when she came to England. I imagine she hoped for a
kind reception from yourself where the baby's birth could be
attested. Instead, the boy was born in an Ipswich cottage with
only Mary Read and her mother to deliver him.'

The Queen groaned, whether with pleasure or dismay I
couldn't tell. 'A royal Stuart. Can it be?'

'Only you can decide, madam.' I went on, 'Mrs Read has no
doubt that Anne was kidnapped on her return to London,
though she does not know by whom. Her daughter Mary determined to go off in pursuit of her friend, leaving the baby in Mr
and Mrs Read's care. When Mary also did not return, they took
charge of the child. They are simple, kindly folk.'

The puffy royal hand took mine. 'Does he thrive? Did you see
him? What is his appearance?'

I nodded. 'A handsome little boy. Dark. Very long-lashed
eyes of a strong blue.'

She said, 'My father had long lashes and strong blue eyes.'

I rummaged in my pocket and brought out a paper that
might have been a page in a church register. A forgery, of
course, but very well done. 'Anne had the boy baptized at once
by an Ipswich priest who entered its name in his book. I was
naughty, ma'am, I fear. I tore it out for you when the parson's
back was turned.'

Queen Ant hunched her great shoulders in wicked approval;
we are partners in secrecy. I put her spectacles on her nose so

399

that she might scan it. The child is registered as James Rupert Dudley Stuart. The mother's name Anne Bard. The father's James Francis Stuart.

If necessary I can produce the priest as well as Mr and Mrs Read, all members of the Brotherhood who would swear they were Joseph, Mary and the Holy Ghost if I paid them. And be believed.

I sheered away then, content to leave her to mull it over. The Queen is not quick. Her mind vacillates like a windvane at the best of times and loathes to make a decision. But once she has settled on a conviction, as well try to push over Gibraltar as to change her. If, given time, she concludes that this baby is her half-nephew we are home.

But have we time? Though I have been absent for only just over two weeks, I am shocked by her deterioration; the fat of her face does not cling to the bones but falls away into folds, like a hound's.

Oh Lord, let the Queen live a little while more.

St John caught me as I went off duty and hauled me off to the garden. 'Where have you been, damn you? I needed you.'

'You surprise me, my lord. I thought Lady Masham has become your mouthpiece in the bedchamber.'

'Abigail's proved a broken fucking reed,' he said, 'Have you found Anne Bard yet?'

'Are we still on that tack? Haven't you yet persuaded the Pretender to become a Protestant?'

'Yes, we bloody are. And no, I bloody haven't. A fine fucking Pretender that can't even pretend. That's all he's got to do; abjure the Pope for five fucking minutes and I'd have him on the throne. Will he do it? No. Merely promises to safeguard the Church of England when he becomes king. I tell him the English would rather have the Grand Turk as king than a Roman Catholic. God, how I abhor men of principle.'

He has deteriorated. The fine bones of his face stand out sharp. The hand which plucked at my sleeve had a tremor, as well it might; it feels the future eluding its grasp. If German George becomes King, St John will suffer the same fate as his enemy, Marlborough. In fact, he will be fortunate if it is merely exile; I've heard Whigs swear they will have his head.

In his panic, he is trying to pack every part of the country's government with Tories so that he is in such a position of power that he can negotiate with Hanover. Whig army officers, Whig board members, Whig committees and, for all I know, Whig night-soil men are being replaced by Tories.

To deflect him from the subject of Anne Bard, I said, 'I think Her Majesty might love you better, my lord, if your wife were less unhappy.' His wife, Frances – he calls her 'Frank' – is a long-suffering woman and Queen Ant is distressed by his desertion of her.

'Would she? Would she?' It seemed to come as a surprise to him. 'Then I shall become a model husband. Frank shall come back to Court to show how happy she is. In any case, the Schism Act will demonstrate to the Queen and all the other backwoodsmen what a good churchman I am.'

The Schism Act is one that he hopes will gather the High Tories behind him. It is to persecute Dissenters. The Act will take their children's education out of their hands and put it in the hands of Church of England schoolmasters. This is desperate boat-burning – if the Whigs gain power after this, they will surely have his head.

Of course, in this he is also tilting at Harley, his esteemed cabinet colleague. The war between the allies and Louis XIV was not conducted with more hatred than the feud between these fellow Tories. Harley is a Dissenter himself; his wife and children regularly attend a Presbyterian church. He will be affected by the Act.

'What will the Earl of Oxford do against that, poor thing?' I asked. As far as I can see, Harley does nothing except drink. There have been times lately when he's been drunk while attending Her Majesty. His face appears as composed as usual but his enunciation is almost unintelligible, while the whiff of port from his breath has mingled with the whiff of brandy from hers.

'Harley's trying to find Anne Bard,' said St John. 'There's still time to present her to the nation as the only solution to civil war. My spies tell me he's sent to Jamaica to fetch some trollop back to England. He appears to think she can identify our Stuart princess.'

Bratchet.

'When? When did he send?'

'Good God, woman, keep your voice down. These are high secrets I'm telling you.'

I fought to be quiet, though the creature howled so loud I could barely hear myself speak. 'When did he send, my lord?'

St John shrugged. 'A while ago.' My agitation calmed his and he smiled at it. 'Worries you, doesn't it? And so it should. If Harley finds her before I do, there'll be no reward for little Miss Bedchamber, whereas *I* will fill your pockets with gold and your slippers with champagne. Have you discovered nobody who fits the bill?'

'I shall redouble my efforts, my lord.'

He nodded. 'And I shall redouble mine. If necessary, I'll kidnap this Jamaican hussy the moment she sets foot on English soil and parade every female at Court in front of her.'

I don't know what he said after that. I broke away from him as soon as I could and went to my room, the creature lumbering around me like a whale dancing.

Bratchet.

I should have killed you that night in Puddle Court. I strangled Effie, why not you?

I pitied you, of course. So small and weak you were. So small and weak, you have pursued us like Nemesis. Every step we took, you have taken. Even to Jamaica. Were you led to Nannytown? Did you stand beside the fireless cauldron as we did? Have you fathomed our revenge?

But of course, it wasn't Bratchet I should have killed. It was that insignificant, low-born soldier who has watched over her every move. It was Martin Millet. If we'd had a Martin Millet on our side, you and I, my dear one, would have escaped the press boat and England's history would have changed.

He is here.

They shipped him back from Jamaica to sniff me out. They

made him one of the gardeners, a station that fits him so well that for a long time I did not notice him.

So plain and ordinary-looking is he that *nobody* notices him at first – and then they do, especially women. Despite his limp. More than one of the females in the household finds herself called into the gardens to ask his advice on horticulture, fluttering her eyelashes as she does it. He answers politely and gravely and ignores the eyelashes.

And Queen Ant has taken to him; like calls to like. Her tastes were always plebeian. We were all dragged to Brompton to watch the display of some contraption he has invented and I was able to study him. He, of course, is my true enemy. I see that now. There is something about him; a steadfastness. Once latched, his teeth will never let go. He's the one who has protected the Bratchet from me all these years; without him she would be dead.

Like the rest of the women, I asked ridiculous questions about his plough, or drill, or whatever it is, and was answered with a weary courtesy. The Queen was charmed. 'Some men waste their whole lives in studying how to arm Death with new engines of horror, Master Millet,' she said, 'but you have employed your labours in a new instrument for the increase of bread.'

Well, well. I have plans for Master Millet and he may live, despite the creature's demands for his death. He will do very well as a guardian. Strange, that a man who has hunted me all these years with the intention of bringing me down, is perhaps the only man I've ever trusted.

Keep the creature from my brain. Let there be blood for blood. After all, we do not wish to take it; we want to give it, to see ours run into the blood of England. Then, though she claws me to pieces, we shall be at peace.

And now we wait on the Queen. Harley nags her to rid him of St John. St John and Abigail nag her to rid them of Harley. All three nag her to contact the Pretender and nag him to change his religion so that the blood of the Stuarts continues to rule Britain.

I, who know her better, hold my tongue in patience though I near bite it in half. Silently I scream at her. I can feel my mouth form the words she must utter: 'I wish to see the boy. Send for the boy.'

Must, must, must. Say it, you full-gutted, gouty, wavering, royal old sow. Say it before that mouth of yours closes for ever. Say it before my hands reach for that fat neck, so like Effie's neck, and squeeze the words out of it. Say it. *Say it.*

She said it last night. Somehow she endured the concert. Carrots wheeled her back from the great hall, nearly dropping – Carrots, like the rest of them, had to stand for the whole of it and then wait for the congratulations to Mr Handel, Mr Handel's return congratulations, the hand-kissing, the word dropped to this courtier then that.

Queen Ant, for once, was in fine fettle. Music soothes her. We undressed her, put on her night robe and cap, attached the harness and, hauling on the rope like canvas-climbers, swung her into bed.

Danvers went to mix the medicine while I placed her elder son's portrait near her hand – she sleeps with it always. As I curtseyed before summoning the night's draught of cold tea, she whispered, 'Fetch the boy.' I turned away, thinking it was my mind had said it. 'Bring the boy to me. Secretly,' she said, 'Send to Ipswich. I want to see him.'

Lord God, why did I pretend he was at Ipswich? It will be at least six days more, to allow for the supposed message and the journey, before I can present him. But I dared not let her think he was close by; she might have sent Danvers or Carrots to check.

Don't let her die yet, God. Let her live six days more.

I took the boy to her an hour ago. The coach I'd sent to Highgate brought him and Jubah to Kensington Palace's back stair. Sarah and Abigail used it in their days of power to get to the Queen unseen, but since the unrest there are two guards on it, mainly, I think, to thwart Abigail who now has to use the public approach.

Tonight the Queen had sent orders to let me pass. Jubah stayed in the shadows. With her black face and clothes she was virtually invisible. A faithful nurse, Jubah, and I hope she will not have to be parted from him.

In all these years I have been careful not to touch him. He must not love me. I am the woman who visits occasionally, that is all. I think I frighten him. But tonight, because the stairs were dark, I took his hand.

'It is very dark here,' he said.

The door was open for us at the top and I inspected his appearance. He is a handsome child with loose black curls and clear, pale complexion. In the clothes I had bought him, he looked very well.

'I hope you will behave nicely,' I told him, 'you are going to see the Queen of England.'

He nodded. Jubah had prepared him.

We went in. Queen Ant had dismissed all the women, saying she wanted to contemplate her soul alone, as sometimes she does, but they had put her to bed first.

Like I did that first time, he flinched at the size of her, but he advanced bravely to the bed and bowed, sweeping off his hat. He'd been told not to speak until she did, but he said, 'Are you the Queen of England?'

She nodded and smiled. 'Are you James Stuart?'

'Yes. But you haven't got a crown on.'

'I keep it in a drawer.' Her voice, which is the only pretty feature left to her, reassured him. She said, 'Can you climb up here?'

I helped him clamber up on the bed. The macaw shrieked and I looked around for the creature. She was there, on the other side of the bed, looking at him and licking her lips.

If she touches him I shall kill her, dead as she is.

'Well, James,' said Queen Ant, 'do you know your catechism?'

'Yes, Your Majesty.' He said the creed for her. He has been well instructed by one of the Brotherhood, a defrocked priest, who gives him lessons in Latin and mathematics in return for free lodging with Jubah. There is a slight trace of Creole in the boy's speech, which he catches from Jubah, but I hoped the Queen would mistake it for a Suffolk accent.

She was pleased with him, I could see. 'What is the outward part or sign of the Lord's Supper?'

'Bread and wine, which the Lord hath commanded to be received.'

Satisfied he was a good member of the church, she asked, 'And who are your parents, James?'

He leaned forward confidentially. 'I think they are dead. But my mother left me a message with Jubah. She's my nurse. She said I must always be worthy of my blood.'

'So you must, James.' There were tears in her eyes. 'So you must. May God keep you.'

I lifted him down and curtseyed while he bowed.

As we went down the stairs, he said, 'She's a very fat queen.'

'Yes, but you behaved very well.'

He said, 'I liked her.'

I must not be proud of him. He is an instrument.

She cannot make him king, my darling. I know that now. Nor would I wish that on him. But she can set him up so high that the fathers of aristocratic daughters will stumble over themselves to gain him for a son-in-law. An earldom at least. He shall take precedence over St John, mere *Viscount* Bolingbroke.

It will be enough to know that his blood will enter the stream of the enslavers, that careless nobility which every day presides over the slaughter of the unfortunate, that has decreed capital punishment for the theft of bread, that ride their carriages through streets where men and women and children die from neglect, that sent a girl into servitude because she was inconvenient.

I want it known that we held hands in that prison cell in Spanish Town, my love and I, and swore that, if we survived, if the child in each of our bodies survived, there should be restitution made through the body of that child.

Oh, Christ who suffered on the Cross, allow this balance of the scales of justice; let our cry come unto Thee.

I shall not see him again except at the last. He looked very small when Jubah lifted him into the carriage.

CHAPTER TWENTY-ONE

AFTER HER daughter Livia was born and weaned, the Bratchet used the last of her prize money to set up a pickle factory in Kingston. It was a long way from Coppleston's but Jamaica's main town was where the glass bottles she needed were manufactured.

She was lucky that in this colonial society women setting up in business on their own were not unusual. Several successful planters were widows who'd inherited their husband's estates, there were women traders and shop-owners in Kingston and, most successful of all, a large black lady known as Mother Sarah who operated the biggest whorehouse in town, restricting her clientele exclusively to white men.

As things turned out, Bratchet's factory didn't have time to be a success but it showed every sign of becoming one. She'd thought originally that she would export to England, but the fast sale of her relishes and preserves in the town alone taught her that, from a very small beginning – her workforce was five free Negroes – with luck and hard work, she could build a pickle empire in the West Indies.

She enjoyed discovering that she was a born businesswoman. What she didn't enjoy was the enforced absences from Livia. For the child's sake, neither she nor Kilsyth wanted to move house to Kingston; it had too many diseases. And Livia flourished at Coppleston's under Kilsyth's doting eye and the care of Sarcy, who was proving herself a better nursemaid than she had a house servant.

If it occurred to Bratchet that she and Kilsyth were being slowly dropped by the social circle of the Liguanea Plain, it was only to feel relief that she didn't have to entertain so much and that therefore Sarcy could devote herself to Livia. Mr and Mrs Chantry were now the only couple who invited the Kilsyths to their house, and vice versa. Kilsyth minded their social isolation, but as the disease increased in his bones he was glad of inactivity.

The Bratchet, in any case, had become something of a liability in planters' company; her independence as an entrepreneur gave her confidence and she was more and more outspoken in her disapproval of slavery.

The one conversion she made to the planters' thinking, if they'd known it, was to join them in hating piracy. Her first attempt at export was a consignment of lime and tomato chutney to Barbados. The barque carrying it and other goods was boarded by pirates on the high seas, and her master killed in defending its cargo. Bratchet had met the master while overseeing the loading of her precious jars; with her workers she had endured the appalling heat while the contents of those very jars – concocted from a recipe of Mrs Chantry's – were chopped, cooked and stirred, she had written out each label herself.

'And now some throat-slitting swab's sitting down to spread my chutney on his biscuit,' she raved at Kilsyth when she got home, 'I hope he chokes on it. May he swing alive till his eyes drop out.'

'And what if it's your friend Sam, or Nobby?' he asked.

It brought her up short. She hadn't thought of that but now she did it didn't make any difference. 'They killed Captain Perry,' she said, 'It's a bastard trade.'

One afternoon in early spring Bratchet left the factory early so that she could celebrate Livia's birthday in the evening. 'Home, Pompey, and quick.'

He was slow helping her into the trap. He looked disturbed. 'You been summoned, missy.'

'What do you mean? Who by?'

His head turned and raised until he was looking up towards the Blue Mountains. 'We's to meet a guide at Gordon Town.'

'Bugger.' She'd waited a long time for this summons; in a sense, she'd come thousands of miles for it. Now all she wanted to do was get back to Livia. If she didn't return from the Blue Mountains, who would look after her baby? The child was crying for her this minute. Had fallen ill. Who cared what'd happened to Anne Bonny and Mary Read? Not her any more. She had more important people to love.

'All right,' she said. She was being irrational. And if she didn't go, she'd spend the rest of her life wondering.

Before they left Kingston, she called in at Johnny Faa's town house and gave one of his servants a note to take to Kilsyth saying she'd be delayed at the factory and wouldn't be home. They took the road north, following the Hope River which cut its way out of the mountains through a deep, narrow ravine.

There were few people on the road. Ferns and plantains were utterly still in the moist air. Cedars, tamarinds and gum trees had struck their roots in the clefts of the crags and hung out over the falls below them. Above the track the limestone cliffs stood out in relief. Bratchet hardly noticed. Her fingers drummed on the edge of the trap. She was getting further and further away from Livia. Well, she still had Porritt's pistol in her holdall. If anybody tried to stop her return to her child, she'd use it.

It was nearly dusk by the time they reached the outskirts of Gordon Town. There were no white people in sight. A black man holding the reins of two mules stepped out into the road in front of them and waved them down.

Pompey helped Bratchet out of the trap and on to one of the mules, then made as if to mount the other one. The man stopped him. 'Stay here. She go alone. With me.' He wore a slave's iron collar but his manner was peremptory.

'How long'll I be away?' Bratchet asked him.

'Day and half a day.'

She turned to Pompey. 'Go back home. Say I'm staying at the Chantrys' Kingston house. I'll explain when I get back. Meet me here the day after tomorrow.' He nodded, then addressed the man in a burst of Creole patois which Bratchet hoped amounted to 'Take damn good care of her.'

With Bratchet's mule's reins in his hand, the man kicked his bare heels into his mount's sides and they jogged away from the road between some slave huts and along a track in the hills. When it became too dark to see where they were going, the mules were halted and tethered, the man threw a rough sheep-skin cape at Bratchet, lay down and went to sleep.

The Maroon, Bratchet was sure he was a Maroon, was young-ish, thin as whipcord, carried a knife in the back of his belt – she saw its shape under his dirty shirt – and hostile. He disap-proved of taking her wherever he was taking her.

Ain't overjoyed myself.

'Asantewa and your *ohene* and I are good friends,' she said clearly at the recumbent figure. She didn't want a mistake about it. She lay down at a respectable distance away and put her holdall under her hand, taking care she could reach inside for the pistol at a second's notice, and went to sleep surprisingly quickly.

There were coffee plantations up here where the slopes were less precipitous, but the way she and the Maroon went the next day didn't impinge on any of them. She wasn't surprised. Goats would have had trouble with it.

She kept her eyes open as her mule edged along the first precipice, watching eagles soar above the abyss below on the same level as she was, then looking down to see if her mule's forefeet could fit on the flange of rock that was the path. It was a matter of inches. 'Don't sneeze,' she begged it. She didn't even want to think about the return journey. The next time they emerged from forest to find their noses over a thousand-foot drop she shut her eyes. And the next. And the next.

They stopped at mountain pools so that they and the animals could drink, but she was given no food. She supposed they were avoiding bridges which, this close to Maroon country, would be guarded by English soldiers. There was an army camp up here meant to contain them. Better if it bloody well had.

When they passed up through the clouds, the Maroon turned round and gestured for her to put on the sheepskin, the first solicitude he'd shown. Human beings had worn it a deal longer than the sheep and it smelled, especially as the cloud vapour moistened it, but she was glad of it. Above the clouds the air was keen.

They were in primeval forest now, the thick, looping greenery that from far away looked mauvy-blue and gave the mountains their name. Under its canopy it was dark as the sun began to go down again. Bratchet's temper became scratchy with fatigue and hunger. 'How much longer? I'm getting tired.'

He didn't answer. A bit further on, he slid off his mule and pointed up a thin, almost vertical path that squeezed between two outcrops of limestone. She was to go on alone.

Bratchet went up on all fours, stones shifting under her feet and starting avalanches of pebbles behind her. A smell of cooking came from somewhere above. She stumbled out on to a bare plateau of rock where a solitary figure sat by a fire stirring something in a pot. The higgler.

There was no greeting. Bratchet was too puffed to make one and there seemed to be a Maroon law against saying hello. Asantewa handed her a gourdful of stew from the pot and a smaller gourd to scoop it up with. It was disgusting; dog, probably, with a soupçon of lizard, but she was starving and ate it.

Asantewa still wore her military hat and bandolier, though both had gained more fetishes and feathers since Bratchet saw them last. She wore an enormous hide cloak and thong sandals on her feet. Apart from that, she hadn't altered a jot since her little boat had grounded on to the pirates' Bahamian beach.

'How's Licky?' asked Bratchet, giving her back the gourd.

'Want to change ever'thing,' grumbled Asantewa, 'All dat rain I make, and he grateful?' She shook her head. 'Dat one ungratitudinous *ohene*.'

Bratchet looked around at the verdant forest. 'And you doing such a good job,' she said.

Asantewa was not amused. 'Why ain't you git?'

'You ain't told me what I want to know.'

The higgler's eyes rolled up, showing only the brown-threaded whites. She moaned. It was alarming. Her pupils came back and regarded Bratchet. 'You goin' git soon,' she said, 'Spirits tell me.'

'I ain't.'

'You is. Navy took the *Brilliana*. Two days back.'

'Oh no.' Bratchet covered her face and rocked back and forth. Gone was her loathing of piracy; Sam, Nobby, Chadwell, men

411

she'd served with on that crazy voyage, facing a terrible death. She smeared the tears off her face and looked up to see Asantewa watching her, unmoved.

The higgler nodded. '*Now* you goin' to git.'

Bratchet cursed the messenger: 'You old besom. All the way up here to tell me bad news? Why didn't you send a message like normal people? I got a child, you know.'

Asantewa nodded again. 'I had a chil' once,' she said, 'Called it Joshua. Want to know what they did to it?'

'No.' Bratchet began to edge away on her backside. 'Please.'

'You listen. That what you come here for, so's I tell you.'

Asantewa was remorseless.

'Navy catched Calico Jack's boat same as they catch de *Brilliana*. Took Jack and them two girls and my Joshua and the rest to Spanish Town. Hanged Jack and the crew.'

'I know.'

'Din't hang the girls.'

'I know.'

'Din't hang my Joshua neither. He slave. He bad nigger runaway. The court say don't hang him, give him to whitey owners, give him to Vinner's brother.'

'Please,' pleaded Bratchet.

'He din' die easy like bubby fever or hangin',' Asantewa said, 'He rebel. He die rebel slave dyin'. They broke he arms and he legs. They tie him to the ground. Den dey burn him, slow. Start at he feet. He don' die till the fire reach he chest. Took three hours.'

The Bratchet hitched herself round away from Asantewa's face. She found herself looking out over Jamaica. From here, over 7,000 feet up, the rest of the Blue range rolled away below her, purple hill succeeding purple hill in gradual descent until they reached the plain and rolled rosily west into a crimson sunset.

The most beautiful abattoir in the world.

Asantewa's voice came from behind her, interested. 'What you do, if they kill your chil' like dat?'

Oh, Livia.

'Die,' she said, 'I'd kill them. Then I'd die.'

412

'Dat very weak,' said Asantewa as if she was marking an essay, 'Dyin' and killin'. That one weak revenge.'

'What did you do then?' asked Bratchet, wearily.

'I send them another chil'.'

Bratchet stayed where she was, hugging her knees and watching the plain darken. The cluster of lights to the south was Kingston. Somewhere beyond it, too small to be seen, the candles of Coppleston's would be lit. Kilsyth would be crooning Scottish lullabies to her baby as he always did to send her to sleep. *We're strangers here.*

'It's cold,' she said.

'I seen ice on this peak,' Asantewa said, 'Highest there is.'

So are you. A stranger. She thought how wonderful Asantewa was, and her people. Wrenched from wherever they came from, they had freed themselves, watching their captors from the cold mountain tops like wolves, waiting. And how terrible.

She shook herself briskly, wrapped the sheepskin more closely about her, got up and helped herself to more of the awful stew. It was going to be a long night.

'Tell me,' she said.

'Drink dis.' Asantewa was holding another gourd. The firelight shone on dark liquid. Bratchet looked from it to Asantewa, then drank it. If the woman wanted her dead, the Maroon who'd brought her up here could have killed her on the journey.

'Now what?'

'We wait.'

They waited. Asantewa built up the fire. Beyond the circle of its light was total blackness, and silence except for the breeze rustling the forest canopy below them. 'Look in de flames.'

She looked in the flames. Asantewa began to sing the same three-note chant that she'd sung in her boat before the waterspout came. Bratchet had no sense of fear, if anything she became bored, although the flesh on her arms and back was tingling. Asantewa began to speak in her limited Creole English but it had become supplemented with description that made pictures in Bratchet's mind.

413

At first she didn't understand. Asantewa was talking about two women called Ananse and Nassuna, one of whom she'd brought to Maroon country herself, the other arriving later.

Anne and Mary stepped into the fire. Anne was still wearing the velvet skirt in which Bratchet had last seen her in Puddle Court, but it was worn and old. They were standing on a high rock. It was this one but in the fire picture it was surrounded by black women.

'Dey got to be baptized, ain't they?' said a voice, 'Can't have two whiteys in Maroon country, kin we?'

Bratchet nodded. 'Got to be baptized.'

There was a huge cauldron and women prancing round it with human-skull rattles. And drums. A lot of drumming. Bratchet's foot beat in time with it. Though the cauldron steamed, the two white women, now naked, climbed into it and climbed out again, unharmed.

'Dey niggers now, ain't they?'

Bratchet nodded. 'Ananse and Nassuna.'

They went away. She saw them on a ship's deck against blue sky but each of them was attached to a thin string that led back to this peak where Asantewa watched them, its end in her lap.

It was evening, one of the soft blue Caribbean evenings and Ananse and Nassuna were lying down, each with a man on top of them, coupling.

'Getting bubbas. They need a bubba before dey too old, don't they?'

Bratchet nodded. They couldn't impregnate each other. It was the sensible thing to do.

They were fighting against boarders now, using cutlasses They were in wide canvas trousers, their hair streaming, in hand-to-hand combat with men in uniform. Their comrades had given up and were being herded for'ard but Ananse and Nassuna fought on, shouting, until Ananse was wounded in the arm and dropped her cutlass. Nassuna dropped hers and ran to her.

There was Pompey. How nice to see him. Holding a candle up in the birthing cell at Spanish Town courthouse. The string from Asantewa on her mountain top that was attached to

414

Ananse faded into invisibility as the younger died. Asantewa twitched the other one and Nassuna flew out of the cell and landed beside her. They talked. Nassuna kissed Asantewa, bowed, and picked up a baby.

Carrying the child under one arm, like a parcel, she walked off the Blue Mountain peak into mid-air and strode towards the sunset, her string still attached to Asantewa's hand. A thicker string ran between Asantewa and the baby, from the old black woman's navel to the child's white one.

'You git now,' said Asantewa and Bratchet woke up. Her head ached so badly she could hardly see. She was freezing cold. The fire was grey ashes, the same colour as the sky. Asantewa was holding out another drink to her, this time water. She drank it and Asantewa massaged her neck so that some of the ache went.

They walked together to the top of the steep track between the rocks. As they stood there, the sky above the dead fire was splintered with light. They turned to watch the sun rise over the eastern sea. It was like being washed in gold.

'Hope,' said Bratchet.

'Vengeance,' said Asantewa.

'How do you know I won't tell?'

Asantewa smiled for the first time. 'You nigger,' she said, 'No need baptize you. You always a nigger.'

Bratchet sat down and wriggled down the incline on her bottom. The Maroon was waiting for her, with the mules.

Pompey clicked his tongue when he saw her, helped her into the trap and tucked a rug round her. She slept most of the way, her head lolling on his shoulder.

She woke up when the trap swerved. Pompey was swearing. He'd rounded a corner to find a line of men walking in the middle of the road beyond it and was now having to drive the horses along the edge of them, taking care a trap wheel didn't foul the storm drain alongside.

Bratchet stretched. They were approaching Spanish Town through the trees that turned the road into an avenue. She paid little attention to the limping line of men as they went past

415

it in the same direction. Her mind was in the Blue Mountains.

Pompey reined in while the slave overseer, who wore uniform, cracked his whip to get the front of his line out of the trap's path. It took a few moments because the men were in legirons and the chain that connected the ankle of one to that of the man behind caused a few to stumble.

Another overseer at the head of the line turned, saw her and waved. It was the gaoler from the courthouse who'd shown them the birthing cell. She waved back and saw that his prisoners, some of them at any rate, were white. The shadow of leaves and the dirt on their faces had made it difficult to distinguish their colour.

One of them, shorter than the rest, turned to see who the gaoler was waving at and she recognized Nobby.

Wait. Wait until I can cope with this. I can't manage.

Pompey shook the reins to urge on the horses, and the trap was past the line in seconds, adding its dust to the prisoners' filth.

She had to cope. She was back in white Jamaica.

'Pull up,' she told Pompey. 'That gaoler, what's his name?'

'Dat Master Stubb.'

'Talk to him. When he comes up I want you to talk to him.'

'What 'bout?'

'Just talk to him, for God's sake.'

She turned in the trap, waiting until the shuffling line was nearly abreast of her.

She shouldn't be doing this. She should drive on. She couldn't. The gaoler, leading the procession, was pleased to see her. She greeted him and he stopped. Behind him, shoulders slumped as the men could stand still for a moment. There were manacles on each set of hands.

She heard Pompey begin a stilted 'How you doin', Master Stubb?' and scanned the faces.

Sweetman. Partridge – with an open wound on his cheek that flies clustered on. They had beards and every one of them was the same colour from the dust of the march from Kingston, as if they had started the process towards becoming corpses. Chadwell, so brave on the night of the storm, who'd voted to sell the captured slaves. Some she didn't recognize.

The gaoler was addressing her. 'Crew of the *Brilliana*, ma'am. Feared through the seven seas for rapine and murder and plunder . . .' He'd been reading the reward notices. 'Fine upstanding gentlemen now, eh? Not so brave now, eh?'

She nodded. *I knew them when they were brave.* They still were. If she were facing what these men were, she'd be crawling, not walking. Grimes, Freeble.

'Taking 'em to my cells . . .' the gaoler was saying.

Johnson. Oh, God, poor Johnson.

'. . . await trial . . .'

Guienne. Their eyes were blank. She supposed she must look very different, just another lady nob taking a prurient interest in men about to hang. What could she do for them? Nothing. Water. She could get them some water. She was looking for Sam Rogers, stretching her neck to try and see the end of the column.

'. . . give 'em hempen collars at Gallows Point . . .'

He wasn't there. Nobby. Blessed Nobby. They hadn't broken Nobby, he was shouting something at the trees. 'I ain' going dunghill.'

There was a cough from the prisoner nearest the trap. She glanced down at a grey-bearded old man looking intently at her. His legs looked too frail for the shackles.

Sam. Oh, Sam. How did you become so small? You were our colossus.

His eyes were the same, they willed hers to stay on them. Very slowly, he shook his head. She was to do nothing, there was nothing to be done. Understand me. Nothing.

Equally slowly, she nodded. 'Drive on, Pompey.'

They went back home another way. She couldn't bear to hear the jeers and abuse that would accompany the prisoners into the main square. Planter society hated pirates – justly, as she'd come to know – for raising insurance costs sky-high. She'd thought she did too.

But the line now shuffling towards its trial didn't consist of faceless villains but of Sam and Nobby, Johnson and Chadwell, men who hadn't started out as pirates, men she'd served with, whose tangled, helpless histories she knew. Who at their trial

417

would bother about why they were in the dock, any more than anyone had bothered to discover the long path that had led Anne and Mary to the same place?

My lads, whatever they've done since. She had a sudden spurt of pride. 'I ain't goin' dunghill,' Nobby had shouted.

'To go dunghill' in Nobby's world – it had been hers – was to mount the gallows begging for mercy. Then it occurred to her. It hadn't been aimless defiance Nobby had been shouting. It had been reassurance; they'd never know from Nobby her part as mutineer and purser of pirates.

She'd never thought they would.

Of Rosier, the Frenchman, she didn't think at all. She hadn't seen him in the line. He'd been there though . . . And recognized her.

Two days later, Bratchet answered a knock on her door. Kilsyth was still upstairs in bed. Sarcy and Livia were round the back of the house in the garden. On the porch steps was a black female slave, who curtseyed.

'Hello,' said Bratchet.

The woman curtseyed again. 'Juno, missy.'

She was thirtyish, and wore a turban and a good dress with a linen apron, showing that she was a house servant, which Bratchet had already guessed; field women lost their looks early. This one was still handsome.

'Good morning, Juno. What can I do for you?' Bratchet waited for the woman to deliver her master's invitation to a breakfast or some other message, though usually they were brought by men.

'Trouble, missy. We . . . my missy got trouble. You help her.' Juno nodded to a figure that was sitting at the bottom of the steps. It was Mary Waller.

Bratchet hurried down the steps and helped the girl into the parlour, Juno behind her. The jalousies were down, only allowing in thin white stripes of sun across the floor. The deep hum of slave chant and the rumble of barrels came from the distilling house up the hill. What air entered the room was high proofed with the smell of rum.

418

Mary Waller broke away from her and sat on a corner stool, not the central couch, as if she were trying to back into the walls. She was staring straight in front of her.

'Mary!' Afraid the girl had been injured in some way, Bratchet knelt down beside her ready to proffer nursing, but one look at her face showed this wasn't physical suffering. 'What is it?'

'I'm in trouble, Mrs Livingstone.' It was said quite normally but Mary's eyes didn't move from a point somewhere over Bratchet's head. Her face stood out white in the shade of the room.

It was the first time Bratchet had ever heard her speak and her voice was a shock, a contralto in Creole which made her seem older than her sixteen years.

But, oh dear, there was only one trouble spoken like that. And Mary, the most chaperoned female on the plain; Waller saw to it. Boasted about it. Helyar would kill her. In that moment Bratchet wanted nothing so much as to protect her. She'd been there.

'My poor baby. Don't look like that. I'll help. I'll do anything to help.'

The girl slumped suddenly, either in relief that she'd been understood or because, in being understood, her situation had become more real to her. Juno, standing still in the doorway, said: 'I tol' you, child. Missy help us.'

Juno was the mother then. This was the woman on whom, if the story was true, Helyar Waller had begotten this white daughter. There was little physical resemblance, but the bond of horror between her and the girl was an almost visible cord stretching from one to the other.

Bratchet stood up so that she could put her arms round the girl. Mary flinched away and Bratchet let her go. 'It's not as bad as all that. Come on, chuck, bear up. No harm's going to come to you, I promise. Oh, *dear*.'

The girl had vomited. She went on staring into space while they cleaned her up, as if somebody else had done it.

Calling Sarcy to stay with Mary, Bratchet took Juno with her and Livia into the kitchen house out in the garden to fetch some lemonade. 'Who's the father?' She looked up when the woman didn't answer her. Oh, God, he's black. That was the reason for the fear; Mary had consented to one of her mother's race. Or perhaps she hadn't consented to anybody. 'Was it rape?' The poor little one; however it happened, Helyar would kill her.

'You help her, missy.'

'I want to. I just don't know what to do.'

With Livia holding one of her hands and a glass of lemonade in the other, they went back into the house. Mary was still staring across the room. Bratchet held the glass while she sipped, Juno kneaded her daughter's hands. Livia got her doll from under a chair and nursed it.

Mary pushed them away. Her words were stilted: 'I came to you, Mrs Livingstone, because you're a woman of the world.'

Am I? She supposed that in Mary's eyes she was the most raffish woman on the plain. She wanted Bratchet's help with an abortion.

Automatically, Bratchet said again, 'It's not as bad as all that.' *I can't. I won't. She's not going to suffer what I did.* Anyway, if that's what the girl wanted of her, she'd have done better to ask her mother or one of the other black women; they were known for performing operations on themselves or each other to avoid bearing a child into slavery. Poor, poor Mary.

She said, 'You shall stay here for a while. My husband and I will go to your . . . your uncle and explain about the baby. He'll come round. He loves you, I know, and –'

Mary Waller screamed, 'You're not a woman of the world.' She got up and rushed at Juno and began batting at her with her hands. 'You stupid nigger. It's only happened to me. I told you. Nobody else. I'm the only person. It's me, it's me.'

Bratchet watched the black hands enfold the clawing, scratching white ones, watched the black mother gather the white daughter to her, heard her croon nursery sounds until the girl collapsed against her and let herself be rocked into quiet. Now she understood.

Oh, my God. Oh, my dear God.

Livia, upset, began to grizzle. Bratchet picked her up. She said, '*Is* she pregnant?'

Juno shrugged. She began leading her daughter to the couch. 'He been goin' into her room a week.'

Bratchet went to the window and pushed open the jalousies to breathe air. She could only smell the stifling sweetness of sugar. Even with the shutter propped to its fullest extent, her view took in merely the ant-ridden boarding of the cellar trap and the roots of the cotton tree like black and white snakes in the strongly defined light and shadows.

She rubbed her cheek against her child's light, fine hair. *I hate this country*. There was too much sun. Too much that was beautiful, ugly, inexplicable, too much fecundity of growth and flowing water, too-naked black flesh, too-overdressed white. It was too . . . unexpurgated.

She said, 'It isn't you. You mustn't think that. It happens.' Jimmy Groves and his daughter in Puddle Court. *And* his grand-daughter, the old bastard. In manor houses, castles, perhaps palaces.

Mary's voice behind her said, 'I shan't go back. I'll kill myself first. I'm staying here. When you go I'll come with you. I've got relatives in New England.'

'When we go?'

'He's going to drive you out. He doesn't like you. Nobody does.' Desperation had done away with shyness, even manners.

Bratchet didn't blame her. She thought she'd known horror enough, but she'd been spared the particular atrocity of incest. 'Does he know you've come here?'

Juno answered. 'We said we gine shoppin' in Kingston.'

'Good. I'll get your room prepared.'

She and Sarcy got bedding from the linen cupboard, carried it upstairs and made up the spare-room bed, then she took Livia in to Kilsyth, plonked her next to him on the bed and told him.

He wouldn't believe her. 'The lassie's hysterical. There's no father would do that to his own bairn. Nor uncle neither. I know ye don't like Waller but, ach, it's against nature.' He looked at the small girl beside him. 'Who'd do that to his daughter?'

'You've led a sheltered life. And she says he's going to drive us out.'

'There y'are then, the girl's havering. She canna stay here.'

But when he came down into the parlour his natural courtesy prevailed. 'Ye're welcome to stay a while, Miss Mary, till ye've settled your spirits. Later, mebbe, I'll send a wee note to your . . . to your folk to tell them where you are.' When she began screaming, he relented again. 'Weel, weel, whisht now, lassie. Nothing will be done until you're more composed.' He looked at Bratchet. 'Well, put her in the spare room.'

By the time they got her upstairs, the girl's eyes were beginning to close. Bratchet left Juno sitting beside her on the bed and went downstairs to find Kilsyth still worrying. 'We canna leave the man to think she's mebbe had an accident.'

'He's the accident, the bastard.' She went out to the kitchen to get some lunch. She sent Sarcy upstairs with food for Mary and Juno, then settled Livia in a pinafore at the table. As they ate, she told Kilsyth of her encounter with the *Brilliana*'s crew.

'I'm sorry for it,' he said, 'but they knew the danger. And the court has exonerated us.'

While Livia took her nap, Bratchet had to do the washing up. Sarcy was nowhere to be found. Upstairs, Mary Waller was asleep, her hand in Juno's, her body shuddering every now and then.

In the heat of the afternoon, Bratchet played chequers with Kilsyth, watching his clawed fingers move the pieces by the knuckle, rubbed them with liniment and went back to the kitchen to experiment with pickling while he looked after Livia. Sarcy was still missing.

She went to bed early, exhausted and worried. After an hour's sleep she woke up, gasping and in a sweat. 'Sarcy!'

'Don't fash yersel' about the besom,' Kilsyth said sleepily, 'She'll be back.'

'No. She won't. Oh, God, Kilsyth. She's gone to Waller to trade Mary for Dinnah.'

He yawned. 'We've no' kept her that hungry.'

'Dinnah. Her daughter. She'll get him to give Dinnah her freedom in return for telling him where Mary is.'

There was nothing to be done. In any case, it was too late. Helyar Waller was already coming up the track at the head of twenty planters with guns and a warrant for Bratchet's arrest on a charge of piracy.

CHAPTER TWENTY-TWO

DANIEL DEFOE, bewildered, sweating and ecstatic, wandered Kingston, questioning dockers on lading, planters on crop yield, naval officers on piracy and black-market women on babies and vegetables.

He bought a white linen jacket with gold braid appliqué on collar and cuffs, which left a large hole in the purse Harley had given him for expenses and an even larger one in the sum he'd been thinking of expending on a cotton dress for Mrs Defoe. But the summer back home hadn't been up to much. She wouldn't thank him for cotton. Whereas he was extremely hot in his best velvet . . .

In the end, he compromised on an Indian shawl for Mrs Defoe and bought a wide-brimmed straw hat for himself to keep off the sun. Excellent quality. Perhaps, when his present difficulties were over, he should start importing them.

The clock in the pagoda steeple of the parish church on the south-east corner of King Street started to chime midday. Reluctantly, he set off up the wide thoroughfare, approving of the grid plan of the streets. If London could be reconstructed on such an efficient system, fewer visitors would be lost to fall victim to cutpurses . . .

He got lost. By the time he rediscovered the house on Harbour Street, John Laws had a carriage waiting for him. '*There* you are, my dear. Just time for a stiffener before we take the open road. Madeira? Claret? Rum?'

Harley had said, 'You're to contact the attaché, John Laws. As you know, he's worked for me before. He's at present in Jamaica, negotiating trade agreements with the French West Indies. Don't be fooled by his manner; the situation calls for the unconventional.'

John Laws was certainly that. When he'd met him earlier in the morning, Defoe's Puritanism had winced at the fluttering fingers and eyelashes, the face-patches and lace. It did so again. 'Do we have to go so soon? I only landed this morning. I was hoping for –'

'So was I, my dear, so was I. Had it not been for Mr Selkirk, I should have been thrilled to show you Kingston, not that I've plumbed quite all its joys myself, being so lately seconded to the West Indies. But go we shall, before Mr Selkirk arrives back from the barber's to which I have sent him. Now then, Madeira? Claret? Rum?'

'Rum,' said Defoe firmly.

'Very well.' John Laws poured golden liquid into a silver-rimmed glass and added a squeeze of lime, 'Though I feel the principle of when-in-Rome depends entirely on whether the Romans piss in it. You'll forgive me if I quaff claret.'

Defoe stared dubiously at his rum. 'Who's Mr Selkirk?'

'Alexander Selkirk . . .' began John Laws, when there was a knocking on the front door. 'Oh, my God, there he is. Out the back, dear heart. Delilah, my little black pudding, answer the door. Give Mr Selkirk my apologies. Called away on government business. Give him some cheese. And rum, lots of rum.'

He took Defoe's glass away, picked up a small portmanteau and hurried his guest past a grinning maid, down back steps and into a palm-treed garden. Peering round the front of the house, they made a sprint for the carriage waiting in the road with its driver. As they drove off, a man appeared at the front door, calling after them.

'Whip 'em up, Nero,' ordered Laws. He turned to call, 'Back soon, Mr Selkirk,' and waved until the dust of their going obscured his view.

'Alexander Selkirk,' he told Defoe, slumping back in his seat, 'was marooned five years ago on a deserted island off the coast of Peru by his captain, a gentleman unknown to me but of whom I have formed a high opinion. Mr Selkirk was recently rescued by Captain Woodes Rogers. Ah, you know Captain Rogers? Yes, well, having rescued Mr Selkirk, Captain Rogers was good enough to land him in the West Indies, where I, the least of the diplomatic corps, was deputed to look after him while Captain Rogers went off to do something nautical in the *East* Indies, as far away from Mr Selkirk as he could get.'

'Boring?' asked Defoe, clinging to the carriage side.

'Boring? My dear, he invented it. Instead of listening to myself expounding on how the world has wagged since he last saw it, Mr Selkirk has been pleased to spend the last few days giving me five years of his experiences – most of them with goats. The island of Juan-Wherever was blessed with goats. Goats, it seems, have fed Mr Selkirk, clothed Mr Selkirk and entertained Mr Selkirk in ways I shudder to imagine. All right, Nero. You can slow down now.'

'Still,' pondered Defoe, 'cast away alone for five years. It would be very interesting to know how he survived.'

'Really?' John Laws raised an elegant eyebrow. 'I'm sure Mr Selkirk will be happy to tell you. Now then . . .'

He heaved his portmanteau from the back of the carriage on to his knee and opened it. Defoe glimpsed a gun case and papers. The papers were extracted. 'Thanks to Mr Selkirk, one's merely been able to scan the letter from my Lord Oxford you were kind enough to deliver, and then make the necessary enquiries, so if you'll forgive me . . . How *is* dear Harley?'

'Ill at ease,' Defoe told him.

'Mmm, I always think sitting on the fence *such* an uncomfortable position. Do tell me, which way is he expected to jump in the lamentable event of Her Majesty's death?'

Defoe blinked. Usually such questions were coded. He wasn't going to confide Harley's difficulties to this scented, beautiful young man. 'The Act of Succession ensures that . . .'

'Oh, *please*. I thought better of you. Here's Mr Defoe, I thought, writer and friend to the Lord High Treasurer, privy to all the secrets. Now I'll hear the gossip, I thought.'

You don't hear much in Newgate. The prison gatekeeper had welcomed him like an old friend. 'Back again, Mr Defoe? And not debt this time. Sedition, ain't it?'

It was. And, like the last time, because the public was too ignorant to recognize irony when they read it. He'd given his tracts daring titles to attract attention: 'Some Considerations of the Advantages and Real Consequences of the Pretender's Possessing the Crown of England', and 'An Answer to a Question that Nobody Thinks of, Viz: What if the Queen Should Die?'.

Anybody who'd read them should have seen that he was putting the case for his own side by comically advancing that of his opponents. The reasons he gave for opposing the Hanoverian succession were so palpably absurd he'd expected intelligent readers to realize they were no reasons at all. The only people they should have annoyed were Jacobites.

He knew better, now. The Whigs had neither humour nor gratitude. They'd laid a complaint. Arresting officers were at his house with a warrant from Lord Chief Justice Parker within minutes, for all Mrs Defoe could do to impede them.

Harley, putting up his bail, had said, 'I think, Mr Defoe, we must get you out of the way until the gunfire dies down.' Then, to Defoe's joy, 'I'll send you to Jamaica to bring back the girl.' And here he was in the tropics he'd dreamed of. It was worth it. He'd cross the bridge of his trial when he came to it. Harley would get him off somehow.

He leaned over the side of the carriage, taking in atmosphere and dust, storing away details and wishing he'd had time to buy a notebook.

John Laws was perusing the letter from Harley. 'Nyumnyum . . . "to assist in all particulars the bearer of . . ." nyumnyum, ". . . to secure the person of the woman known as Mrs Livingstone Kilsyth believed to be living in Jamaica." Yes, well, according to my information she is now on the Coppleston estate.' He poked Defoe with his elbow. 'What's she done?'

'How do those women carry so many articles on their heads?' asked Defoe in admiration, watching the road.

'Practice, I imagine. What has our Mrs Kilsyth done, Defoe?'

Defoe wondered how much to tell him; on the other hand he could hardly withhold too much information from a man deputed to help him. 'My Lord Oxford believes she can assist him in the identification of some matter. She was sent to the Low Countries on his behalf some years ago . . .'

'That's right. I knew it . . . pockmarked little wench. Terrible name, if I remember. Pocket, was it?'

426

'Bratchet,' said Defoe.

'That's right. Turned up at m'house at The Hague when I was attaché. I remember the Scot. Great big lad. Nearly caused a riot. Jacobite, as I learned afterwards. Married her, did he? Fishy, the whole thing. Are you at liberty to tell me any more?'

'No,' said Defoe. 'Look, that's coffee. Those red beans laid out to dry. I was told about them. Fascinating.'

'Isn't it, though,' said Laws. 'Enjoy the view while you can, m'dear fella. M'duty in this pest hole is completed, thank God, and so, when we have secured the person of Mistress Bratchet, is yours.'

'Can't we stay a bit?' asked Defoe.

'According to these instructions, we are to return her to England with all possible speed. So we'll carry them out and go back to Kingston to catch the very next boat, don't you agree?'

'Can't we stay overnight at Spanish Town? I should very much like to see it. An officer I met this morning told me pirates are imprisoned there. I should like to see . . .'

'I think not, dear,' said Laws. 'It's as well the governor's away visiting his opposite number in Barbados, or we should be bound to inform him of our doings which, in turn, would involve us in protocol that would take days. My Lord Oxford stresses not only the urgency of this mission but its secrecy. We'll eat as we go and . . .'

Surprised by Laws's firmness, Defoe salvaged what he could. 'On pineapple? I'd dearly like to taste a pineapple.'

'. . . just secure our quarry, and flee.' Laws sighed. 'Taking pineapples with us.'

'A cabbage tree,' exclaimed Defoe. 'I'm sure that's a cabbage tree. They have to fell the entire tree, you know, because it dies when you cut out its top.'

'Do they?' John Laws produced an exquisite lawn handkerchief which he laid over his face, 'If you'll forgive me, Defoe, I shall reflect for a while on the interesting subject of goats.'

The clouds that had been building up all afternoon were gaining anemone colours from the setting sun. Even Defoe was

427

tiring of a world that consisted entirely of sky and sugar cane, and beginning to wonder what happened if one was benighted in it. His bones ached from the springless bouncing of the carriage over ruts.

A peculiar resonance was rising from the endless fields, a sort of hum. What insect could be so loud at evening? Frogs, perhaps. He'd heard about the frogs.

Laws wouldn't know. He leaned forward and tapped the driver on the shoulder, raising a puff of dust. 'Are those frogs I hear?' Good Lord. The man was afraid!

'Ent frogs, massa. Them's drums.' Nero's free hand plucked at his lips. 'There's trouble. Dey sendin' message.'

'Maroon drums?' He'd heard about Maroons, too. 'What message?'

Nero shook his head. 'Kin' read drums. But I don' like 'em.'

Neither did Defoe. Whatever the message, it carried menace. And was getting louder. Flocks of disturbed birds rose from the cane. A line of rats raced across the track ahead of them. The drum beats now seemed to be coming from all points of the compass and directing themselves straight at him.

Tales of cannibals and stewpots lost the magic they'd held and lodged sickeningly in his gut. Coincidence? No. His enemies had pursued him and hired savages with sharpened teeth and spears to still his pen for ever.

Panicking, he shook John Laws awake. The young man was unperturbed. 'Whiggish cannibals? A *teeny* bit unlikely, I think.' However, he hauled his portmanteau back on to his knee and got out his gun case. 'Duelling pistols. Carry 'em everywhere. *De rigueur* in the diplomatic corps, my dear.'

They primed them and held them carefully downwards as the carriage jolted onwards. 'How far to Coppleston's now, Nero?'

'Up there, massa.' The driver pointed with his whip to a track on their right winding out of sight into hills that were becoming indistinct with mist as the twilight temperature fell. In the distance – how far away it was difficult to judge – was a small patch of sharply defined lights. As they looked towards it, they saw added twinkles. Seconds later, the air carried the report of pistol shots to them.

'Ye-es,' said John Laws, 'my informant this morning told me the Kilsyths had been making themselves unpopular. They seem to have overdone it. Ah well.'

To the dismay of Defoe, whose instinct was to hide in the cane, Laws ordered the carriage up the track. Drums, lights and the occasional exchange of shots grew stronger as they jolted up it. Now they could hear dogs barking.

Perhaps we should call back tomorrow, Defoe just managed not to say. He'd not bargained on entering a war; rounding the next bend they'd be in the middle of it.

'Stop here, Nero,' said Laws, 'Turn the carriage round and be ready to go when we come back. Keep out of sight.'

He got down and held up his hand to help Defoe alight. 'I think we'll go on foot from here, dear. No, leave the pistol. From the sound of it, there's enough guns abroad already.'

Defoe wished John Laws had stayed in the pigeonhole he'd put him in; effeminate young men should shrink from violence, not advance on it. He followed the tall, mincing figure round the corner and towards the house and the crowd of angry men gathered outside its gate . . .

Inside the dark house, Bratchet made the rounds of Copple-ston's defenders, giving them drinks. In the bedroom above the parlour, Mary Waller crouched by the window, pistol in hand.

'Are you all right, Mary?'

'I'll kill him, you know.'

'You damn nearly did.' They'd had to make Mary's post here, looking out to the north and away from the crowd, in case she did it again. They'd had no idea she possessed a gun until she'd produced it at the west window and shot at Helyar Waller approaching below. Luckily, she'd missed her father, instead killing the dog he was holding on a leash.

'I'm not sorry,' said Mary defiantly.

Bratchet patted her head. 'Neither am I.' It hadn't looked a nice dog; it was trained to hunt slaves, as were all the others that now added their snarls to the racket of the drums. And the shot had sent Waller back to the healthy side of the gate. 'What's happening here?'

'Nothing.'

Outside, just beyond the cottonwood tree, slaves from the sugar mill had gathered to watch the scene at the gate. Moonlight touched the black sheen on bare, muscled arms and iron collars. One of them would have alerted the drummers to send a signal to the Maroons.

God, don't let Licky come. She didn't want a massacre of either side. He'd be too late in any case. It was a long way to travel from the Blue Mountains and the standoff couldn't last much longer; the planters would rush the house any moment. That they hadn't already owed nothing to the defenders and their guns, but was because the drums had disconcerted them; they were afraid of precipitating a revolt.

Johnny Faa had already ordered the slaves back to their huts, threatening to set his dogs on them, shouting at his black overseers, the 'jumpers', to whip them into line. But, while the slaves showed no sign of attack, neither did they retire; lashes from the jumpers hadn't shifted them. They stood where they were and eventually Johnny Faa had admitted defeat and gone back to the gate.

Nevertheless, and surprisingly, Coppleston's fire power wasn't proving negligible. Kilsyth had given Juno one of his fowling pieces and put her at the east window over the hall while he took the position of most danger in the west bedroom window facing the gate.

He himself had offered for Mary's horse pistol, which was the best gun in the house, but she'd refused to surrender it. It was some sort of justice that the man she'd tried to shoot with it had been the one who'd given it to her in order that she could protect her virtue against lustful blacks while out riding. She'd brought it with her when she escaped – to kill herself, or him, if he caught up with her.

Pompey had produced an antique fowling piece with a barrel like the end of an ear trumpet, given to him by one of the courthouse judges as a farewell present. Its recoil had done nearly as much damage to him as its birdshot had inflicted on the attackers.

'Are you all right, Pompey?' She could see his cap of grey-wool hair against the hole he'd made in the jalousie of the south bedroom window.

'Fine, missy, I is fine.'

She poured him a glass of punch. 'I'm sorry I got you into this.'

'Don' you trouble yosself, Miss Bratchie. They call Pompey wutless ol' nigger. I show 'em wutless.'

Bratchet took her jug to Juno in the hall window, sitting with Kilsyth's gun across her knees as if she did it every day, and then joined her husband where he knelt by the sill in the west bedroom. 'Is Livia all right?' he asked her.

'Wonderful.' The child had been woken by the firing, but had merely said 'Bang' and gone back to sleep, her small posterior in the air, her cheek on her doll.

'How's the spirit o' the garrison?'

'High. Pompey actually seems to be enjoying himself.'

'So am I. I'll teach yon callants their manners.' It was a Highland reprise of Pompey's 'I'll show 'em wutless'.

Had they come to arrest him, he would have gone, albeit protesting. But the information had been laid not against Kilsyth, but against Bratchet. He and Helyar Waller had met on the porch – distrusting the armed men Waller had brought with him, he had refused to let them beyond the gate.

'I'm sorry, Kilsyth,' Waller said, 'I'm here as chief magistrate with a warrant for the arrest of your wife,' and proceeded to read it.

As with Anne Bonny and Mary Read the charge was of 'piratically, feloniously and in a hostile manner, attacking, engaging and taking the barque *San Martine* off the coast of Florida . . .'

'We were at war wi' the bloody Dagos,' Kilsyth's roar had interrupted Waller's reading. 'Yon was an act o' war. And I was wi' her at the time, ye great gowk.'

The sunset behind Waller had made a corona round his curly fair hair; with his brutal face shadowed, he'd had the outline of a saint. 'Whether she knew it or not, there was already an armistice between us and the Spanish. And the depositions name your wife only.'

431

'And whose depositions may they be?'

'A Frenchman called Rosier, now in custody, and that of an honest man, John Faa.'

'Twa pirates, then.' Kilsyth's accent grew more Scottish the angrier he became, 'I'd not try a dog on the word o' sic.'

But, allied together, the two depositions were, literally, arresting: Rosier's that Bratchet had willingly cooperated in piracy; Faa's that she'd had in her possession valuables gained from it.

There was worse. Waller declared, 'I have also had information that she has entertained, in this very house, the nigger who calls himself King of the Maroons, a wanted outlaw. Furthermore, she has seduced my daughter into this same house with the intent of poisoning an innocent young woman's mind against her family.'

Sarcy.

'Ye incestuous bastard, the lass came willing.' The shout had carried to the crowd beyond the gate and Bratchet knew they were done. Now Waller's reputation would depend on proving her a criminal who'd corrupted his daughter; he dare not rest until he had.

'I warn you, Kilsyth. We are prepared to use force.'

'Then ye'll have tae use it. And get off my bloody steps before I use a bit mysel'.'

Waller retired for consultation. Soon after he'd led a rush at the house. Which was when his daughter had shot at him. There'd been an exchange of fire that had hurt nobody but had forced the assailants back to their present position.

'I'll have to go,' Bratchet said reasonably, 'Somebody'll get killed.' *Livia, oh, Livia.* 'Anyway, we can't get to the well. There isn't enough water in the house to stand a siege.'

'Ye'll be taken to nae prison while Livingstone of Kilsyth's alive tae stop it.'

She rubbed her face against the top of her husband's head. 'You and your hopeless causes,' she said. She knew what she should do; she should walk quietly out of the house and give herself up. But Waller would see to it that she was refused bail. And what would Livia do without her if she never came back? Her child was the priority.

For the same reason, she could feel only sympathy for Sarcy's treachery. If it were her daughter and grandchild who were slaves and she could gain their freedom by betrayal, she'd betray. She'd betray anybody. Besides, there was Mary Waller to consider. Surrendering that poor girl to a life of abuse was more than she could bear.

Licky might come in time. But if he did, the bloodshed would be terrible. And her responsibility. Oh God, how had it all happened? What had led her to this?

She heard Kilsyth say: 'Mebbe the governor'll get word of this humudgeon an' come to scatter the vermin. Hamilton's a Scot and a civilized man.'

She didn't remind him that the governor was away in Barbados. It wouldn't make any difference.

Kilsyth said, shifting, 'There's two more rascals come to join the pack.'

She peered out. Two figures were walking up the track to join the group at the gate. She was puzzled by a sense of *déjà vu*, but supposed they must be planters she'd seen at one of the gatherings.

'Lord aid us, what've ye put in this brew?' Kilsyth had taken a sip of the punch she'd poured for him, 'It's fit for pigs.'

'Everything.' She'd emptied into lemonade the remnants of most of the spirits they had in the house.

Her husband grinned at her. 'Send some out to Waller.'

'I do understand your position,' Laws was saying, sweetly and loudly, above the drums, 'but I hope you'll understand mine. Here's Sir Daniel Defoe, the Crown's own envoy with the Crown's own warrant for the detention of this female, and I'm sure you wouldn't want him to return to Her Majesty to tell her that her subjects had disregarded her instructions.'

Defoe adopted his sudden knighthood with a raised chin, and put his hand on his sword hilt. The planters weren't sure at all. He could see that, to them, Laws personified colonial administration; the unnatural dandy who grew effete on their taxes. But because he personified it, he was giving them pause. Here was the authority that could send or withhold soldiers for their

433

protection, the government that could make their trade with international agreements, or break it.

'We've our own warrant,' said Helyar Waller, 'and we can detain the nigger-loving bitch safe enough without your help.' There were growls of agreement from the other planters. They had the excitement of men half-drunk. Defoe noticed hip flasks being passed round.

'I'm sure you can, *sure* you can,' Laws told him, 'but the Queen, after all, has a teeny say in the matter, don't you agree? Whatever the woman's done, be sure she will be returned to you for punishment – if she *can* be returned after Her Majesty's finished with her.' His wink left Bratchet swinging from the gallows.

'If it's tha' serious,' Johnny Faa broke in eagerly, breathing brandy, 'we can dispose o' the slut oursel'.'

'It's a matter of state, you see,' said Laws, 'Justice must be seen to be done where it's been flouted most.' He became businesslike. 'Now then, what I suggest is this. Sir Daniel goes into the house on his own, to reason with her. What about that?'

He took Defoe by the arm and drew him away, as if leaving the planters to discuss the matter. 'You've got about fifteen minutes,' he said, 'I won't be able to hold them longer. See if there's a back way out. Smuggle her down to the carriage. I'll meet you there.' He raised his voice. 'Now then, Sir Daniel. A flag of truce, I think.'

He walked up to one of the planters – '*Would* you mind, dear?' – took his hunting musket off him and attached his handkerchief to its barrel. 'Off you go. We'll be waiting.'

A man totally sure of his course has the advantage of those who aren't, but it was clear the planters wouldn't be confused for long; there was a resentful murmur as Defoe began his walk up the path.

'Tell the bitch if she don't come out, we'll blast her out,' one of them called after him.

This, then, was adventure. He'd written about it, dreamed of it, Defoe the Dauntless. It's sordid. Where the romance? Where the high courage? Somewhere down in his ankles and refusing to support the rest of him.

It was a long, long path. The cacophony of the drums terrified him. The planters' dogs terrified him. The black, closed faces of the slaves staring at him from under the tree up the slope to his right were the fire waiting for him if he leaped from the planters' frying pan.

Into his mind came the disjointed memory of this morning – a week ago – when he'd first arrived at John Laws's house and commented to that gentleman on the fineness of the day.

'My dear,' Laws had said, 'You don't know how tired you'll be of saying that.'

He was tired already and there'd only been one day. Resentment spurted through him that he was among these alien stinks, plants and people because of a Cockney drudge. He, Defoe, mover of political thinking, the man for his times, dead in a squalid encounter, waggling a white flag.

They'll get Swift to write my epitaph.

Appalled at this new horror, he sprang up the steps and rapped at the door-knocker. *Something sardonic and witty to be remembered long after I am.*

The door opened halfway. 'Yes?'

'My Lord of Oxford's compliments,' he said, quickly, 'And I'm sent for the Bratchet.' Lord, he sounded like a dog-walker. Still, the thing was to get in. Before the buggers back there rushed the place.

The door opened wider and closed behind him. Facing him in the moonlit hall, a lantern in her hand, was a beautiful woman. 'Bratchet?' he asked, incredulously, and corrected himself, '*Mistress* Bratchet?'

The candlelight was gentle to the pocks on her face which had, in any case, gained a bloom from the sun, as the rest of her had acquired poise. Tired, anxious as she must be, she possessed a still assurance that came from intelligence and, yes, kindness. Whatever her past adventurings, they had left no sign of sluttishness on her. He'd wondered why Kilsyth had lowered himself to marry a maidservant; now he knew.

'Come up.' She held the light high so that he could follow her up a dark Jacobean staircase. The house smelled of rum and mildew but from the dress of the woman ahead of him came a scent of orange-flower and, oddly, pickles. She showed him into a dark room where a man knelt by the window, using its sill as a rest for a fowling piece.

'Kilsyth, it's Daniel Defoe. Do you remember me?'

The Scot didn't turn round. 'Aye, I recognized ye as ye came up the path. It's me in the stocks now, Defoe.'

Strange. He'd forgotten that first meeting, only recalling the encounter at Puddle Court. The whirligig of time . . . Defoe the saviour said gently, 'I've come to rescue your wife, Kilsyth. I've come to take her home.'

'Did Martin send ye? I could ay depend on Martin.'

'Yes,' said Defoe immediately. 'He persuaded Harley to send a message to the government envoy in Kingston.' In a situation so extraordinary, extraordinary lies were necessary – and believable. 'A man called John Laws. He's out there now, persuading them to let her leave.'

'I know the man. A mimsy, but with a head on him. They'll not let her go, though.'

'No. I'm to take her out a back way and meet him down the track. He's got a carriage.'

Beside him, the woman called Bratchet said, 'Livia and me aren't leaving you, so don't think it. We'll solve this somehow.'

Kilsyth ignored her. 'There's a cellar leads out under a tree on the north side. Its doors are mebbe stiff. I'll keep the bastards occupied whiles ye're raising them. I'll meet ye in Kingston.'

'I'm not going,' the woman said again.

'Come here, Defoe.'

Defoe joined him at the window. Outside, Laws's pale lemon jacket stood out among the buff colours of the planters' clothes. He had his back to the house, facing the angry men, his hands flirting in gesticulation. Through the hammering drums it was impossible to hear voices but the planters' mouths were opening and shutting in ugly, silent shouts as they patted their guns. Their dogs had caught the unrest and were bounding to the lengths of their chains. Undoubtedly, Laws had underestimated the length of time he could hold off an attack.

Kilsyth was looking up at him. 'Take her and the wee one. An' God preserve ye to keep them both from harm,' he said softly, 'Mebbe I'll meet ye in Kingston, mebbe I'll not.'

Afterwards, Defoe was to say that in that moment he looked for the first time into the eyes of a condemned man who was happy with his sentence. He nodded.

'Grand. Give me that musket. Then get to that bloody cellar. Bratchie, bring me all the guns in the house. Primed.'

In the doorway, Defoe paused to watch the wife protest, the husband speak quietly to her, saw her nod, saw the tears on her face, saw her put a jug of some drink on the sill, saw Kilsyth put down the fowling piece long enough to raise the jug, like a chalice, with hands that had become misshapen into claws, saw the Bratchet lean down to kiss him – and went.

An elderly black man carrying a lighted candle showed him the cellar and together they stood on a chute that led to the flat wooden doors in the ceiling. Earth and seeds had settled in the crack where the doors met and matted it with weed as strong as chain. They found a stave from a broken barrel and hit at the doors with it – in rhythm with the drums.

Defoe dropped his aching arms. 'They won't shift.' His efforts had brought dust powdering through the crack. Its fall increased instead of lessening. 'My God, they've heard us.' Somebody above was scrabbling at the other side of the doors.

The black man picked up the stave and gave a complicated rap on the underside of the doors. Thumps from above came back in the same sequence. The black man gave him a piano-key smile. 'Brothers.'

Leaving the rest of the work to the black man's relatives, Defoe glanced behind him to check that the Bratchet was ready for departure. She had a child in her arms, nodding sleepily against her shoulder. There were two more women, a white one and a black one. 'Lord, who are these?'

'They're coming with us.'

One woman and a child to take across enemy lines, he'd bargained for. Three . . . as well give him elephants and call him Hannibal. Weakly he said, 'Well, cover that one up.'

'Of course.' Bratchet gave the child to the black woman and ran back upstairs.

The girl was as fair as the Bratchet, but whereas Bratchet's

437

hooded cloak was dark, her friend was in pale colours with a light straw hat. Dammit, so was he. He snatched off his hat and, groaning, rubbed his palms into the dirt of the cellar floor and smeared them over his new coat.

Bratchet came back with a deep-purple shawl and tucked it round the girl. 'Pompey, when we're out you must go to the stables and saddle the horses. Wait for him.' She turned to Defoe, pleading for reassurance. 'There's no warrant for him. They'll let him leave when they find I've gone, won't they?'

'Sure to.'

She wasn't convinced. 'They're angry. They might do anything.'

'It's you they're angry at, apparently. You only endanger him by staying.' There was a tearing sound from above his head and the doors shifted. 'Put the candle out.'

When the doors rose, the noise of the drums, which had sounded in the cellar as muffled booms, came rampaging in, gaining a pitch which bewildered the brain. They would incite the planters' madness now, rather than inhibit, he thought. They were inciting his, or he wouldn't be going out into the exposing moonlight trailing women behind him.

Black hands reached down to help him up. Outside, he found himself encircled by slaves and beneath the branches of an enormous tree which allowed the moonlight through in dapples.

Peering over black shoulders, he could see the edge of the crowd at the gate round the front of the house. One of the dogs which had been pulling on its leash changed direction and began trying to rush towards the tree. He could see it slavering as its master hauled it back. The man glanced to where the dog was indicating. Lord, don't let him loose it. Don't let him loose it. It was a terrible dog. It could see him. It could hear the women being lifted out of the cellar. Its owner was looking directly at him. Then the man gave the dog a kick and turned back to the interesting scene at the west window.

Pompey was out now. He put his mouth close to Defoe's ear. 'He say wait till he begin firin'.'

Begin firing then. For the love of God, fire. Grouped like this in the open, even with the wall of slaves around them, it could only be seconds before they were seen. From the front of the house came the crack of a shot. Defoe saw a man next to the man with the dog fall down. Immediately there was another shot. Then a fusillade from the planters.

A slave pushed him. 'Git.' He got. Another slave, a woman, had his sleeve and led him away from under the tree. Like a phalanx, the slaves moved with him. He was the soft part of the tortoise, they its shell. He didn't look round to see if the women were following; he didn't care any more. If the dogs were loosed . . .

Now they were running. His female guide was scrawny and naked from the waist up, he followed the shine of her back with devotion, panicking when he lost it as they passed between the shadows of bushes. He fell over roots, he got up. His feet moved in time to the drums. His legs were drumsticks beating the earth. He bumped into the woman as she stopped and looked back. He pummelled at her, 'Get on,' and looked back with her.

They were halfway down a hill on which the moonlight shone with empty calm. At its brow there was the reflection of an unmistakable glow. Something was on fire over the other side of the hill, where the house was. There was a kerfuffle from the group in the rear. Slaves attacking Bratchet. No, trying to stop her running back. He saw them lift her and the child and carry them on.

They completed a wide arc which brought them out to where the carriage stood, Nero beside it. Coming down the track towards it from the opposite direction was the lone, lemon-jacketed, lace-frilled figure of John Laws.

Pompey arrived in Kingston at dawn the next day, weeping, with the corpse of Kilsyth in the trap beside him. It had three bullet holes in it. The one that killed him had gone through the throat. A stray bullet had set fire to the house, Pompey said. The planters had rushed it then, and found Kilsyth bled to death, which had sobered them. They had dragged the body out and made no objection to Pompey taking it away. They had, in fact, hastened him to do so.

439

John Laws wouldn't let Bratchet stay to bury her husband; the naval cutter that he'd commandeered to take them to England was due to sail with the afternoon tide. As he said to Defoe, 'If we wait to sort through the legal complexities of this little fracas, we'll be here for months.'

A local carpenter hastily constructed a coffin in which they took the body with them on board. Bratchet had wild ideas of carrying it to Scotland and burying it there, but again John Laws prevailed. Delicately, he pointed out that there hadn't been time to line the coffin with lead. 'Give him to the sea, my dear,' he said, so she did.

The only matter in which Laws didn't get his own way was in Alexander Selkirk's insistence on travelling home with them.

The cutter revictualled at Boston in Massachusetts, which was where Laws put Mary Waller and Juno into the care of the authorities, charging them to find Mary's relatives for her.

When they landed in England a month later, Livia was taken away from Bratchet. Who was responsible for parting her from her child, she wasn't sure; 'My lord's instructions', they said, when they met her on the quayside.

'Ah, yes,' they said, as if she were on a list, 'Mistress Bratchet. Yes, my lord requests that you come with us immediately. No, not the child. We've made arrangements for it.'

Defoe was carrying Livia down the gangplank for her. She lunged too late as one of the men took the toddler from him and hurried off with her through the crowd. Bratchet ran after him, screaming, and was caught by the two other men and bundled into a coach.

'This is an outrage, gentlemen,' Defoe had been bundled in after her and protested from the floor between the seats, 'Who is responsible for this?'

'Tell her the child's being well looked after, will you?' shouted one of the men over the racket Bratchet was making. 'She's going to get it back, for God's sake.'

Through the last tiny window in her mind, she saw their faces; young, childless, official, genuinely puzzled that she should make a fuss when she had their assurance no harm was intended.

'The matter's urgent, you see,' the other one said.

Urgent? Urgent was having a lovely man give his life for you and your baby, urgent was transferring every nerve you had into the body of your daughter. Urgent was seeing her face crumple with fright as they took her away. They didn't know what urgent was.

She showed them. Blackness shut out everything but urgency as she kicked and writhed and screamed and begged for her baby back, until she was limp and lay on the coach floor, twitching and uttering soundless whimpers – by which time an embarrassed Defoe had gone over to the side of authority and was trying to explain to the official-looking young men that she wasn't mad.

'Tired from the voyage, I think,' he was saying, 'and only just lost her husband and, well, you know what women are like about their little ones.'

The young men gave tight, understanding smiles. Women.

Defoe lifted her up and wiped her face. He spoke slowly so that she could understand him. 'These gentlemen are taking us to Kensington Palace. Kensington Palace? The Queen is dying, they say, God rest Her Majesty's soul, and you and I are required there.'

He leaned closer and whispered. 'It'll be to identify you-know-who.' At her incomprehension his mouth formed the words 'Anne Bard.' Then formed two more: 'Anne Bonny.' He glanced round crossly at his companions: 'Can't you see the lady needs sustenance?'

It hadn't been in their arrangements, but they agreed, though reluctantly, and stopped the coach long enough for one to purchase sausage and bread from a wayside stall while the other went into a tavern and bought a jug of ale.

In the minutes they had alone, Defoe said, 'If it is true that your Anne is in the palace, you must tell us, my dear. It can do no harm now, surely, whatever her reasons have been for remaining incognito. Indeed, it may exalt her. You would wish that for her. The situation is pressing, as they say. England is on the brink of civil war. Your country needs a new claimant for the throne on whom everyone can agree. You can see that?'

441

Bratchet could see nothing except Livia held hostage, crying for her. 'Give me my baby back.'

Defoe became exasperated. 'You shall have her back. They've said so. You can hardly expect to take a squalling child into a palace where a queen is dying.'

One of the men, clambering back into the carriage, said, 'Isn't she prepared to cooperate yet?'

It might have been a genuine enquiry. Bratchet heard it as the threat of a blackmailer. She nodded. When she wouldn't take the food or drink, the two men and Defoe shared it among themselves.

Entering the City they had to pass through a cordon of horse and Dragoons. Inside it, the militia was out on the streets; a late father's uniform hanging loose on his son's thinner stomach, swords being eased in and out of scabbards that hadn't been put on since the Glorious Revolution, tarnished epaulettes trying to gleam in the lowering July sun.

The militia had set up road blocks for the fun of showing that it could, thereby adding to delays in traffic already enhanced by the continued presence in the capital of the great and the good who, at this time of the year, were more usually settled in their country houses preparing to shoot game. Messengers bearing the Queen's blazon swerved their horses around the congestion, galloping council directives to all points of the compass and adding to the sense of crisis.

During one of their enforced stops, a militia sergeant put his head through the coach window. 'Who and where?' he asked, with assumed ennui.

'The Queen's business,' one of the young men told him, shortly.

'Mine an' all. An' if I don't like it, I can take you to Newgate. So now then. Who and where?'

'This lady and gentleman have just arrived in the Port and are required at Kensington Palace. I suggest you let them get there.'

'That's a bloody lie for a start. There's a 'bargo on all shipping.'

'There's no embargo on the navy,' said the young man, slowly and distinctly. He produced a warrant with a large royal seal. 'And if you don't let us through I can take you to the Tower.'

They were waved through. Impressed, Defoe asked, 'An embargo on shipping? Are we expecting the Pretender to invade?'

They were new and elevated secretaries; discretion was their stock in trade and they enjoyed it, but Defoe was Grub Street; by the time they'd reached the Gore, he was as au fait with the situation as they were.

Yes, there was a very good chance that the Pretender would invade; he'd already set out to join his fleet on the French coast. To combat him, troops had been recalled from Dunkirk and Flanders. The Tower was being reinforced. The army was camped in Hyde Park. Nobody knew which way anybody would jump. Would Louis back James's bid for the crown and invade, or wouldn't he?

Nearly the entire high command of the army and navy had been replaced, at Bolingbroke's behest, with men who might or might not be Jacobites when it came to it. But when it did come to it, since sailors and soldiers trusted their former officers more than their new leaders, would the army or the navy obey them?

It was chaos. Defoe found himself wanting very much to go home and cuddle Mrs Defoe. No, they told him, he was needed at court where there was even more confusion than in the country. Bolingbroke was definitely for the Pretender. That is, he would be if James changed his religion, which James was still refusing to do.

Harley . . . well, my Lord Oxford was my Lord Oxford; you couldn't be sure what he would do. Anyway, it wasn't a matter of political difference between him and my Lord Bolingbroke, it was a street fight. The two of them were virtually bawling in the dying Queen's ear, each trying to order her to dismiss the other.

The one thing he couldn't learn of the two young men, though he tried, was for whom they were acting. 'Are you in my Lord Oxford's office?' he asked, as if merely interested, 'Or St John's, I mean, my Lord Bolingbroke's?'

They didn't answer. *They don't know, by God. They're like the rest of us, waiting.* It would depend on the street fight. Even in the time it had taken them to drive from Kensington to the Port of London and back, Harley might have prevailed on the Queen to dismiss Bolingbroke. Or vice versa.

He changed the subject. 'And Her Majesty?' Confusion again. She was making a will, well, she might be making a will, it was rumoured she was making a will, setting aside George and leaving her throne to her half-brother.

'But her will can't set aside the Act of Succession,' said Defoe, the law-abider.

One of the young men looked straight at him. 'The hell with the Act of Succession,' he said, 'It would form public opinion. The people love her.'

It came to Defoe that he did too. In the rocky terrain of English history, her reign had provided one firm and level plateau. They had all rested on it, catching their breath.

More than ever, he wanted to hug Mrs Defoe and smell the smell of cooking cabbage that permeated his house. 'I really think I ought to go home and change. I'm somewhat travel-stained.'

'You're also on bail,' one of them reminded him.

Oh God, so he was. He'd forgotten. His mind split in two, like his country. Which monarch would get him off? Was it too late to save his bacon and cheer for James III? Should he hot-foot it to Hanover and kiss the hand of George I?

He looked towards Bratchet. She held the answer. If there was an answer. With her help he could be Defoe the Queen-maker. Pityingly, he saw that she was deaf and sightless in her misery for her child. He sighed. The ladies, bless 'em. Useless in politics.

They were taken to a room that was an antechamber to the antechamber to the bedchamber, a large and rather ugly room, ill proportioned, the ceiling too high and its length too long for its width, more a hallway.

It was where the Queen had received the less-noble dignitaries among her subjects, mayors and guilds presenting loyal addresses and such, and from which she could make an easy retreat to her bed. Windows ran along one side, looking out on to a terrace of parterres. On the other, on either side of a great, unlit fireplace, hung a series of tapestries depicting the voyages of Ulysses. At the far end were double doors leading to the antechamber and bedchamber.

Defoe and Bratchet were put at the other end – 'Wait there' – on hard little gilt chairs near a door under a high minstrel gallery beneath which hung a superb, ormolu bracket clock.

There were a lot of people in the room, mostly men, talking low in groups, though not as many as in the antechamber beyond, which, Defoe saw, peering, was crowded yet even quieter. Late afternoon sun coming through the long windows, which were closed, added to the body heat. 'She's still alive, then,' said Defoe.

Nobody spoke to them. The secretaries did not come back. Defoe scanned the faces, recognizing some, trying to fathom whether Whig expressions displayed more contentment than Tory or vice versa. After an hour, he gave up and left Bratchet in order to mingle.

He came back to clutch the back of his chair for support. 'Harley's out.' He sat down with a thump, staring into a Harley-less future. 'She ordered him to break the White Staff three hours ago.'

He was wondering aloud. 'Should I go home, do you think? But suppose they're waiting to arrest me? It was Harley stood my bail.'

The Bratchet didn't see, didn't hear, didn't care. The crowd was lessening. On the supposition that the Queen would outlast the night, people were returning home to the reassurance of their dinner tables.

'No,' said Defoe the optimist, 'I won't go yet. The Staff isn't Bolingbroke's yet. And my Lord Oxford remains a privy councillor. The Queen's a woman. She may give the Staff back to him.'

By seven o'clock the room had nearly emptied, and so had the antechamber beyond. A sweep of men in caps and fur-lined gowns flowed through the door behind Bratchet and Defoe, up the antechamber's antechamber towards the bedchamber, leaving a train of apothecary shop smells behind them. 'The doctors,' said Defoe.

When they swept out again, he made another foray of enquiry.

'She has pain and heat in her head and her nose bleeds. They've cupped her. She prefers that to leeches. They think her improved. She's asked for her hairdresser.'

On their left a pink Ulysses struggled with pink Trojans as the dying sun suffused the room. A lady in a high cap went through, followed by a small Negro boy carrying a tray of combs, brushes and pomander bottles.

'The hairdresser,' said Defoe.

Liveried footmen came in with long, flaming tapers to light the sconces. One of the doors beyond the open doors between the antechambers was flung back. A woman filled the doorway. A sweet voice said, 'I can walk, Danvers, I thank you.'

She was enormous. The ivory-coloured mantua that hung from her shoulders and trailed on the floor either side of her made her outline more gigantic yet. A cap, stiffened at its front into a fan, sat like an exclamation on top of a head as round as a pumpkin. She teetered her mass forward on tiny feet. The hands on the end of the tree-trunk arms were so delicate they might have been grafted on from the body of a child.

Defoe the courtier took off his hat and sank to one knee. Bratchet sat where she was. Queen Anne wobbled towards them, two bedchamber women hovering either side with their hands juggling to catch her every time she swayed.

'Kneel,' hissed Defoe at Bratchet. She didn't, but neither did the Queen notice; her eyes were intent on something above their heads. Six yards away, she stopped still. Defoe involuntarily turned to look upwards. Someone must have entered the minstrel gallery.

But it was the clock. She was looking at the clock. They listened to its mechanism tick a full two minutes of her life away before the woman she'd called Danvers said, through tears, 'What do you see more than ordinary, madam?'

The Queen slowly turned her head to the enquirer but her eyes remained on the clock. Danvers screamed. The other woman ran, calling for help. Defoe and two footmen helped the women support the Queen to her bedchamber. Defoe stopped discreetly at the door, standing back to allow through a running group of men and women, but stayed as long as he could to overhear what the duty doctor might say.

Bratchet sat on.

Coming back, Defoe told her, 'I heard the Duchess of Somerset ask how she did and she said, "Never worse. I am going." She's unconscious now. They're bleeding her and Lady Masham has collapsed in a faint.' He was in tears, but excited, and forgave himself for being so. After all, this was the most important play in Europe, and he was in the pit of its theatre. He said, 'Poor soul, she's but forty-nine. Younger than me.'

At midnight, a harassed major-domo on his rounds asked them who they thought they were and what they were doing. Defoe said they were there at the behest of the Viscount Bolingbroke – it being no longer politic to name Harley. The major-domo was disdainful but allowed them to remain where they were. 'You'll have a long wait, I hope. Her poor dear Majesty's rallied again.'

They sat on. None of the household was allowed off duty, so that those footmen who'd been in attendance all day were beginning to flag and slid to the floor to sit with their powdered heads on their silk-covered knees. Those who were fresher woke them when the tap of ivory staff on marble floor presaged the arrival of the major-domo.

Bratchet was moaning and attracted the attention of the major-domo on his next round. 'What's the matter with the woman? She can't stay here.'

'Where then?' asked Defoe, 'She's under my Lord Bolingbroke's orders to keep in sight of the antechamber.'

'Up there.' The major-domo pointed the way to the minstrel gallery above the clock.

The gallery was approached by a door in the corridor outside, which led to a winding and lethal staircase set in the wall. On its other side was a corresponding staircase. In the middle it bellied out into a half-circle on which musicians stood to play. Defoe hoped they had a better head for heights than he did, the place gave him vertigo; its balustrade came only crotch-high and allowed an uncomfortable view of the expanse of marble floor twenty feet below.

Nothing seemed to be happening down there. Dare he go home?

Not least, he wished to change his linen; he didn't want to usher in a new reign in anything but his best. He could hire a hackney and keep it waiting to bring him back. If the bailiffs were sieging his house, he could get in through a back window. He'd done it before.

He explained his intention to Bratchet, fetched her some ale from the buttery, told her where to find the water closet, and set off, not knowing whether she'd heard him.

Bratchet's mind was in torment. Nothing had been as terrible as this. Not the loss of Martin, not the death of her husband, nothing had been as terrible as this.

Defoe was back, newly shaved and gaudy, full of tremendous news. 'The Whigs have told Bolingbroke: "You have only two ways of escaping the gallows. Either you join the honest party of the Whigs, or you give yourself utterly to the Pretender. If you do not choose the first, we can only imagine you have decided for the second."' Defoe shook his head with admiration. 'The Whigs are gaining ground. It looks like Hanover.'

Bratchet didn't move.

Defoe pulled her chair back a little from the balustrade and turned it to face him. 'I've been home, mistress,' he said clearly, 'Livia's there. They gave her to Mrs Defoe. She's been fed and is now fast asleep in one of our old cots. She's well and lusty. When this is over, we'll go straight to see her.' It would have been Harley who arranged that, he thought, before he went. Harley always admired Mrs Defoe, bless her.

He had to repeat what he'd said. 'Your child is with Mrs Defoe. She'll be safe with Mrs Defoe.'

'Yes,' said Bratchet, at last, 'I know she will.'

He helped her down to the buttery to eat. The place was in such confusion nobody questioned their right to be there.

448

Stablemen, grooms, gardeners, stewards, valets, table-setters, chandelier-dusters, hobbling retainers who hadn't attended Court for years, had congregated with the rest of the household to wait for their Queen's death.

In a sense, it was theirs too. A new staff would come in with the new king, be it James or George, and who knew if he would pay their pensions. And, genuinely, they loved Queen Anne. Most of the women and some of the men were weeping like children, there was worry on most faces, a few were drunk.

'Do you see Anne Bonny Bard?' asked Defoe.

Bratchet shook her head.

'It's not too late, my dear,' he told her, eagerly, 'It will take weeks for either Hanover or Stuart to come. I could rally the country in that time for a new Queen Anne.' There was such wildness in the air that anything was possible.

She shook her head. 'She isn't here.'

Well, it had always been a long shot. Harley wasn't often wrong, but his belief that the woman had infiltrated the Court was obviously the beginning of his errors. Never mind, it had brought him, Defoe, to the heart of things as it fluttered into its death throes. What a tale he'd have to tell.

He escorted Bratchet back to the antechamber's antechamber. Colour had come back to her face; she was no longer the hag she'd become when they'd taken her child; indeed, she was beautiful again and seemed content to see the death out. They all trusted Mrs Defoe. Besides, he dare not leave with her until whoever had commanded her presence, Harley or Bolingbroke, gave them permission to go.

They sat together in their original position, beneath the clock. The bedchamber doors were closed. Dawn light enfeebled the flames in the sconces and they were snuffed. A footman raised one of the windows, allowing in the warble of a thrush sitting on a box bush in one of the parterres, and the smell of roses. The major-domo clouted the footman over the head and ordered it closed, as if the thrush had been committing *lèse majesté*.

'What day is it?' asked Bratchet.

'Saturday.'

449

'What month?'

'July. It is the thirty-first. Yesterday was the anniversary of little Gloucester's death.' Defoe thought Poor Queen, she would have been low. She will be glad to follow her son, glad to follow all her dead children.

'I lost track of time.'

He said, 'I think it's stopped.'

The doctors swept on their medicinal way through the room to the bedchamber.

'The doctors,' said Defoe and went on one of his forays.

'She's had the benefit of vomiting three times by the help of cardis. Dr Arbuthnot tells me it is the best symptom she's shown and they've laid garlic to her feet to help the pain in 'em. They've ordered her head shaved but while it was doing she fell into a convulsion, or it may be an apoplexy, but came to when they bled her. They're thinking of blistering next.'

'Poor Queen,' said Bratchet.

Both antechambers began to fill up again. There were a lot of churchmen around, hoping it would be they who would be called to give the last rites. They really had an excellent seat. The advantage of this chamber was that people talked more freely and loudly; in the other they kept their voices to whispers for fear of disturbing the quiet of the bedchamber. Here there was an echo which brought conversation skipping along the marble floor to his waiting ears.

From beside him, the Bratchet asked: 'When you went home, did you see Martin Millet?'

'No, shh,' he said, and went back to listening.

'. . . She hasn't given Bolingbroke the White Staff yet . . .'

'. . . She'll never make him First Minister. As soon to give it Old Nick.'

'. . . She might . . .'

There was a hush. Bolingbroke had come through the door behind Defoe and Bratchet and stood for a moment so that everybody could see him. He wore black, which suited him, but with a tastefully coloured waistcoat to show that it was not mourning. His head was raised, his smile brilliant, his walk, when he began his progress through the rooms, carelessly elegant, its effect only spoiled by the plump dough-faced man who followed him shouting invective.

Harley was drunk but for once his speech was clear; with nothing to lose he was flinging charges and hatred at the back of Bolingbroke's head. 'Corruption,' he said, 'peculation, disloyalty, treason . . .' The sins reverberated round a room in which not a soul moved or blinked.

The odd procession went into the second antechamber, Harley still shouting until the bedchamber door shut in his face. There was an audible and multiple gasp as everybody started to breathe again. The major-domo moved forward and led Harley away. Before he went he was heard to say, 'Where's Masham? I shall leave that female as low as I found her.'

'She is not here, my lord.'

As they passed back through the door by Defoe, he heard the major-domo add: 'I hear she is gone to rifle St James's while she yet can.'

In the appalled excitement that broke out when the two had gone, Defoe, for once, had no regret that he had chosen the losing side. *I shall right you, dear master*. His pen had long annoyed Bolingbroke and the wolf pack he led. Defoe, the Dissenter, scourge of High Tories, would dissent and scourge them to the end, though it meant the Tower.

And perhaps it wasn't the losing side. Bolingbroke had emerged from the bedchamber, still smiling, still unruffled – but there was no White Staff in his hand. He nodded to acquaintances as he went, asked a question and strolled towards where Defoe and Bratchet sat.

Lord, not the Tower. He hadn't meant it.

'Mistress Bratchet?' Close to, he seemed to have a fever; there were red patches high on his smooth, long cheeks, but he bowed to Bratchet as if all he'd wanted in the world was to meet her.

Bratchet stood and curtseyed. Defoe stood and bowed – slightly.

'In all the comings and goings, have you recognized the woman we are calling Anne Bonny, my dear?'

'No, my lord.'

451

'What is the most precious possession you have, Mistress Bratchet?'

'My daughter, my lord.'

'Will you swear on your daughter's life that if you do see Mistress Bonny you will come to Golden Square and tell me?'

Bratchet smiled at him. 'I swear that I will.'

Viscount Bolingbroke smiled back at her, bowed again, and went on. As he passed Defoe, he said, 'You seedy little man.'

Defoe was triumphant. 'He hasn't received the White Staff. He's lost. Do you see how I am his enemy? Oh glory.' He paused and frowned. 'What can he mean by *seedy*?'

As if Bolingbroke had infected the rooms with his fever, decorum disintegrated. The major-domo tried to hush the chatter but kept being called into the bedchamber where there was activity which, to judge from his face each time he emerged, did not please him.

Defoe barged his way through the crowd to stand near the bedchamber door. 'All sorts are entering Her Majesty's presence by the back stair,' he reported, thrilled, to Bratchet, 'Someone has persuaded her to knight a farmer, or he may be one of her gardeners, a yokel. I could not find out who he is – nobody seems to know.'

A little later there was another sway of the crowd, more exclamations. Defoe went off again and returned. 'Now she's created a new peer. The Earl of Cullen.'

The major-domo emerged, a broken man; protocol had gone by the board. He came to stand for a moment at the side of Defoe and Bratchet, by now the only constants in his collapsing world. 'A gardener,' he said, 'a knighthood for a bloody digger. She's wandering, poor lady, and being taken advantage of. At least they've smuggled the varlet out by the stair. And now a peerage for . . . Excuse me.' He hurried back to the bedchamber doors which were opening.

'. . . the Devil is the Earl of Cullen?'

'. . . Cullen? Sounds popish to me . . .'

'. . . Who the Devil is he?'

'. . . Here he comes . . .'

The major-domo was bowing out backwards. He turned and

with sweeps of the top of his staff stalked ahead, clearing a path for the newly created peer. Behind him came a small boy, and behind him a bedchamber woman.

'*That's* the Earl of Cullen?'

'He cannot be more than seven. Eight at the most . . .'

At the end door, the major-domo stooped to talk to the new earl. 'Her Majesty's patent will be copied on to the patent rolls, my lord. You will be introduced to the House of Lords at the next Parliament.'

'That will be very nice, thank you,' the small boy said.

The major-domo blinked, but his training held. 'Probably on a Tuesday or Wednesday. According to custom. After prayers.' He turned to the bedchamber woman. 'Has he somewhere to go? Someone to look after him?'

'I believe he lives in Highgate, my lord, with a nurse. She is outside.'

'But who *is* he? . . . Oh, never mind. Does the boy know he now has estates and a sizeable income?'

'Shall I tell him, my lord?'

'Do so.'

While they were talking, the boy's eyes wandered and fixed on Bratchet, perhaps because she was sitting and nearer his height, perhaps because she smiled at him. He came over to her. 'I'm very hot,' he whispered.

'It *is* hot,' she whispered back, 'Perhaps you could loosen your coat and take off your gloves.'

The bedchamber woman came over, smiling, and ushered him to the door. 'This way, my lord. Let us find your nurse.'

The tempo increased when he'd gone; speculation, astonishment rose to a pitch more suited to a tennis court than the antechamber to a deathbed.

'. . . must be a commoner . . .'

'. . . a by-blow of somebody important . . .'

When it was announced that the Earl of Shrewsbury had received the White Staff from the hand of the half-conscious Queen, there was a roar that shook the clock.

Defoe danced. 'A middle man, by God! Agreeable to Hanover *and* England. She's made her wish known. It's Hanover!' He

453

recollected himself and sat down, pumping Bratchet's hands up and down with one of his own. He pointed with the other. 'Look at them. Look at the relief.'

People were shaking hands, clapping each other on the back. Jacobites were quietly leaving, but without haste. If the ante-chamber represented the country, England would wait quietly enough for George of Hanover to come and rule it.

Queen Anne died early the next morning, on Sunday, 1 August 1714. It was still dark. Her subjects in the antechambers lolled on tables and window sills, others slept standing up. In the bedchamber were gathered two duchesses, all the bedchamber women, Lady Masham, the Bishop of London with chaplains, seven doctors, members of the privy council and cabinet, and footmen.

Perhaps there was an announcement but Defoe and Bratchet didn't hear it. They were asleep themselves. What brought them to their feet was the stampede. As if somebody had shouted 'Fire', the antechambers were emptying at a run. Privy councillors hurried by, already consulting their timepieces and making arrangements. Scurrying bishops were instructing their chaplains about the ringing of bells and services. Men who had stood for forty-eight hours scampered off in a release of energy to be first with the news.

In less than two minutes the antechambers were empty. The bedchamber doors were left open and figures were bustling about it against the glow of candles. It was the most indecorous thing Bratchet had ever seen. Appalled, she said, 'How can they be so . . . so rude?'

'My dear, there is much to do,' Defoe told her. Tears rolled down his cheeks. 'The regents must make the country safe in case the Pretender *does* attempt an invasion. All must be put in readiness for the new king. Then there's the mourning arrange-ments, the obsequies, flags at half mast, cannon, the bells, mes-sengers to carry the sad news. I must write the dear soul a valedictory ode . . .'

Bratchet sat down. 'They could let her get cold first.'

'The Queen is dead, long live the King,' explained Defoe. Yes, an ode of welcome to George, a splendid one, ready for his arrival. And a new suit . . . Aloud he said, 'I wonder if we dare go. There is still time for a coup, I suppose, but whether Harley or Bolingbroke will be in any position . . . Perhaps we could risk it.'

'I'll stay a little longer,' said Bratchet, 'Kiss Livia for me. She's safe with Mrs Defoe.'

Defoe was relieved. 'Yes, that would be the best thing. There may be tumult yet and the streets chancy. I'll go and assess the feeling and come back for you.' He kissed her hand and walked at funeral pace through the door. Once outside his feet could be heard quickening in the corridor until he was running, towards a new reign.

From beyond the windows came the faraway clatter of carriage wheels, the crack of whips and the call of coachmen encouraging their horses to gallop. An eggshell dawn came in through the windows until the major-domo shut it out again by ordering the shutters closed. Some of the sconces were snuffed. A bell began tolling in the chapel, to be taken up by churches further away.

The antechambers' dimness intensified the light in the bedchamber where shadows moved around a mound on the bed covered by a sheet. Two elderly women, the layers-out, went by, carrying baskets. The doors of the bedchamber shut behind them.

The major-domo and one of the bedchamber women emerged, carrying diaries and papers and a small brass-bound box. The major-domo's voice echoed round the empty room. 'It seems a shame.'

'The duchess agrees. Those were her orders. Unopened.'

A footman was called to light the fire, which caught at once. 'It might be her last will and testament,' said the major-domo.

The bedchamber woman said, 'Private letters, I think.'

'Oh well.' Tenderly, the major-domo leaned down and put the papers and the box on the flames.

The box was shabby. Bratchet knew it well; Anne Bonny had brought it to Effie Sly's house where it had remained. The bedchamber woman was the one who'd walked behind the little Earl of Cullen. Bratchet had seen her before too.

Four men in carpenters' aprons came in dragging another box, this time immense and almost square. They knocked. The bedchamber doors opened to let the coffin in, then shut again. Bratchet got up from her seat, walked to the fireplace and lifted out the box. It was slightly scorched but intact. She put it under her cloak and went back to her place.

After a while, the major-domo came out. 'You still here?' he asked incuriously. 'She's going to St James's now. I want this room cleared. Watch from the gallery if you must.'

It took eight men, with difficulty, to carry the coffin the length of the rooms to the door. Their gasps for breath came up to where Bratchet now sat, looking over the gallery balustrade.

Those of the household who were still left formed two ragged lines to watch its progress, some weeping, but most of them too tired to show anything except a desire for sleep. As it passed out of the door below Bratchet, there came the only graceful gesture of the night: the major-domo took his staff in both hands and broke it over his knee. He looked around at the lines of men and women. 'Thank you,' he said, 'You can rest now. And God rest Her Majesty.'

They went. The doors of the empty bedchamber stayed open, its candles remained lit. There was nobody left. Through the darkening palace came the sound of slamming doors, then quiet. Bratchet sat on, waiting. But not for Defoe.

A sconce lit the tapestry on the wall to her left where Greeks attacked the towers of Troy. How long had that war lasted? There had been a similar arras at St-Germain-en-Laye and dear old Dr MacLaverty had recounted Ulysses' adventures from it as part of her education. Ten years. Not as long as the war in Flanders, but long enough. And Ulysses still had a long way to go, right along the length of the room, through monsters and swine, sirens and enchantresses, until he came home to Ithaca and the patient Penelope.

'You were Penelope,' said Bratchet to the flickering light in the bedchamber. 'You hated war, too. You wanted them all home.'

But the other Anne, she had been Ulysses. Wrenched from

456

the normal she had fought with all the courage and cunning of the great adventurer alongside the friend who had joined her from her own Odyssey. Not male souls in female bodies, but women finding joy in hazard, like Kit Ross, women enlarged.

There had been no room for her. There weren't supposed to be women like her.

Below Bratchet, the clock ticked away the interregnum. Would there be a place in the new reign for a Mistress Ulysses?

No. It would be a man's reign. *Unless we're Mrs Defoe, men destroy us.* They had destroyed Anne Bonny and Mary Read.

Twenty feet below her, the gold knob of the major-domo's broken staff lay where he'd thrown it, touched by a sliver of sunlight coming through a crack in the shutters. Alongside it was a glove dropped in the rush to get away.

Somewhere in the silent palace a door shut with an echo. There was the sound of shoes tapping briskly from a long way off, turning into the corridor outside, nearing. Tread on the stairs coming up. The door to the gallery opened. Confident, tidy steps approached Bratchet's chair and stopped behind it.

'Hello, Mary,' said the Bratchet.

From my cottage window I heard the bells in St Mary's tower begin tolling for the death of Queen Anne. I could see the carriages sweeping out through the palace gates, turn towards London and race off. The Queen is dead. Long live Whoever. When William the Conqueror died, his courtiers were in such a hurry to greet his successor they left his body naked on the floor.

They gave Anne a coffin at least. After the rats had all gone, it came trundling out through the gates on a gun carriage and headed for St James's with only a few outriders and the Lord Steward in attendance. The panoply would come later, the black-plumed horses, the pall bearers, the muffled drums and the rest. When there was time to arrange it. When the politicians had finished scrambling for places under the new king.

God rest her, I thought. She was a nice woman. Why she'd knighted me at the last, I couldn't think. Services to agriculture? It hadn't been that good a drill. But they'd sent a flunkey to the cottage. 'You're to come at once, Mr Millet. No time to change. Quick.'

We went via the famous back stairs and into the bedchamber. It was filled with people. She was on the bed, hardly conscious, with her hand plucking at the sheets like my father's had just before he died.

'Is this him?' somebody said. I was ushered to the bedside where a doctor was feeling her pulse. There was a young boy there, very small and bewildered but standing straight.

A bedchamber woman leaned over her. 'He's here, Your Majesty. Martin Millet.'

Her eyelids were half closed. One of the lords at the foot of the bed, the Lord Chamberlain I think, came up with a sword in his hand and put it on the bed, its handle towards her hand. 'Are you sure, Your Majesty?'

The eyelids flickered. There was a movement of the head. 'Very well.' To me, he said, 'Kneel down.'

I knelt and the sword was angled so that its hilt stayed in her hand and the tip of its blade rested on my shoulder.

'Your Majesty?' said the Lord Chamberlain.

A sigh came from her mouth. You could just make out the words 'Sir Martin'.

'Rise, Sir Martin,' said the lord. I rose.

'Her Majesty wishes you to be guardian of the Earl of Cullen during his minority,' said the lord, 'The papers have been signed already. Do you consent?'

He had his hand on the head of the boy. The Earl of Cullen looked at me and I looked back. 'If that's what Her Majesty wishes.'

'Very well then. You may go.'

I grinned at you, James, if you remember, and said 'Hello', but somebody grabbed me by the sleeve and took me away. Her major-domo opened the door to the back stairs for me. He looked as if he'd have been happier to kick me down them. 'What's it all about?' I asked him.

'God knows.'

So I went back to my cottage, no wiser than I'd gone, though, apparently, somewhat better class, and sat at my ground-floor window and listened for the bell, and kept a vigil for the soul it tolled for, watching the dawn come up on a new age.

It also came up on a hackney carriage that cantered into the silent street with Daniel Defoe leaning out of its window.

'I forgot to tell you,' he shouted.

'What?' I had to wait while he made the driver turn round, ready to chase back to London.

'Mistress Bratchet's back. She was asking after you.'

'Back?'

'Harley,' he explained, 'wanted her back. Useless now, of course. Oh, and Kilsyth's dead. Can't stop.'

'Where is she?' I yelled.

The hackney was already picking up speed. I saw him pointing towards the palace. 'In the antechamber. Had to leave her.' His voice came faintly over the horses' hooves. 'Take her home.'

I pushed aside the solitary guard who tried to stop me at the palace entrance. 'Get out of my fucking way.'

Inside the palace the windows were shuttered and it was dark. There was nobody about. The place echoed. I didn't know where to go. I'd kill Defoe if I ever saw him again. At least I knew where the buttery was. I collared a page who was asleep on its floor. 'There was a woman waiting in the antechamber. Where is she?'

'Get off, sir, I'm tired.'

I shook him. 'Where is she?'

'She was up in the gallery.' The page hung limp in my grip, yawning. 'She won't be there now.'

'Show me.'

Stumbling, he took me to a corridor and pointed along it. 'That door there.' He yawned again, put his back to the wall and slid down it and fell asleep. There was a staircase beyond. I went up it two at a time, bad leg or no. I slammed through the door at the top. And stopped.

There were two women in the middle of the gallery ahead, standing close together on a bit that bellied out into a platform. A chair lay on its side near them. Bratchet had her back to the drop, the balustrade pressing into her skirt. Light from the

459

room below lit the back of her hair but left her face and the woman opposite her in darkness.

I saw the other woman look at me and turn back to Bratchet. 'Here's Master Millet come for you.'

Bratchet didn't look. 'I know.'

'I never had a Martin Millet.'

'I'm sorry,' Bratchet said.

'I didn't need one.' She raised her voice. 'Tell him to stay where he is.'

I didn't dare breathe. She only had to push and Bratchet would be over. It was a long way down.

As if she were resuming a chat over a garden fence, Bratchet said, 'So whose is he?'

'It doesn't matter.'

'I don't mean the father. I meant, is he yours or Anne's?'

'I told you,' said the dark woman, 'it doesn't matter. He's ours, hers and mine. She was my only love. We wanted children together.' She shifted impatiently. 'There was only the one baby left. When I escaped the prison. We rode to the midwife, the Maroons and I. There was one baby alive. She said the other died. I don't know which of us bore it. I hadn't seen either in daylight. It doesn't matter.'

Bratchet nodded.

The woman took a thick roll of papers from her sleeve and handed them to Bratchet. 'Give this to Millet. It's my journal. It will interest him.'

'Thank you.'

The woman frowned, like someone trying to remember a shopping list. 'Well, I think that's everything. Is *she* there yet?'

Bratchet glanced down. 'I can't see her.'

'I think the best thing will be to drown her.'

'Oh, Mary.'

'Yes,' said the woman, 'that will be the best thing. I shall go to the sea with her. She'll follow me. She keeps following me.'

'There's nobody there, Mary.'

'She used to be Effie Sly,' said Mary Read. 'You kept following me too, Bratchet. She hates you. She wants you dead.'

I measured the distance between me and the women. Three

strides. It'd take three. By the second, Bratchet would be over the edge.

'It's time to say goodbye,' said Mary, and put her hands on Bratchet's shoulders.

I got ready to take the leap of my life.

Bratchet kissed her. 'Goodbye, Mary. I never told them.'

'It was nice of you,' said the dark woman, vaguely. 'Tell Millet to take care of our son, Anne's and mine.'

'We will.'

'Goodbye, then.' She brushed down the front of her dress, turned and walked tidily to the door at the far end of the gallery. It closed behind her. I heard her shoes tapping down its staircase.

I walked up to the platform, lifted Bratchet further into the gallery, righted the fallen chair and sat down on it. After a while I said, 'I ought to go after her. For Aunt Effie. Trouble is, every time I leave you, you get in some other bloody mess.'

'The sea, she said,' said Bratchet, 'She's going to the sea. She's going to walk into it.'

I got up and held her. We were both trembling. I said, 'Who's the Earl of Cullen?'

'He's her son. Or Anne's son. She persuaded the Queen. Mary said she'd been her favourite bedchamber woman. She had you knighted so that you can be his guardian. She thought a lot of you.'

I rocked her quietly for a while. 'Let's go home.'

She said, 'Anne slept with Calico Jack, Mary slept with Joshua, Asantewa's son. They didn't care which. They wanted their own children. She said they had to use men because they couldn't make each other pregnant.'

'Come on, my love.'

Bratchet bent down and picked up a brass-bound box that had been hidden by her skirt hem and cradled it. 'She hopes the boy is Joshua's. It's to be their revenge, hers and Anne's and Asantewa's.' She shook her head in wonder. 'No child can be a revenge.'

She looked down at the box in her arms. 'They were going to burn this. I took it out of the fire. It was Anne Bonny's.'

I took the box from her. 'Let's leave now, Bratchie.'

She couldn't stop talking, although what she said was causing her horror and she spoke the words as if she were trying not to vomit. I think she had to tell me then because she wanted rid of it so that it need never be mentioned again. 'They planned it after Anne died at Spanish Town. That's why Asantewa got her away. She said they wanted the blue blood of England to be coloured by the black blood of slaves. Like the dark thread they twine into hawsers, she said, a rogue thread. Sooner or later there'll be a black child born to the aristocracy, she said. "He's our revenge," she said.' She looked up at me. 'She's mad.'

That she bloody was. I said, 'Don't think about her any more, Bratchie. Let's go.'

She shook her head. 'Even they don't see it. After all they've been through. They think it's a stain. It isn't. Look at Licky. England could be proud of someone like him.'

I had to stop her crying. 'I don't know but what the Queen didn't knight me for myself,' I said, 'She was very pleased with me. I've invented a new seed drill, Bratchie. A machine to stop the waste of broadcasting seed.' I told her about the trouble with the hopper, explained the spindles, tongues, road wheels and funnels and bored her into being calm.

She began to laugh.

'Will you like being Lady Millet?'

'I'll love it,' she said.

'I'm sorry about Kilsyth, Bratchie.'

She nodded. 'So am I. He died to save me and Livia. That's our daughter. We had a baby. They took her to Mrs Defoe's.'

'Let's fetch her and take her home.'

'And the Earl of Cullen,' she said, 'And his nurse. Mary said she was called Jubah.'

'God Almighty,' I said, 'I'll have to get a bigger house.'

'And the Earl's to marry an heiress. So Mary said.'

'He can marry who he likes. No ward of mine's going to be somebody else's revenge.'

'And if he wants to marry Livia?'

'She can marry who she likes and all.'

'I love you,' she said.

'You always did.'

At the bottom of the stairs she paused to look towards the quiet, empty bedchamber.

'I hope she's at peace,' Bratchet said, 'She gave England peace at last.'

'I don't know much about royalty,' I said, 'but she beat the Sun King hollow.'

We went out of the palace into a Hanoverian morning.

CHAPTER TWENTY-THREE

THERE IS something eerie in the fact that I finished writing this narrative today, 14 July, 1717, the eleventh anniversary of Aunt Effie's murder.

I set down the last sentence an hour ago and then added a postscript for James. Yet I'm still sitting here, at the desk in my study where I've sat so often in these last twelve months, writing on.

Partly, I suppose I've got used to writing; it has been a way of keeping my mind away from the pain in my leg when I couldn't sleep. And partly, I am filling in the time until midnight. Just in case there should be a recurrence of those strange and unsettling events that took place in this house a year ago. If Aunt Effie should want to repeat her performance, I want to be awake to contend it.

So far, thank God, it has been as contented a day as all the others that make up my life now. Even more contented. A proud day. Squire Narracott rode by, ostensibly to inquire after my health and drink my Madeira. Towards the end of the conversation, he asked casually whether he could borrow my seed drill when it comes to the winter sowing.

Bare-faced impertinence, of course. Last spring he was bruiting it about the village that I was mad. Drilling with a machine? Couldn't I be satisfied with the time-honoured method? What did a common – very common – soldier know about farming? Was I not flying in the face of God Himself?

But I noticed he often rides past the fields down by the river where I've done my drilling and can see for himself that by sowing in neat lines the weeds can be kept down and the ground made friable more easily than if crops are allowed to come up anywhere, as they do by broadcasting.

'Use much seed to an acre, that machine of yours?' he asked. He booms like a bittern.

'Two pounds.'

It shook him. He uses nine or ten pounds to the acre and still has a large proportion of ground unplanted, while the rest grows so thick it doesn't prosper.

It was gall and wormwood for him – asking me for a favour. His disapproval of the way I run my household wasn't improved when Lady Millet and the Earl of Cullen came galloping through the hall, hallooing, dragging a miniature cart containing my baby daughter, with Livia running alongside and whacking them with a ribbon whip.

'It's my younger daughter's birthday,' I told him. I snatched Aimée from the cart as it went by and carried her to the door to say goodbye to Narracott and heap some coals on his head. 'I shall be most happy for you to borrow the Millet drill, Squire.'

I stood on the steps, enjoying the sunshine and kissing Aimée's fat cheeks, until he'd passed out of sight beyond the oak that was blasted a year ago – we've planted honeysuckle round the stump.

When the roisterers came back, we were joined on the lawn by Barty Bates's boys and the Nutley children for cake and a toast to Aimée's continued good health in lemonade. The youngest Nutley, who's six, said, 'Pa says Aimée is an odd name. Heathen French, Pa says.'

A typical old-fashioned Dissenter, Will. And if I'd imposed Bless-the-Day and Lord-be-Praised as given names on my children, I'd be chary about criticizing anybody else's choice. But he's entitled to his opinion.

As a matter of fact, we did have difficulty naming the child at first. I suggested Morgan Le Fay, but Bratchet said it was the name of a girl who'd been a bloody clinchpoop then and wasn't any more. She suggested Brilliana, but no child of mine's going to be called after a goat, however fetching. Eventually we decided on Aimée because it's Bratchet's true first name, though she won't use it. 'Bratchet' is good enough for her, she says, and affronts the Narracotts.

She'd made some drop scones – the boys were gallant enough to try one each. Despite the months with Licky in the galley, Bratchet's a dreadful cook.

'What's the matter with 'em?' she asked suspiciously.

'I think you dropped them too far,' James told her.

Luckily, Mrs Nutley had made the cake.

So it's been a golden day. No sign of Effie Sly – so far. The house was restful, its old bones still basking in the day's heat, when I retired to my study to finish the manuscript after everyone had gone to bed. It still is.

As I sit here, waiting for midnight, I can smell the honeysuckle round the poor oak. There's a barn owl perched on the stump. For me, writing the tale for James has laid most of its ghosts. I wish Bratchet would read it so it could do as much for her, but she's set her mind against remembering. 'I'm staying in the here and now, where I'm happy,' she says, 'and no bugger's going to take me back. Not even you.' There's a lot of Puddle Court still in the Bratchet.

It isn't as easy as that, of course. Now and then she has nightmares, though she won't say what happens in them. I'd do a great deal to stop them for her, but the only thing that can do that is time. I only have one nightmare, awake and sleeping. I'm standing on the balcony above Queen Anne's antechamber watching Bratchet face Mary Read, her back to the drop. Time won't take that away.

It was a relief when they fished Mary's body out of the Pool of London a few days later. Superstition, I know, but when I finished copying out extracts from her journal for James, I burnt the thing. She may have been hardly done by, but she turned evil. I left out some of the worst bits.

I left out another thing I know. That Livia is my child. She looks like me, poor little thing, apart from her hair which is as

465

blonde as her mother's. Mrs Defoe says she's my image. Bratchet has never said so. After all, Kilsyth died for her and that child and she's a woman who pays her debts. It's too late to pay him mine, but if our next child's a boy I'm going to call him Livingstone.

Bratchet came in an hour ago to ask when I'm coming to bed. 'Still scribbling?' she asked, 'You don't finish that bloody book soon James'll be too old to read it.' She looked at the pile of papers which make up the manuscript. 'Won't be able to lift it, neither.'

I made her come in and at least read the postscript which I've penned to our ward. She leaned her chin on my head while she did it, her finger moving along the lines of the page.

' "Dear James, I see now that I didn't write down this narrative so much for you as for me. Old men forget, Shakespeare said, and I suppose I wanted to remember. Writing it down helped me to bring it back, good, bad, stinks, sights, sounds, things you don't really need to know but which are precious to me because I shared them with Bratchet." '

She kissed the top of my head. 'Bit sentimental, ain't it?'

'I'm a sentimental man,' I told her.

' "What you really needed to know from me can be put into a few sentences. It may be that you are the son of a black man called Joshua. If not, your father was a pirate, Jack Rackham. Your mother was either Anne Bonny, who had royal blood in her veins and died in prison in Spanish Town, Jamaica. Or she was Mary Read, whose dead body was taken out of the Pool of London two days after Queen Anne died.

' "You have to know this, James, because there is a possibility that you or your children will have a black child." '

Bratchet clicked her tongue. 'You might dress it up a bit for the boy.'

'How? He's got to know.'

She read on. ' "I hope you will love it. If anybody ever says to you that blood is thicker than water, tell them they're wrong.

' "I said to you once that we couldn't love you more if you were our own. It's still true, just as I love Livia as my own

466

daughter. Who begets whom doesn't matter. When we sat beside your bed during your bout of scarlet fever last year, when Livia fell out of the apple tree and bumped her head and I carried her home, those were moments when I knew I couldn't do without either of you. It's the loving that counts, and the dependency on each other.

'"Anyway, I don't think black blood in the nobility would do it any harm. Joshua, who may or not have been your father, was the brother of the man we knew as Licky who is as royal as any man I've ever met and still, as far as we know, rules over the kingdom of a free people. His blood is as good as the Stuarts' any day."'

'That's a fact,' Bratchet said, wiping her eyes. 'Better than the Hanoverians' and all.'

'I don't think George is doing so badly,' I said, 'considering everything.'

She put her chin back on my head while she finished the letter. '"I know which I'd be prouder of. James II was a limited man. So is his son, the Pretender. In fact, all the Stuarts, as Daniel Defoe says, were a unchancy crew. Except Queen Anne, bless her. She was the best of them. And she's dead."'

Bratchet stopped breathing on my head. 'That's nice,' she said, 'Bit pompous Sir Martin here and there, but it's nice.' She sat down in the chair by my side. 'It's not going to be easy for him, though, is it?'.

'No,' I said.

'Or his wife, when he gets one.'

'No.'

'But it's right about Licky's blood. He was a royal man.' She brightened. 'If he does father a black baby and can't keep it, perhaps he could give it to us.'

'Always room for one more.'

She got up. 'Well, finish it and come to bed. How you going to sign it?'

'"Your loving guardian?"'

'"Your loving guardian and father,"' she said. 'Don't stay up too late.'

Now she's gone, I've opened the little brass-bound box that

Anne Bonny Bard brought with her to England ready to put the manuscript in. I burned the papers that were in it.

Down in the screen passage that leads to the hall, the grandfather clock is beginning to wheeze, ready to chime midnight. It doesn't look as if Effie Sly is going to do her haunting this year. Perhaps she never did.

I'm strangely reluctant to lock the manuscript away. It's a form of goodbye to all the people in it. Some I'm glad to lock up but there's others I'd like to see again. The only one I will is Daniel Defoe – he's coming to stay next week. Some trouble over a debt, I gather.

There's the twelfth strike. Time to finish the postscript to James and go to bed.

May God have you in his keeping, James, my son
Your loving guardian and father,
Martin Millet

AUTHOR'S NOTE

The official Admiralty records of the trial of Mary Read and Anne Bonny are not extant. There's no doubt that the two women existed, or that they turned pirate, but the stories about them rely on a pamphlet printed in Jamaica some time after the trial, and on *A General History of the Robberies and Murders of the Most Notorious Pyrates* by Captain Charles Johnson which was published even later.

And Charles Johnson was Daniel Defoe. If truth conflicted with legend, Defoe was the man to print the legend. In my opinion, he could not have had access to the details of Read's and Bonny's lives that are recounted in his history.

He was as interested in criminals as he was in everything else, perhaps more so; unusually for the age he lived in, he was fascinated by daring women. The real, and necessarily extraordinary, truth about Mary Read and Anne Bonny eluded him, so he made it up. (He needed the money anyway.)

What was good enough for Defoe is good enough for me, so I concocted my own story for the two women in order to weave it through the reign of the also extraordinary – and underrated – Queen Anne, best of all the Stuarts.

To do it I have involved real people: the Queen, of course; her two warring ministers, Harley (Earl of Oxford) and St John (Viscount Bolingbroke); her two warring women, Sarah, Duchess of Marlborough and Abigail Masham née Hill; Daniel Defoe, William Greg, Kit Ross, Captain Blackader, Francesca and Dudley Bard and others, in a fictional murder mystery.

There is more than one suggestion in contemporary accounts to suggest that Queen Anne indulged in spiritous liquors. It's hard to blame her; the twelve years of her reign were harassed, especially the last one when Bolingbroke and Harley were quarrelling virtually across her deathbed.

Sarah and Abigail fought tooth and claw to dominate her. Both of them were wooed by vested interests trying to sway the Queen in their direction. Anne's reputation has suffered through the apologia Sarah later wrote about their relationship – almost a character assassination.

In fact, the last of the Stuarts wasn't as persuadable as Sarah made out. But while Elizabeth I made her prevarication look like strength, Anne's looked like weakness. Yet 'Can any think me so blind as not to see through these things?' she said of the attempts to manipulate her.

Despite the war in Europe, Anne's reign brought a standard of calm and respectability to England which it never knew before. She refused to let either Whig or Tory party persecute the other too far. There were no political executions during her time. She presided over the Union of England and Scotland. She saw herself as the mother of her people and wished that all of them would play happily together.

It seems possible that Prince Rupert of the Rhine did make a morganatic marriage with Francesca Bard, the sort that was prevalent in Europe at the time. Francesca was certainly received with all honour at the Court of Hanover by Electress Sophia, Rupert's younger sister, though later she left Germany and settled down with the Jacobite exiles at St-Germain-en-Laye, but I'm quite sure she was not involved in any plot other than to put James Francis on the throne. (He was the Old Pretender, incidentally, father of the Young one.)

From there, I've speculated on what might have been. If Francesca and Rupert's son, Dudley Bard, *had* married before his death his child might well have had a better claim to the crown than the Hanoverian who became George I. It is true that the offspring of morganatic marriages are not supposed to be eligible for their father's or mother's titles, but it would have been the bloodline that mattered to those who set such store by a Stuart succession.

In order to squeeze the story into the reign I have concertinaed a few dates, so that Anne Bonny and Mary Read stand trial rather earlier, and Defoe finds himself in the pillory rather later, than really happened.

Whether Alexander Selkirk and Defoe ever met, as I have them do on a ship returning from the West Indies, or whether Defoe ever went to the West Indies, nobody knows. Selkirk's own account of his years as a castaway on the island of Juan Fernandez was going the rounds and would have been widely read. But it was Daniel Defoe, in *Robinson Crusoe*, who made the story immortal.

It's worth pointing out that the death of Joshua, as it is recounted by his mother on page 412, was in fact visited on a real runaway slave.

READ MORE IN PENGUIN

In every corner of the world, on every subject under the sun, Penguin represents quality and variety – the very best in publishing today.

For complete information about books available from Penguin – including Puffins, Penguin Classics and Arkana – and how to order them, write to us at the appropriate address below. Please note that for copyright reasons the selection of books varies from country to country.

In the United Kingdom: Please write to *Dept. EP, Penguin Books Ltd, Bath Road, Harmondsworth, West Drayton, Middlesex UB7 ODA*

In the United States: Please write to *Consumer Sales, Penguin USA, P.O. Box 999, Dept. 17109, Bergenfield, New Jersey 07621-0120.* VISA and MasterCard holders call 1-800-253-6476 to order Penguin titles

In Canada: Please write to *Penguin Books Canada Ltd, 10 Alcorn Avenue, Suite 300, Toronto, Ontario M4V 3B2*

In Australia: Please write to *Penguin Books Australia Ltd, P.O. Box 257, Ringwood, Victoria 3134*

In New Zealand: Please write to *Penguin Books (NZ) Ltd, Private Bag 102902, North Shore Mail Centre, Auckland 10*

In India: Please write to *Penguin Books India Pvt Ltd, 706 Eros Apartments, 56 Nehru Place, New Delhi 110 019*

In the Netherlands: Please write to *Penguin Books Netherlands bv, Postbus 3507, NL-1001 AH Amsterdam*

In Germany: Please write to *Penguin Books Deutschland GmbH, Metzlerstrasse 26, 60594 Frankfurt am Main*

In Spain: Please write to *Penguin Books S. A., Bravo Murillo 19, 1° B, 28015 Madrid*

In Italy: Please write to *Penguin Italia s.r.l., Via Felice Casati 20, I–20124 Milano*

In France: Please write to *Penguin France S. A., 17 rue Lejeune, F–31000 Toulouse*

In Japan: Please write to *Penguin Books Japan, Ishikiribashi Building, 2–5–4, Suido, Bunkyo-ku, Tokyo 112*

In South Africa: Please write to *Longman Penguin Southern Africa (Pty) Ltd, Private Bag X08, Bertsham 2013*

READ MORE IN PENGUIN

A CHOICE OF BESTSELLERS

Under My Skin Sarah Dunant

In a culture where no one wants to grow older and where everyone believes in the cosmetic power of the knife, Hannah Wolfe is an alien visitor, tested to the limit by a case of sabotage which turns to murder. 'Cunningly plotted to keep you riveted to the very last page' – *Independent*

Harvest Celia Brayfield

Three women – Grace, Jane and Imogen – who all made the same mistake: loving Michael Knight. A TV star, a public figure but also, in private, a serial adulterer, Michael is driven to destroy the women whose love he craves. Now, as friends and family gather to celebrate his birthday, Michael reaps what he has sown.

To Lie with Lions Dorothy Dunnett

In the sixth book in the House of Niccolò series, the English are shaking themselves free of the Wars of the Roses; France and Burgundy face each other across the Somme; and Venice, with Cyprus her unwilling daughter, attempts to stem the growing threat of the Ottoman Turk. 'Imaginative, scholarly and compelling' – *Mail on Sunday*

When Christ and His Saints Slept Sharon Penman

The Empress Maude and her cousin Stephen of Blois. Both are courageous, stubborn and passionate. She quick-tempered, imperious, heir to her father's kingdom. He gallant, popular, indecisive, but a brilliant battle commander. Only one can have the throne of England . . .

Children of a Harsh Winter Janet Cohen

On a bleak, urban wasteland three children formed a bond that would outlast all the traumas of their youth and the success of their adult careers. 'A powerful novel of contemporary Britain . . . will keep you reading to the end' – *Daily Express*